THE

# SILVER THREAD

Kylie Fitzpatrick was born in Denmark and grew up in
the UK, the US and Australia. She lives in Somerset with
her daughter, and tutors on the Creative Writing degree
course at Bath Spa University. Her previous two historical
novels have been published in ten languages.

# THE
# SILVER
# THREAD

## KYLIE FITZPATRICK

HEAD
ZEUS

LONDON

First published in the UK in 2012 by Head of Zeus, Ltd.

Copyright © Kylie Fitzpatrick, 2012

9 7 5 3 1 2 4 6 8

A CIP catalogue record for this book is available from the British Library.

ISBN (HB): 9781908800121
ISBN (TPB): 9781908800138
ISBN (E): 9781908800862

Printed in Germany.

Head of Zeus, Ltd
Clerkenwell House
45–47, Clerkenwell Green
London EC1R 0HT


www.headofzeus.com

*For my parents, Philippa and Bryon, with love.*

The Way of Heaven is to benefit others and not to injure.

Lao-Tzu (sixth century BC)

# 4 April 1841

The grey walls of Millbank receded until they were a dark huddle on the edge of the world. The sun spread across the water, refracting into shards where their oars dipped.

A light that would leave scars.

The Thames snaked towards the sea, carrying the procession of rowing boats, in each a huddle of silent women. The last boat was piled with luggage of modest proportions; canvas sacks, wicker baskets and battered hat boxes. And a single trunk.

The small liberties of freedom – a walk to the market or an idle afternoon in the sun – were hopes once. Now a length of ribbon would seem like freedom. Still, what could be worse than Millbank prison?

For those who had left their children, there was only the grief. Against this, the guilt of any crime was incidental.

At the mouth of the river the currents collided, creating ridges of tidal water frilled with dirty foam. The Thames was opening to the sea. The white water churned like a bilious stomach. Behind the boats, the rising sun traced a copper edge along rooftops and chimneys; a burnished London; a trick of the light.

There was time for one last glance at the receding city; a moment to take in its outline and shape. Once the entire world, London now looked no larger than a page in a picture book, and so pretty that it might be the Otherworld.

All of a sudden the light changed, revealing the new factories along the banks, their chimney stacks exhaling wraiths of smoke, their pipes leaking into the inky river.

Ahead of them lay an unfathomable voyage and a land beyond the seas. This farewell to London might be for ever. Now, there was only the sea, and the shadowy form of a ship appearing through the fog. Drawing closer still, they could read the name painted at the towering prow of their new prison.

*Rajah.*

# I

# Linen

I am told that in your country, opium smoking is forbidden under severe penalties. This means that you are aware of how harmful it is. So long as you do not take it yourselves, but continue to make it and tempt the people of China to buy it, such conduct is repugnant to human feeling and at variance with the Way of Heaven.

'Your country lies 20,000 leagues away; but for all that, The Way of Heaven holds good for you as it does for us, and your instincts are no different from ours; for nowhere are men so blind as not to distinguish what brings profit and what does harm.

*From a letter to Queen Victoria from*
*Imperial High Commissioner Lin Zexu, 1839*

# Flax

*I arise today*
*Through the strength of heaven;*
*Light of sun,*
*Radiance of moon,*
*Splendour of fire,*
*Speed of lightning,*
*Swiftness of wind,*
*Depth of sea,*
*Stability of earth,*
*Firmness of rock.*

St Patrick (fifth century bc)


*D*o not think of him.

Rhia had been not thinking about William all afternoon and it showed. She squinted: the pattern was crooked.

Everything was out of shape lately. *Serpentine*, Mamo would have said. *Life does not always beat an even rhythm, Rhiannon. It meanders like chords on a harp.* The resonance of the old woman's voice seemed to move the air. She could almost be in the room. Rhia let her paintbrush drop into the tray. She had tried to resurrect the pattern all afternoon and it still looked as wrinkled as silk moiré. Now the light was only fit for catching swirls of dust, the sun so low that it filtered through the canvas, making her pigments as translucent as coloured glass.

She blamed William. He should not have called.

It could have been a day given, with the front room all to herself and nothing to do but paint. It could have been. The question was, would her father understand that she'd had to tell William what had happened in Greystones all those years ago? It was unlikely.

To Connor Mahoney, truth was a holy thing. So was chastity. And marriage. This was the kind of rhetoric he had brandished since Rhia was old enough to irk him. She had always been expert at it. She understood, now, that it depended on the nature of the truth, and that discretion outranked honesty. Sadly, she possessed neither.

A carriage bell tinkled and, not for the first time that day, Rhia wished herself in Greystones, walking barefoot on the shale, listening only to the sea and the gulls.

Connor Mahoney's boots tapped briskly up the stairs.

Rhia removed her smock. She paced to the front window. She smoothed her hair in its reflection and paced back to the fireplace. There was absolutely no need to tell him that she had upset his cherished William. It would all blow over and they would be married next February as scheduled. The time for having a say in such matters was past – the fact remained that no one else had offered. The fact remained that she had not fallen in love.

Or else, she had not fallen for love.

Rhia shivered and cast about for her shawl. The air had moved again.

Mamo despised cynicism.

Connor Mahoney's voice murmured in the hallway, talking to Hannah. Rhia retrieved her shawl from the floor and turned to the fire, her back to the door. She softened her gaze, looking for shapes in the flames, dancing like dervishes. She willed them to lend her their grace. Rhia could sense her father's

5

mood through the wall. He was unusually irritable lately. This was most definitely not the time to tell him that she had insulted her fiancé.

The door opened.

'Rhia.'

Strange how you could tell someone was angry with you just by the way they spoke your name. She could think of nothing she had done to rile him lately.

'Father.'

His jaw was squared for a fight. His anger made him look old and ugly, though his frame was trim and his thick hair still as bright as copper. He snapped a folded piece of paper at her. 'I've had a letter from William.'

Rhia had not expected this. 'From William?' Her voice sounded high and unnatural. The letter must have been written as soon as he had left her.

'He has withdrawn his offer,' said her father.

'Withdrawn his—!I am to be ...' Rhia strode to the door and back, smashing a pipe dish to the floor with her skirts. She took a breath. 'I am not a *property*,' she spat. The flames had lent her nothing. She clenched her fists, took another breath and suddenly felt like laughing. She lowered her eyes and stared hard at the pattern on the Persian rug. It only reminded her of her failed painting. Persians could design patterns fit for the feet of a goddess.

'Until you are married, you are *as my property*, and I will not have you become a burden on this household.' He was almost choking on the words but they hit their mark. He had never called her a burden before. He would regret it, she thought, though with almighty self-restraint she held her tongue. She would say the wrong thing and he would see that she was unrepentant – relieved rather than ashamed.

6

He paced between the cutting table and the wall of shelves where the cloth was stored, his hair falling across his spectacles, his cheeks hot with emotion. He was not finished. 'You should have been married years ago, and now I wonder if anyone will have you.'

Rhia had wondered the same thing herself.

He stood with his back to her, talking to the bolts of fabric. 'William O'Donahue is a respectable and successful merchant. He would have been a great asset to this family – to the business.'

Rhia flinched. Restraint be damned. 'Is that what this is about? The *business*? William is a dullard who does not dare to wed a woman who is cleverer than he. I'm *glad* I need not see his face each day!'

Her father spun and glared at her, his eyes burning. 'I did not raise you to have opinions! If it were not for your … were it not for your mother's family, then you would be like any agreeable Dublin girl. Instead, you read the papers and tour the city like a milkmaid. I see now that you have deliberately offended William in order that he be forced to cancel the engagement. What in tarnation did you say to him?'

'I did no such thing! I would not.' Rhia lowered her voice. 'I told him what happened the winter Michael Kelly was arrested.'

Connor Mahoney was silent. When he finally spoke, his voice was hoarse. 'You told him that you helped those tenants; that you made a Protestant landlord look like a blackguard?'

Rhia held his gaze. She had only done what anyone with an ounce of compassion would have. The weavers were being evicted because their rent was not paid. It was the middle of winter. They might have starved. They would certainly have frozen. She had taken them to Mamo's cottage. Not long after, Michael Kelly's boys torched a shipment belonging to the same

7

landlord, a tea merchant. He, the landlord, came after Michael, who broke his nose. Michael was transported.

Her father was glaring at her. She had not answered him. 'Yes, I told him,' she said quietly.

'Foolish girl. O'Donahue is a business associate of the man Michael Kelly assaulted.'

'All the more reason not to marry him.'

'You are a devil in petticoats!' He slammed the flat of his hand on the table.

'And you are a damned tyrant! I should have married Thomas Kelly, at least he loves me.'

He had once.

'You will not breed with a weaver!' He strode to the door and stopped with his hand on the knob. Without looking at her he said, 'We shall discuss this further when your mother returns. I will dine at my club.'

He left the room.

She stood shaking with anger, her fingernails digging into her palms. 'I am not a child!' Rhia called after him, but the second she heard the front door close she collapsed onto the Chesterfield, feeling every bit a child. He was right, she should be married by now. William O'Donahue was from Belfast; he had not encountered her reputation before they met, and now she had turned him against her.

Hannah knocked before she entered. She had no doubt heard everything, even if she hadn't had her ear to the door. She scurried about more than was necessary, poking at the fire and lighting the lamps. 'Will you have supper in here, miss?

'I'm a devil in petticoats, Hannah.'

The maid chuckled. 'Well I never heard that one before. He's only in a mood.'

'He's been in a mood for months. This time last year we

would never have closed the front room for an entire day. And now I've turned away the only man in Dublin who might have married me.'

'I'll tell Tilly to make dumplings,' Hannah said, and hurried away as though nothing could be more pressing.

Rhia crossed the room and picked up her paintbrush. The motif was a spray of orange and yellow calendula. If she could make it right, everything else might straighten out too. When her father got home they would make amends. They never slept on a quarrel.

At the sound of Hannah's voice, Rhia's eyes flickered open. She was on the Chesterfield and Hannah was leaning over her, reeking of tooth powder and glycerine. 'There's a fire!' she puffed breathlessly. The candlestick in her plump hand tipped dangerously. Its flame cast skittish shadows around the walls and was the only fire in sight, as far as Rhia could see.

She swung her feet to the floor in a tangle of skirts, catching Hannah below the knees. The maid clutched the arm of the Chesterfield to steady herself; Rhia stumbled around in the dark. There was something she had to remember. What? Shouldn't there be smoke? She found the door to the hallway.

'Quick, Hannah, wake the others, we must get everyone out of the house!'

'It's not in the house,' puffed Hannah, following her. 'It's at Merchant's Quay. The night-soil men saw it.'

The storehouse.

Rhia ran up the dark hallway towards the stairs, though she couldn't think why. Boots? She collided with the banister in the dark, hitting her head and cursing. She could do without boots.

Hannah was behind her when she turned, her nightgown as voluminous as sailcloth. 'I've got Tom hitching up, and his

9

brother's taken the steed to fetch your mam. Don't forget your cloak! And where's your blessed boots? Merciful heavens, and Mr Mahoney's not home yet ...'

Rhia stopped. This was what she needed to remember. 'What is the time, Hannah?'

Hannah didn't know. She had found the boots and followed Rhia back down the hallway chattering anxiously. She mustn't worry – her da would still be at his club, he wasn't exactly going to be at the quay after the soil collection, was he? And would she please put on these blessed boots? It was the first of November, after all.

Rhia stood at the front door, fumbling with the clasp of her old red cloak. There was no time to button boots. Of course he would still be at the club. He would be playing another game of cribbage, or talking about the new looms; or he'd decided to have another brandy or two because his daughter wasn't to be married to a tea merchant after all.

Outside, Tom the groom had hitched the two-seater and the horses were shifting and snorting restlessly, their breath trailing mist in the air. Tom was bleary-eyed, his pale hair in a tangle beneath his cap. He reeked of poteen. He nodded when Rhia climbed up beside him and slapped the reins before she was seated. The horses lurched forwards and she clutched the hammercloth to stop from toppling backwards. She searched her mind for a prayer.

The chaise almost tipped as they clattered through St Auden's Gate and past St Patrick's. Rhia glanced at the cathedral. Would the saint give a damn about an irresolute Catholic?

*Save our storehouse and I'll stop the cursing.*

Was it enough?

*And I'll attend church.*

They'd reached an unsafe speed. Rhia looked sideways at

Tom, tilted forwards, enjoying himself: the groom was a lunatic at the reins even when he'd not been at the drink. She should take them from him, but she wasn't sure that she'd do any better. The mare was on edge; her ears pricked back.

'Slow down, Tom! She'll bolt if she gets any faster.'

Tom nodded. 'Aye, we'll not stop before Kilkenny if Epona bolts. But I reckon Mr Mahoney's at the storehouse.'

'He's not. He's at his club.'

'He's not. It's gone two.'

Rhia's heart pitched. The club closed at one. 'Well then he's gone to the quay to supervise the firefighters.' This seemed reasonable.

The sky above the waterfront was lit up as if all the saints of Dublin were swinging their blessed lanterns above Merchant's Quay. As they rounded the corner of the last alley, Rhia braced herself to see the entire waterfront ablaze. But only the Mahoney storehouse was burning. This was somehow more devastating.

Rhia leapt clear of the chaise before the wheels stopped. Connor Mahoney would be close to the front of the crowd, perhaps with the *gardaí*. She pushed her way through the press of spectators, their faces glowing eerily in the blaze. A wall of flames rose from the stone foundations where only yesterday had stood a wall of brick. The air was poisonous with fumes, the heat staggering. The quay was lit like a carnival, with people still arriving to watch along the opposite shore.

She could not see him.

She darted between fists of spectators, trying to see beyond the line of *gardaí* keeping the crowd back. She searched the faces of the men by the waterside. He must be on the other side, closer to the storehouse, but she would have to get around the *gardaí*. She moved along the edges of the crowd, as close to the furnace as she could get without being overcome by the heat. She might have got a little closer but someone grabbed her wrist, twisting it like a rope. The rough, unwashed wool of a *garda*'s tunic was suddenly in her face.

'*Tuilli!*' She spat before she could remember her wager with the saint. Perhaps cursing in Irish didn't count?

'Who are you calling bastard, you wee tinker?' The *garda*'s expression was as dirty as his face. Rhia held his gaze and tried yanking her arm away, but his fingers pressed into the flesh of her wrist.

'Loose your hand or I'll bite it!' she snapped.

His hand was like a slipknot, fastening tighter when she twisted. He was strong. A ghost of a smile twitched at his lips. 'You don't want to be getting too close to a burning building, now. It could all come down faster than your legs can carry you away.'

'*Please!* It's my family's storehouse. I'm looking for my father!'

'You're never the Mahoney lass?' The raised eyebrows and swift appraising glance said it all. Her hair would be like a bird's nest – it always was after sleep – and her favourite cloak was old. Her feet, she suddenly realised, were bare. The dark looks of the Black Irish came from her mother's side, and Black Irish were as good as tinkers to many Catholics. People thought them of dark nature, as well, which was occasionally useful.

'There's a bold-hearted *garda* gone in after your da. An hour ago.'

*An hour.* The words crushed the breath from Rhia's chest like a lead corset. The *garda*'s grip held her upright.

'You mean …' She would not say it.

He nodded grimly. He expected the worst.

She should pray. Mamo would not counsel prayers to saints.

St Patrick had chased the true religion from Ireland and stolen the sovereignty of women. That's what Mamo said. She would say that fire, being elemental, was the business of the creatures of the Otherworld. Connor Mahoney said Mamo was without religion. To Rhia the stories were just as credible as the immaculate conception and an immortal carpenter. She stared into the fire for the second time that evening, though this time looking for a different kind of grace. For a heartbeat the flames sculpted a heat-white sylph, twisted like a crone. Had she called it from the crucible?

*Cailleach*. Death.

It was only a fire trick; air warped by heat. Rhia had outgrown dragons and enchantresses and vaporous creatures, and all but the most persistent ghosts. She closed her eyes; opened them. Just flames.

She looked around for a means of escape. There was none, so she bit the *garda*'s hand. He tasted as bad as he looked. He bellowed and drew back his other hand, but seemed to think better of hitting her. She might be Connor Mahoney's daughter after all. He twisted her wrist a little tighter instead, making her wince.

'Why has your mam not come?' The *garda* was watching her closely. Did he really think her a tinker, and if he did, then why not let her go? She just might be Connor Mahoney's daughter.

'She's not in town.' The rents were due and more weavers were in trouble. Brigit Mahoney's swift, charitable hands at the loom might not save them, but, in spite of her husband's disapproval, she wouldn't stand by and watch another eviction. The mechanised loom might be the pride of Belfast, but it was enemy to the Greystones pieceworkers.

Rhia suddenly remembered Tom. He could explain who she

13

was to her captor. She scanned the crowd hopefully, but her heart sank when she saw him. Tom had joined a nearby group of spectators who were passing around a flask. The fire had drawn a sizeable crowd from the rookeries as well as from the opposite shore. It was an amusement.

'Cheaper than the penny gaff,' said the *garda*, following her gaze.

The stink of charred cloth filled the air. Rhia remembered Mamo telling her that they'd used linen rags as tinder, because it burnt well. The smoke was in her eyes and lungs. She felt hollowed out. Along with the great timbers of the storehouse, she was dragon's prey. It suddenly struck her that the assurance society's men were not here. She elbowed the *garda*, who narrowed his eyes. 'Where are the firefighters?' she demanded.

'They went home.'

'*Why?*'

'Building's not insured.'

'The building *is* insured!'

He shrugged. His look said that biting him again was not advisable.

It was impossible; Connor Mahoney was unerringly conscientious; *fastidious*, even. He would not forget to keep up the assurance payments. Rhia shook her head, disbelieving.

Eventually, the *garda* eased his vice a little so his dirty nails did not bite into her flesh. Again Rhia tried to snatch her arm away; his grip tightened in response. She did not try again. The fire lessened but continued to burn through the night.

She watched and waited as though her father's life depended on her not taking her eyes from the flames. This time she was certain she saw Cailleach. The hag's hair was a mantle of blazing flax, and her fiery gown trailed the ruin like the tail of the dragon. She was terrible and beautiful; her face as white as ash, her lips as red as embers.

Was she here to take Connor Mahoney?

'*Bring him out or ...*' What? What bargaining power could she possibly have with Death? Threaten to marry a Catholic? She almost had.

The *garda* was looking at her. Had she spoken aloud? The figure vanished into the flames, leaving Rhia blinking away hot tears.

The heat diminished and the flames settled. Darkness lifted just as suddenly, or so it seemed, and the smoking ruin was exposed. The storehouse, yesterday unyielding and constant on the waterfront, was a carcass. Bricks, timbers and thousands of pounds' worth of new linen all reduced to a fine white dust, waiting to be carried away by the smallest breeze.

Brigit Mahoney arrived as dawn exposed the ashen rubble. Most of the crowd had drifted away. Only vagabonds, a few sailors and the *gardaí* remained. Brigit embraced Rhia, but could not speak. Her face, normally so carefully composed, was creased with fear. She was almost in her fiftieth year but her features might have been carved from well-preserved wood. She seemed smaller today, her shoulders rigid.

Brigit was looking at Rhia's feet and Rhia followed her gaze. They looked like marble in the half-light. She had barely noticed the aching chill of them until now.

'I didn't feel the cold,' she mumbled.

'Then perhaps they are frozen. My calfskin slippers are in the carriage. There is a flask of tea.'

Rhia returned from the carriage shod and carrying the stoneware flask. Her mother was talking quietly to the *garda* who had detained her. He glanced up at Rhia wearing an expression that said he believed her, now. They shared the steaming brew with the remaining men. None spoke Connor Mahoney's name.

They waited. No one wanted to be the first to lose hope, but there was no sign of life from the ruin, and barely a flame. 'The lawn at the cottage is like a Persian carpet,' Brigit whispered. 'The pink and scarlet rose petals are scattered everywhere.' She was trying to evoke something beautiful; to soothe them both. 'And the leaves from the maple and the copper beech. I thought you might come with your paintbox ...' She trailed off with a choking sound, her fingers flying to her lips. Rhia followed her gaze. The body of Connor Mahoney was being carried from the skeleton of the storehouse on a makeshift bier by two *gardaí*. He was black as a sweep and as still as death.

Her mother gripped her hand so hard it felt as if the bones would crack. They walked towards the bier, which was being lowered gently to the ground. Those gathered stepped back to let them pass. Connor Mahoney's left leg was twisted so badly that it looked as though his trousers were stuffed with rags. His face was a dark mask.

The moment was an eternity.

Brigit sank down beside her husband and kissed his blackened lips as though they were alone together. '*Leannán,*' she whispered, *my love.* Her little shoulders finally collapsed. Rhia knelt beside her.

'He is alive,' said the young *garda*, black from head to foot. 'He is alive.'

Rhia laughed and her mother wept. The *garda* beamed and thumped the young hero on the back, handing him the flask. The boy told them how they had passed the night. The fire started at the bottom of the building, he said, when Mr Mahoney fell down the stairs, dropping a tallow into a basket of oiled linen. In the fall he'd broken his leg, and by the time his rescuer arrived the cellar was their only hope. It was, providentially, connected to a tunnel that led deep into an old vault close by the river. A tiny vent; perhaps a rat's entrance, had allowed them to breathe plain air when the room filled with smoke.

The boy waved off their thanks and praise and looked uncomfortable. He did not seem to think it remarkable that he had saved a man's life. He was merely disappointed that the flask contained tea and not whiskey.

Someone was despatched for the infirmary coach.

Rhia watched her mother take the coarse blanket that was offered and place it gently over her husband. She brushed his hair from his eyes, lightly, and dusted ash from his shoulders.

The *garda* who had detained Rhia smiled before he walked away. She smiled back. Cailleach be damned. Tonight, after all, there had been grace.

# Flannel

Morning sloped into the ramshackle docks. Rhia walked away from the quay as if she could leave the night behind, but its smell lingered, threaded through her hair and the wool of her hood. The infirmary coach was drawn away by four drays, carrying Brigit, pale and weary, clasping her husband's hand. Rhia sent Tom back to St Stephen's Green. He didn't look well on his night of thrills and cheap potato whiskey, but she couldn't summon the energy to reprimand him.

The water trade started to gain momentum along the docks and she felt soothed by the commotion. She pulled her hood forwards, for invisibility, but a young fisherman still tipped his cap and grinned foolishly, following her with his eyes until she'd passed. It was hard to be invisible in a red cloak.

She sifted through the ruins of the night. What if the *garda* had not found the cellar hatch? What if it had been Connor Mahoney's time to die?

She stopped still.

It was Samhain. How could she have forgotten? This was the night when the dead awoke whilst the living slept. When the Others were abroad. If Cailleach had not come for her father, then for whom? She pulled her cloak closer and kept walking, faster now.

The smell of burnt cloth seemed to be all around her. She tried not to think about all that linen turned to cinder. It was a disaster. But there was clearly some confusion about the assurance society – her father never forgot to pay his accounts.

Their quarrel would continue to trouble her until they had made peace. They were too alike; both pig-headed. He'd usually bring home a lace fichu or a length of silk after a dispute and say that he regretted his words. Rhia would then apologise for whatever heated remarks she had made and that would be that.

She had never wanted to marry William O'Donahue. She had sensed what kind of man he was beneath his manicured respectability; his oiled whiskers and London tailoring. But she had not sabotaged the engagement. Perhaps she should not have confided the events of that cold January night, seven years on and still so sharp in her memory and her heart; she had carried the couple's babe to Mamo's cottage, in awe of its wee hands. The weaver's landlord was, like Connor Mahoney, a member of the United Irishmen; an alliance of Protestant and Catholic traders against the English stranglehold on Irish produce. She had made the man look heartless. (Never mind that he was.) She had made herself seem unattractively active. There was a difference, her father said, between being rebellious and being a rebel. Mamo had been proud of her.

William had found the affair highly distasteful, and made it clear that his sympathy rested with the landlord, rather than the tenants. After all, they had not paid their rent for three months. In turn, Rhia made it clear that she considered him as pitiless as any man who built his fortune on the ruins of honest labour. He had looked startled to hear her disagree with him. The memory of his expression cheered her.

The eye-watering stink of the port area made her nostalgic. As a child, she would often beg to accompany her father when he was supervising a linen shipment, and thrill to inhale the reek of wet canvas, and to get close enough to a sailor to smell the tar on his breeches and the tobacco on his breath. She loved to hear the creak of leather straps on wicker, as basket upon basket of Mahoney Linen was hoisted onto the deck of a sleek tea clipper, bound for London. The sound always sent a shiver through her; it signalled the beginning of a journey to a place so exotic and mysterious that it might as well have been the Otherworld: London. But one had to cross the Irish Sea to get there.

The sea.

Whenever Ryan visited Dublin, Rhia begged him for tales of the capital. London had cultivated her uncle, who had always been elegant but was now worldly and sophisticated. He made the capital sound like the most intoxicating city in the western world. Ryan would not be receiving their shipment of linen at China Wharf this season, nor finding buyers for Mahoney's sheerest cambric or heavy damask. Irish linen was not Ryan Mahoney's only enterprise, of course. He also imported wool from the continent, cotton from India and silk from China.

Along the port market, Rhia took refuge in the familiar, nodding her greeting to the barrow-keepers who recognised her; guilefully dodging the vendors you could smell from a distance, their pails filled with cockles, jellied eels and herring. The everyday muddle of wastrel beggars, canny merchants and bleary-eyed passengers calmed her.

Beyond the fishermen bartering with prostitutes, Rhia saw something that made her woes seem trifling. A line of female convicts, a queue of sagging brown flannel, shackled and surrounded by *gardaí*. Their pale faces stared vacantly, as though they had already departed their land and kin. Their utter hopelessness. For a moment, Rhia was one with them. The sensation was so strong that she clutched an upturned drum to steady herself. Such feelings only ever got her into trouble. She could do nothing for these women. She turned away, thinking of Michael Kelly, whose wife and son had not seen him for nearly seven years.

She arrived at the last market stall. Nell the fryer was up to her elbows in fish scales. Her flesh wobbled from her chins to her buttocks every time she slammed a fat trout or glittering salmon down on her block. On her fire was a griddle pan and in it was a fillet of something that had, a few hours before, spent its last night swimming up the Liffey. When she noticed Rhia, Nell gave her a sparse-toothed grin and wiped her poxed hands on her apron.

'Rhia, me lovely! You look half dead. Set them skinny haunches down and take a draught.'

Rhia did as she was told, and a dish of fried whiting was slapped down in front of her. Nell cocked her large head and squinted. 'Well, what the devil is Rhiannon Mahoney doing in the port market at sparrow's fart?'

Rhia burst into tears. She had been perfectly all right until she saw the women. She was quickly enfolded in Nell's mighty bosom, which radiated fish oil and love. 'There there, blossom. There there. Is it a blackguard? Or is it your da again?'

Rhia took a deep draught of warm porter, and then, amidst sobs, told Nell her troubles. Nell always knew how to make things right. She was astonishingly well-informed about the world for a woman who had never left Dublin. She had survived the last epidemic of the pox, which invaded the rookeries around the port like the Norsemen, taking all of her family from her. The world came to Nell; she heard of its farthest reaches from sailors and traders, whores and thieves. Nell the fryer's fish was legendary.

'I believe the business was in need of a prosperous son-in-law,' Rhia concluded. 'We have less custom with each new season because we charge more than the factories. People don't care that hand-woven linen is of better quality, they want what's cheapest.' This made Rhia weep all over again. She would not make such a spectacle of herself in the presence of just anyone. Better to be thought brazen than hysterical.

Nell cocked her head the opposite way, tutted and sighed. 'These machines will be the finish of honest labour. Take heart, blossom, bricks and cloth are easily made, but boldness is not. A lady is as limp as a dead trout without it. A lady such as yourself, with knowledge of a trade, can earn her living – husband or no – though I doubt your da would have it. Now take yourself home before your mam finds you missing. The woman has cares enough without you giving her more. But first, you finish that fish!'

Rhia did as she was told, then she hugged Nell and left the port market.

She took the shortest route home, behind the rookeries. A band of ragged urchins followed her until she stopped and told them that she thought them brave to be abroad so early after the night of the witches. 'I'm on my way home from a witch's gathering,' she added, 'and if you don't leave me alone I'll turn you all into beetles.' They ran off laughing and squealing.

Beyond the rookeries was the dyers' quarter, where bolts of cloth were hung out to dry all along the alleyways: saffron, scarlet, indigo and emerald. Rhia the child had thought the dyers' streets an enchanted forest. No one looked twice at her red cloak here. It was here that she had once imagined days as pieces in a quilt made of all colours and cloths; some days were bright and delicate, others discoloured and ruined.

Today was dove grey, and silk. A melancholy cloth that whispered and rustled and liked to be mysterious. Who could say what it foretold.

# Yarn

Michael Kelly pulled the brim of his hat down against the sun. Even at the end of a November day, the broad corridor of George Street was sunlit and lively. Most of the shopfronts were now shuttered, but striped awnings were hoisted at all hours here, all the days of the year. In Sydney, no draper, confectioner nor bookseller left goods displayed in their windows. Cloth faded, vendibles turned rancid and paper crisped.

Michael had an uneasy alliance with this remote shore, his home and his prison. A man would be a fool not to hold some regard for the unseen in Australia; for ancestral heroes and sacred places. Disrespect for the wildness of the land had cost many a convict his worthless life.

When Jarrah told him about the Altjeringa – the 'religion' of the original Australians – Michael was not surprised. He had felt it. The place was overrun with spirits, some freshly slaughtered and others which had apparently been around since the world's dawn. In this alone, Australia was like Ireland; the gods were inseparable from the land. It had taken Michael years of scrutinising Jarrah, the only Original he knew, to even begin to see it.

The craving for home used to spoil his gut when he caught sight of the watery horizon. But now the silvery shale of Greystones and the wistful mauve of the Wicklow Hills were so remote that he barely believed they existed. Here, the beaches were met by tow-headed cliffs and laid with pale sand, and the mountains to the west looked dangerous. The sky was of a blue so striking that it seemed unreasonable such a colour should occur in nature.

Michael couldn't say that he'd miss Sydney, but the colony had an unexpected anarchism that he approved of. He supposed this was the natural condition of a place whose population was cobbled together from the lawless outcasts of other societies. Shackled together, he thought wryly. The place was damned beautiful, too, for a prison.

There was a carelessness about the George Street shopgirls who jostled past him on their way to the cocoa rooms at Circular Quay. Their bare arms were linked, their hair loose and their gait typically defiant. Sweethearts were more daring here, children louder and men more violent. The public behaviour of the colonists was unique. Sydney was unlike any place Michael had known, and he'd known plenty.

He had a lot of time, lately, for the past. It seemed to press against him with more force the closer he got to leaving. As a young, wayfaring sailor, he'd taken whatever commission he could to avoid the stationary industry of weaving. He'd seen the ports of Europe and Africa and had got as far as Bombay with sherry and tobacco from Bristol. The cargo was not for sale. Rather, it was destined for the cellars and pipes of the gentleman of the East India Company. His father called him home before he was near ready, because of a contractual arrangement with the Dublin Mahoneys. Then he met Annie. After that, Michael only went to sea in his dreams, or spinning salty tales for Thomas and young Rhia Mahoney, who begged to hear them again and again. Over the years his stories grew bigger and more embellished, but their scoundrels were usually the same – the Merchant Venturers who controlled the Bristol docks.

It was after he'd spent a few days in Colaba, the thriving colonial port of Bombay, that Michael began to reflect upon the dark underbelly of profit. It was the stinking slums behind the stately offices of the East India Company in Bombay that did it. He could not fathom how, when the merchants of Dublin and London were investing so much capital in Indian produce, the children of Bombay had rags for clothing, no food, no books nor schools and slept in the street.

In the port taverns where the British traders took their drink, Michael learnt that the very *gentlemen* whose sherry and tobacco he had accompanied across the Indian Ocean, were forcing Indian farmers to grow poppies. The arable land remaining for food crops was negligible. Five thousand chests, containing one hundred and thirty pounds of resin each, left India annually for China on the ships of British merchants. This single commodity provided the commerce upon which the empire prevailed. Michael could barely fathom how many poppies were grown, how many farmers and farmers' children it took, to accomplish this feat. All in the name of commercial expansion.

He'd only realised the full extent of the crime when he happened upon an opium den in St Giles. That was the first time he'd seen a hollowed out man; a living carcass emptied of spirit. He'd seen many more since putting to sea with a ship load of condemned men. He'd seen truer crimes committed by wealthy industrialists than by any of the petty criminals who populated this town. The tea merchant who had sent him down was running opium from Calcutta to Canton, then collecting his China tea and shipping it to London and Dublin. It was the dogs in doublets Michael was after bringing down; that much hadn't changed.

The toil of a sailor had mettled his body and his nerve, but it was nothing to how the last seven years had sharpened his wits. He might be more than fifty now, but he was as able as he had ever been. His skin was browned like leather, and on the rare occasion that he caught a glimpse of his reflection in a glass, he was always a little startled by the way his face seemed etched with those years.

In the sandy, darkening street, children played skittles with pebbles and seashells, and built fortresses from driftwood. Contrary to the mutterings he'd heard about the offspring of felons, these children weren't as lawless as those in the slums of Dublin and London. Michael reckoned it was because their playground stretched from the golden sands to the silver-green scrub forest, where they could chase small marsupials and brilliant parakeets, and hunt for insects too large to keep in a jar.

At its western rim, the settlement was skirted by a large saltwater lagoon which provided the natural boundary between the land that had been claimed by the city and that which was still occupied by the Altjeringa. Only children dared to cross to the other side of the lagoon and to fish for turtles with the Originals, who were magnificent hunters.

Jarrah occasionally agreed to be a tracker for the constabulary, though an escaped convict was more often found dead than alive. His tribe, the Eora, had inhabited the coastal hunting grounds until Phillip saw fit to tenant them. Michael was not entirely alone in his empathy for the Originals; there was many an Irishman in Sydney who knew what it was like to be turfed off his land by an Englishman. He was in awe of them. Jarrah could find a trail after a sandstorm, a deluge or a brush fire. But if he himself didn't want to be troubled by white men, he simply became invisible.

The convicts assigned to cattle stations and who tilled the

barely arable land, told stories of old men standing on one leg, still and naked as statues, for over an hour, spears poised, waiting for some creature to emerge from its hole. They shook their heads as they described young hunters, little more than babes, creeping through the dry underbrush in pursuit of a possum or reptile, moving as silently as their own shadows. Michael had not come to this land to claim it as his own, so it was clear to him that these uncanny people honoured the red earth and belonged to it in a way no Christian ever would.

Dan, the wool draper (who had served his sentence and opted to stay), was on the footpath outside his shop. 'Lovely evenin', Mr Kelly.'

''Tis so, Dan. How's the trade?'

'Can't complain. Though if I did, I'd say it's not exactly the temperature for wool.'

'Aye. You shipping it yet?'

'We'll be sending our first home-spun to Bristol come end of the month. There's a yarn dyer up near the barracks now.'

'Thought about Dublin, have you?'

'Can't say as I have, Mr Kelly, why's that?'

'Well, there'd be many a Dublin merchant happy to buy yarn or spun cloth and not give his silver to the Crown, if you take my meaning.'

'I do. Well, I'll give it some thought.'

'You do that, Dan. Regards to your wife.'

The wool draper tipped his cap and finished bolting his shutters, and Michael continued on his way to the Harp and Shamrock.

The hot, dry breath of the day lingered, and Michael was thirsty. The seasons were topsy-turvy here, so November was a month already expectant of the scorching summer. George Street was neat and new, the sandstone, quarried from the nearby cliffs, still pale and unweathered. Here were all of the commodities of any city in the western world, yet it was so far east as to not be thought a part of that world. Few would believe that each day he passed by more banks and churches than one would find along a carriageway of equal distance in London; that he lived in an attic above a professor of the pianoforte and harp, and next door to livery stables; that there were French baskets and fancy biscuits to buy. He had not expected this of the colony. He had heard only of lawlessness and scurvy, both conditions that he had encountered before and had little regard for. To be sure, there was crime and illness here, and worse, but then, there was an underbelly to the veneer of civility and respectability of *any* prospering place.

Occasionally, the children playing on George Street scattered to one side of the road to avoid a bullock dray piled high with shafts of wheat or merino fleece, or a landau containing one of the Hebrew bankers from Pitt Street.

Or that rarity, a lady.

Such creatures always stopped a game of skittles. The picture of white muslin and a pale straw bonnet caused most eyes to swivel, Michael's included. The sight of a lady, even the wife of a merchant, was like a cool balm in this overheated land. She might be regarded with envy or curiosity; resentment or lechery; or simply because she was clean as new linen – a welcome tonic for eyes that, like his, looked upon men, masonry and wood shavings all day, and at night upon an inky letterpress.

Michael walked wide of the footpath to avoid a game. Some days everything reminded him that wealthy men caused the suffering of children. The opium traders would never see the gallows nor the stinking belly of a convict transport. Michael never thought he'd clap eyes on the breed in Sydney, but there was more land here than an Irishman could dream of, and that meant merino, cedar and wheat, and trade with India and China.

It meant silver.

Everyone wanted silver. It was the only currency the emperor of China would take for his tea. Had it escaped the attention of the few good men in Whitehall that the West thrived on a stimulating brew that financed the East to dull its wits on opium? Perhaps Britain intended to colonise China by making its population oblivious.

Michael sighed at his own unhappy preoccupations. Annie would have told him to find something to be pleased about and to keep his mind where his boots were. Well, right now they were on the way to the Harp and Shamrock, and that was something to be pleased about.

# Jacquard

The upstairs parlour had the best view of St Stephen's Green which was, this morning, clad in diaphanous fog. Serious-looking gentlemen with black coat-tails and walking canes appeared and disappeared like apparitions. They were not (not as far as Rhia could tell). These were men with earthly concerns in offices and chambers. It was the time of day when the light could be fleetingly incandescent. If she narrowed her eyes and focused her mind, a shape might just emerge from the shifting patterns amongst the trees and the mist. She had not opened her paintbox since the fire; had not looked upon the world with an eye to light and shade; colour and shape. Her mind would not be coaxed away from its troubles.

Ryan's letter lay where she had dropped it on the window seat. Rhia picked it up and read it again, pacing in front of the window.

China Wharf
London

7 November 1840

My dear Brigit,
I was grieved beyond measure by your news, and deeply regret that I cannot leave London this month. How like you to look immediately to your blessings: my brother's life, your mother's cottage, yours and Rhia's skill and experience.

I have taken the liberty of discussing your situation with a recently widowed friend. Antonia Blake is a woman of good character with considerable knowledge of the trade. She is of the abstemious Quaker faith, but you will never meet a more generous soul. Her husband Josiah, my friend and associate, died tragically early in the summer whilst in India on business.

Mrs Blake has invited Rhia to reside with her in the City of London, a vibrant and exciting quarter of the capital. She says she would enjoy the company of another woman. It is plain that she is missing Josiah terribly. I would offer lodgings myself, but have recently given up the City address and moved into my offices at China Wharf.

Antonia assures me that there are an abundance of positions for young ladies of good character advertised daily in the London papers. Would you consider allowing Rhia to come? A young woman as bright as she would easily find a post as a governess or companion, and I know Connor is anxious that she marry. In a modern city such as London it is still possible for a spirited twenty-eight-year-old to find an eligible husband! It is something you might consider, at any rate.

I must continually remind myself that I will receive no shipment of linen from Dublin this autumn, but the trade is changing rapidly. The import price of American cotton has recently plummeted due to London clothiers and drapers stocking the new blended fibres. This is an exciting time and an ever-expanding enterprise. Of course, I have been trying to convince my brother for years that there is no future in hand-woven cloth.

Connor confided the state of Mahoney Linen to me in the summer, and I had by now hoped to provide some means of rescue, but it is complicated. It is not only because I am not convinced traditional methods have any future, but because my finances are temporarily inaccessible.

Do let me know what you decide with regard to Mrs Blake's offer. I would love to have Rhia in London, but the decision must be made by you both.

God bless you and may His grace be with you in your troubles.

Ryan Mahoney


Rhia bit her lip and glanced back to the Green. There was still no sign of her mother. What exactly was 'the state of Mahoney Linen' that her father had confided to his brother? It sounded ominous. Was this why her mother was being so sparing of the tallow and the gaslight, and had instructed Tilly to boil a leg of mutton clean to make another meal of it? As usual, no one had told Rhia anything.

She folded the letter. She should not have read it. Her mother had left it on top of the dresser knowing full well that Rhia used that mirror to braid her hair, so she could hardly be blamed for her curiosity – her *blessed interestedness* as Hannah called it. Her father called it unbecoming. She didn't miss his opinions on what the female mind was and was not suited to, but she missed not having his quiet proprieties running the business. Without him, nothing felt right.

She squinted at the Green, searching for a distraction, trying not to think about Ryan's letter. How did this house appear to those who passed by? An elegant house, built in the time of the first King George, painted white in the London fashion; the house of a successful merchant.

Was it all a lie?

Her mother should be back from the infirmary by now. Rhia was impatient to know how long it would be before they opened the front room for trade again. She was restless and bored and tired of not being told things. She suspected that this was no different to being a wife.

She'd only been out on Epona to escape Hannah's long face. She'd given up on trying to make Hannah smile after being chided for her blessed cheerfulness. The entire household was in a mood. The mare was no better. She sensed Rhia's restlessness, which made her frisky if they left the cobbles for the fields. Rhia wasn't in the mood for jumping stiles.

She couldn't decide if Ryan's proposal made her feel anxious or excited.

It would mean crossing the sea.

It was all very well standing at its shore with her feet on the land. The idea that a boat was safe at sea was laughable.

Rhia looked around the room for something to occupy her. Only the coal fire here in the parlour was lit, now that the downstairs rooms were closed to customers. The ivory-papered walls and pale rose furnishings were restful, but she had spent too much time here lately and it was beginning to feel like a cage. She had scoured her father's bookshelves for something she hadn't read, and had found Tilly's secret hiding place for her penny journals. This proved to be a waste of time, since Tilly had ripped out all the most interesting pages for fear someone would find them.

On the upside, since the fire Rhia had read the *Irish Times* daily without having to defend her 'blessed interestedness'. The shipping news was still dominated by the events unfolding in the Port of Canton between the British Navy and the Chinese war junks. It was enthralling reading, though she supposed she shouldn't feel this way about another war. She wondered what opium was like. She'd taken laudanum for a week once and it had rendered her practically senseless. Yesterday, there had been an essay on a new fad called photogenic drawing. It required the use of a light box, parchment, silver nitrate and salt. She could not imagine how on earth a portrait might be effected from such an unlikely recipe.

Brigit Mahoney was easy to spot from a distance in her pea-green cloak. As she drew closer, a triangle of colour flashed beneath it. She was wearing purple. This was not a good sign.

Purple was not an everyday colour for Rhia's mother. She wore it when she needed courage, such as on the days when she took tea at the linen hall with the other Catholic merchants' wives. Brigit was hurrying along the path that meandered through the Green. As she passed, one or two gentlemen turned to catch a second glimpse of her small, swift figure. She did not have the look of a Dublin lady. She wore plain dresses in solid colours, and although she always delighted in the season's prints, she rarely took more than a passing interest in a fashionable sleeve or corsage. Rhia, on the other hand, took note of every new conceit.

She still had the letter in her hand. That was foolish. By the time she had run up the stairs and replaced it on the dresser, Brigit was in the front hall. Usually, Rhia could judge immediately how the invalid fared by the depth of the creases etched between her eyebrows.

'He is not improved, then?'

Her mother brushed a loose strand of hair from Rhia's eyes. 'A little.'

It wasn't true.

'The physician says he might recover more quickly were he cheerful. He frets ceaselessly that he has let us down, that he has,' she hesitated, 'caused the ruin of the company.'

'*Is* the company ruined?' Rhia could not take her eyes from her mother's face as Brigit hung her cloak and smoothed her hair. The air turned cold, as if all the shadows in the house had gathered in the front hall to hear her answer. 'You're wearing purple.' Rhia's voice sounded accusing, even to her ears.

'There are things that need doing in the front room. Will you help me?'

The room was bathed in darkness. Brigit pulled the curtains open and let in the morning light. The long cutting table in the centre looked forlorn and the Chesterfield only reminded Rhia of the night of the fire. This room was where all of the public business of Mahoney Linen was conducted.

She wandered to the wall opposite the door, which was lined with deep shelves, bowed under the weight of rolls and rolls of damask, jacquard, chintz and cambric. She ran her hands over plain and patterned linens of different ply and quality; some woven, others printed. Prints were the Mahoney mainstay and Rhia loved them all; tea party florals, Indian paisleys, modern abstracts, this riot of pattern and colour had always delighted her. She'd gazed at prints for years without realising that she was learning composition. Later, for detail, she went to *Culpeper's Herbal*. She became preoccupied with the way that quality of light changed the natural world, from the silvery Greystones shale to Dublin's flaxen autumns. She had a portmanteau full of designs for repeat patterns. It was an amusement, though. Designing textiles was not a woman's occupation.

Brigit was standing in the middle of the room looking at the shelves with her hands on her hips. Rhia made herself sit on the Chesterfield and fidgeted with her sleeve. She took in the lay of the room as though she had never before noticed it. Memories paraded before her. The entire front of the house always smelt of flax, and she had spent her days here for as long as she could remember. As a child she had sewn pretty scraps of cloth into miniature quilts for her dolls while her parents ran the business. Sometimes she'd sat quietly in the corner with her paintbox and tiny easel, listening to the clip of Brigit's shears and the scratch of her father's fountain pen. Thomas had made the paintbox and easel for her, only then he became annoyed when she started to copy from Culpeper instead of walk with him. Still, it was years before any of her botanicals were recognisable.

Brigit was still gazing at the shelves as if trying to decide something. Rhia stood up and walked the length of the room and back, twice. She wanted to ask about the letter, but her mother seemed too deep in thought. When Brigit turned round, she looked wretched.

'Rhiannon.' She only called Rhia this when something was wrong.

'I know about the letter. I read it,' Rhia said.

'I knew you would. Today I asked your father to tell me the truth. We were in debt to several creditors before the fire, which is why the rather expensive assurance policy was cancelled. A false economy, as it turns out. The loss of the stock and storehouse has ruined us. We have agreed that we must sell this house and move permanently to Greystones.'

Rhia was not prepared for this. She walked over to the window. The fog had lifted and the Green was lively with costermongers and nannies with black hooded prams. Her composure fell away. 'Why didn't he tell us?'

Brigit looked at her imploringly. 'Don't be angry. He was ashamed. He believes he has managed the business badly, but it is simply a result of the times. Our methods are becoming old-fashioned. It is not so awful. We are blessed to have Greystones. You always wanted to spend more time there.'

Rhia tried to grasp what this all meant. 'But how will we live?'

'We will manage. You forget that I spun wool before I met your father; I still have deft fingers and there are Mamo's sheep. Thomas Kelly can weave a broadcloth as fine as any I have seen, and Michael will have served his sentence by next summer.'

Rhia struggled to take it all in. It was now clear why her father had been so angry over her broken engagement. She felt like a criminal. 'And I turned William O'Donahue against me.'

Brigit shook her head firmly. 'A man such as he would probably have dishonoured the engagement once the state of our affairs was known. You were lucky to escape that, though I would never say so in front of your father.' There was little she would dare to say in front of her husband. Mamo had always been disgusted by it.

Brigit had said nothing of Ryan's proposal. Surely she wouldn't want Rhia to go? She would want her to stay and spin wool. The offer was tainted, anyway, by the governess thing, and besides, she was not nearly clever enough. The only Latin that interested her was the names of plants, and her French was poor. 'What about London?' she ventured.

'You would have to spend a night and a day at sea to reach Holyhead.'

Rhia shuddered. It was settled, then.

Brigit kissed her on the forehead, then left her alone to wrap herself in whatever cloth this day of change might represent.

Rhia absently rolled up a bolt of pretty jacquard that was on the cutting table and picked bits of thread from the floor. She glimpsed herself in London. She had always dreamed that she would visit the capital with her husband, travel being one of the few advantages in having a husband at all. Of course, the likelihood of marrying was increasingly remote, and her dreams always conveniently overlooked the inevitable sea crossing.

As to love, it was clearly a condition that had originated in the minds, rather than the hearts, of poets. Everyone knew that aside from a dowry and annuity, husbands preferred a tepid nature and an agreeable tongue. Or a tongue that always agreed. These were graces that Rhia neither possessed nor could become interested in fostering. What was to love in that? Perhaps she was destined to be a governess living in the house of a Quaker after all.

# Satin

On the way to Pudding Lane, Antonia Blake was inconveniently overcome by emotion. She took out her handkerchief, neatly side-stepping some unidentifiable filth in the street (one advantage in having one's gaze cast down).

On certain days it seemed that she had only just received the news of Josiah's death. Today was such a day. She focused her mind fiercely on short ends of ribbon and bias binding. The theatrical costumer had seemed pleased when she first approached him. Not because he had heard of prison reform or Elizabeth Fry's charitable works, but because it relieved him of the extra bother of disposing of unusable cloth. All the better of course, he said, if it was put to some purpose beyond rag picking.

The Pudding Lane costume workshop was a cluttered front room, in the corner of which was a trestle table and a huddle of straw and cloth mannequins. Onto these was pinned and stitched all manner of regalia; the buttons and braid of a Napoleonic tunic, a cascade of scalloped flounces for a Shakespearean heroine and an ass's head made from horsehair.

Antonia always felt acutely plain when she visited the costumer. He made no secret of his fascination with the lack of ornament on a woman of means, and his eyes usually roamed unashamedly over the cut and cloth that she wore. She imagined he was, over time, working up the courage to enquire after her faith. Quakerism was clearly something of a mystery to one whose living was derived from the decorative and theatric. He would know that those of her faith refused to bear arms, pay tithes on church land, or take the sacraments, and as such were heretics of a kind. He would also know, as all seemed to, that the Society of Friends excelled in business and were amongst London's richest bankers and wealthiest merchants. This was all Antonia herself had known about the Friends before she met Josiah Blake.

It was not to be the day for a conversation of this kind. The costumer was in a state of distress, which was not unusual. He was habitually fearful that he might not complete some assignation or other before a dress rehearsal. Today, a bodice had been cut for an actress whose waist had expanded, following her recent success in Drury Lane. She was, he explained mournfully, sustaining herself on suppers of meat pies and cream cakes rather than the bread and tea she had used to make do with. The costumer gave Antonia her sack of cloth with only a cursory glance at her grey linen and starched white collar. As he did, he complained of the complexities of inserting a panel of satin so that the elegant line of the décolletage was not lost. She could not help but take a step closer to his table and look at the pieces of the troublesome bodice. She was relieved to have something, a salve, to occupy her mind.

'It might be that you could insert two narrow panels here and here instead,' she suggested, 'then it would look as if you were deliberately making something of the new seams.' The sweaty little man was staring at her with utter disbelief. She did not look like she knew a thing about the cut of a corsage. Antonia laughed at his expression. 'My father is a mercer,' she explained. 'There are often shirtmakers and seamstresses in his showroom, measuring silk around their paper pieces so as not to waste an inch of precious cloth. I no longer take an interest in fashionable clothing, but I hope that I still have an eye for silhouette and ... contour.'

'You have indeed. You are most gracious to share your expert eye with me, Mrs Blake. Why, I believe you have solved the riddle of the thing! Is your father a London mercer?'

'His emporium is in Manchester.'

'Then you will have come to London when you married.' It was a clever means of extracting information without appearing to enquire.

'Yes. My late husband was a cotton trader. The trade was how we came to meet.'

The costumer looked embarrassed. 'I am sorry for your loss. I did not realise.'

There was no salve. Why, today of all days, should she have to be reminded? 'You could not,' she said quickly. 'And I must be getting on. As ever, our organisation is most grateful.' Antonia hurried away before her composure was undone by a conversation with a relative stranger. She was overcome by small things. She could still not completely believe him gone. How could he be gone?

Josiah had upheld the excellent reputation of Quaker merchants and was a man of his word. He had been among the first to voice an opinion on the trade ban with China. It was a Quaker ship that had triggered the sea battle that now raged near Canton. The captain of the *Thomas Coutts* had refused to acknowledge that the British Navy's blockade of the Pearl River, preventing Chinese trading vessels from passing, was legal. The Pearl River was the only means of reaching Canton, the most important port in the East. The Blakes, like all Quakers, considered themselves outside of the dispute between the Emperor of China and the British East India traders. They were bringing cotton and wool into Canton, not opium.

When she was seated in the privacy of a Hackney cab surrounded by her bags of cloth, Antonia leaned back and wept. She had been mercifully distracted at the costumers, but in the dark privacy of the carriage there was no longer the need to pretend. She need only be composed by the time she reached the Montgomery emporium, her next appointment. Composure, like charity, whether heartfelt or not, was her shield. Beneath it skulked fear and loneliness, always measuring her faith and her strength.

When her handkerchief was wringing wet and her eyes dry, Antonia felt calmed. She straightened her back. There were women in far greater misery than she, locked away in pitiful conditions in dank, subterranean cells. Some waited to be hanged, and others to be sent far away from their children. It should fortify her to think that, by her hand, the suffering of another might lessen.

Antonia was cheered to find Mr Montgomery on the shop floor in his shirt sleeves. Mr Beckwith was up a ladder arranging bolts of pearly silk and sleek cashmere. Grace Elliot, the assistant, was behind the counter, her face drawn as tightly as her stays. Antonia was accustomed to her airs. It was a peculiarity of Londoners that they were affronted by appearances to the point of prejudice. Northerners were more robust in their judgement, and not so easily fooled by a myrtle green petticoat or a candy stripe bonnet.

Mr Montgomery smiled so warmly when he saw her that she felt her heart lurch.

'Mrs Blake! What a happy coincidence that I should be here for your visit. I have asked Miss Elliot to put aside some remnants for you. Is your carriage on Regent Street?' He turned to

Mr Beckwith, who had come down the ladder and was smiling shyly at Antonia. 'Francis, would you bring the sacks from the storeroom?'

They were as unalike as two gentlemen could possibly be. Mr Montgomery was tall and lean with an abundance of pewter hair and a fondness for Savile Row tailors. It was unusual to see him without his coat and, in spite of herself, Antonia admired the breadth of his shoulders. Francis Beckwith was slight and balding, his mud-coloured suits always ill-fitting. Josiah had considered Beckwith the cleverer of the two; he'd thought that, without Beckwith, Montgomery would not be known as king of the mercers.

'Tell me, Mrs Blake, what progress have you made with Mr Talbot's mysterious potion? I admit that I am baffled by it, though it has captured the imagination of London as thoroughly as a scandal.' He was looking at her as though her opinion on such things mattered.

'It does seem to be the latest sensation, doesn't it?' Photogenic drawing had captivated her from the moment Laurence, Josiah's cousin, showed her his experiments with the calotype process. After that, she begged Laurence to instruct her every time he visited. She still found it extraordinary that light could pass through a small brown box and form a picture on the wall opposite. But to now be able to transfer the light onto paper, as Fox Talbot's famous innovation could, was simply wondrous. Laurence had been lodging in the house since the news of Josiah's death, and the entire third floor was now their calotype laboratory.

'Speaking of photogenic drawing, what of our experiment?' Mr Montgomery was smiling. He had no idea what he was asking of her. She was surprised, also, that he considered the experiment to be *theirs*. He had been merely one of her subjects.

Mr Montgomery was conveniently distracted by a customer. How could he understand? Early in the spring, just before Josiah had sailed for Calcutta, Antonia had decided that she wanted to take her experimentation a step further; to *capture* a negative image via its exposure to light. On a bright day soon after, several of Josiah's colleagues, including Mr Montgomery, gathered at Cloak Lane to discuss a joint venture. Antonia had, that day, not only asked the gentlemen gathered to donate cloth scraps and factory ends to the Convict Ship Committee, but also to be her subjects. In the spirit of supporting the new science (or perhaps to humour her), five gentlemen, including Josiah, allowed themselves to be arranged in a tableau in the garden.

The negative was now carefully preserved in a silk wallet, as advised by Laurence. The paper looked no different at all after its exposure, though he said this was normal. And now, with the recent arrival of her licence, Antonia finally had permission to bring the image to paper. Or, to use the expression coined by Mr Talbot, to make a representation. How could she, though? How could she bear to see Josiah's face gazing back at her, as though a ghostly portrait had been painted *after his death*. One day she would feel brave enough to expose the negative, and Josiah's face, to the light. She would be exposing her heart to the truth in a more tangible way than her faith had ever done. Grief, Isaac said, eventually evolved from refutal to acceptance. He would know.

Mr Beckwith returned from the storeroom lugging two bulging sacks. While he fastened them, Antonia noted that Mr Montgomery had donated some exceedingly high grade remainders. He had been more generous than usual since Josiah's death. For this, Antonia liked him even more. Too much, perhaps. The pattern on a roll of jacquard caught her attention and she drew closer to examine it. When she looked up Mr Montgomery was watching her.

'Wonderful, isn't it? French of course, but one day I will have my very own collection.' He was interrupted by another customer, so Antonia thanked Mr Beckwith and left hastily. She was not herself.

When she was back in the quiet of her carriage, she ordered her thoughts. She might soon have another lodger. By Ryan's description, his niece Rhia was an unconventional young woman. Had she been hasty in inviting a stranger and a foreigner into her house? Antonia sighed at her own fearfulness. She should be hopeful rather than anxious. It would be enjoyable to have a female companion with whom she could discuss the trade, rather than the quantities of vinegar and linseed oil required for furniture polish.

Antonia delivered her cloth at the Meeting House and took weak tea with the sombre British Ladies Society, as the convict committee liked to call themselves. Quakerism had, at least, saved her from the helplessness of her gender and class. She approved of the Quaker view that equality and respect were due to women. The integrity of God's guidance was, of late, a more difficult ideal to uphold. Without Josiah, how could she now be certain of it?

Her gaze shifted and she became aware of the passing view. This part of the City of London was always humming with activity. The Gracechurch Meeting House was in between Lloyds Bank and the Bank of England and only two streets away from the Royal Exchange. All along Lombard and Cornhill were coffee houses where bankers, merchants and stock jobbers met to discuss the shipping news and the international marketplace; to buy and sell Jamaican sugar, West Indian tobacco, Australian wool and China tea. Antonia lived in the City and passed through the banking district almost every day, but she never grew tired of it. There was an invigorating briskness to the quarter that may well have as much to do with the amount of coffee consumed as with the nature of its industry.

As she passed the Jerusalem Coffee House, she was certain that she saw Isaac through the window. It was hard to mistake him. He was a large man; not corpulent, but tall and broad of frame. He was deep in conversation with another gentleman, whom she recognised as one of the bankers at Barings. Josiah had forsaken all ties with this bank upon discovering that currency from the sale of opium was deposited in its vaults. For the use of the Crown. Antonia was startled. Why would her husband's close friend, a Quaker, have reason to meet with such a man? She turned away, chastising herself for her lack of trust. Of course Isaac would have a perfectly sensible and morally sound reason for his actions. She was not herself.

# Calico

Juliette inspected herself in the only looking-glass in the house. The sight did not cheer her. Mrs Blake only ever used the glass in the hallway to fasten her bonnet or brush lint from her dull costumes. It was a shame for someone like Mrs Blake to be without vanity. To have the purse for silk but to choose wool seemed against the natural order of things. Surely the whole point of wealth was in flaunting it. Her mistress was pleasant-looking, though certainly no stunner, and would look well in India green or Lavinia blue.

Juliette leaned a little closer to the glass and smoothed her flyaway brown hair. She looked every bit as unquiet as she felt, though she tried so hard not to be anxious. Ever since Beth said fretting made the flesh flee from your bones. If the reverse were also true, then it explained the scullery maid's contented roundness. Beth's cheeks were like pink apples and she had a beam as round as a laundry tub beneath her black calico skirts. Black did nothing for Juliette. Today, her narrow face had a red spot high on each cheek and her forehead looked like crumpled linen. She examined her every angle and flaw until her gaze reached her hands. Her knuckles were as white as a boiled joint from the fastness of her grip where she clutched the letter.

She turned away from the disappointing portrait in the glass and marched the length of the hall. She did this another three times before she heard the jingling and huffing of carriage horses, and then the clip of sensible boots on the stone stair.

Immediately, Mrs Blake looked concerned, which made Juliette feel better.

'Is something amiss, Juliette dear?'

'Not amiss. Not exactly. But the afternoon post has come ...' Juliette took the grey mantle and the grey kid gloves, noticing the unnatural shine to Mrs Blake's eyes. She had been weeping again. She showed no other sign of it though; she was not one for self-pity.

'It has arrived!'

'Well the postage mark is Sydney Town.' Juliette's voice quivered. This letter had been long awaited.

'You've not opened it?'

'Oh no, it is addressed to you, and my reading's no better than my writing.'

'Well, then. Shall we brew some tea and sit at the table in the kitchen. It seems cruel, I know, to make you wait just a little longer, but I think it wise that we are composed and have a tonic at hand.'

Juliette hurried away to put the kettle on the range, unable to stand still a moment longer. It had been Mrs Blake's idea, that they – she – write to the Quakers in Sydney, to ask after the situation of her mother, Eliza Green. If Eliza had survived, she would by now be a free woman for five years since serving her seven year sentence.

When they were both seated in Beth's gleaming kitchen, and Beth had left to sweep out the larder, Juliette laid the letter on the table. They both looked at it nervously. It lay innocently on the smooth pine, but its contents might, at any moment, be deeply affecting. Mrs Blake had been so kind, and was so concerned, that Juliette felt almost as afraid for her disappointment as for her own. She put her hands up to her cheeks as the seal was broken and a plain, yellowish page removed.

Friends Meeting House,
Sydney Town

4 July 1840

My dear Mrs Blake,

Pertaining to thy letter, written on behalf of thy domestic servant Juliette Green, we have, these past months, made certain advancements into discovering the whereabouts of her mother Eliza Green.

Eliza Green was assigned to private service after passing four years at the House of Correction for Females in Parramatta. Whilst there she worked in the laundry, cleaning linen for the hospital and orphan school. As far as we can ascertain, Eliza Green remains unmarried, is healthful, and is now engaged by a squatter with a sheep station at Rose Hill, some miles west from Sydney.

Upon hearing that her beloved daughter, Juliette, was enquiring after her, the lady was overcome by emotion and told our Quaker sister (who visited the station) that she was hopeful to return to mother England but could not find the means for her passage. This is a sad truth which strikes many of those who have served their sentence here and in Van Diemen's Land, and is more common to the women, for the men can often work the passage home.

She bade us send to her daughter the most heartfelt love and blessings, and her ardent wish that they shall see each other again in this life. She promises that never a day passes that she does not think of her and offer a prayer. She was most comforted to hear that her daughter is no longer in the

workhouse but has found a position in a respectable household.

The Friends here are wholly at thy service to convey any
further correspondence to those who have need of comfort.

Thy interested Friend,

Mary Warburton

Juliette laughed and then cried and then she seemed to be
doing both at once and couldn't stop. She clasped both hands
over her mouth, worried that Mrs Blake would think her hysterical. Mrs Blake only handed her a pristine white cambric
square and, serenely, poured tea into each of their cups.

'There, there. It is perfectly reasonable to feel overwhelmed,
after all. Your poor mother. It is wonderful news, and a relief,
yet at the same frustrating and terribly sad. You must not feel
that you are in any way responsible for her situation, I hope
that you do not? Juliette?'

But Juliette knew that she was responsible. Eliza had only
been thieving so that her daughter would not go hungry. She
was less certain, though, if she was also accountable for her
father's death. It was the memory of that evil day that finally
overcame her, and, in spite of wanting to appear sensible, she
put her head in her hands and wailed.

# Merino

The ale house was as rowdy as ever and the Lafferty boys had the corner table. Their fiddle and tin whistle were out already. Every face was familiar. Many were assigned, like Michael; beholden to wait out the last years or months of their sentence in private service. They would be sheering merino, or working in a quarry or boot factory or, like he, as a carpenter on one of the many new public buildings on Macquarie Street. There were many here who would never go home, even in the unlikely event that they could pay for their passage. Once you had a ticket of leave, wages were better than in Ireland or England and a redeemed convict with a trade or even just an able body, was assured a good living.

Michael had never once considered staying on. Mostly because of Annie. He'd been living like a free man for almost two years, assigned to the governor's building agent, and it was not a bad life. The harshest sentence had always been being away from his wife and son. Annie's hair might be grey now, like his own. And Thomas, who was little more than a lad when Michael was arrested, now a man. His son, a man.

The letters from Thomas came every few weeks with news of Annie, Greystones and the Mahoneys, and were Michael's most treasured articles. Thomas never wrote plainly of the activities of his men, it was too risky, but he managed to convey whether they were safe and had been successful. Most of the underground news from Ireland came from the steady stream of new arrivals, and this fed Michael Kelly's small, secret press in the form of a monthly pamphlet.

The dark brown bitter that they called porter tasted more like charred malt, but at least at the Harp and Shamrock you could be certain to never encounter a colonist. Here all Irishmen, be they free settlers, prisoners or pardoned, were treated as equals. The bar was lined with the men without a choice; the survivors of '98, the biggest uprising Ireland had ever known. They were all old men now, and their exile was political and unrepealable. They lived to tell anyone who would listen of the way things had been for them when they arrived. Michael had listened a good many times, at first out of interest and then out of sympathy. Now he just pretended he was listening. He had a good picture of the barren shanty town Sydney had been, once, where the prisoners were always hungry and where people were either killing or being killed by the natives. Michael had heard, more times than he cared to mention, of subterranean isolation cells, and water pits where a prisoner was unable to sleep for fear of drowning; of leg irons and lashes and the godawful loneliness. It was the loneliness, they all agreed, that was the worst.

Many of the political exiles were educated men and they had put their idle wits to use making life difficult for the governor's military and constabulary. It was from their solidarity and rebellion that Michael had the idea for the basement press, and the veterans of the Harp and Shamrock were his most faithful readers.

Oscar was behind the bar with a jug at the ready for refills. His round face shone with good humour and perspiration. He nodded as Michael approached. 'A pint is it, Mick?'

'Aye. The black stuff. It's what I look forward to all day and when it touches my lips I always wonder why.'

'The water,' said someone.

'Aye. Too much lime,' someone else chimed.

'Lucky to have the bloody water. We didn't have fresh water in the early days.'

'Well it's not as if it's a good supply even now, is it, Sean? Not with the bore about to run dry and the piping gone to rust.'

The conversation was always the same. No one really minded that the stout wasn't as sweet as it was 'back home', since it did the same job, but it was necessary to remark upon it. It united them. It also saved thinking of some topic for conversation whilst the drink was being poured. At the end of the long, labouring day, no one really felt like talking. At least not until they'd emptied a pint or two, so it was better that way.

Michael took his jar to one of the upended barrels that served as tables, and lit his pipe. The Laffertys had struck up a reel and he tapped his boot absently on the straw that covered the wood floor. His never-idle mind moved towards the evening ahead, but before he could assemble his thoughts, Will O'Shea shuffled over.

Even when he was pickled, which was most of the time, Will was good for a yarn. He had been a razor-witted Dublin journalist in his youth, until he wrote one too many scathing commentaries on the British in Ireland and was summarily picked up and dumped in New South Wales.

'On your way down the Rocks, Mick?' Will had his eye on Michael's tobacco tin, so he pushed it towards him.

'Aye.'

'Awful quiet down there.' Will took a pinch of tobacco and pressed it into his pipe.

'Aye.' Michael nodded thoughtfully. He'd noticed it too. If there was a job on, he was bloody well going to get to the bottom of it. He was no whistle-blower, but if the orders were coming from London, then he'd make it his business. 'Let us know if you hear of anything, won't you, Will?'

Will chuckled and puffed on his pipe. 'Nothing else to do.' They assessed the new builds on Macquarie Street, and agreed that the timber from the cedar logs being floated down the Hawkesbury were magnificent. When Michael had drained his glass and Will had packed his pipe again, he left and headed for the Rocks.

The Rocks, the slum area at the bottom end of George Street, was overlooked by the homes of merchants and entrepreneurs. These honey coloured villas were perched right up on the tops of the ridge and as far away from the slums below as was physically possible. From their roost, Michael Kelly imagined that it was simply a matter of keeping one's eyes directed out to sea, rather than to the rookeries below. Then a wealthy man might conveniently forget that his citadel rose up, both metaphorically and literally, from the tenements of the poor.

As Michael passed by the huddled, flimsy hovels loosely defined as 'cottages' in the lower Rocks area, he felt the same vague uneasiness he'd felt for the last week. These huts were a patchwork of rough-hewn timber, roofing iron, sea chests and canvas. They had no guttering or sewage and they opened onto alleys which were unpaved and undrained, and where all manner of filth collected. In this neighbourhood many cottage industries thrived in amongst the homes of the Irish and English poor. Michael knew exactly where one might find coiners, unlicensed pawnbrokers and 'financiers'. Sydney was a competitive market for forgers and tricksters, and for thieves of varying skill and audacity.

All was still suspiciously quiet in the Rocks; the characters who were usually seen sauntering up towards George and

Elizabeth Streets at night, looking for an unsecured fob watch or a carelessly tied reticule, were either staying in or, more likely, were otherwise engaged. A big job meant someone was in from London or Calcutta; the cities between which most of the empire's silver was shipped. If it was a big job, then someone who would never, ever, let their identity be known was running it. Someone who would think nothing of having nosy bastards like Michael silenced. He'd have to be careful not to let his interest show. It offended him that so many traditions and trades were being laid to waste. The suffering and degradation made him sick, and when he saw the clippers and barques of the East India Company or Jardine Matheson docked in Sydney harbour, he wanted to hang them all from the jib by their prissy white cravats.

Michael arrived at a row of slightly better class housing – whose windows had shutters that could be fastened by a bolt and whose walls were wide planks of native hardwood. When freshly hewn, it gave off the faint scent of eucalypt, which was a welcome respite from the rotting funk of the Rocks neighbourhood. These dwellings had underground rooms, originally excavated to keep food from spoiling so quickly. It was in one of these cellars that Michael spent his evenings.

The cottage in question belonged to Maggie, his oldest friend in the colony, and someone he didn't ever expect to see again when he left. The fact that she was also the madam of a well-run brothel was of no consequence. One had to make a living. Since the upstairs trade was profitable, Michael's rent was low; and Maggie no more cared what he got up to, than he did she. There were so few women in the settlement that purchasing the company of one of them was perfectly sensible, being as it provided everyone involved with a reward of some kind.

Michael knew as soon as he took the latch from the gate that something was amiss, because the windows were shuttered and bolted. The gas lantern that normally flickered on the verandah, informing punters that all was well, was not lit. His guess was that the law had been to visit. It almost certainly wasn't a small-time brothel they were after, so what did they want? Information, perhaps. Maggie was doyenne of the streetwalkers, and the street was the conduit of the Sydney underworld, a criminal network that had imported its highly skilled practitioners from the most infamous of London's prisons. Something was definitely up.

# Paisley

The stair timbers creaked. Rhia put the pen down silently, hardly breathing. Its silver shank rolled across the table, then rolled back towards her, coming to rest at her fingertips. The fountain pen was a gift from Mamo, but until now, Rhia had been too afraid to use it. She had thought it foolish to imagine that using a gift from her grandmother might call her from the grave. The pen was graceful and decorative, and the knot-work of its engravings glowed like illuminations. Even perhaps a little brighter than they should by candlelight.

The stair creaked again. Mab was fat enough to make the stairs groan, but Mab wouldn't move from the stones by the hearth until there was cream in her dish. It could only be Mamo again, moving through the house, doing whatever ghosts did in the faraway hours. *The faraway hours.* Strange that she should remember. It had been their secret name, long ago, for the time when the household was sleeping. Mamo had told her stories to help her sleep, which kept her awake. Mamo had also taught her a little rhyme to keep ghosts away, but Rhia couldn't remember it now.

The shadows scattered as the door creaked open. Mamo's spindly legs were clad, as before, in her husband's too-big long johns. She'd worn them to bed from the time that he died until her own death, and had insisted on being buried in them. The underclothes of a dead man might seem unconventional nightwear to some, but to Mamo it was perfectly sensible. She was from the hills and had always complained that the cold sea mist coiled around her bones. Her husband had been from the sea, being Black Irish and, supposedly, descended from the wrecks of the Spanish Armada. Mamo had liked to think him *silkie*. The silver braid of her hair was draped across her bony shoulder and half-hidden by her old paisley shawl. Her feet were, as usual, bare.

Mamo stood for a minute looking at Rhia's drawing book open on the table. 'You're expecting a visitor?' Her grandmother could never simply say 'are you drawing?' Any artistry must be a visitation from Cerridwen, muse of the bards.

'Not tonight. I thought I'd write. Say goodbye to Thomas.'

Mamo looked at the page. 'You've not much to say.' She couldn't read, but anyone could see that the parchment was unmarked. 'Don't be a milksop, Rhiannon. Say goodbye to his face.'

Rhia sighed. She knew that she should.

Mamo was still looking at the page. Her neat little walnut face was smoother, as though she'd grown younger in death. She traced a crooked finger over the knot-work on the pen, as if it were a pattern in cloth. It was a simple triple knot; the oldest of designs; the sign of the goddess. Mamo turned away and knelt by the wood basket, looking for faggots. 'Write to me,' she said.

Rhia laughed. 'But you can't read! And besides you're—' Should she state the obvious? Better not. Mamo was easily offended.

Mamo clicked her tongue in annoyance. 'Keep what you write. You can read to me when you come home.'

'I could.' Rhia knew that she probably wouldn't, and besides, she didn't want her grandmother, or any ghost for that matter, waiting for her when she came home. She was finished with ghosts. Or so she had thought.

'Good.' Mamo sat down. 'Now, I've a story.'

Mamo's stories were drawn from some boundless ancestral hoard; tales that had been told and retold by generations of bards. Some had never even been written down; others weren't entirely Irish and weren't entirely Welsh, like Mamo herself. She professed to be descended from the *Tuatha de Danaan*, the tribe of the great goddess Anu and the preservers of her stories. Connor Mahoney had always left the room when Mamo talked about the *Tuatha*; whenever she did, her grey eyes turned dark as granite.

'There is a story about Rhiannon I haven't told you; from after she fell in love with Pwyll and brought him to the Otherworld and after she was wrongly accused. After these things happened, she became the wife of Manannán, god of the sea.'

Rhia thought she knew all the stories of Rhiannon, her namesake who travelled between the world of the Others and the world of men. She knew that she rode a white mare and wore a purple cloak and that three magical birds always accompanied her. She knew that Rhiannon was, mysteriously, separate from but also part of Anu, and that her life was beset by troubles and betrayals because she had to become strong to do the work of the goddess.

She listened to Mamo's story, but it was long and complicated and full of Gaelic names, and Rhia's mind wandered. In only a few hours she would be leaving for London. Mamo had visited only once before, on the first night. She insisted Rhia go, and Rhia, just as adamantly, insisted that she would not. They had argued about it half the night. In the end Mamo said that it was her house and that she didn't want Rhia in it. If

Rhia didn't go, she said, she, Mamo, would stay. That did it. It was time, her grandmother said, for Rhia to undertake the night sea journey.

Brigit had been stunned by Rhia's announcement that she would go to London after all, but she didn't ask what had made her change her mind. Perhaps she didn't want to know.

'At least your mother agreed with me about your naming,' Mamo was saying. Her father had wanted to name her Mary. 'Goodness knows, she needs to stand up to him more,' Mamo shook her head. 'I didn't raise her to be stupid.'

'She isn't stupid. She only thinks it's respectful.'

'Respectful!' Mamo spat. 'It is not *respect* to surrender, it is respectful to respect oneself and one's spouse equally.'

Rhia did not want a lecture, or another tirade against her father. 'Tell me the rest of the story of Rhiannon and Manannán,' she said.

Epona stood as still as a statue and accepted an apple graciously while Rhia saddled her in the stable-yard in the half-light. Her soft grey ears were twitching as though the mare could hear the altered rhythm of Rhia's heartbeat; as though she knew something was different.

Only the baker's lamp was lit as they rode through the village and down to the sea. Thomas would be awake, though, and at his loom. The shale was glistening, the tide receding. The moon was new; a dim crescent, barely visible in the pearl grey sky. The sea sighed rhythmically. Rhia pressed her heels gently into Epona's flank and the mare tossed her head and picked up her hooves. Rhia leaned lower over her neck and they moved as one until Epona was at a canter, her hooves rattling the shale like castanets. Rhia's hood fell back. The air was sharp and salty and its damp clung to her hair. She closed her eyes for a moment.

*The night sea journey.*

The journey to the farthest shores of one's fears. It was the sea itself that Rhia feared most.

The Kelly cottage was on the outskirts of the village, in the next cove, with the sand instead of shale at the back gate. Michael Kelly had once said he needed to see the ocean to remember that there was a world around its shores: doubtful he would need to be reminded of the fact again.

As children, Rhia and Thomas would sit on stools by Michael's loom and watch him. He taught them how to weave and told them that flax was one of the oldest fibres in the world. He showed them how the soft, flexible stem of the plant needed to be soaked to separate the fibres, allowing for a much finer yarn to be spun. Flax was a peculiar fibre, and much harder to spin than wool and cotton. Spinning it by hand pro-duced a superior cloth because a spindle and hands as deft as Annie Kelly's could produce yarn of any weight, whereas machines could only produce coarse yarns. Annie Kelly spun all grades of linen yarn; finer for lace and cambric and damask, and coarse yarn for rope and paper and canvas.

Rhia arrived at the back of the cottage and tied Epona to the gatepost. The building was the shape of a barn and larger than most of the weavers' cottages in Greystones. Thomas saw her through the window and beckoned her to come in. He was at the loom. The Kellys worked long hours. They produced such perfect repeat patterns that their cloth was always in demand.

The back door was never latched. The long narrow room that looked out across the Irish Sea was sparsely furnished to make way for two ancient looms, one for linen and one for wool, each hewn from gnarled oak and dark with age. There was a large hearth in the middle of the room and from a hook above the spitting flames hung a blackened pot. A bright copper kettle shone like a lantern on its stone ledge. The scene was so familiar that Rhia wanted to cry at the thought of leaving. Neither Thomas nor Annie stopped working when Rhia let herself in. She did not expect them to. The rhythms of the loom and the spinning wheel were not to be interrupted without good cause.

'Morning.' Annie smiled. She smiled no matter how much she missed her man or how much yarn was left to spin. 'There's broth in the pot, and you know where the bread is.'

Thomas said nothing as Rhia fetched herself a bowl of broth and a hunk of warm soda bread from the cheese cupboard. She sat on a stool by the fire next to Annie's spinning wheel and watched Thomas's foot treadle up and down and his hands fly across the shafts as though they were an extension of his body. He had his mother's colouring – wavy chestnut hair and milk-white skin. His hands and forearms were strong and sinewed. He was always quiet, but his silences had moods. Rhia could tell he was brooding.

Annie looked from one of them to the other, wound her bobbin off and dropped it into the basket at her feet. She touched Rhia's shoulder. 'I've linen to boil. Don't go away for ever, will you? You'll be missed.' Annie kissed her on each cheek and gave her a swift hug and then hurried away.

Rhia swallowed back her tears and moved closer to the window near the loom. She waited for Thomas to speak. He finally took his foot from the treadle.

'Well, Rhia.'

'Well yourself.'

'Will you come back to us do you think?'

'What a thing to say! Do you really think I'd leave for ever? I don't want to go. I've no choice.'

He laughed bitterly. 'My pa had no choice. You've been wishing yourself in London since you were wee.'

It was true. 'But this is not how I wanted it, not to seek a position.'

'Aye, and I'm sorry for your troubles, but you've no idea how you've been blessed. You've not had to think about how to pay for your kid slippers and your silk ribbons. It won't be so bad, you've a quick mind – you're inventive.'

'But I'm not polite. All of the Londoners I've met are polite. And I'm not clever enough to be a governess.'

Thomas only shook his head as though this didn't warrant a reply. He looked away from her towards the waves breaking across the beach. Epona was pawing the sand at the gate. 'She'll miss you,' he said, jerking his head at the mare.

'You'll be careful, won't you Thomas?'

He didn't answer. He led a small group of Catholics who met secretly to plan insurgencies, just as his father had done. He and his men wrought their own brand of justice on the English Protestant landlords who behaved unjustly towards their tenants. Their actions were often violent and always unlawful, and Rhia didn't ever ask about them. She heard things, of course, and that was bad enough. Lately, she'd also heard that Thomas had a sweetheart; the sister of one of his men.

'I hear you're courting Fiona Duffy.'

He ignored this. 'What of your painting? Have you more ideas?'

Rhia smiled. 'Only a hundred. But I've not picked up my brush for weeks.'

They had climbed trees and bathed naked and searched for fairy rings. Thomas had watched her first experiments with pigments, sitting on the forest floor in the autumn or amongst the long headland grasses in the summer. He had admired the silken skin of a wet shell with her, and the scribble of veins in a dry leaf. He'd made the easel and paintbox for her sixteenth birthday. That was when he'd asked Rhia to marry him. Connor Mahoney did not allow him in the cottage for the rest of the summer.

They were silent until the fire spat loudly, making Rhia jump and interrupting the awkwardness of the moment. Thomas went to the cheese cupboard and returned with a package wrapped in brown paper. He gave it to her. 'Don't open it now. Not till you're on your way. I'll not say goodbye, as you've said you're coming home. You know the hearth's always lit here.'

'I know.' She took Thomas's hands until he pulled away and returned to his loom. He didn't look up again. He kept his head bent low – lower than normal – over the shafts.

Epona walked up the headland as though she was hitched to a cart, and seemed to slow even more as they neared the cottage. Perhaps she had sensed that something was amiss. Rhia turned to take a last look at the beach; at the gulls circling above the red and yellow and blue fishing boats. She turned back and saw her father. He was sitting in his wicker chair looking out across the bay as he'd done every day for a week, unheeding of the weather. The weight of his failure was patent in the stoop of his shoulders.

They had pretended, thus far, that the quarrel had never happened. It was easier. She'd had little time to dwell on it once the decision had been taken to leave Dublin, and Connor had not returned to St Stephen's Green to witness the empty echoing rooms and the tears of Tilly and Hannah. He had been released from the infirmary only last week. Rhia and Brigit had done everything themselves. There was enough from the auction of the Dublin house and contents to settle accounts, but not much more.

Rhia could delay the moment no longer. She jumped down and kissed Epona on the nose. She gave her a withered apple from her pocket and a light tap on the rump. The mare knew how to find her own way to the yard, but she went reluctantly, her head hung like Thomas's had been. Rhia turned away quickly.

Her father looked up at her with his head tilted and attempted a smile. 'I wish you wouldn't go, Rhia.'

'It's not for ever.'

'To think of you seeking a position. And with no husband to provide for you. It's shameful.'

Rhia resisted the temptation to argue. 'It is fashionable,' she said as if she were only off to the opera. 'Women of every class work in London. I've read about it.'

He shook his head. 'Who will marry you now?' It was as if she had not spoken. He would never understand because he did not want to. The restraints of class and the roles of men and women were traditional and non-negotiable; like weaving. Linen should be hand-woven and that was that. It was dangerous ground. Rhia kept her tone light, with effort. 'The coach will soon be here. Will you come up to the house?'

'No, the place smells of your grandmother today. It is depressing me.' Rhia was too surprised to respond. He looked so mournful, so sorry for himself that she almost smiled. For the first time she saw his obstinacy as a weakness rather than a strength. He was not prepared to yield even a little to see the world as something other than that which he ordained.

'Then I'll say goodbye.' She leaned over and kissed his forehead. He took her hand and held it so tightly, so that she wondered if he would let her go. When he finally did, he looked away, back to the sea, so that neither could see the other's emotion. He was really letting her go, perhaps only because he had not the strength to prevent it. Rhia felt a mix of sorrow and elation. Was she really going to be in charge of her own life?

She turned away and started to walk back up towards the cottage.

'Rhia!' he called out weakly. She turned.

'You are brave and kind for a devil in petticoats.' His eyes almost twinkled, just for a moment.

'I'm sorry about William.'

'He wasn't good enough for you.'

Rhia rushed back and threw her arms around her father and then ran up the hill.

Her trunk was already beside the front door. She and her mother had lugged it down the stairs on their own. They were both much stronger since the move from Dublin. Brigit was at one of the three spinning wheels by the hearth. Now that Rhia was leaving, two of the village women would come in to spin. Her mother looked up. 'There's a new loaf.'

Rhia thought Mamo might still be in the house, but she didn't seem to be. She was probably with her sheep. 'I've eaten at the Kelly's,' she said.

Brigit nodded. 'We should have a jug, then.'

It was what they did in the evenings when there was a spinning circle, but this was a special day. Rhia got the stoneware jug from the larder and filled it with porter from the tap in the barrel, then put it on to the ledge by the hearth to warm.

Mamo's downstairs parlour was much cosier than any of the rooms at St Stephen's Green. The furnishings were simpler and the fabrics older and softer. There were books on tables and faded rugs on the wooden floor and Rhia's easel in the corner. The room smelt of the lanolin and lavender Mamo had used to put in her hair to make it soft.

Rhia went upstairs to change into her travelling clothes and took a last look around her childhood room. It was neat, which was unusual in itself, and it felt empty without her paintbox on the table and her books by the bed. There were no clothes strewn across the old blanket box. She could see the sea from the window, but she turned away before she could think too hard about it.

When she came downstairs, Mamo was at her old spinning wheel, but if Brigit noticed the wheel turning she said nothing. They sat together quietly. Brigit passed Rhia the jug and sighed. 'I didn't realise how I've missed the oily feel of wool through my fingers.'

Rhia, too, liked the feel of wool. 'Will you try out some new weaves?'

Mamo chuckled. 'You can treat worsted to make it pretty as silk,' she said. 'And it costs much less. Tell your mother that.' Rhia shot her a look.

'I've spoken to Thomas,' said Brigit. 'I'll have him weave some samples.'

They talked until the coach wheels were to be heard coming up the hill, and then until there was no ignoring the jingle of the reins and the snorting and stomping of the horses outside.

There were no tears, they had each shed them privately. Their emotion was present only in its constraint; in the tautness of speech and the gripping of hands.

'Don't forget to write,' whispered Mamo in her ear. 'Remember, there is always something to feel grateful for. *Always*. Be in the world but not of it, Rhiannon.'

This made no sense to Rhia. How could one be *in* the world but not *of* it?

Brigit pressed a purse into Rhia's hand and put a finger to her lips before she could protest.

She stepped up into the coach. In a moment it was rumbling down the drive towards the Dublin road.

Mamo stór,

The *Irish Mail* has arrived in Holyhead without sinking. I was so bilious until this morning that I didn't once consider the fate of the Spanish Armada. Manannán's kingdom is in ceaseless motion and I cannot imagine how sailors ever manage to walk upright.

There is little to see of England on a November evening but fog and a barrow-seller or two, but there is thankfully a tavern on the quay, from where I write this. It feels a little bold, venturing into a tavern on my own, but as I have crossed the sea, what is there to fear in a port tavern? So far no one has either approached or reproached me.

The window is grimy with sea mist and soot, but I can just see a row of black hansoms beneath a gas lantern, waiting to drive passengers to the overnight rail service to Euston. It departs at midnight and it is barely ten o'clock. I am told the railway is nearby and, since I don't want to encounter certain passengers from the crossing, I am taking comfort in a glass of porter and a slice of cold, rather greasy, pigeon pie.

At lunch today (besides the pie, the only meal I've eaten since I left) I shared a table with a party of London ladies who had been in Dublin for a Protestant wedding. I was seated beside Mrs Spufford, who informed me that travelling unchaperoned is a terrible thing for the reputation of a young woman, and that I must endeavour to learn certain proprieties if I expect to be welcomed into polite society. If *she* is an envoy of the la-di-da league (that's what Thomas calls them) then English society isn't so polite after all.

Manannán took revenge on my behalf. Mrs Spufford dipped her spoon into her minted pea soup just as the boat tilted, causing both ladies and bowls to slide sideways. The contents of the spoon landed in her décolletage and I laughed before I could help it. No one else did. Mrs Spufford looked at me as though I were something sticking to the sole of her slipper. Presumably, a well-bred young Englishwomen would have found no humour in a pea green décolletage. Mrs Spufford and I did not speak again and the other London ladies took the opportunity to practise their repartee, which still stings my vanity.

*'You are from the trade, Miss Mahoney? Why, my upstairs maid comes from a linen family.'*

*'Ireland really is becoming civilised, I had no idea I would be able to buy silk stockings in Dublin!'*

They droned on with their pretty spite, and I let them. I simply could not be bothered wasting my wits on the creatures, besides I'm weak and weary from being rolled around like a brewer's tun. I thought they'd forgotten me by the time the custard pudding was served, but their best insult was yet to come.

*'How fortunate you are, Miss Mahoney, that your complexion is so dark. It is tiresome being fashionable at times; always taking care to protect one's delicate pigmentation.'*

I entertained myself by imagining their coils of lacquered hair as the stubs of Lucifer's horns. I am beginning to wonder if being Irish and therefore Catholic might be a disadvantage in London. Of course, *you* know I'm no Catholic, but that is our secret. I was curious to know what English ladies liked to talk about. Now I know: breeding, and the allowances of people one aspires to know; idle people who pass their time redecorating their homes and themselves. I cannot imagine the conventions and niceties I am ignorant of. I hope Antonia Quaker is no minion of polite society.

I can see the contents of the hold of the *Mail* being transferred to wagons; but there seem to be more sacks of grain than of mail. It looks as if I have just crossed the Irish Sea with all of the wheat, oats and barley of the nation. It is not just Irish linen that is channelled through London. Perhaps I should be grateful that British law has not actually forbidden women to read the papers. I wonder whether it is because if she read of the ruthlessness of his trade, a woman might turn against her industrialist husband.

I suppose I should curb my blessed interestedness and get into one of those ominous-looking black carriages. By morning I shall be in London.

# Weave

The sleeping compartment was the size of the water chamber at St Stephen's Green. It was close to midnight and Rhia couldn't be bothered with fastenings and button hooks. She doubted that she would sleep.

The carriages clattered and hissed all night, halting at one lantern-lit station after another. Crates and trunks and bulging brown canvas sacks stamped with the insignia of little Queen Victoria were loaded on, before the train lurched off again. The rhythmic activity and increasing nervousness kept Rhia awake. It seemed that in no time at all grey mist hung over fields soft and eerie in the dawn. The silhouettes of stone walls and sinewed trees reminded her of home. This, surely, was a good sign.

She must have dozed, because the light was suddenly strong and stark and the scene from the window unsettling. The soft landscapes of daybreak could have been a dream. Forests and fields had been replaced by slag heaps and flatlands, interspersed occasionally with a dairy farm or a mill. Then the straggling hovels of the city's fringe-dwellers appeared; wattle and daub with a bleak yard that ran up against the railway. Sometimes a scraggly hen or two; a skinny goat; a mongrel pig. Could this be London?

The flimsy housing became denser, and more portraits of slum life lined the track. A woman in her nightgown and cloth cap pegged out her laundry for all the world to see; a barrel-chested man washed his hair from a tin pail. Children sat on piles of stones and rubbish, waving as the train passed. They jumped and shouted with excitement when Rhia waved back. She felt a creeping cold. She had never imagined the capital would have poverty worse than Dublin.

The train was creeping so slowly that they must be nearing Euston. Rhia's spirits lifted in anticipation of seeing Ryan. His liveliness was always infectious; his costly habits reassuring. Whenever her uncle came to Dublin he brought China silk, French lace and Portuguese wine. And he knew how to make her laugh, a restorative now absent in the Mahoney household. If it was possible to resurrect Mahoney Linen, then Ryan would know how.

She now wished that she had taken the time to remove her clothing last night; her ribs were sore from the chafing of her stays. She inspected her hair in the speckled oval of glass beneath the luggage rail. It was still more or less braided and only needed a pin or two. She washed her face in the tiny basin and changed her long, lace-up walking boots for the shorter, buttoned boots that were in her carpet bag. They had a pointed toe and pretty heel and they instantly made her feel better. She was ready.

Thomas's parcel was beneath the boots, and she sat and eyed the carpet bag, suspecting that Thomas's gift would only lure her into the homesickness she was taking such care to evade. She would have to open it sooner or later. Rhia rummaged in the bag and drew out the brown paper square tied with string. She put the parcel on her lap and took a deep breath, then immediately wished that she hadn't; there was a funk in the air; something sulphurous or rotting. When the paper wrapping was peeled away, the folded underside of a heavily woven piece of cloth was exposed. Rhia unfolded it, holding her breath. She knew what this was. Unfolded, the piece covered her knees; a two-foot square of a high grade chintz. The linen upholstery was impeccably woven and as vivid as a botanical garden against the green alpaca of her travelling costume. The pattern was achingly familiar. It was *her* design, from a long, long time ago; a time when she still believed in fairies and did not mind ghosts. She had spent weeks perfecting it before giving it to Thomas as a gift. He had woven it. She was overcome. The design was of curling boughs laden with golden fruit and birds of jewel colours. It was, she remembered, intended to be the Otherworld, where the magical birds of Rhiannon woke the dead and put the living to sleep.

Thomas had written a note on a square of the stiff paper used for carding yarn:

Anam Cara,
Do not forget who you are.
Thomas Kelly

He liked to be mysterious. How could she forget something that she didn't know? Rhia replaced the chintz in her carpet bag. She felt fortunate to have such a friend, troublesome though he was. But she wouldn't have married Thomas, in spite of what she'd said to her father, because when they were lying naked on the prickly forest floor she hadn't wanted him to touch her. She had, regrettably, told him so, and Thomas hadn't spoken to her for the whole, long summer. It wasn't just because she was the daughter of a clothier and he was a weaver; they were, like Rhiannon and Pwyll, from different worlds in other ways besides. They both knew that she would never be happy to have a simple life, and Thomas made no secret of the fact that he thought her spoilt.

She thought of William O'Donahue. Had she wanted *him* to touch her? She thought not. She had been taken by his manners and sophistication; with the allure of his profession. How fickle she was. With Thomas she was her true self; as bad-tempered or whimsical or inquisitive as she felt. William had clearly not cared for her blessed interestedness. She shivered to think that she might have married a man who would have wanted only a fixed smile in an expensive bonnet.

The locomotive steamed through the northern reaches of London, the slums had become red brick terraces; row upon row, mile after mile. Rhia felt her stomach somersault, and it wasn't the pigeon pie. What was the house of a Quaker like? Would the furnishings be austere and uncomfortable? There would almost certainly be no modern conveniences such as pumped water or gaslight. She expected that Antonia Blake would disapprove of her fondness for fine cloth and her aversion to church services.

The dirty stains of industry on the sky reminded her of ruined linen and of how much her life had changed already. The oily smell of the fog only worsened as the heart of the city approached, and she wondered how anyone could feel healthful in such a place. She heard again Mamo's whisper in her ear. She must find something to be grateful for, and quickly.

The train slowed and the sky disappeared completely. Above the densely crowded platform a large, proud sign read: LONDON EUSTON.

# Tartan

Rhia stepped into the fracas on the platform and was practically knocked sideways by a liveried footman. The man was laden with hat boxes and parcels, and was so anxious to keep up with a madam in a striding fur pelisse that he didn't even stop. The next thing Rhia knew there was a hand beneath her elbow. She swung around defensively, but it was only Ryan's smiling face that greeted her. He had easily approached without her noticing. She was so relieved to see him that she threw her arms around his neck, making him laugh.

'Rhia dearest, welcome to London!' He gestured towards the disappearing footman and the general mayhem. 'I assure you that the city is not all such an abomination, nor as ugly as its northern approach.' He propelled her swiftly across the platform, dodging urchins and passengers alike with an alacrity that didn't seem feasible, given the conditions.

'It isn't at all what I imagined,' was all Rhia could manage. She didn't have time even to look at Ryan properly until they reached the relative calm of the reception hall. She thought he looked uncharacteristically haggard, but still the picture of a successful bachelor. He wore long polished boots, a mustard yellow cravat and a rakish frock coat. Aside from his stylish clothing and the fact that he oiled his russet hair, Ryan Mahoney looked much like his brother, with an Irishman's pale, freckled complexion and wiry build. In nature, though, he was passionate and frivolous, quite the opposite of her father.

'We'll escape this unholy commotion just as soon as your luggage is in the porter's office,' Ryan assured her. 'My carriage is waiting in the avenue.' She nodded and her gaze was drawn upward to the vaulted grandeur. Fields had become flatlands and slag heaps for this. Should she be more in awe of the human achievement or the resilience of the natural world? She felt small suddenly, and more than a little overwhelmed. She needed to wash the salt from her hair and the soot from her skin; to move without her stays creaking and to sleep somewhere motionless, then everything would be all right. She had barely slept for days.

'Not every station is as grand as Euston,' Ryan was saying, watching her. 'It is the new darling of the London and North-Western Railway and not a farthing has been spared.'

Perhaps he thought that she was made speechless with awe at the industries of men?

He chuckled. 'If you think it is crowded now, you should see the platforms in August, prior to the beginning of the shooting season in Scotland. I always think it a wonder their prey doesn't hear the racket from the highlands and flee for the season!'

Rhia felt a little like prey herself. After what seemed an interminable wait, her trunk was located and they stepped into the street. It was a commotion. Carriages, omnibuses and carts jammed the thoroughfare and the footpath was crowded with every manner of basketseller and barrow. A little girl with a tangle of hair and a basket of chestnuts tugged at Rhia's cloak as Ryan towed her towards his vehicle. Everywhere she looked were billowing chimney stacks and blackened stone. She had expected classicism; elegance. She at least had the heart to smile at her own naivety.

Her portmanteau was strapped to the back of Ryan's sleek burgundy landau, and a tartan rug tucked over her knees. They set off. She could feel Ryan's eyes on her. She tried to hide her disappointment. 'I ... look forward to seeing more of the city,' she said without conviction.

'And you shall, within moments!' The landau lurched into the stream of vehicles and didn't slow until they had almost collided with a milk cart. Rhia glanced at Ryan. His lips were pressed into a thin line and he was frowning as though he was miles away. His face looked thinner, she thought; his jaw sharper. He needed a shave. He caught her eye and smiled instantly.

'I can hardly believe that you are finally visiting the capital. There is so much I want to show you. We'll walk by the Serpentine and shop at Piccadilly and go to the Royal Opera. You'll have a smashing time. I'll wager you are in need of it. Now, tell me of my brother's health and how your mother is managing. And of your intent to secure a position, which I find most admirable.'

Before Rhia could remind him that this had been his idea not hers, Ryan was talking again. He seemed harried. 'As I said in my letter, I regret that I could not accommodate you myself, but I was spending so much time at China Wharf that there was no point in the upkeep of a second household. I have sufficient room for desk, bed and storage, and usually dine at my club, all of which suits my bachelor ways estimably!'

Ryan manoeuvred the landau, more swiftly than seemed necessary or safe, past another wagon laden with crates and barrels. It was a mystery how the narrow roads could withstand so many vehicles. Bloomsbury, he was saying, was a citadel of garrets, accommodating more hungry writers, thespians and *artistes* than even the halls of Trinity College. He pointed out the sleek homes of merchants and the premises of a gentleman he knew. He enquired after Connor and Brigit again, as though he'd forgotten that he already had.

Rhia told him their news, occasionally distracted as her eyes skimmed across the rooftops of London. Industry marched on the inner city like a militia of chimneys. Shadowy tenements housed pitiable shops in their front rooms, some with a rickety table out front displaying trinkets and bric-a-brac, from stacks of yellowing catalogues to tins of scavenged boot buttons. This was not at all the city she had imagined. She caught Ryan's eye and wondered if her disappointment showed.

'London is a fickle mistress,' he remarked wryly. 'One moment you are seduced by her and the next rejected.' It seemed a melodramatic statement and Rhia wondered if he was mocking her. She nodded absently as her eyes followed a chariot drawn by a pair of sleek bays. It looked to be driven by an oversized hat; its plumage so excessive that it could have been the nest of a sea bird.

She barely had time to take in the cut of the walking dresses and short cloaks that swirled along Hatton Garden before Ryan said they were on Cheapside. Every second shop now seemed to be a tailor or milliner or corset-maker, as if the economy of the city revolved around cloth and clothing. She had, so far, provided a vivid account of the Merchant's Quay fire and described the physical and worldly well-being of her parents. 'My mother,' she concluded, 'intends to earn a living from wool. The Kellys have a broadcloth loom.'

Ryan looked thoughtful. 'Then I must assign a clipper of merino to Dublin as soon as possible.'

'But merino wool is awfully expensive …' Rhia was secretly relieved. She had hoped he would offer to help.

'Prices have been falling. The sheep thrive in the warm

climates, but not only in the southern Continent. Merino is now the primary export from Australia, you know. It is being blended with silk and cashmere. The fleece is more expensive to purchase, but the yarn can be sold for thrice as much as English wool.'

'Then you don't think it wise to try and revive Mahoney Linen?'

Ryan sighed heavily. 'I was never as sentimental about the family legacy as your father. I'm relieved that he was its heir. Had Connor and I been less ... disposed to disagreement, I might have stayed in Dublin and been a partner, but that was not to be. As you know, your father is as devoted to tradition as I am to progress. It is 1840, a new decade! The linen industry – the whole cloth trade – has progressed rapidly. Mahoney has been disadvantaged in choosing not to mechanise.'

True or not, this seemed harsh. 'And so will any discerning tailor be disadvantaged, not to have good quality linen to cut,' she retorted.

'There are other cloths, Rhia. New blends of fibres are being machined all the time now. *Progress* is the word you will hear more than any other in London. Besides, the loomed linens are not so poor in quality as your father would have us believe. The trade is changing. The world is changing.'

Rhia did not want to be thought old-fashioned, but she didn't believe, either, that there was no place for tradition in the new world of the machine. She might have pressed her argument further, but the streets had changed again. She sensed that they were passing through an important part of the city.

'This is Cornhill.' Ryan named the quarter as though this was explanation enough for its vibrancy. The street was pulsating with hurrying clerks and gentlemen wearing polished

leather hats and top coats with fur collars. Whatever its industry, the quarter clearly had a vital purpose.

The landau turned into a narrow, shadowy road, aptly called
Cloak Lane, and stopped outside a flat-fronted red brick terrace. They were only a hatch of streets away from Cornhill. Of
course! Mrs Blake lived in the City of London. They had just
passed through the banking district. She felt a small thrill to be
lodging so close to the heartbeat of the capital.

The subject of Antonia Blake had not been raised at all during the journey from Euston, but now that she was to meet her
puritanical hostess, Rhia felt her nervousness return. Ryan patted her hand absently. 'You will never meet a kinder soul than
Antonia. Did I tell you that her husband's cousin is also lodging at Cloak Lane? He is a professional portraitist.'

'A painter!'

'No, not a painter. Laurence Blake is thoroughly modern.
He makes photogenic portraits.'

Before she could reply, Ryan was reaching for the door
knocker. It was the wrought head of a mythical beast with a
ring through its nose, and the first sign that the Blake household might not be as ascetic as Rhia had expected.

She braced herself as the door swung open.

# Cambric

Antonia frowned as the front door hinge creaked. It was an unsettling sound; she must remember to drip a little linseed onto it. She completed the last neat column of entries swiftly as she listened to the arrival of the Mahoneys.

'Good morning, Juliette!' Ryan boomed his greeting with unnatural cheer, no doubt in response to Juliette's dour airs.

'Morning, Mr Mahoney sir. Miss.'

Antonia stood. She smoothed her skirts and patted her hair and stepped into the hall. She waited for a moment in the shadows, not wanting to interrupt before the moment was right. Juliette was holding a ruby red cloak; but Rhia Mahoney was obscured behind her. The colour of the cloak spoke volumes about Antonia's new lodger.

'Mrs Blake says you're to go straight to the morning room where it's warm. She'll be with you presently.' Juliette took Ryan's top coat and then showed them inside.

When Antonia stepped into the morning room, Ryan was warming himself by the fire and Rhia was examining the photogenic landscape on the wall with her back to the door. It was the work of one of Laurence's colleagues. Rhia turned. Antonia was surprised. Rhia looked nothing at all like her uncle; her features were strong and dark; not pretty, but striking. She was small. Elfin, almost. Her gaze was a little too direct to be entirely respectful or genteel. In fact, if Antonia didn't know better she would describe those dark eyes of hers as fey.

Ryan made introductions and Rhia gave the landscape a parting glance before stepping forward and extending her hand, which Antonia took.

'Do you like the photogenic drawing?' she asked, not knowing what else to say. 'Isn't the paleness of the trees eerie,' she continued. 'Don't you think?'

'Yes,' Rhia agreed, though she seemed almost suspicious when she glanced back to the picture. What a peculiar creature she was. She tore her gaze away and looked around appreciatively. 'It is a pretty room,' she said. 'How clever to paper the walls in such a warm colour. It's just like a field of wheat with the sun on it.'

This pleased Antonia. She had taken great care with the room. It had seemed necessary to redecorate it after Josiah's death. The walls were amber with a pale lemon leaf pattern, and were hung not only with photogenic drawings but also – most recently – with several of the Madonnas from her collection. Josiah had not approved of icons. The French oak armchairs by the hearth were upholstered in bright saffron. The breakfast table was set back a little from the front window and laid with delicate white china. The morning room now felt lit by the sun even when only thin winter light strained through the lace curtains.

Antonia took in Rhia's travelling costume at a glance. Stylish but not showy. She imagined that she herself seemed out of place in her own pretty room. Her usual sombre grey was so dark that it was almost black, relieved only by a white collar. Her brown hair was, as always, parted in the middle and pinned back in a neat, net-covered mound. She thought fleetingly of a time when she had worn cloths that rustled and whispered, when pearls had clicked softly at her neck. It surprised her, to be reminded of her former self. Was Rhia Mahoney going to bring ghosts into the house?

Antonia forced a bright smile. She was the benevolent hostess. 'I expected you a little later, but then, I should have remembered that your landau is as swift as a racing chariot, Ryan.' Ryan bowed and smiled. He was as debonair as ever, even though he looked dreadful. Too much claret at his club last night, no doubt. He was uncharacteristically quiet.

Antonia took Rhia's arm and guided her to the breakfast table. 'Come! You must be hungry and weary after your long journey. How wonderful it is to finally meet you. I confess that I have heard much about you from your uncle, so I feel that I know you a little already. I'm so pleased to have you here, Rhia.'

'It was kind of you ...' Rhia seemed to be struggling to find something to say and Antonia realised with relief that her guest must feel just as awkward as she did.

'Not at all. I am in dire need of companionship. It is a blessing to have Laurence, though he is often abroad on business. Silence only echoes silence, and having empty rooms seems a crime when so many are homeless.'

While they were talking, Juliette, silent as an apparition, had placed bread baskets and cut glass pots on the table. It was a simple breakfast of preserves, baked white bread and dark continental coffee. While Rhia buttered her bread and sipped a glass of coffee, Antonia considered an appropriate topic for conversation. She could tell that Ryan was preoccupied, which improved the choice considerably.

'What a charming dress. You look rather like a forest nymph in that mossy green.' She suspected that the fashionable panel of white cambric in the corsage had been inserted, but one did not speak of frugality in London. Rhia's dark eyes lit up mischievously.

'The forest nymphs I have seen wear little more than bracken and spider's webs,' she said. She took another bite of bread and marmalade and was talking again before she had finished chewing; 'I've not narrowed the sleeves enough, but the cambric is Mahoney.'

Antonia felt like laughing. Was this lack of decorum an Irish trait – or just Rhia? She knew next to nothing of Celtic customs; Ryan was so thoroughly a Londoner. Whatever had she got herself into? If this was to be an adventure, then so be it. She was sorely in need of one. 'I wondered if it was Mahoney cambric. I was dismayed to hear of your family's misfortune. I have, in the past, bought Mahoney linen myself. The quality was always the best available. Cloth itself is the better half of the entire business of fashion.'

Rhia looked pleased by this, and nodded in agreement. 'Isn't it just? Some of the styles I've seen this morning surely serve only to inform the world that one can afford a lady's maid. Who could fasten herself into such a narrow bodice?'

Rhia would be an entertaining companion, but Antonia was still vaguely unnerved by her. There was something a little *wild* lurking beneath her élan; and she had only been half-jesting when she made the forest-nymph remark. She smiled, though, and pursued the topic. 'Our sex have, sadly, been led to believe that a true lady is helpless. Yes, it is impossible to be fastened into stylish underclothing without a maid, and without stylish underclothing, a lady is not an acceptable shape—'

'Unless she go hungry,' Rhia enthused. 'I know Dublin girls who won't eat another potato until their corsets can be laced to sixteen inches. Someone should tell them that the children of farmers have nothing but potatoes to eat and are as thin as a rail.'

Rhia was clearly not amongst the potato-starved, she had flesh in all the right places and was in the process of buttering her third breakfast roll. Antonia was relieved that they had found some common ground, even though it was at the expense of Ryan's interest. He had been listening with dwindling patience and now he was restless. He rose to his feet.

'I leave London this afternoon. There is a new cotton mill in Essex that I want to inspect. I'll be away for a day or two. You two have much to discuss. I'll call later in the week, Rhia.'

Antonia was reminded of something. 'Before you go, I have some shipping documents that are perplexing me. I am attempting to understand Josiah's methodology, Ryan. Would you cast your eye over them? If you haven't the time, I can ask Isaac.'

'But of course, by all means. Then you are planning to keep the business going? Surely you do not intend to trade on your own, Antonia?'

'Eventually. Why not?' She did not say that she had not yet found the strength and faith that she knew it would take; or that she was praying for courage.

Ryan looked bemused but had no reply. Rhia looked full of admiration. Antonia turned away with a small smile.

From Josiah's office, she could hear snatches of the conversation in the front hall. Rhia said something in a soft voice, to which Ryan replied, 'Don't object when someone offers you money, my dear! I only wish I could give you more, but I'm in rather a fix at the moment.' Antonia was surprised. She had always considered Ryan Mahoney to be a cautious investor. Perhaps he was not suffering from an excess of claret after all. She rolled up the document and tied it with a ribbon, then bustled down the hallway so as not to surprise their private conversation. She handed Ryan the scroll. 'I might be being obtuse, but it appears from this ship's log that the *Mathilda* is still in the dry dock in Calcutta.' Ryan frowned at this and then looked as though he was going to say something but thought better of it. He put it in his coat pocket thoughtfully, then smiled briefly, though his eyes were already distant.

'Good day to you both. Enjoy London, Rhia.'

Antonia stood at the door with Rhia, who was leaning in the doorframe as though it were supporting her. She clearly needed to bathe and sleep.

They both waved as Ryan's landau pulled swiftly away, his hair lit from behind, like one of her Madonnas.

# Devoré

The ivory brocade around the bed was swaying gently as though a draught had passed through the room. Rhia examined the embossed pattern sleepily. The arabesques danced and shimmered with the light behind them. It gave her an idea.

Yesterday, after breakfast, Mrs Blake had disappeared into the depths of the house, leaving Rhia to wash and unpack. A buxom girl called Beth, who was much more jolly than the thinner maudlin one, had offered to draw her a bath, but Rhia was too bone weary to bathe. She lay down on her bed and instantly fell asleep. The first time she woke it was dark, and she listened to the city; peddler's bells and hooves on cobbles and carriage wheels creaking. She wrote a line or two to Mamo, describing the household, and must have fallen back to sleep in the early hours of the morning.

Now she pulled back the bed curtains and tried to judge the time by the angle of the sun glancing off the rooftops. She looked around the room, appreciating all over again the dark Oriental furniture against the pale biscuit walls. It was just as cosmopolitan as it had seemed yesterday. The chest at the foot of the bed was engraved with characters like those printed on the wrapping of China silk. Josiah Blake had probably travelled regularly to the Orient if he was in the cotton trade. What manner of man had he been and how had he died? She had meant to ask Ryan about Antonia's husband, but he had been in such a strange mood that she'd forgotten. The room, Rhia decided, had the qualities of the mistress of the house; plain but elegant, restrained yet worldly. At some time during the morning her fire had been lit and her washbasin filled with clean water. Her gaze came to rest on a clock on the mantelpiece. It was past ten! She had probably missed breakfast. She hurried to wash and dress and took the stairs two at a time, almost colliding with an abandoned bucket and mop on the downstairs landing.

The table in the morning room was laid for two. Perhaps she was not too late after all. As soon as Rhia entered, Beth bustled in, wiping her hands on her apron. 'Morning, miss. Mrs Blake's already abroad. She and Juliette are making their visits. She says to tell you she'll be back at tea time.'

'Their visits?'

'That's right. They collect cloth for the convict ships, from shops and such.' Beth lowered her voice. 'And they visit *prisons*.' She paused for effect and arched an eyebrow. 'You wouldn't catch me walking free into Millbank or Newgate. *Evil* places.' She shivered melodramatically. 'Anyway, your breakfast is on the table. It's only bread and marmalade and such, that's what Mr Blake has – *young* Mr Blake that is, of course, because there's no other, not any more ... But I can cook you eggs or porridge if you prefer.'

Rhia could tell Beth didn't want to cook either eggs or porridge. 'I expect you've better things to do,' she said.

Beth looked surprised, and then pleased. 'Well, yes I have,' she said importantly, and disappeared quickly before Rhia could change her mind.

Rhia sat down at the breakfast table. Mrs Blake had left a copy of a broadsheet, the *London Globe* open on a page that she presumably thought would interest Rhia. This was clearly not a household that disapproved of women reading the papers. The page was divided into narrow columns of print so minuscule that it was almost illegible. She bent over it. A commodious property was being let in Regent's Park, complete with chaise house, water closet and counting house. It would cost one hundred and fifty guineas for five months. A parish in Limehouse was seeking to contract a butcher who could supply mouse buttocks, maiden ewe and ox beef without the bone; suet included. A respectable officer's daughter could teach the globes and French grammar and the rudiments of Latin. This lady was apparently qualified by accomplishments and education. Rhia sighed. What chance did she have against a respectable officer's daughter?

She felt a cold breath on the back of her neck, as if a door had opened behind her. She turned, but directly behind her was only the photogenic drawing of tall, pale tree trunks, like the columns of a classical temple. Yesterday, she had imagined she'd seen a shadowy figure amongst those unearthly trees. She'd been overtired of course, and besides, who'd ever heard of an apparition in a *painting*. Of course it wasn't exactly a painting, though it was very like one. Perhaps it was all those pictures of the Holy Virgin on the wall that had thrown her. Their presence unnerved her almost as much as the trees did. She turned her back firmly on the photogenic drawing, and the Madonnas, and saw a man standing in the doorway watching her. A real man, not an apparition, though she was beginning to worry that she might not be able to tell the difference. He was a smiling, boyish man with very blue eyes. She had no idea how long he had been there.

'You must be Miss Mahoney.'

'And you must be Mr Blake.'

'Please call me Laurence. Antonia does. Quakers don't believe in formalities.'

'Then I suppose you should call me Rhia.'

'Very well,' said Laurence, beaming.

'But I thought it was impolite in London to call a stranger by their first name?' This was just the kind of etiquette she had been dreading.

'Then we must pretend that we are old friends.'

Rhia laughed. She liked Laurence Blake immediately, with his carelessly tied cravat and crumpled shirtfront. He held a top hat in one hand, as though he was on his way out. With the other hand he attempted to smooth a hillock of dark blond hair.

'I hope I am not disturbing you,' he said, suddenly awkward.

'Oh, I'm pleased to be disturbed. I might otherwise be forced into looking for a position.'

'I see,' he said, though he didn't look as though he did. 'If you need further assistance in the matter, then perhaps you will permit me to join you for breakfast.'

'But the table is laid for you.'

'That's because Beth is a gem, even though she is constantly grumbling about not being a downstairs maid or a housekeeper. I was going to visit the stationer in Cornhill, but it can wait. Besides, it is raining.' He sat down opposite her, his very blue eyes hardly leaving her face. 'Might I enquire what profession will be so fortunate?'

Rhia sighed. 'I am to be a governess.'

Laurence chuckled as he poured her coffee from the samovar. 'Surely it will not be so awful?'

'No, it probably won't.' She buttered another roll, feeling self-conscious. She searched for something else to say. 'Mrs

Blake says that you make photogenic portraits. That sounds far more exciting.'

'Oh it is, and I'm a fortunate fellow to have made a career of something so jolly agreeable.'

'Is your studio close by?'

'I'm using one of Antonia's rooms for now.'

'Then you are making portraits in this house!'

'Why yes.' He looked pleased by her enthusiasm. 'I am recently arrived in the capital from Bristol, you see, though I used to visit regularly. In fact, it was your uncle who urged me to come to London when Josiah ... died.' His lips twitched for a moment and he lowered his eyes, but he recovered his humour quickly. 'Antonia is quite a devotee of photogenic drawing. Now tell me, Miss Mahoney – Rhia – how does London seem to you?'

How did London seem? She considered this. If London were a cloth ...

'Like devoré, I think.' Was this being too clever? Did Laurence, too, think this unattractive in a woman?

'Devoré?'

'A cloth whose pile is—'

'Ah, I do know what devoré is, but only because the weaves that allow light to filter through make extremely good subjects. Antonia likes experimenting with lace, for example; it is very *photogenic*, as we say.'

'Then Mrs Blake also makes photogenic drawings?

'Indeed. But tell me why London is like devoré.'

'It is as rich as velvet, but in parts the bare cloth is exposed.'

'Poetic.' Now he was looking at her as though she were some specimen beneath a glass.

'Can you really make photogenic drawings of cloth?' she asked.

'Would like to see one?'

'Oh yes!'

'Then you shall, as soon as I return from the stationer.'

Laurence drank his coffee in a gulp, bowed flamboyantly and was gone.

Rhia coiled a strand of hair around her finger thoughtfully. It felt coarse and reminded her that she had still not bathed. She went looking for the kitchen.

Beth seemed proud to inform her that there was a 'bath room', and led her to the back of the house. It was a recent addition at Cloak Lane, the maid explained. The piped water came into Mrs Blake's basement and it was carried upstairs and heated in coppers, then transferred to the porcelain bath. No wonder Beth wanted Mrs Blake to employ a downstairs maid.

The bath was of such a dimension that a small body could easily recline, and the room was warmed by a rotund iron stove in the corner. A brass rail was fixed to the green-tiled wall near the stove and draped with a white linen bath sheet.

Inside it, Rhia sat with her knees to her chest. It felt strange being in a room that contained only a bath. She felt acutely aware of her naked, honey-coloured limbs. Did she feel this way because of Laurence Blake? He had looked at her as though she was something unfamiliar. He thought her uncultivated. He would marry a pale English girl with a demure smile.

The steam hanging in the air reminded her of the Atlantic fog that had wrapped itself around the *Irish Mail* as it carried her away from Dublin. She hugged her knees more tightly as though to protect herself against homesickness. But now the green tiles reminded her of the Wicklow forests, and she could feel their clean breath in her lungs as though they had taken root in her; inhabiting her blood and bones.

She heard Laurence return, and she held her breath, listening. Did he hesitate outside the door? Surely not. His boots tapped briskly up the stairs. She heard more footsteps and a soft rap on the door and then Beth's voice. 'Mr Blake says go up when you're ready. He's on the second floor at the back.'

Rhia dried herself and dressed hurriedly, and dried and braided her hair in front of the fire before she went in search of Laurence. The second floor was laid out like the rest of the house, with a landing and housemaid's closet in the centre and two large rooms either side. He was in the south-facing room. The room had little furniture, and a large Turkish rug covered the dark floorboards. The rain had pattered rhythmically on the windows all morning, but now sunlight fell across a long table that stood against the wall. Laurence's tall frame was bent over its surface and he straightened when she came in, his hair falling into his eyes. Rhia could not decide if he was handsome or not. She assumed that his gaze was presumptuous, but it didn't bother her.

'Ah, Miss Mahoney. Rhia. Welcome to my calotype workshop!'

'It sounds like a torture chamber.'

'On the contrary, calotype, in Greek, means "beautiful picture". Come and see for yourself.'

There was a row of pictures on the table, and they certainly were beautiful. Disturbingly so. Somehow this science or wizardry could conjure the membrane of a leaf; the delicacy of a piece of lace and, most extraordinarily, a number of miniature portraits of sombre-looking gentlemen. These, Laurence explained, were a new enterprise: calling cards; an idea he had picked up in Paris where, he said, the personalised calling card was *de rigueur*. The shadowy lace fichu, the scallop of crochet and the broderie anglaise, he said, were Antonia's.

'But how is it done?' Rhia breathed. She was unable to take her eyes from the pictures. They looked as though they were rendered, oh so delicately, with the steadiest hand and the finest black and brown ink.

Laurence looked pleased. 'It is, supposedly, a secret,' he stage whispered, though she could tell it was one he had no intention of keeping. 'Fox Talbot has patented his calotype process, so one must apply for a special licence to be able to make a certain type of photogenic drawing. He has discovered the means by which one can make several copies of a picture, using a single exposure. I don't expect you to know what any of that means, but perhaps you would like to watch me transfer an image.'

It was true, Rhia had no idea what he was talking about, and she could only nod and sit down on a stool by the table. Transfixed, she imagined how these motifs might look printed onto linen but then remembered that, here, she was no longer the daughter of a linen clothier. Who was she, then? She concentrated on the motifs. They would look even better printed onto silk, but she was not the daughter of a mercer, either.

Laurence was explaining how the paper that he had brought back from the stationer must first be treated to make it 'light sensitive', and that this chemical process must be undertaken at night and by candlelight to achieve greatest success. He had some paper that was treated already. 'It is best to use a parchment with a smooth surface,' he said, as he took a sheet from a writing box, 'and to keep the treated paper away from the light. You will soon see why. I will show you a simple experiment. The more complex transfers, such as portraits, require the use of a lens and a light box.'

He laid the paper on the table and placed a dried frond of wheat on top of it. Within seconds the paper began to darken, and quickly turned black. After no more than a minute, Laurence removed the frond. The feathery outline remained, in all its filigree detail, pale and perfect against the inky paper.

Rhia watched Laurence do the same with a small posy of dried flowers, and then with a scrap of curtain netting. She lost track of time and was surprised when Beth puffed into the room with a tray of cold cuts and boiled eggs and pickles. This, she explained, was how Mr Blake always took his lunch and she hoped it would do. Rhia assured her that it would. She was too excited to be hungry.

When she asked Laurence if he had any more photogenic drawings she could see, he laughed and pointed to a large chest of drawers against the opposite wall. 'Be my guest. I have some letters to write and accounts to address, but stay as long as you wish.' He sat at the end of the table with his writing box and inkpot and was soon absorbed, though Rhia felt his eyes on her occasionally.

She opened one drawer after another. The first was full of portraits; gentlemen in high-backed chairs or with a woman standing behind them. The women stood behind in the family tableaus, too. There were children in sailor's stripes, and por-traits of newly-wed couples with frozen smiles. In another drawer were representations of instruments and teacups; samo-vars and candlesticks, vases of roses, seashells and even a shelf full of books. Another drawer was filled with pictures of London and Paris and Rome; cities that Rhia knew only from paintings.

When Antonia appeared, Rhia was sitting in the middle of the floor surrounded by pictures of bridges, wrought iron gates, landscapes and every type of masonry from angels to gargoyles.

'I see that you have been introduced to the industry of the household,' said Antonia.

'An industry of light amongst the dark industries of the factories,' Rhia replied. It sounded melodramatic, even to her ears.

Antonia only nodded. She crossed the room and put on her spectacles to look at Laurence's new work, and he looked up from his letter writing as though he'd only just noticed her.

'Hello, Antonia. Have you been out saving condemned souls?'

She smiled but still said nothing and Laurence put his head back down. Rhia wondered if she had offended. Antonia returned to where she was sitting. 'Industry is a double-edged sword, isn't it? It has liberated some and ruined others. Will your family continue to trade?'

'My mother is spinning wool. When my father is well enough we might ...' She was not sure what they might do. Everything was uncertain. She had hoped Ryan would help, but she now suspected that he had cares of his own. In fact, she wondered if he had moved to China Wharf not only for convenience, but because he could not afford the upkeep of his house.

Mrs Blake was looking at her kindly. 'There is absolutely no reason why you and your mother cannot achieve the same standard of excellence, with or without your father. I am intent on doing so myself.'

Rhia sighed. 'I would not know how.' She wished she did, and that she was the kind of woman who would think nothing of riding camels across a desert, climbing icy mountains and exploring Africa without a crinoline.

'We are bred to believe the opposite,' Mrs Blake continued. 'It is the demands of women that keep the cloth industry lucrative. It is fallacy that only the men who run the trade benefit from it. We clothe not only ourselves, but our families and our homes when we have little else to keep occupied with. We sew, we embroider, we mend. We desire harmony and novelty in the house because it is here that many of us will spend our lives; those of us who do not know that we have a choice.'

Mrs Blake had taken off her spectacles, folded them and put them in a worn pouch. 'I'm afraid I will be out this evening – I have a meeting. Will you be in, Laurence?'

He looked up. 'Hm? This evening? I expect I'll be at my club.'

Rhia was relieved. She was itching to capture the patterns that were chasing around in her head.

At the door, Mrs Blake turned and gave her a bemused look. 'My husband always said that one could achieve a thing merely by believing it possible.'

Rhia wanted to ask about this man whose belief had not, after all, prevented his death. 'I wish I had met him,' she said instead.

'Yes,' Mrs Blake said, and hurried away.

# Gossamer

The cartridge paper lay on the table by the window, where Rhia had spent the previous evening. The real test of a new design was always in how it looked the next day. If it still seemed a good thing, then one could start thinking about colour. She squinted at the pattern of swirling leaves. It looked different. They appeared to be curling, as though they were autumnal rather than new, green leaves. She was not sure that she liked this. Was there some eidolon abroad in this house, that tampered with pictures? She was reminded of her dream last night. In the dream, she was at the table, drawing, and Ryan was with her. They were having a conversation about Australian merino and he had insisted that she must arrange to send some to Brigit – he was far too busy to do it himself, he told her, and pulled his watch from his pocket as if to show her just how little time he had. Then, all of a sudden, he had disappeared into the flames in the fire.

Downstairs, the breakfast table was laid but there was no one in the morning room. Rhia darted a quick glance at the picture of the trees and felt unreasonably relieved to find no shadowy figure lurking in amongst the pale trunks. She had meant to ask Laurence where this ungodly place was.

The *London Globe* was folded neatly on the table and a fragrant thread of steam coiled from the samovar. Rhia braced herself and opened the broadsheet to the classified pages. The situations advertised looked just as unappealing as they had the day before. She simply had no idea how one went about securing one. She had never once imagined the necessity would arise. Perhaps Thomas was right, she was spoilt and mollycoddled. Mamo had certainly thought so. Ryan would advise her. He had given her five pounds, which was generous, on top of the purse from her mother. She would easily last until the spring if she were careful.

Rhia's attention strayed to pages where advertisements for powders and ointments promised to resurrect, restore and vanquish for only a few pennies. She was engrossed when Antonia joined her smiling brightly, all traces of yesterday's melancholy masked by decorum and briskness. Rhia had rarely seen her Quaker host stop moving. Perhaps this was how she managed.

'Good morning, Rhia. It seems as though I barely saw you on your first day in London. I'm suddenly terribly busy deciphering Josiah's ledgers, on top of my usual charity work, and then there are regular Friends meetings to attend.'

Another etiquette. 'You attend regular meetings with your friends?'

Antonia smiled. 'It is what Quakers call themselves. Ourselves.'

It seemed a strange expression. 'I think you are brave, to trade without your husband.'

Antonia sighed. 'I have barely begun, and I am not so brave as I may appear. It took me months to find the nerve to merely enter his room.' She spread butter neatly on a slice of toast. 'Grief has wearied me.' Antonia wore her sorrow so lightly, as though to protect others against it, but its weight in the house was palpable. At least it was to Rhia. She searched for something more to say.

'I've never seen so many faces of the Holy Virgin,' she said carefully. 'She looks different in each picture, don't you think? In that one she is pale with yellow hair, and in the one next to the trees she is dark as a Moor.'

Antonia looked at the icons as though she had never considered this. 'Yes. Curious. I've always loved them, though iconography is considered by many Quakers to be idolatrous. I don't personally believe that aspects of the divine are incarnate in holy images. But you are quite right, Mary does appear in the form of every woman.'

Rhia wanted to say that maybe the Virgin *was* every woman, just as Anu apparently was. 'I envy your belief,' she said.

'Oh, I was not born to it. My family are Anglican. I prefer the simplicity of Quakerism.' Rhia wondered if she was trying to convince herself of something. 'The problem is, the inner light is not always bright enough to show the way.'

Quakerism seemed anything but simple.

'Then you think that is what faith is – a light?' said Rhia.

Antonia poured their coffee, watching the fragrant liquid spill into the white china cups. She put on her spectacles and cast an eye over the front page of the *London Globe*. Rhia waited. Antonia eventually took off her spectacles.

'I believe that faith is like walking in the dark; guided only by one's inner light. But all I am truly certain of is that any compassionate God must surely want us to bring our love to the poor and the suffering rather than spend it all on prayers to a plaster statue.'

Before Rhia could reply, Laurence appeared, looking bleary-eyed and even more dishevelled than he had the day before. 'Good morning, ladies,' he said, drowned out by the loud hammering of the door knocker. He groaned at the sound, and put his fingers to his temples. Juliette hurried past the door to the hallway.

'It is too early for the morning post,' Mrs Blake said with a frown. 'Who could be calling at this hour? What *is* the hour, Laurence?'

Laurence retrieved a tarnished fob watch from his waistcoat pocket. 'Just after nine. Ungodly. I hate morning meetings.' He yawned and sat down nodding gratefully as Mrs Blake poured him coffee.

They listened to the front door creak, and to the low murmur of voices. Rhia shivered and, involuntarily, glanced at the photogenic trees. As she had dreaded, the shadow was there again, like the imprint of a figure between those pale trunks. She closed her eyes and felt icy cold.

*Cailleach?*

When she opened her eyes Juliette was standing by the table with a folded piece of notepaper, which she gave to Laurence. She hurried away as though she, too, was afraid of its contents.

Laurence unfolded the note slowly and read it. Rhia watched his face. Antonia was bent over the newspaper, sipping her coffee, seemingly oblivious. The note slipped out of his fingers and fell to the table, and he put his hands over his face. Antonia looked up and took off her spectacles.

'Laurence! What is it?'

He pushed the notepaper towards her. She read it and then put it down, so slowly.

Someone had died.

Mrs Blake reached for Rhia's hand and clutched it fiercely.

'Ryan,' she whispered.

It was a hoax. Someone had written the note as a jape; an amusement. It was disgraceful. Laurence was already on his feet.

'He is dead,' said Antonia, dazed.

Rhia shook her head. '*No.*' Had she shouted? She could neither think nor move. Antonia was still holding her hand, so she pulled it away and stood up abruptly, knocking her chair back. No one moved to pick it up. Antonia put her head in her hands.

Laurence looked as though he might faint. 'Who has this note come from?' Rhia asked. It was a surprisingly sensible question.

'From a friend who is a journalist of the *Globe*. He says that the dustlady who has rooms at China Wharf found Ryan's body and sent him a message this morning.'

'But why would she tell a journalist?' asked Antonia.

'Yes, why?' Rhia echoed. It was clearly a hoax.

Laurence was shaking his head. He could not answer. He was death white and the skin on his face was shiny with sweat.

Rhia suddenly remembered, relieved, why it was impossible for Ryan's body to be in London. 'But my uncle has gone away; he *told* me.'

Laurence's voice broke. 'I must visit China Wharf directly. Perhaps Mrs Bribb, the dustlady, is mistaken.'

Rhia was clutching the back of her chair for support. 'Of course she is mistaken.' The pitch of her voice was brittle, as though it might easily break.

'Mrs Bribb has concluded, somehow, Rhia, I can barely say it … She believes that he died by his own hand.'

Such nonsense.

'I'm coming with you,' Rhia said.

'With respect, it is not advisable. It will be unsettling.'

'With respect, I *will* come with you.' Laurence looked surprised, or perhaps shocked. Either way he was not pleased, but Rhia didn't care if she alone made her entire gender unattractive.

'Very well. Dillon is at a coffee house in Cornhill and suggests that I meet him at a nearby tavern.'

Antonia stood and hurried from the room and when Rhia and Laurence entered the hallway she was waiting for them, holding Rhia's cloak and Laurence's top coat and hat.

They must have walked the length of Cloak Lane and a distance along Cornhill, though Rhia could not recall it by the time they were taking a seat in the window recess of a public house. The tavern was almost empty at this hour, but for a huddle of ragged old men seated around a table with a flagon of claret and a deck of cards. They probably did so every morning. For them, today was a day just like any other.

Laurence went to the bar and returned with two small glasses of spirit. 'Brandy,' he said, when Rhia looked at it blankly. He drank his measure in one. 'Dillon will be an asset in this situation,' he said, as though that might make a difference. She nodded.

'How did he – my uncle … ?' she began, though she was not sure that she wanted to know.

Laurence looked away from her, at the window. 'Did you know that Ryan collected antique firearms?'

She shook her head in bewilderment. She was sitting in a shabby tavern with a man she barely knew who would soon accompany her to the place where her uncle lay dead. Perhaps she was dreaming. She followed Laurence's example and drank the rest of the brandy down in one.

The tavern door swung open and a man entered. Laurence waved limply at him.

The journalist crossed the room, his boots striking the floorboards with purpose. Even the card players took notice. He wasn't bohemian, but he wasn't concerned with convention, either. He wore a long, battered leather coat and the toes of his boots were pointed more sharply than was fashionable and badly in need of shoe black. His black hair was tied back and, although he appeared relatively youthful, there were furrows of tension on his face. He was as pale as any newspaper man and had a general air of arrogance and impatience. He extended his hand to Laurence and gave Rhia a small bow.

'Rhia, this is Mr Dillon. This is Ryan's niece, Rhia Mahoney,' said Laurence. 'She insisted on coming,' he added. Laurence had been watching the street and now he tapped on the window, beckoning to a straw-haired boy who was loitering on the footpath.

'I had not realised that Ryan had family in London,' said Mr Dillon politely, though his curiosity was too sharp to miss.

'And I did not realise that he kept company with gentlemen of the press,' she countered. 'I have just arrived,' she added, holding his gaze. Did he think her an imposter?

The boy from the street appeared at their table. 'Yes, mister? Want yer 'orse groomed, is it? I can shine them winkle-pickers, too,' he said cheekily, jerking his head at Mr Dillon's boots.

'Find a cab and have it collect us outside, lad,' said Laurence offhandedly, pressing a copper into his hand. The boy nodded, grinned and disappeared.

Rhia listened to Dillon tell Laurence, in a low voice, how he had come about his discovery. He had recently visited Ryan to discuss some kind of business (what?) and, early this morning, Mrs Bribb the dustlady had found his calling card. She hadn't known who else to turn to. He was cut short by the arrival of the hansom, whose driver sat whistling cheerfully and dusting off a battered pork-pie hat.

They were soon amidst the crowds and commotion of some arterial road, and then suddenly at a standstill behind a mail coach. Laurence craned his neck out of the window and sighed with exasperation.

'The coachman is changing horses, it looks as though one is lame.'

Rhia nodded, hardly hearing him. Dillon had taken a notebook from his coat pocket and was flipping through it as though looking for something, and Laurence kept his head out of the window, occasionally issuing another exasperated sigh.

The noise and motion of the street seemed to be receding. The air moved as gently as a coil of smoke on the outer reaches of her vision, and Rhia felt the lightest touch, like the caress of a feather on her arms, which left her flesh crawling. Was she just seeing her own shadow?

'Miss Mahoney, are you well?' Rhia had not realised that she was slumped in the corner of the carriage. She felt like retching. The vision was quickly gone and the smells of damp horsehair and old tobacco in the carriage were suddenly overpowering. She sat up slowly. Laurence had pulled his head back in and both men were looking at her. She nodded and turned away, pretending to find something of interest through the window as they started to move again. She could feel Mr Dillon's eyes on her and knew that he was going to speak to her and she wished he wouldn't.

'Are you feeling equal to answering some questions, Miss Mahoney?' He spoke gently enough but didn't wait for her to answer. 'It is critical that we do not waste a moment, because once Scotland Yard are informed, we might have no access to your uncle's room, his effects or – and I'm sorry to put this so bluntly – his body.'

His manner of speech was vaguely familiar, but it took a moment to place. He had the same lilting accent as Mamo. Welsh. She should not be surprised, she had heard that any Celt in London who wasn't a beggar, a cobbler or a tailor was certainly a journalist.

'Did you know my uncle well?'

He ignored her. 'Please tell me what you and Ryan spoke of last you met.'

Rhia felt her guard rise. 'What did *you* speak to him of last you met?'

He shot her a surprised look but didn't answer.

'Besides,' she said with a shrug, 'I fail to see how what my uncle and I speak of affects you.'

'I would not expect you to, Miss Mahoney. Perhaps I should rephrase my question. Did you notice anything unnatural about your uncle when last you saw him?'

Rhia caught Laurence's eye. He looked as though he might interrupt, but seemed to think better of it. She bit her lip, remembering Ryan's leave-taking. 'Yes. He was … he seemed troubled. Even—' She stopped herself. She was talking to a newspaperman, after all. He might even be a penny-a-liner. She should be protecting her uncle's privacy, not telling a man she barely knew and whom she was already suspicious of about his affairs.

Both men were watching her, waiting for her to say something more. Rhia pulled her cloak around her and looked down at her hands, silent.

Laurence spoke, softly. 'Dillon can be trusted, Miss Mahoney. He is here to help. Please tell us what you think.'

She believed, at least, that Laurence could be trusted and if he thought she should talk to the journalist then, she supposed, she must. 'I thought he seemed worried.' She would not tell him about Ryan's financial circumstances, it was simply none of his business.

Dillon nodded thoughtfully. 'And what about this letter, Blake?' he asked, turning to his friend. Laurence looked at Rhia almost apologetically.

'He'd had a letter from Josiah. Antonia knows nothing of it – she would only fret. It was posted from Bombay and written only days before he drowned. Ryan would tell me nothing more about it but that its contents were extremely worrying.'

Dillon nodded thoughtfully. 'We should try and find it, before the Yard does.'

Rhia looked out of the window. They were on a bridge. She wished she could take some pleasure in the carnival-like bobbing of boats on the river and the elegance of the stone spires and turrets along the skyline. She could feel Dillon's eyes on her as they crossed the river. She had not made a good impression and she did not care.

# Brocade

In a lane that ran between two brick storehouses, a huddle of street girls rearranged themselves hopefully. Bosoms were hoisted and hips tilted, but when it was clear that the carriage was in China Wharf on other business, they returned to slouching and gossiping.

The hansom halted outside a nondescript black door and Rhia alighted quickly, relieved to be free from the oppressive silence of the carriage.

Mrs Bribb, a sallow, harried woman, answered their knock surrounded by children. She was clearly relieved when Mr Dillon introduced himself and his companions. They followed her up a circular stair of blacked iron to the first floor where the grassy smell of raw silk was unmistakable.

Outside the only door on the landing, Mrs Bribb jangled a brace of keys looking for the right one. She shooed away the children who, Rhia realised, were hanging about because they wanted to have a look at the dead body.

'Could you tell us how you came to find him, Mrs Bribb,' Dillon coaxed quietly as she hesitated with the key at the ready.

'He said he'd be leaving Tuesday evening, and isn't it strange, because I was certain I heard the door below. I came this morning to clean around, as I do when Mr Mahoney's away, and I find him,' she made the sign of the cross, 'on the floor and one of his peculiar old firearms *in his hand*. Merciful heavens! I'm still in a blessed dither. I've not touched a thing, I wouldn't, not in the presence of the dead.' She turned the key in the latch and the heavy door creaked open. Rhia steeled herself against whatever sight awaited her inside.

They entered a variegated forest of giant, freestanding rolls of cloth of every imaginable weave, quality and pattern. Indian, Chinese, French and American. Devoré and brocade, worsted, lawn and damask. By the door were several rolls lying on their side, still wrapped in hessian and rope as though they were newly arrived. Rhia bent over one impulsively and pulled away a little of the hessian. It was silk, embroidered with a pattern of swirling autumn leaves. The pattern was almost identical to the one she had drawn last night. She remembered her dream about Ryan and shivered. She moved away quickly, following the others through the upright bolts of cloth, barely looking at it. She could take no pleasure in it.

Mr Dillon navigated confidently towards the source of light against the far wall and Rhia wondered how long ago he had been here and what his business with Ryan was. It was now clear that the room occupied the entire second floor of the storehouse.

The body of Ryan Mahoney lay at the foot of an enormous mahogany desk. He was on his front with his arms at right angles to his body, as though he had raised them to break his fall. In his right hand was a pistol with a silver barrel and carved ivory hilt. The weapon looked deviously beautiful, as though it might have beckoned to a man who was weakened by desperation. There was a dark spillage on the floorboards beneath Ryan's left armpit and under his head. It took Rhia a moment to understand that it was blood. She felt her legs quiver. Ryan's bloodless face was turned towards the pistol, and looked as though it was modelled from tallow, but for a rime of dark red where it rested. His eyes were, mercifully, closed.

It was true. He was dead.

She had needed to see it, but it turned her cold until she had to clench her teeth to stop them from chattering.

Mrs Bribb shuddered and crossed herself again. 'I never liked them pistols and such.' She cast a wary glance towards a cabinet whose upper shelves displayed the prizes of Ryan's collection. 'No one heard the shot, so it must have been when there was a ship in. There's all manner of fuss then, and everyone down by the water.' Mrs Bribb was edging away, towards the door. 'I best be getting on. Call when you're done here and I'll lock up.'

Mr Dillon bowed to her as graciously as if she were a dowager. 'Sincere thanks, Mrs Bribb. Perhaps you would be so kind, when you notify the constabulary, as to not tell them that anyone else has been to call?'

'Don't you be worrying about that, sir. I won't breathe a word of it and neither will any of my brood. We know better, around these parts, than to do the bobbies any favours. Good day to you all and God bless you, miss, in your sorrows. I'll be brewing a kettle of strong tea downstairs, should you need it.'

Mrs Bribb disappeared. Dillon was walking in a slow circle around the body as though measuring something, while Laurence sat, white faced, on a packing crate. Rhia looked around for something to focus on, besides the body. The front end of the storeroom was spacious and shabbily comfortable and contained the basic requirements of a home. There was an expensive-looking leather armchair at one end, and beside it stood the dresser containing the pistols. At the opposite end was a small range and a pine table. The desk and a French day bed were in between, beneath the row of long windows. From here, one could look down over China Wharf and across the Thames.

Rhia remembered Ryan's leave-taking two days earlier. The light had touched his hair in such a particular way, the suggestion of a guarding angel. He said that he would see her at the end of the week and she had detected no ambiguity; no hint of what was to come. This must have been an act of desperation. How could she not have seen it coming? What if she could have done something to prevent it? She felt sick.

She wandered amongst her uncle's belongings. Her gaze lingered on an immaculately tailored coat and polished leather top hat hanging up on hooks, travelled to white shirtfronts and collars that Ryan would never wear again. She forced herself to look at the fatal firearms, the quality of craftsmanship clear even to one as ignorant as she. These were unexpected objects of beauty, whose parts were variously of polished woods, figured ivory, silver, gold and nickel.

Rhia imagined, fleetingly, that she smelt lanolin and lavender and its familiarity comforted her. A small draught lifted a scrap of white on the floor beneath the hooks; a calling card. Had it been there a moment ago? She picked it up. On it was printed the address of the Jerusalem Coffee House on Lombard Street in Cornhill. On the back was a series of numbers and an oriental character. She put the card in her reticule absently and when she glanced towards the other end of the room she caught Mr Dillon watching her. He looked away.

She was drawn to the long windows that stretched the length of the room. The view was of storehouses and rooftops, and a web of masts and rigging behind them. She imagined Ryan watching a shipload of cloth being unloaded, contemplating his own death. The thought was terrible. What level of despair preceded the wish to die? The masts swayed gently with the river tide and she had another sickening thought. Her father. How would he bear it?

She closed her eyes and lowered herself to the floor, back to the brick wall beneath the window. She willed the veil to lift as it had on the night of the fire. Perhaps Others could help her, be they ghosts or spirits or whatever creatures roamed the Otherworld. What purpose did they serve, except to be a nuisance to people such as herself? But there was no disturbance of the air now; no wisping in the reaches of her vision; only the harsh world of the living. She became aware of the low murmur of voices from the opposite end of the room and turned to find that both men were watching her. No doubt they thought her deranged by grief. Perhaps she was. She got to her feet slowly, and felt her shoulders hunch. She pushed them back with effort and walked towards them, keeping her gaze level; averted from Ryan's body.

'Is there anything?' she asked, hoping there was nothing and that they had decided it was an accident after all.

Mr Dillon answered. 'A cursory search has unearthed nothing, but it is a task in itself, as you can see.' He gestured to the towers of documents and ledgers and correspondence on the desktop. 'I am curious about the finer details of Mr Mahoney's death. I would like to spend a little longer here, if you do not object?'

How could she object? There was no one else to call on. 'Of course. I am grateful. I am at loss …' Her voice was unreliable again so she left the sentence unfinished.

Laurence took her hand and it seemed perfectly natural. 'Miss Mahoney, might I advise you?' Rhia thought she saw a glimmer of his inherent waywardness, in spite of his pallor. He was clearly remembering his attempt at advising her earlier.

'It would be a relief.' She smiled as best she could.

'There are arrangements to be made and it is crucial that we attend to them quickly. You must keep busy. No priest will question Ryan's right to a proper burial if we keep the circumstances of his death to ourselves. And we must take some advice on funeral arrangements. We will visit the good Mrs Bribb and her kettle of tea. She will know which church your uncle attended.'

Rhia agreed, partly because there was something else she wanted to ask the good Mrs Bribb. She turned to Mr Dillon. 'Please don't keep things from me, no matter how disturbing you think they might be. I am equal to the truth.'

'Yes, I can see that you are.' He paused. 'May I ask what has brought you to London?'

The question was blunt and Rhia felt, as she had in the carriage, that it was she who was being investigated.

'I had hoped to find a position, but now ...' She looked out of the window and bit her lip, unable to continue. She had no idea what, now.

'If you have come this far, Miss Mahoney, perhaps you might see how much further you can go?' This was unwarranted advice from a stranger, and it irked her. She might have retorted, but she hadn't the spirit. Mr Dillon's expression was unreadable. He bowed politely and turned away to examine some papers on Ryan's desk.

Mrs Bribb's residence was a narrow annexe at the rear of the building, looking out onto a tiny alleyway where a band of scruffy children were playing. She tidied around in her small, cluttered kitchen, and then stood with her hands on her hips inspecting Rhia. 'Will you be needing something for hysterics, miss?'

Rhia couldn't help a small smile. 'Do I appear to?'

'Not as far as I can see, but then, well-bred ladies don't

always show it. I have a syrup I take myself when they' – she gestured towards the alleyway where it sounded as though a cuff fight was in progress – 'get the better of me. It's only hyssop, skunk cabbage and Solomon seal root with a little ginger.'

It sounded vile. 'Tea will be fine, I think.'

'And you'll need some victuals.' Mrs Bribb set about preparing a tray of apple jam and cheese and a slightly stale knead cake. Rhia took a bite or two, to be polite, and when she had made a show of being strengthened by jam and tea, she remembered her question.

'Mrs Bribb, you said you thought my uncle might have fired his pistol when there was a ship in?'

'Well, it seems the perfect time, if you take my meaning.'

'Because of the noise?'

'That's it.'

Rhia frowned, trying to grasp something that kept sidling away from her. 'What time *was* the last ship in?'

'Tuesday evening.'

'Where was it from?'

'Bombay, I believe.'

'And was any of the cloth delivered to him?'

'I believe so but I couldn't say, miss. I don't take an interest, generally. There's merchant's storage on the floors below and above Mr Mahoney's, so there's always comings and goings.'

Rhia could feel Laurence's eyes on her.

'What are you thinking, Miss Mahoney?'

'I honestly don't know. Would my uncle have gone to the trouble of receiving a shipment of cloth, and then … ?'

'I see.' Laurence nodded, but Rhia could see that he thought she was distraught. She could not shake the idea that he might have received some news that had distressed him, perhaps tipped the balance. Mrs Bribb gave them directions to the chapel of St Andrews, three streets away. They thanked her and left.

The elderly priest at St Andrews answered the door of the priory, tousled and yawning and smelling of Communion wine. He squinted at them as though he had not seen the light of day in a week, but assured them that there was a place in the small graveyard, just as there was a place in the hereafter, for all members of his flock. It transpired that Ryan Mahoney had been a generous patron, and had thus purchased his place in heaven and a respectable burial.

Before returning to his meditations, the priest directed them a little farther along the river to Spice Quay, where they would find a cabinetmaker. Rhia did not question this peculiarity until she and Laurence were on their way.

'Do you think the priest thought that we wanted some furniture made?'

Laurence smiled wanly. 'Cabinetmakers in London are, often as not, also funeral directors.'

The cabinetmaker's workshop rang with the sound of hammering and sawing and smelt of wood shavings and linseed. For three pounds, a respectable but low-key burial was arranged for the following Tuesday. It occurred to Rhia that this would be one week exactly after her arrival. Three pounds would purchase a hearse with one horse, a stout elm coffin, and a coachmen and bearers with hatbands and gloves.

Laurence paid the cabinetmaker so swiftly that she had no time to protest. He assured her that it was a privilege to be able to spend a few pounds on a friend. He took her elbow and led her to their carriage. The driver in the pork-pie hat was smoking and whistling cheerfully. He'd bagged a good long fare today.

Rhia watched the sun hover above the river as they crossed

Blackfriars Bridge, sprinkling its dying light across the dark water. It took all her strength not to shrink into the corner of the carriage.

The streets were dark and shining with gaslit drizzle by the time they reached Cloak Lane. When Juliette opened the door, Rhia walked past her without removing her cloak. She felt as though she were weightless. She reached the bottom of the stairs as Antonia came to the door of her husband's study. Without warning, Rhia sank to the bottom stair, no longer weightless, though she was relieved to be sitting.

'Juliette! Fetch my smelling salts!' Antonia and Laurence reached her surprisingly quickly, and Rhia wondered why they were in such haste when she'd only sat down on the stair. With Antonia at one elbow and Laurence at the other, she was half-carried up the stairs and to her room. Laurence whispered something before he left, but she neither knew nor cared what it was.

Juliette took a buttonhook to the side of her bodice nimbly, and Antonia unpinned her hair. The company of these women was soothing, but she had never felt so far from her mother's arms. She wanted to go home. In the space of one day, London had been transformed from a place brimful with life and expectation, to a place where death visited the unwary.

She floated into sleep, aware that there was someone beside her. Antonia? No. This woman's hair was like strands of sea mist and she wore a girdle woven of seagrasses and coral, from which hung pieces of shell. Rhia decided that she must be asleep, since it was unlikely that she was dead. Ryan was dead. One shell looked like a pearly key in the shape of a simple, three part knot; the same knot-work that was on her silver pen. Rhiannon's key to the Otherworld.

# Chine

Michael woke, as he often did, in the basement of Maggie's brothel. The first thing he laid eyes on was the great, dusty cog of the Stanhope with its ink-blacked rollers and wooden press levers. He lay for a while, musing that he hadn't seen any of the Smith boys around for a few weeks and remembering little tasks that needed attending to. He'd noticed, for instance, that there was a small chip out of the top of the letter R, which made it look like a K. The only type-blocks he could find on George Street were wooden, not lead, and hand-cut, and his paper came from the butcher's shop at the quay. He enjoyed hand-setting, inking and printing the text as much as he liked writing it. It all gave him great satisfaction and had kept him from despair on many homesick nights.

The cast iron Stanhope press might have been the largest object ever stolen by a pickpocket. Before its arrival in Maggie's basement, it had gathered cobwebs in the abandoned offices of the *Defender* for a year before it came to Michael's attention. The *Defender* was a short-lived newspaper enterprise, being a publication with Irish sympathies and liberal views. Few who had an interest in its contents could afford a penny for a weekly. Michael liked to think that the Stanhope had been liberated, rather than stolen, and returned to its true calling.

The pickpocket in question was Joey Smith. Joey and his two brothers had all ended up in Sydney, though none of them had intended to, and they had all come from London on separate transports. The family name was contrived, since the Smith boys didn't know who their pa was, or even if they all had the same one. They had come about the name because it suited their profession. If they had used the full name of their professional calling, *fingersmith*, then they'd have more trouble from the law than they did already.

The pamphlet was always two double-sided pages, and was distributed, monthly and secretly by a couple of the newspaper boys from the *Sydney Herald*. The boys were the sons of Irishmen who had been transported for being intelligent and ideological rather than for other crimes against the English. Ironic, since the *Herald* was a newspaper for the gentry, whose editors were ministers of the very faith that persecuted (and prosecuted) the newspaper boys' fathers. Michael had pointed this out to Will in the Shamrock once, and Will snorted and replied that ideology turned clever men into drunks. It was a fair point, seeing as they were surrounded by clever drunks.

Maggie's basement was made of clay bricks and there was a blessed chill on its musky, subterranean air. As Michael rose and stretched and buttoned up his braces, he spared a rare thought for the furnace from whose fires these bricks had emerged. He had been assigned to the brick-firing pit, along with other convicts who weren't half dead after the voyage. They'd nicknamed the brick pit Hades. The punishing days in Hades had acclimatised Michael quickly to the soaring temperatures that baked the earth during the Antipodean summer. He was still not accustomed, though, to the approaching Australian Christmas.

He started to climb the staircase to the kitchen, then stopped for a moment to appreciate the silence. Sunday was a day of blessed quiet in the brothel. Usually in the morning there were half a dozen or so of Maggie's girls sitting around in their stays and flimsy housecoats, drinking tea and talking about last night's custom. It was always rough talk – some of the things these girls came out with would put a Bristol sailor to shame. Michael occasionally found himself pitying the poor sod who couldn't get a cock stand, or who was puny enough to make a room full of prostitutes laugh.

This morning Maggie was alone, and it looked as if she'd just had a wash in the copper pail outside, because her wavy brown hair was dripping wet, making the thin fabric of her dress stick to the curves of her shoulders and breasts. It was chinois, Chinese silk, he could spot the stuff a mile off. He'd bought Annie some once, on his travels. Maggie liked expensive things, and what she wore was always cut to show off her best features. Modesty was no virtue when you made a living from fucking.

'Good morning to you, Michael.'

'Nice and quiet.'

'Aye. The girls are like family – it's good to be rid of them now and then.' Maggie looked at Michael with an expression she reserved for their rare moments alone. 'Of course, not for as long as you've been separated from yours, my love.' She put the iron kettle on her little black range. 'Will you stop with me for lunch? I've a treat.' She nodded her head towards the open door to the back verandah and Michael took a step closer to see what it was. Trussed at the legs and hanging from a cross-beam was a wild turkey, already plucked. He let out a low whistle.

'And that's not all,' Maggie grinned. 'I've been saving a bottle and, given that it's a few weeks till Christmas, I'm willing to start the festivities early.'

'It's good of you, Maggie.' It was tempting all right.

'Well, Michael Kelly, if only you'd allow me to, I'd show you greater pleasures than turkey and Rio whisky.'

Michael sighed good naturedly. 'We both know how that conversation ends.'

Maggie chuckled. 'It could end anyway you want it to.' She uncrossed her legs slowly, watching to see if his eyes could stay on her face as the chinois slid away from her thighs. He held her gaze only with difficulty.

Maggie shrugged as if to say he'd come to his senses one day, and got up to make his tea. Her range was the envy of every housewife in the Rocks who had to cook over an open fire. There probably wasn't another for miles around. She moved slowly; her hips round and smooth beneath the silk. She knew he was watching. It wasn't as if he'd never been tempted to forget himself in her bed, and he'd been no saint in Sydney. The loneliness got to them all eventually, but that was years ago and he'd regretted it. He'd never bedded any of Maggie's girls, though. It wouldn't have been right. There was only one woman, even to the ends of God's earth, for Michael. He could only barely recall Annie's face now, but her heart still beat with his. It always had. It wasn't as if his body no longer wanted to explore the hidden inlets and darker caves of a woman, but he was old enough now to be able to more or less master his cravings. It was only Annie that his *heart* ached for.

He sat and drank Maggie's fragrant tea while she put the turkey in the oven. Tea was a luxury in Sydney; but Maggie always had a good supply. She knew people. She could get hold of just about any victuals, be they contraband, rare or imported from the farthest shores of Africa. She also knew the talk on the street. Her girls got a bonus for keeping her informed of anything interesting they heard from a punter who momentarily forgot himself.

The morning whiled away nicely while Maggie did her chores and Michael read over his draft for the next pamphlet, making notes. There would be more news from Ireland next time a ship was in. Maggie eventually sat down and poured herself another cup of tea. It was some time since they'd had a quiet stretch together, and Michael wondered if she had any information for him. 'No more trouble, since the raid?'

'Nothing. As you know, the lads had no clue what they were looking for – they rarely do, these young bobbies who think just because they're the law, that they're clever along with it.'

'Lucky for me, otherwise they'd've had me for the Stanhope.'

Maggie laughed. 'They didn't even know what it was, bless 'em. I told 'em there had been a shoemaker living here and it was some contraption for mending boots he'd left behind.'

Michael grinned, enjoying the thought of outwitting the Sydney constabulary, who, aside from his mate Calvin and his hand-picked boys, were mostly thugs in uniform. 'It's still awful quiet down the Rocks.'

'Know what you mean. There's something keeping the boys off the street and it smells profitable, but best to keep your nose clean of the big jobs, Michael. Think of your ticket of leave.'

'It's all I think of. But I'm curious. Besides, if the likes of the Smith boys are caught up in something too clever for their limited wits, then I want to know who's paying.'

Maggie sighed and retrieved the whisky bottle from her cheese cupboard. She poured them each a measure, and from the way her lips were pursed, he knew that there was something she wasn't telling him.

'All right, Maggie, out with it.'

'Will you promise to leave it alone if I tell you?'

'Not a chance.'

'Sweet Jesus, you're a bloody fool.' She sighed. 'But you're a likeable fool, and I don't want you getting in any strife.'

'I tell you what, if I get another seven years, then I'll build you a little lean-to out the back, just like you always wanted – somewhere to get away from all the fuss of the business.'

Maggie laughed. 'I'll tell you. Though not for a lean-to, but because I know that you'll just go asking somebody else and it's dangerous. All I know is that there's been crates of something godawful heavy being carried into Mick's place down on the junction road in the wee hours, and I've never known merino yarn to weigh that much.'

'Mick the Fence?'

She nodded.

'So Mick's in. It's high-end robbery, then.'

'Aye.'

Michael frowned. 'As soon as there's comings *and* goings, then there's bound to be some activity on the harbour.'

'You're only one man, just remember that when you feel your bile rise against the *industrialists*, as you call them. It's all very well writing your pamphlet and encouraging the spirit of rebellion, or whatever it was you called it, but you interfere with a powerful man's profiteering and you'll be crucified.'

'It was good enough for Jesus.'

'Don't joke about this!'

Michael could see that she was in earnest and felt mildly remorseful. 'You mustn't fret for me, Maggie. I can't help the way I'm made, and if there's something I can still put right, then I will. You won't be able to change it.'

She looked at him, eyes hard as nails, and a moment of understanding passed between them. 'I see.' She poured them each another measure. 'Then here's to your damned crusade and may you live long and be returned to the lucky woman you love.'

'And here's to you, Maggie, as fine a woman as ever ran a brothel, and may you find love for yourself.'

She threw back her head and laughed as though this was the funniest thing she'd ever heard.

I woke in the faraway hours and thought I smelt your smell again. I couldn't sleep so I watched the candle flame until patterns danced from it onto my paper. More leaves, as though every last leaf must fall.

Daylight has filled the shadows. It will soon be time for Ryan's burial. It has been four days, and each day I've felt that I should be with him. What if he had something else to tell me? Antonia wouldn't hear of it and no doubt thought me unhinged, even after I explained that in Ireland a family member would always be accompanied until burial. She was shocked, though she tried to hide it, when I told her that dead bodies needed to be protected from thieves and medical students. And from fairies you would say. She assures me that in England anatomical medicine is respected by the public, and there is a ready supply of the dead.

It feels as though a lifetime has passed, though it is only a week since I arrived in London. Mrs Blake and I sat together in her morning room on Friday afternoon and dipped our quills by turn into her ink pot. She composed an obituary notice to be published in *The Times* and then, while I wrote and rewrote the letter to my mother, she wrote to Ryan's friends and associates on black-edged stationery. The wake will be held after the service this morning.

On Saturday I went to the Petticoat Lane market for black crêpe and green velvet ribbon for a tabard, and sat sewing in the morning with Mrs Blake and Juliette. Juliette is habitually miserable. She barely speaks and hunches her shoulders as if she alone bears the sins of all Catholics. Her gloominess irks me now that I am so wretched myself. I have sewn a tabard trimmed with green ribbon for the coffin and a mantle for myself. I can barely bring myself to wear a black gown, but I must. Only for the burial though, because Ryan told me that he found the excessive mourning habits of the English extremely dull. I would prefer to wear the print I saw in his room, of golden leaves spinning across emerald green. This was a cloth more symbolic of death than black crêpe; a reminder that the falling leaves of autumn sustain the tree that bears new leaves in the spring.

A gentleman by the name of Dillon has taken it upon himself to mediate with the authorities. Laurence trusts him. I only hope I have not been a fool, telling him as much as I have. Both men have been looking for a letter, written to Ryan by Mrs Blake's husband before he died, and now I cannot stop wondering what it contained. Perhaps it will explain Ryan's strange mood on the day before he died. I believe he was in some kind of financial difficulty. Someone is on the stair. I will write more anon.

# Ribbon

Rhia closed her drawing book and ran her hand over its red cloth cover. It contained designs and sketches of ideas. Now, the 'letters' to Mamo were interspersed with drawings of ivy on stonework and winter roses. It felt odd writing at first, but now it seemed the most natural thing in the world. She even wondered if Mamo had always intended that this was how the pretty pen with its shining knot-work would be used.

There was a light rap on the door and Antonia appeared carrying a breakfast tray.

'You are dressed already,' she said, surprised.

'I couldn't sleep.'

'Nor I. Laurence left an hour ago for China Wharf. Isaac has offered to collect us in his carriage. I thought I'd make sure you had time to dress, but I can see that I needn't have worried.' She took the tray to the table and stopped still when she saw Rhia's painting.

'Is this your work?'

Rhia nodded.

'But, this is *accomplished*! I had no idea. I am quite astonished. So delicate. Such inventiveness. You have an eye, my dear.'

Rhia was pleased to be praised by someone like Antonia, who clearly had an eye herself. She joined her at the table and squinted to assess the worth of what she had painted. The leaves were in different shades of blue, more like spiralling arabesques that whorled across the page like candle flames in a draught.

Antonia was leaning over the table, examining the design more carefully. 'Extraordinary that one colour can have so many moods.'

Rhia nodded in agreement. 'I once bothered a dyer until he would name every blue in his workshop, probably in the hope that I would go away.' She pointed out different jars in her box. 'This is pearl blue and that one mazarine and that is ultramarine. The names were given to different shades of Indian indigo by the dyers of the last century. Before that there was only woad.'

Antonia was listening intently. 'Wasn't that what the Irish painted themselves with before going into battle?'

'It was. To frighten off the Romans. Perhaps we should try it on the English ...' Rhia trailed off, remembering that she was talking to an Englishwoman, but Antonia was smiling.

'You are well-read,' was all she said, and she didn't seem displeased.

'Too much so, according to my father. When he is angry he says that no man will have me. And I *have* made him angry rather a lot.'

'Some men are at loss to know what to do with a woman who can think for herself. They cannot help it. They are bred to believe that they are our intellectual superiors, and to be proven otherwise would topple their world from its perch. But topple it we must! I hope that you will never consider marrying a man who does not want you to think for yourself.' Antonia was quiet for a moment, looking at the blue arabesques. 'Do you have others?' Rhia nodded and unearthed her binder. She had been unable to bring herself to leave behind all her paintings, they were like a journal; each one reminding her of the day it had been created. Antonia examined design after design, exclaiming over knot-work roots, brightly coloured vines and twirling ribbons of lilies. She said she loved them all, so Rhia showed her the chintz from Thomas. Antonia seemed quite in awe as she trailed a finger along the golden feather of a bird, and then a bough laden with jewels of fruit.

'How wonderful,' she breathed finally. 'My dear, this is a treasure. You must never part with it!'

They ate a little bread, though neither had the stomach for it, and then waited in the entrance hall until they heard bridles clinking outside.

Rhia was intrigued by Isaac Fisher immediately she stepped into the carriage. He wore a flat-brimmed hat and the white neck tie that made Quaker gentlemen resemble clergymen. He was large, though not corpulent, and the shoulder length hair beneath his hat was greying brown. His gaze was distant, but his handshake firm. He only spoke to ask where Laurence was, and after Mrs Blake explained that he had left early to supervise the casket bearers, they rode across London Bridge in silence.

In the small, overgrown churchyard of St Andrews, there were perhaps a dozen gentlemen in black hats and coats, but Rhia recognised only Mr Dillon. He stood a short distance from those gathered at the grave. She suspected his presence was more than a mark of respect for a man he had barely known. Did he expected to find some clue here, amongst her uncle's mourners, or did he already know why Ryan had taken his own life? He caught her eye and bowed deferentially.

The casket bearers arrived and discharged their sombre duty impeccably. Rhia was glad that she had decided not to be present when Ryan's body was nailed shut into his coffin. It was kind of Laurence to offer to oversee the formalities, particularly as he seemed a little nervous about doing so.

Rhia would only have feared for her uncle's comfort and the lack of air within the casket. It was foolish but she could not help it.

Laurence was at the front of the queue of bearers, his hand resting beneath the front of Ryan's coffin as gently as if he were carrying a precious object. The priest seemed vaguely inattentive and kept trailing off as though he had forgotten where he was or what he was doing. The service was brief. Before the casket was lowered into the earth, Rhia stepped forward and draped her crêpe tabard over it. As the dirt was shovelled carelessly into the grave, Laurence came to stand by her side. They watched until only a corner of ribbon was poking through the brown dirt. It was the green velvet ribbon disappearing into the gaping earth that was Rhia's undoing. The irrevocability of it. Her knees suddenly felt like aspic. Antonia rested a hand beneath her elbow, and each held the other up a little straighter than they could have managed alone.

The mourners stirred when the last clods of earth were in place, and two men approached. The taller had the self-assured air of a successful gentleman and looked aristocratic. His companion was slight and a little stooped, and more modestly attired. Rhia took him to be a clerk.

'Good morning, Mrs Blake,' said the tall gentleman. 'And this must be Miss Mahoney?'

Rhia saw Antonia's hand flutter to her hair before it was corrected. Who was this man who made the Quaker self-conscious? Antonia composed herself quickly and smiled her gracious smile.

'Yes, this is Miss Mahoney, Ryan's niece, and this is my husband's cousin, Mr Blake.' Antonia introduced the gentleman as Mr Montgomery, a mercer of Regent Street, and his associate as Mr Beckwith. Rhia had not heard Antonia Blake use formal titles before. Was she doing this for Mr Montgomery's benefit? And if so, what of her Quakerly values? Rhia extended her hand, which Mr Montgomery took. His clear hazel eyes met hers for only a moment, but she felt a small thrill at their intensity. It must be useful, as a mercer, to have such an effect on women – his clientele being largely female. He turned to Laurence.

'Ah, Mr Blake, I heard you had moved to London. Your reputation precedes you. I understand you are making great advances in the photogenic field.'

'Indeed I am,' said Laurence. 'If you would like a portrait or a personalised calling card, I am at your disposal.' Even Laurence seemed a little in awe of the man.

'But Mrs Blake has already taken my portrait! Or rather, she took a group portrait in her garden in the spring.' Mr Montgomery turned his handsome face back to Antonia. He was in the region of fifty and had an abundance of pewter hair and a toffee-cream complexion. The corners of his eyes were crinkled to suggest he often smiled. Mr Beckwith barely raised his eyes. He was either painfully shy or overcome by emotion. Perhaps he had been fond of Ryan.

'I have done nothing with the negative yet,' said Mrs Blake eventually, softly. 'It is not transferred.' It was clear that she did not want to talk about the portrait, which made Rhia even more interested in it.

'My deepest commiseration for your loss, Miss Mahoney,' said Mr Montgomery. 'Your uncle was very well liked. He will be missed. Sadly, Mr Beckwith and I have a pressing engagement elsewhere and cannot attend Cloak Lane, but I would very much like to make your acquaintance. I know it is abominably short notice, but you must, all three, agree to be my guests this Saturday for supper.'

'That is gracious,' said Antonia. She looked at Rhia, flushing. Laurence was clearly pleased, so Rhia nodded.

'Splendid! Shall we say eight o'clock?' Mr Montgomery strode away through the churchyard with Mr Beckwith hurrying behind him. He looked rather magnificent, with his polished leather top hat and black mourning coat. It must be English broadcloth. The quality, Rhia had to admit, was superior even to that woven in Wicklow. His patent boots and the silver tip of his walking stick flashed in the sun, affirming that he was a man who had money and who liked to spend it. There was something reassuring about this.

The vision of the ribbon in the brown earth would not leave Rhia as they returned to Isaac's carriage. It was a symbol of renewal, she decided, and of hope. If today were a cloth, it could only be green velvet.

At Cloak Lane, Beth and Juliette wore starched white aprons and caps, they curtsied and took top coats and hats and showed guests down the hall.

The fire was lit in the drawing room, at the centre of the house. Rhia had not yet seen this room in use. Like any drawing room, it was a statement of the prosperity of the household, but it seemed out of place in the Blake household. The carpet was deep rose and the curtains heavily patterned damask. The furnishings were teak and mahogany upholstered in red velvet, and the walls were papered in dark green. The room was conventional and did not have Mrs Blake's lightness of touch. Rhia felt, instinctively, that this room had been Josiah's and that it had not been used since he died.

Several gentlemen, whose names Rhia immediately forgot, approached her and offered sympathy and condolences and murmured a few kind words about Ryan. They drifted off to converse quietly in huddles by the fire, on the ottoman or by the windows.

Antonia brought her tea in a cup and saucer of pink china, so fine that it might have been made from a sea shell. Neither of them spoke for a time. Rhia was puzzling over the drawing room and Quakerism. For all of the simplicity of their faith, the Blakes unashamedly embraced the accessories of wealth.

'You must be thinking about Ryan,' Antonia coaxed.

Rhia almost felt guilty that she was not. 'No. Is it true that Lloyds and Barclays are Quaker banks?'

Antonia looked puzzled. 'Yes.' She nodded slowly. 'But affluence can be a consequence of ethical trade as much as large-scale production. The real error is in being without charity, which is, after all, what God intended for us.'

'How can you know what God intended? He has not been in direct conversation with anyone for almost two thousand years!'

Antonia had the good grace to smile before she said she must fetch more of Beth's barberry tarts and ginger loaf cake. Rhia suddenly longed to be like her; to believe in something wholly and unquestioningly; to follow a creed that made sense of life and death, instead of hovering between the worlds of the living and the dead. On the other hand, wearing grey and brown for the rest of one's life seemed a high price to pay for unwavering faith.

Laurence and Dillon appeared and were, for a time, deep in conversation with Isaac Fisher. When Antonia went to the kitchen, Dillon approached Rhia. He was dressed respectfully in black, but his boots were as narrow and pointed as ever.

'May I speak with you for a moment, Miss Mahoney?'

'Of course.' She wished he wouldn't, as her tone probably implied. She was tired. She caught Laurence watching from the other side of the room, frowning, though he smiled quickly when their eyes met. She felt unsure of herself and wished someone would bring out a fiddle or tell a joke about Ryan. She could not help admiring Mr Dillon's apparent disregard for social graces.

'It is remarkable that your arrival in London should coincide with your uncle's death,' he began, and she braced herself. 'Is it possible that the circumstances which brought you here were connected to his … situation?'

Rhia felt a surge of anger which seemed to fortify her. 'If you think my arrival in London somehow contributed to my uncle's—' She didn't manage to finish before Mr Dillon interjected.

'That is not what I said. I only wondered if you could tell me more about the circumstances that brought you here.'

Rhia bit her lip and felt foolish. 'If you must know, my family's business in Dublin collapsed and I have come to London to find a position as a governess.'

'A *governess*?'

It was evident that he did not think her suited to the profession. Perhaps he thought her too shallow or not cultivated enough? She clenched her teeth. 'Yes, a *governess*.'

'I see.'

She thought she saw the shadow of a smile and that did it. 'I have some questions of my own. Please tell me what your business was with my uncle and why you are so interested in his affairs?'

'It is a fair question,' he agreed. 'I only wish I could be of more assistance to you. As to your uncle's estate, by law, the property of someone who commits self-murder should immediately be seized by the Crown. The gentlemen from Scotland Yard who visited China Wharf have now issued a report to the coroner. There is, however, a period in which the circumstances of death can be attested.' He had neatly side-stepped her question.

'What is there to attest?'

'That is what I intend to discover. Perhaps your uncle felt he had no choice but to take his own life. Meanwhile neither you nor your family will be allowed access to the will or any of your uncle's assets and neither will his lawyer be permitted to release documentation of his legal holdings.'

'I had not given such things any thought.'

Mr Dillon looked surprised. Did he not believe her?

'There is one other matter,' he said. 'I think Mr Blake has told you that we failed to find the letter. I blame myself, in part, for having to ask you this, but please cast your mind back to last week when we went to your uncle's rooms. I should have told you at the time not to touch or move anything. Was there *anything*, Miss Mahoney, that you noticed; that seemed out of the ordinary or out of character?'

Rhia could think of nothing, and said so.

I see. Thank you. I wish you well in your new profession.' He bowed and went to pay his respects to Antonia. When he left, without a backward glance, Rhia breathed a sigh of relief.

What had he meant about the 'circumstances of death'? Presumably he intended, somehow, to discover what had gone wrong in Ryan's personal or professional life. *Was* there anything she had noticed at China Wharf? She remembered the calling card she had picked up from the floor. Although it was probably nothing, she could do some investigating of her own; at least discover what the numbers and the oriental character meant. It might make her feel less helpless. Dillon's interest in Ryan's affairs made her uneasy, and she was now regretting telling him anything at all.

# Armozeen

Juliette's fingers were icy cold as they brushed Antonia's neck. Antonia shivered. Juliette finished fixing the lace fichu and stepped back to inspect her work. She looked pleased, as she always did on the rare occasions that Antonia wore a pretty collar or cuff. The fichu was decorative, not her own choice, but Antonia did not want to insult her hosts by appearing too abstemious. Personally, she cared not if every other female at the Montgomery supper were clothed in rainbows. Or so she told herself.

'I *am* sorry, madam, I tried rubbing them together to warm them, but they're just cold hands and there's nought I can do about it.' Juliette's penitence was occasionally irksome, yet it was what had drawn Antonia to the girl. She had not intended to employ a maid on her charitable visit to the Manchester workhouse. Had she thought that she could save Juliette? It seemed arrogant, now.

'It is not important. No doubt it prevents me from becoming complacent. It is a blessing to have you. Now, is the collar straight? And what about my hair? You know I rely on you to be my looking-glass.'

'You look very fine, madam, though not *too* fine, of course!'

Antonia smiled. Juliette seemed to have untangled some of the emotion of her mother's letter, but there was still that *something*. Antonia could still not bring herself to ask about the death of the father, though she often longed to. She must be deferential, and tread lightly. Was this what God wanted – that no creature should be affronted by another? She was disturbed to feel so weary of righteousness.

The others were waiting in the hall. Rhia was dressed in straw coloured corinna; a silk so ornately figured that it resembled embroidery. Her shawl was of deep, rich maize. The tones set off her inky hair and olive skin as though she were some harvest deity, and Laurence could barely drag his eyes from her. Antonia vaguely recalled a tale of the survivors of the Spanish Armada who had left a strain of their fine, dark looks in Ireland. She felt like a dried-up wheat shaft by comparison. For a moment she longed for the ephemeral pleasure of vanity.

'You look handsome,' Rhia said. She was looking at her quizzically, and Antonia felt her colour rise guiltily. The plainness of dress was originally intended to be a protest against fashion and its wasteful and fickle demands, but that had been in response to the lavish adornment of the last century. It struck Antonia that, without Josiah, these virtues might have lost their meaning. She smiled as sincerely as she could.

'Mr Montgomery is sending his carriage.' The ring of hooves on the cobbles interrupted her. 'And here it is. Remarkably punctual.' She busied herself with her gloves and bonnet to hide her confusion.

Rhia gazed out of the carriage window as they travelled along Holborn and Oxford Street, though there was little to see but drizzle and carriage lamps. She had now drafted two letters to prospective employers; one to a vicar with two young daughters in Finsbury and the other to an elderly widow in Kensington who had advertised for a young lady companion. The latter position, Antonia guessed, might be too staid for someone with Rhia's restlessness. At least Quakerism actively encouraged women in the workplace. At least the Friends would not disapprove of her trading on her own.

'What sort of establishment is the Jerusalem Coffee House?' Rhia asked suddenly.

'It is a meeting place of sorts,' Laurence began, looking to Antonia for help. The world of trade was of little interest to him; unless it was a study in chiaroscuro. 'It is where bankers, investors and merchants and people who work for the Royal Exchange all meet to buy and sell stocks and shares,' Antonia explained. She envied Laurence. She wished that she, too, could focus on light and shade to the exclusion of all else. The irony of the metaphor did not escape her. Focusing on the light alone seemed as problematic as becoming lost in the shadows. They fell into silence again. No one was in the mood for a dinner party.

The Montgomery residence was one of a number of mansions in Belgrave Square, in the vicinity of Buckingham Palace Gardens. They passed through imposing iron gates attended by a footman, and stopped at the bottom of several broad marble steps. These led to a columned portico and double doors of polished oak.

The doors were opened by a starched maid as pretty as a china doll, and they stepped into an austere entrance hall with a tiled floor and walls papered in patterned jade and peacock blue. Very theatrical, Antonia thought, feeling like a domestic servant in her plain, corded armozeen.

They were delivered to a vast reception room. Every wall hung with French tapestries. Here, the dinner guests gathered to listen to the pianoforte, played by a flaxen creature in a froth of sugar pink tulle. Isabella Montgomery was soon to come of age but looked fresh from the nursery with her pale, sausage ringlets and limpid, cornflower eyes. She turned to look when the new arrivals were announced. She struck a wrong key and giggled nervously.

Close by, perched on regal chairs, were Mr Montgomery and his wife Prunella in magenta silk and a tiara. She averted her eyes pointedly when they grazed Antonia's skirts. She had the same cloud of sunflower hair as her daughter, but her eyes were glassy with whatever she sipped on so urgently. Mr Montgomery seemed strained.

The dinner guests were seated on a row of upholstered chairs and Antonia recognised the gaunt couple as Lord and Lady Basset; he being one of the East India Company's representatives in Canton. The Bassets were a part of *Society*, and Antonia did not miss Lady Basset's eyes widening when a Quaker and a foreigner took their seats beside Mr Beckwith and Isaac. At least Laurence had oiled his hair, but his shirt-front was just as creased as ever. She had no idea how he managed to look so consistently rumpled when Beth went to great pains to iron and starch his shirts.

Isabella hammered the pianoforte keys and Antonia caught Isaac stealing looks at her. His mouth twitched as another stray chord escaped. She looked away quickly, lest she giggle. Was it just her feeling of displacement, or was the tension in the room palpable? It was a peculiar company, and she thought Mr Montgomery brave to gather them together.

Isaac had been attentive on the day of the burial, mindful that another death had cut her to the quick. The actuality of Ryan's suicide had not completely registered – Antonia felt only disbelief. Surely they should have seen the signs? Had they all been neglectful? She had noted Ryan's odd mood but had just assumed that he was feeling the pressures of commerce. It was clear that Isaac felt the same remorse. He had been colleague and friend to both Ryan and Josiah. He lived with grief, too, having lost his wife to typhoid fever two summers ago.

Isabella finished playing and Mr Montgomery took charge, since his wife was already in her altitude. He guided Antonia by the elbow to the dining room, and she felt her skin tingle at his touch through the thick fabric of her sleeve. To esteem him was no crime, but she must be doubly careful to be proper – not because she cared what people thought, especially, but because she was aware of her own vulnerability.

Mr Montgomery had seated her next to him. 'I am delighted to see you abroad in society, Mrs Blake. Am I to believe what Mr Fisher tells me – that you mean to run Josiah's business?'

'Of course. I have been more involved in the trade than you perhaps realise.' Why was Isaac discussing her affairs with Jonathan Montgomery?

'It shouldn't surprise me, given that your creed is so intent on reform.'

'I am disappointed that you think it reform! It is merely a mark of respect on the part of both husband and wife that a woman should take an interest in such things.'

'Indeed, forgive me. Quite so.' He sighed heavily and Antonia felt her heart lurch. If his wife were more often sober she might take an interest in his own affairs.

'We must speak more on the subject of commerce, soon,' he added as he pulled back his own chair. 'Perhaps your husband mentioned our newest enterprise?'

'I am not up to date. No doubt he intended to when he … returned from India.'

Her host looked down at his plate, shaking his head. He must miss Josiah too. Her husband had been well-liked even though he was outspoken on the subject of ethics. He would not be associated with anyone who was not similarly principled. Antonia wanted to say something soothing. 'I have been thinking about the portrait in the garden. Perhaps you would like a representation of it?' She trailed off when she caught Isaac's eye. He looked disapproving, and she wondered if he thought she was being too familiar. Isaac looked away quickly and said something to Rhia, his expression earnest and the movements of his large hands slow and deliberate. She had seen him at the Jerusalem with the banker from Barings! She had completely forgotten the incident, so much had happened since. Isaac was listening to Rhia's impressions of London, as was doe-eyed Isabella Montgomery. Antonia could not hear much above the clink of cutlery and crystal, but heard him say, in his slow, resonant voice, 'Irish linen, being an import, can hardly compete against English, but it is favoured in Germany, a nation that appreciates fine-spun cloth as much as it favours quality in all things. Britain is less concerned about quality than with reducing cost and increasing production and profit.'

As they were served their first, extravagant course – chestnut soup and baked sweetbreads – Mr Montgomery leaned towards Antonia.

'I would very much like a representation of the portrait, Mrs Blake. Are you progressing with your photogenic drawing any more than when last we spoke?'

Antonia saw Laurence's head turn at this. 'I am not, Mr Montgomery, though I've not lost interest by any means. I have merely … paused. As for the portrait, the paper negative looks very much like it did before. I'm not sure if I was successful because I've not yet been brave enough to find out.' She turned to Laurence, who did not yet know about the portrait. 'Perhaps it is too late?'

He shrugged. 'If the iodised paper is carefully preserved,

you should be able to expose the latent image even several months later,' he assured her.

'That is fortunate indeed. You see, the tableau in the portrait included Josiah.' She gazed at her soup. She had not discussed the photogenic drawing with Laurence because every time she thought of the possibility of having Josiah's image brought back to her, a terror seized her. Her husband would never return. This ghost image of him could only be a reminder of the fact. When she looked up, Mr Montgomery's expression was so tender that she could hardly bear to meet his gaze.

'I am still baffled by this means of drawing by the use of light and silver salts,' he said. 'Tell me how the method of Mr Talbot differs to that of the Frenchman.'

Antonia was relieved. This was safe territory. 'Daguerre favours the use of a copper plate coated with silver, which darkens when exposed to the light. Rather like an etching on the metal. Mr Talbot's method fixes a negative image onto a paper template that can generate any number of copies. Am I right, Laurence?'

'Quite. With the Talbot method, one picture might be circulated as widely as a woodcut image stereotyped in plaster. In fact, once Mr Talbot releases his patent on the calotype process, photogenic drawing will no doubt be in use by the London papers and journals.'

'Fascinating,' said Mr Montgomery, still watching Antonia, as though she were the object of his fascination. She was anxious to deflect his attention, even though she had sought it in the first place. She lowered her voice when Laurence turned away.

'Are you still looking to create an exclusive range for the House of Montgomery?'

Mr Montgomery raised an eyebrow. 'I am. The Parisian designs are always very modern, but I tire of being led by the French.'

'Perhaps you would consider a female artisan?'

Mr Montgomery looked shocked. 'Mrs Blake, are you petitioning me?'

She laughed. 'Oh, not for myself, no. For Rhia Mahoney.' She rather enjoyed his astonishment. She could not have devised a better test for his character had she tried. Did he have the gall to consider employing a woman for such a position? She could only wait and wonder how he would respond.

# Corinna

The main course had only just been served and Rhia had already eaten too well for a boned bodice. She looked around the table. Mrs Montgomery's tiara tilted comically, or tragically, and her voice was too loud as she explained some obscure rule of whist to Lady Basset. Mr Beckwith and Isaac Fisher were engaged in a heated discussion over the opium trade. Rhia had given up interjecting. Her opinion was inconsequential and Lady Basset's disapproving looks were becoming irritating. In fact, she was certain that Lady Basset had whispered something unkind about her to Mrs Montgomery, because her hostess kept glancing at her suspiciously.

By now they were feasting on wild duck and roast hare and something the serving girl called 'an Indian dish of fowl'. The meats came served with broad beans and baked Spanish onions and truffles with champagne – the latter, they were informed, a delicacy the Montgomerys had recently dined on in Paris and hoped their guests would enjoy. Rhia did not. The flavour of the truffles was strong and earthy and the champagne unpleasantly heady. The claret had sufficiently improved her endurance of Isabella's company. Isabella seemed very taken with her, and thought her *emancipated*. She whispered the word as though it both terrified and excited her. Rhia was enjoying being thought liberal and exotic, but then again a dairymaid would appear so to Isabella who was as cosseted as a little princess – it seemed that she went nowhere without a chaperone. Isabella asked endless questions about the journey from Dublin, her eyes wide and her voice breathy. 'What an *adventure*! Papa should never allow it. How I *envy* you.'

Rhia was only partly listening while Isabella tinkled on about a forthcoming tea party in honour of her birthday. The neighbouring conversation between Isaac and Beckwith was much more interesting. Isaac had raised his voice.

'The fact remains, Francis, that it is as unethical to attempt to buy China silk under the emperor's nose as it is to export our cotton to China. The trade ban is law as far as I'm concerned.'

Mr Beckwith fixed the Quaker with a look that seemed to hold meaning for the two of them alone. Rhia intuited that this was a well-rehearsed conversation. 'The treasuries of China and Britain are inextricably linked, as we know,' he said carefully. 'The ethics are complicated, of course, but didn't gentlemen of your … *persuasion* once invest in cotton that was picked by Negro slaves?' Mr Beckwith seemed almost embarrassed to point this out. 'I am merely arguing the case for commerce,' he hastened to add.

Isaac was silenced as though he had suddenly thought better of his argument. Rhia caught Antonia's expression of dismay and was puzzled. There was some undercurrent that she was missing.

Mr Beckwith looked down at his dinner plate as though he regretted drawing attention to himself. She'd gathered that Mr Montgomery's associate was a sage of the financial markets. It was curious that Beckwith and Montgomery were also friends, since they seemed of vastly different social talents.

Antonia was looking pained. She addressed Lord Basset almost curtly. 'The East India Company, of course, would wish the government to protect the opium trade, which is an enormous advantage to them.'

'And to the British nation,' he spluttered, his face turning the same colour as the veins on his thin nose.

'With respect,' she persisted, 'I know bankers who conjure China as the new British Raj.'

'But the Raj is a huge success,' said Lord Basset. 'The populations of China and India should be grateful for our civilising influence.'

Rhia snorted and before she could stop herself, said, 'Then you cannot know that it was a Chinese delegation that started the Renaissance in Italy?' She was making herself unattractive again, but what was the point in having illicitly read her father's entire library if she could not put the knowledge to use? 'Surely the fact that opium is a slow poison means something to the East India Company.' There was silence.

Lady Basset stared daggers at Rhia. Rhia glared back and took a large, inelegant, swallow of claret to stop herself sticking her tongue out.

It was Isaac who broke the silence in his low, unhurried voice. 'Of course, without the need to sell opium to buy tea, the silver crisis could be averted, couldn't it, Francis?' Mr Beckwith looked up from his plate and replied in his lilting northern accent. 'It is true. The entire reserve of the Bank of England is earmarked for the trade.'

Prunella Montgomery put down her cutlery with a clang, and turned to her husband. 'The Union flag has become a pirate flag,' she said, and then lifted her glass to no one in particular. There was an awkward silence for a moment before Mr Montgomery laughed. 'Yes, my dear, or so Mr Gladstone says.'

Rhia lifted her glass in accord, but no one else did. She had already made a spectacle of herself, so it made no difference what she did now. 'Then it seems that Mr Gladstone is the only man in Whitehall who is more concerned with the humanity of the matter than with its economics,' she said. Even to her own ears, her tone was brittle and accusing, but as far as she could tell, the British *were* behaving like pirates. Lady Basset had a sudden coughing fit and Rhia thought she heard her say 'impudence' or 'impertinence' between splutters.

'It is also,' Antonia remarked, 'a matter of conscience, a quality rare in a politician.' A look of affinity passed between them. If Antonia did not think less of her for being opinionated, then Rhia didn't care what anyone else thought, including Laurence, who had drained his glass nervously twice since the debate began.

Mr Montgomery was now looking at her as though trying to decide something. Perhaps he was making a mental note not to invite her to another dinner party. Cold lemon pudding and damson tart were served in silence. It was a relief, afterwards, to adjourn to the drawing room with only the women. Lady Basset was now studiously ignoring her, which suited Rhia very well. She was unrepentant.

They drank over-sweetened café noir and liqueur, and Isabella chattered ceaselessly about the royal wedding, although it was months ago, and how very *small* Queen Victoria looked beside Prince Albert in all the drawings, and wasn't it remarkable that someone so tiny, and even younger than she, should be queen of an empire? Everyone nodded but no one seemed to be listening. Mrs Montgomery was now comprehensively intoxicated and was sitting with a faraway look and a fixed smile. She was obviously accustomed to the condition, because the only thing that gave it away was the occasional swaying of her torso. Lady Basset looked bored and irritated and Antonia was clearly exhausted. Rhia hoped that she would want to go home soon. Their eyes met. Antonia leaned towards her conspiratorially.

'Mr Montgomery would like to see your portfolio.'

Rhia was suddenly awake. 'My portfolio – is he in need of a draughtsperson? But how did he know?' She trailed off, confused for a moment before she realised that this must be Antonia's doing.

'He told me some time ago that he was looking for a textile designer.'

Rhia was speechless. Antonia merely looked pleased with herself. How was it possible that a Regent Street mercer would even consider a designer with no experience, let alone entertain the thought of employing a female?

'Mr Montgomery wants something a little special, something that is not imported from Paris. Don't forget, Rhia, that some of the most exquisite and famous designs for silk were by Anna Maria Garthwaite.'

'That is true.' She had of course heard of this famed designer, a favourite of the regents of the last century.

'Does it interest you?'

'Oh yes! But I cannot call myself a professional.'

'Yes you can. Perhaps not measured by experience, but experience is not everything and I have seen your work. I am always uplifted to see a woman employ her talent and her wit. I'm certain that God did not intend that artistic fulfilment should be entirely for the gratification of men.'

Rhia was overcome. The evening had been a strain and now, for some reason, she was close to tears. 'I have not known what to do, what to expect of London, now that—'

'Expect anything. London offers everything or nothing, depending on one's fate.'

It was so like something Ryan had said. As if the hopes and

desires of so many were merely tricks in a game of whist. 'Then you believe in fate?'

Mrs Blake sighed. 'To some degree. One must find the fragile balance between directing one's energies and accepting what is bestowed. Or taken away.'

Isabella was attempting to follow their conversation with a petulant frown. 'You are both too serious! Miss Mahoney, you *must* visit again and see Mama's pretty collection of cloth that Papa brings back from the Orient. It is worth thousands, apparently. Mama says I can choose a length for my birthday gown.' Suddenly, Isabella clapped her hands with delight. '*You* must come to my birthday party!'

'When is your birthday?' Rhia asked, trying to sound interested.

'Oh, not until February, but one must have something to look forward to.'

Rhia smiled wearily and Antonia suppressed a yawn. Surely it was finally a respectable hour to withdraw? Antonia stood up and Rhia sighed with relief.

In the darkness of the carriage, silence finally felt natural. Mr Montgomery had seen them out and asked her bring her portfolio to Regent Street soon. The thought filled her with exquisite terror.

Laurence was sitting next to her and she could feel his discomfort. He was probably cross with her for being so opinionated at dinner. He had spent the days since the burial in his studio and didn't seem to know what to say to her, though he was always unerringly cheerful at breakfast. He took lunch upstairs and dinner at his club.

'You are very well informed on the China Trade, my dear,' Antonia said softly, as though she were reading Rhia's thoughts. 'I approve,' she added. 'Perhaps you would be interested to read

Laurence's friend Mr Dillon's column in the *Globe*. He writes on commerce and City matters, you know, and has some quite unusual opinions.'

'Yes, he does rather,' agreed Laurence with a wry smile. 'Too clever for me, though.'

They fell into silence.

As they passed a carriage lamp, Rhia noticed Antonia's expression. She looked as though she needed her bed, perhaps to be alone with her private memories of her husband. She often seemed formidably self-possessed but now she looked fragile and uncertain. She was only human after all.

15 December 1840

The moon is new. I've come to the morning room in the faraway hours to see it from the window. The house is silent and still, but sometimes the shadows move as if they are trying to catch my attention. Whatever they want to show me is always just out of reach. I should understand these things. You would probably say that I could if I wanted to. All I know is that I have not yet found my place in this world, because I feel the undertow of another.

There is a picture in this room that troubles me. It is as though a ghost has entered it. The ghost is black, and it beckons to me, as if wanting to be found. This makes no sense. Tonight I tried your hex for warding away unwelcome spirits. I have trouble with the Gaelic, so I hope I haven't accidentally invited it to stay ! As luck would have it, just as I was finishing, Juliette the morose walked in. I've no idea what she was doing up in the night, but I know she heard me because she looked at me as if I'd grown horns and then she fled. I suppose I've frightened her, but that is easily done.

I have spent days walking. There is a labyrinth of alleyways that lead to Threadneedle Street to the west and Petticoat Lane market to the east, past taverns and coffee houses. Different alleyways are filled with different smells; fresh brew, fried kippers and yeast cakes, the lingering note of the evening's strong ale or sour wine. I have passed by the noisy, busy workshops of coach builders, cartwrights and sedan-chair makers. Yesterday I stopped to watch a fan mounter and became spellbound by the movements of his hands. It is such a delicate craft, attaching silk to wood. Surely there could never be a machine for making fans?

In the market place there is always shouting about the superior quality of baked goods, flowers and cheeses, sausages and ribbons. There is a bent crone who wears black and sits on a stool at a rickety table making lace. I always stop to watch because her wrinkled hands move so quickly that you can hardly see her wind the thread onto the bobbins. Her lace looks as fragile and silken as a spider's web.

There are many nimble fingers within a league of Threadneedle Street, sewing lapels and collars, pockets and sleeves, hems, button holes and gloves. They hang waistcoats and shirtfronts in their front windows or on cloth mannequins on the footpath. The livelihood of so many is dependent on a tailor's needs. I suppose it is sensible that an entire quarter of the city be dedicated to one trade. I remembered the talk at the Dublin Linen Hall about the forthcoming trade in ready-made coats and shirts. I expect gowns will follow, but I cannot imagine how anyone will find a thing to fit without being measured for it.

The mercer Mr Montgomery has asked to see my designs, and I have spent days choosing which drawings and paintings to show him, and have some new designs. The city has unexpected graces. In the garden behind the house is a sweep of ivy, clinging to the pale stonework as though it were embossed. I have also been taken by the silhouette of wrought iron against painted masonry. At Petticoat Lane market, overflowing barrows of lavender, geraniums and winter roses drop their petals like bright tears onto the dark cobbles.

I cannot pretend that I don't long for the sound of Epona's hooves on the shale, and even for your stories. Sometimes I badly want to come home, but I could not leave now, not without knowing what made Ryan take his own life. The unanswered question binds me to London. I've heard nothing from the journalist, Mr Dillon, not since the wake, but Laurence assures me that he has not forgotten us. I suppose he is busy. I still want to make enquiries of my own. I have been so weary.

There is something else, too, that I want from London, though I didn't know it until the possibility became so very real. It will make you smile, because it was you who named me after the goddess of sovereignty: when I return to Ireland, I want to have a profession, and I do not mean that I want to be a governess.

# Silk

In print as in person, Mr Dillon was discourteous but insightful. He took liberties with politeness that must make him enemies in the City. Rhia looked up from the paper to consider his words. Thousands of looms had become idle or completely out of employ because the free trade laws already allowed unlimited imports of silk from the Orient, and now French producers also wanted a piece of the English market. Such a treaty would mean the end of London silk production and another large community of weavers along with it. It was just the same as what had had happened in Ireland. Today's report had a sting in its tail.

If any good has come from the shameful behaviour of the British Navy in the Pearl River, then it is that China silk is not so readily available in London. The downtrodden Spitalfields weavers, therefore, might have a chance to mend their broken looms and feed their children. It is clear that the appetite of industrialists for capital and empire will poison the economy of this country just as they have poisoned the River Thames, ruining the London fishing industry. We might take a moment to reflect that many of the pirates on the river were once fishermen, and that many of the convicts who find themselves in Australia were once weavers.

Rhia wondered if Mr Dillon had any reason to be personally affronted by the iniquities of commerce, or if he was just generally disagreeable. She finished her coffee and remembered that she had left her portfolio upstairs.

Laurence was coming down the stairs as she was going up. He might actually have slept in the same clothes he was wearing yesterday, and his hair was more or less standing on end. It was hard not to smile at his haphazard ways, and she liked to think of him as a kindred spirit, preoccupied as he was with the illusory. He was by turn full of boyish good humour or lost in another dimension entirely.

'More walking today?' Laurence arched an eyebrow and his eyes ran over her indigo linen before he remembered his manners. Rhia had taken extreme care over dressing and her bed was a tangle of discarded dresses. She had needed to try on everything at least once in order to know exactly what one wore to the Montgomery Emporium. She was unreasonably nervous.

'Yes. Regent Street today.'

'Ah.' Laurence nodded. 'The dragon's lair.'

'That doesn't help, Laurence. Why do you say that?'

'Full of shining things, mercer's shops. I dare say that working for Montgomery would suit you better than being a governess though. I don't believe I've ever seen a governess wear a red cloak.' He looked at her suspiciously for a moment. 'Dillon tells me there's a Welsh horse-goddess named Rhiannon.'

'There is,' she agreed, surprised that Mr Dillon had found cause to mention it.

'Then shouldn't you be riding through London in your red cloak!'

'I'd be afraid to ride a horse along Cornhill. I might be knocked off by a wagon or an omnibus.'

'I think, Miss Mahoney,' Laurence said with mock gravity, 'the sight of you would be more likely to cause the wagon and omnibus to collide with each other.' The doorbell pealed down the corridor just as Rhia wanted to enquire after Mr Dillon's interest in goddesses. Beth bustled past, grumbling about not being a housekeeper.

Laurence took out his watch. 'Drat. That's my ten o'clock. Good luck. I hope we can discuss the merits, or otherwise, of your new profession anon.'

As she approached Fleet Street, Rhia's thoughts returned to Dillon. She supposed the printing presses of the *London Globe* chugged away somewhere here along with those of the city's other newspapers. If Threadneedle Street was home to the cloth trade, then here was the heartland of the printed word; the journalist's quarter. She wondered if Mr Dillon's meeting with Ryan and his crusade against free trade might be connected.

Fleet Street, with its blackened stone and teeming thoroughfare, had the same vitality as the banking district but the grime of the East End. Today, Rhia felt part of it. Everyone seemed on their way to a pressing engagement, anxious to achieve something or other – or anxious that they would not achieve that something or other. She had a pressing engagement herself, and the sun was shining in December, and the fiddle player outside the printer's shop was wearing a tea cosy as a hat.

When she reached Regent Street, she began to worry that not making an appointment revealed a lack of decorum. He had said to drop in any time, but even so ... Then she began to worry about the fact that Mr Montgomery hadn't wanted her to make an appointment. Perhaps it meant that he was not that interested in her work at all. In the end she just put Mr Montgomery and his emporium from her mind and focused on the shopfronts.

Every imaginable commodity, from coloured ink and parchment to buttons and buckles, was on display behind panelled glass. This was the destination for all the produce of Threadneedle and Fleet Streets. There were ladies everywhere. Their bonnets matched their crinolines and reticules, and they walked arm in arm, or gazed into the windows of jewellers and confectioners, or peered at passers-by from the windows of cocoa rooms. These women, surreptitiously eyeing-up the costumes of others, were the raison d'être for Empire. It puzzled Rhia that the English liked to use French phrases, since they didn't seem to particularly like the French. She put up the hood of her cloak and hurried along, wishing that she didn't care that she hadn't had a new gown all season.

By the time she reached the emporium, Rhia had remembered her nervousness. The House of Montgomery had by far the most chic premises on Regent Street, with its curved, faceted front window and gold lettering. The sophisticated Mr Montgomery would think her too inexperienced, or too young, or too old or too female. Or he would think her just another fool with a dream. She thought of Nell the Fryer. Rhia was, at very least, not as limp as a trout. She clutched her portfolio closer and stepped into the lair.

The emporium shimmered as though the walls were woven of light. They were shelf-lined and stacked with roll upon roll of silk. Linen and wool had a simple, earthy beauty, but silk, with its ineffable mystique, filled her with desire all over again. No wonder the Byzantine queens and noblewomen had coveted the miracle fibre, apparently strong enough to wear as armour.

A gaunt assistant stood behind a counter at the far end of the shop, her head bent as though she were reading something out of sight. She looked up as Rhia approached and said, 'Can I help you?' with pointed disinterest. She was thinner even than Juliette.

According to Beth, Juliette ate more cake than Rhia, but this spindle of a girl had the transparent skin of the fashionably starved. Her sleeves were so narrow it was a wonder she could move at all. The girl inspected Rhia's cloak as though she had every right to, given that she had arms like pipe cleaners. Rhia felt frumpy and old-fashioned.

'I'm here to see Mr Montgomery,' she said, hoping fervently that he wasn't in. The girl dropped her head, like a flower drooping on a thin stem, and tinkled a brass bell. A moment later, Mr Montgomery appeared, looking as handsome and immaculate as ever.

'Ah, Miss Mahoney. A pleasure to see you again.' If he was surprised to see her he did not show it. 'Would you like refreshment? Miss Elliot can brew us some tea on the spirit stove.' He looked at Miss Elliot, who did not appear pleased to be making Rhia tea but obediently disappeared through the doorway from which he had emerged. 'I see you've brought your drawings. Shall we sit over here?' He gestured towards a corner where there was a divan area for weary shoppers.

Rhia perched rather than sat, and put her binder on the table. She felt mildly nauseous. Mr Montgomery sat opposite, looking at her expectantly. 'Well,' she said. She could think of nothing else to say. She untied the ribbons that fastened the binder and laid out as many sheets of patterned cartridge paper as would fit on the table top.

Mr Montgomery said nothing as he picked up a design at a time, examining the harmonies of colour and motif closely before picking up another. Miss Elliot arrived and put a cup and saucer on an occasional table for Rhia, and then hovered for a moment before she returned to the counter.

Mr Montgomery continued to appraise each design silently. He nodded occasionally and made small grunting noises that she could not interpret, so she simply laid out more, until he had seen everything in the binder. When she had tied the ribbons again, she dared to look at him. Her heart sank. He was looking at his fob watch. She had tried. At least she was not a trout.

'Miss Mahoney.' He hesitated and Rhia braced herself. Why on earth *would* he employ her, when he had all of the designers of Paris to choose from? She looked him in the eye and dragged her lips into a smile.

'Miss Mahoney, these designs are unexpectedly … accomplished. I had not anticipated … I did not expect such a talent from a woman. I must think this through.' He rose. 'It has been exceptionally quiet on Regent Street since this wretched business in Canton, but I will certainly think this through. Now, I am late for an engagement. Thank you again for calling.'

He nodded to Grace as he crossed the floor and then took his top coat and walking cane from the stand by the door and strode away.

Rhia stayed where she was for a moment and took a sip of tea. The girl, Miss Elliot, was eyeing her with slightly more interest and a measure of suspicion. But then something caught her attention in the doorway and her face was transformed. A young man in shirtsleeves and a flat cap had come through the door grinning like a lunatic. When he reached the counter he leaned over and gave Miss Elliot a kiss on the lips. Rhia stood up to leave. When the man noticed her he took a step back from the counter quickly, looking at Rhia sheepishly.

'You needn't worry on my account,' she said. I'm not a customer and I'm just leaving anyway.'

He grinned at her, relieved that he hadn't got his sweetheart into any trouble. His teeth were in lamentable condition. He nodded as though he'd figured something out. 'I expect you've come about the position, have you?'

'I have.'

He nodded. 'Once me and Grace are wedded, she won't be needing the shop work.'

Rhia frowned. 'Mr Montgomery is looking for an assistant?'

Miss Elliot was looking at her ever more suspiciously. 'I thought you said that's why you were here?'

'No, I heard he was looking for a textile designer.'

She snorted. 'So that's what all those pictures were. I've never heard such a thing. A lady who designs! Anyhow, the next two seasons are already ordered from Monsieur Bertrand.' She gave a derisive shrug, busying herself beneath the counter with some phantom task. Perhaps she was just naturally unfriendly. Hunger, probably.

'You're Irish,' Sid said, as though he thought himself some kind of genius.

Rhia nodded and, not knowing what else to do, extended her hand. 'Rhia Mahoney.'

'I'm Sid. You're new to London, Miss Mahoney?'

'I am.'

'I hear there's some fine taverns in Dublin.'

'I've seen one or two.'

His face lit up with an idea. 'I know what, Gracey!'

'What?' She looked suspicious.

'Miss Mahoney here should come for a negus at the Red Lion Saturday night.' Miss Elliot shrugged again. It was clear she didn't like the idea, but perhaps she would pull in her horns if she understood that Rhia wasn't after her job.

'I'd be happy to, though I've no idea what a negus is.'

'Really?' Sid looked astonished and Miss Elliot released a long-suffering sigh.

'You're forgetting that she's foreign.' She turned to Rhia. 'It is mulled wine, of course.'

'It's better than it sounds then.'

Sid laughed and Miss Elliot frowned and returned to her rummaging.

He tilted his cap back and leaned over the counter and kissed Miss Elliot, making her blush. 'I'll see you both Saturday, then. Cheerio!' He departed with a comical swagger and Miss Elliot watched him until he was out of sight, love struck.

Rhia searched for something to say. 'Where is the Red Lion?'

'Covent Garden,' she said sulkily. She looked down, and traced a thin white finger along the brass ruler on the edge of the counter. Rhia felt corn-fed beside her, but she wouldn't think of giving up Beth's ginger loaf. She bade Miss Elliot farewell.

When she was out on the street, she allowed herself to smile. Mr Montgomery had liked her designs. It was a start. A shoe-shine boy caught her eye and tipped his cap at her with a wink. 'Lovely day, miss.'

She winked back at him. 'It is a lovely day.'

# Serge

On a whim, Michael took the pathway between the shipyard and a huddle of poorly built bungalows that housed the Port Authority. The entire area was deserted, but he knew someone who would be working Sunday just as if it were any other day of the week.

As Michael expected, Calvin Hughes was sitting on the verandah of the last bungalow before the stretch of sand that led down to the bottle-green water. He was smoking a whalebone pipe and had his boots up on the rail and his chair tilted back at a precarious angle. His official, navy serge tunic was unbuttoned and his black policeman's cap sat on the floor near the chair.

'Evening, Cal.' The chair shuddered for a moment as the policeman, startled, brought his boots to the floorboards with a thud. 'Christ, Michael! Frightened the bejesus out of me.'

'Mind if I join you?'

'Certainly bloody not. Fancy a brew?'

'No thanks, mate. I seem to be making a habit of consecrating the sabbath on Maggie's imported. Be a shame to sober up too soon.'

Calvin chuckled and puffed on his pipe. He looked at the deserted beach with a sigh of satisfaction. 'Not a bloody soul abroad. Had a couple of blackfellas roasting a goanna in a sand pit earlier. Don't see them much on the shore these days. Gave me a piece too. Tastes like a fish one minute and poultry the next. Bloody decent of 'em, I thought, considering what bastards we are.'

'They know who you are.'

'They know that this strip of shore is safe, at least, and that while I'm still breathing there won't be any shooting of blacks. So what brings you down to my beat, Michael?' Calvin's 'beat' was the port area, including Customs and Convicts – the greater proportion of newcomers to the colony. He had half a dozen or so hand-picked constables working for him, who were mostly as decent as he was himself. Calvin's port authority was an oasis of humanity in a desert of misery. For all of its modern enterprise, Sydney was still a prison to most of its inhabitants. The undercurrent of resentment was ever-present.

Calvin was around the same age as Michael and had been in Sydney for almost thirty years. His posting to the colony was intended to be temporary and he had agreed to it reluctantly. But then he'd fallen for the raw beauty of the place and, having neither family nor a sweetheart in London, had chosen to stay. He'd seen it all, the massacres and the starvation and the absconders to 'China'. In the early days, a series of escapes were inspired by a peculiar notion that to the north-west of the settlement, a river separated Australia from China. In the imaginations of the desperate Irish, the great land across the river contained everything they desired: freedom, kindness, tea and civilisation. Primarily, though, it was women they were after. Amongst the several hundred who undertook the journey to China, few survived, and a trail of human bones still littered the route they had taken – a reminder to others that the Australian interior was more hostile even than British law.

'It's curiosity that brings me, as usual,' Michael replied.

'Oh?' Calvin took his pipe from between his teeth and cocked his head. 'You got something for me?'

The two men had an arrangement. Calvin 'failed to notice' the harmless lawbreaking which Michael turned his hand to, and in return the Irishman kept the Port Authority informed of any serious criminal activity he came across.

'Not sure. It's been awful quiet down the Rocks.' Michael had decided to hold back on what Maggie had told him for now, since there was a fine line between what Calvin could and couldn't ignore. Mick the Fence was well known to the Sydney constabulary, but he was also notoriously professional and unerringly careful. If he was running an operation, you could be certain it was clever and imaginative and that he'd keep his own hands clean. It would be more productive to watch the harbour and find out exactly what was going to be shipped out, if this was, as Michael suspected, what the enterprise involved.

Calvin nodded thoughtfully. 'I don't much like quiet – it just doesn't seem natural in these parts.'

Michael felt the same way. 'It's just a feeling I've got at present, nothing more.' He paused for as long as seemed prudent before he introduced his motive. 'Don't suppose you've come by anything that might interest *me*?'

'Can't say as I have. Got a little project on myself, but he's not local.'

'Is that right?'

'A Manx sailor I took in for smuggling some black gold a few years back. Told him that if I ever saw his filthy breeches on my patch again, I'd see him dance upon nothing.'

'Then he's come back for his own hanging?'

'I think he's on the run. I've got nothing on him, so I just locked him up for a night when he was senseless on rum. One of my men had a friendly chat with him and tells me he was frightened and swore he had nothing to do with the death of the Quaker, off Bombay.'

'That right? Would that be a Quaker who didn't die a natural death?'

'Correct. A Quaker who didn't die a natural death and who clearly knew something he shouldn't have.'

'A trader?'

'Cotton.'

'Got a name?'

'I'm working on it.'

'You got any men keeping an eye on the inlets to the south, Cal?'

'I don't have enough men just to watch the harbour, Michael. Why?'

'Could be your man's hiding out in one of them.'

'Is that the only reason?'

'I don't know. But when I do, I'll be sure to tell you.'

'I expect no less. Now, since Maggie Long has seen fit to squander her good liquor on you, and in the spirit of the approaching season, I suppose I should keep you in your cups?'

'I'd appreciate it, Calvin.'

The blazing sun sank mercifully low, and the two men sat on the verandah watching the sea turn from clear green to inky blue, and the ghostly white ruffs of tide glimmer as they cascaded to the sand. The cliffs to the southern reach of the harbour paled in the twilight and the spiky silhouettes of shrubs along the shore rang with cicadas. A sweep of fruit bats descended on an outcrop of papaya, squabbling and rustling the fronds of the palms as if they were being blown about by a strong wind.

On the days when Michael was at his best, he felt privileged, as well as punished, to have seen a land so wild and so untouched by the polluting industries of men. He wondered if he would miss it, when he went home.

# Cloth

Fresh snow had fallen on the night market at Covent Garden, turning it ghostly white under the carriage lamps. Plum duffs and gingerbread and sugared almonds all looked better by gaslight. They sparkled in their little paper cones. Rhia bought some gingerbread and stopped to watch the courting pairs and young men singing odes to ale. The trees were laced with snow and the lamplight soft with fog. Everything seemed a little magical until a gang of urchins darted in front of her, playing a game with the carcass of a rat.

When Laurence gave her directions to the Red Lion, Rhia had almost asked him if he would like to accompany her. But he was already dressed for a night on the town, or rather, he had oiled his hair and looked vaguely less dishevelled than usual.

The tavern was along one of the alleyways off the square, and smelt of woodsmoke and mulled wine. Rhia stopped inside the low door for a moment to allow her eyes to become accustomed to candlelight. A branch of mistletoe hung on a string from a low ceiling beam and an enormous plum cake sat in a bed of holly behind the bar. A blazing fire cast flickering shadows, and the room was rowdy and merry. Judging by the noise, the Red Lion was a trade workers' alehouse. It was the second time Rhia had entered a tavern on her own since leaving Dublin. Her father would despair.

Sid beckoned Rhia over from a snug by the fire. Judging by the angle of his hat and the glint in his eye, he was something of a libertine – but he had a kind smile, in spite of his teeth. 'Won't you sit down, Miss Mahoney, and let me fetch you a beverage. Will you have some sherry, or a negus?'

'I'd prefer a glass of stout, if you don't mind.'

'Mind? Why, I'm pleased to see a lady take a proper jar.'

Grace giggled nervously as he left them alone. 'Don't mind Sid, he's just fresh. But he's a good heart.'

'I can see that he has.' The girl's temper seemed vastly improved by the contents of the empty glasses on the table, but she still eyed Rhia warily.

'I hope you don't think me bold, but don't you think … isn't it unlikely that Mr Montgomery would want to employ … someone such as yourself?'

'Such as myself?' Rhia wondered where the conversation was leading.

'I mean, for a woman. Well. How will you marry, if you have a trade?'

'Perhaps I won't. I wouldn't mind.' Rhia shrugged as nonchalantly as she could. 'I don't really think of it.' This was only partly true, in that she hadn't thought of it lately. She must just get used to the idea that she wasn't the kind of woman men liked. She wasn't convinced that marriage was of any real benefit to a woman anyway.

'But, you cannot have a family unless you are married.'

'It is physically possible.'

Miss Elliot blushed.

Rhia was no expert on less-than-immaculate conception. She and Thomas had discussed it as children, piecing together what little each of them knew or suspected. They had concluded that the entire business was unfeasible and had not, that day in the forest, managed to prove or disprove their theory. She could hardly imagine the kind of love that might lead to an act of such momentous intimacy. It all came back to love, of course, the greatest problem of all.

Before Rhia could think of anything to say to help cool down Miss Elliot's burning cheeks, Sid returned with a glass of stout and a slice of plum cake for each of them.

'Christmas cheer to us all,' he said as he lifted his glass.

'Christmas cheer!' they chorused.

'And it will be the first Christmas I've not spent in Change Alley for a good number of years.'

'Where is Change Alley?' Rhia asked.

'Well, the truth is, Miss Mahoney, the actual place don't exist, not any more. There was a fire that got the better of the alley, fifty years back, but my pa still remembers it from when he was a lad. My granddaddy was a jobber, like me. It all happens at the Royal Exchange now.'

'What all happens, and what is a jobber?'

'You ask a lot of questions, for a lady.' Sid grinned and Rhia could tell that he was pleased to be the expert at the table. 'A jobber is a stock jobber, and its punters like me give advice to the traders and financiers and the bankers who have more silver than they know what to do with. Jobbers know what's going on in the market – what's good to buy shares and stocks of, and what's good to sell for a profit. You'd know a little about the marketplace if you're from the linen trade, Miss Mahoney.'

'Almost nothing. I know that shares in Irish linen have fallen very steeply.'

'That'd be because English linen is cheaper.'

'But only because England can afford bigger factories and better machines!'

Sid shrugged. 'That's the thing – there's always somebody going to do it better and cheaper.'

'Perhaps cheaper, not better.'

'As you say, I wouldn't know about the quality of the cloth, I don't need to, you see, since I've got my Gracey to advise me on it.' He gave his fiancée a suggestive smile and for a fleeting moment Rhia ached for something that she didn't know – had never known. Men liked women like Grace Elliot, with skin pale enough to blush and a fragility that made them feel strong.

'It's cheap goods most people want,' Sid was saying. 'Before the fire, Change Alley was where all the coffee houses were, and that's where all the buying and selling went on. There's only one or two coffee houses left in the banking district, down around Cornhill and Lombard Street. The main one's the Jerusalem.' Rhia was suddenly alert. The calling card she'd found on Ryan's floor was from the Jerusalem Coffee House.

To her astonishment, when she looked up from her glass she was met with the sight of Laurence and Mr Dillon entering the pub – as though in remembering that day at Ryan's flat she had conjured them. Laurence was beaming. He had known she would be here. When they reached the snug, to her even greater surprise, Mr Dillon slapped Sid on the back. He greeted Rhia and Grace politely before disappearing to the bar. Laurence squeezed in next to Rhia while Sid and Grace cooed over each other.

'You look smashing.'

'And so do you,' she said lightly. She found that it was easier to play along with Laurence's harmless flirtations than to resist them. Besides, she liked him and even if she wouldn't make him a good wife she didn't mind being admired.

'And I've not even asked you how you fared with the dragon,' he added. Rhia darted a meaningful look at Grace and frowned at Laurence. He nodded and winked and put his finger to his lips conspiratorially. Grace was preoccupied with Sid, though, and had heard nothing

'Miss Elliot works in the emporium,' Rhia whispered.

'Oh, I *see*,' he whispered back.

'Mr Montgomery seemed to like my designs, he said he'd think about it, and then he rushed off somewhere.'

'These dragons are extremely busy creatures, you know.'

'Speaking of dragons, I've been meaning to ask you, is Mr Dillon always so aloof, or is it just the effect I have on him?'

Laurence looked taken aback. 'I'd not noticed him being aloof!'

Rhia laughed. 'You wouldn't notice if your own boot buttons were undone. But you've answered my question. It must be me.'

Laurence looked towards the bar. 'I suppose he does brood. You should have seen him when we were students, though. I used to wonder, on certain mornings, if I should call on him and make sure he hadn't died, poetically, in the night. He's a very level-headed chap though. He's at his worst when he's personally affronted by something, like this business in the Pearl River.'

'But *why* is he personally affronted by it?'

'His younger brother was a scholar who lived in Canton.' Laurence trailed off as Dillon arrived and placed a jug of porter on the table and a glass of sherry for Grace who hadn't touched her plum cake.

'Oh good man,' said Laurence. 'Rhia was just asking about your piece on the war.'

Dillon shot her a surprised look. 'Do the economics of war interest you, Miss Mahoney?'

His tone made her bristle. 'We are all affected by economics.

My father paid excessive duties to the Crown for the privilege of exporting his linen, so I am merely curious to know how the Crown is spending his taxes.'

Mr Dillon's eyes crinkled. Rhia almost fell off her chair – so he had a sense of humour after all. 'A fair point, Miss Mahoney. In fact, it is something that is lately being called capitalism that interests me. It is a relatively modern industry, and one that is killing people.

*Capitalism.* The word sounded inauspicious.

'Could we talk about something a little less profound please,' said Laurence. 'I have no affinity with numbers.'

'Indeed you don't, Blake – as your recent trip to Paris demonstrates.' Mr Dillon looked at Rhia with a raised eyebrow and a wry smile. 'Mr Blake has purchased a collection of daguerreotypes from a Paris dealer I am convinced is a thief.'

Laurence laughed. 'Come, Dillon, you've already bored Miss Mahoney with talk of the City.'

'But I'm not bored at all,' Rhia assured him. She was beginning to see that there was a whole side of trade that she knew little about. In effect, people bought and sold goods without even laying eyes on them, and it wasn't even because they particularly wanted the commodity, but because they wanted to build their own little empires in trading with them. As if one wasn't enough. 'In fact, Mr Dillon, I would appreciate it if you would explain to me why I should have no faith in banknotes.'

He was immediately serious. 'It is more a question of the actual capital represented by the paper money, Miss Mahoney. The Bank of England is really only a holding house for a limited amount of coin and bullion, and when a major trade route such as the South China Sea ceases to operate, there is a domino effect. The balance of capital and debit topples and the vaults are emptied very quickly.'

'Do you mean if I deposited my silver in a bank and then wrote a note of credit, it does not represent an actual transaction?'

'Precisely. Your silver ceases to exist once it is deposited in a bank.'

'But then banking is a charade!'

'Of course,' said Dillon coolly, as though it was something everyone knew. 'I suggest you make payments with actual coin rather than notes of credit until the silver reserves are replenished. The vaults aren't entirely empty, don't worry,' he said when Rhia widened her eyes. 'Quantities of silver enter London daily from the Calcutta exchange; opium money mostly, but it is only here to be laundered so that the Crown can honestly say that the revenue from opium is not being used outright to purchase tea.'

'But there's silver coming in from the colonies too,' said Sid. 'Land is fetching a good price on the eastern shoreline of Australia, and the wheat and wool markets are attracting investors. The Calcutta exchange sees plenty of revenue from Sydney, but maybe some punter is just robbing the wealthy squatters in New South Wales!'

Rhia was piecing all of this together. 'But I thought the emperor of China declared the opium trade unlawful.'

Dillon shook his head in disgust. 'It makes no difference. The transactions just take place offshore. The black gold, as it is called, is taken to a depot ship anchored at Lintin Island in the Gulf of Canton. The ships are large, with crews of fighting men. The Chinese silver that pays for the opium is deposited on an armed ship, and then transferred to a barque or a clipper and taken to Calcutta.'

Rhia shook her head. 'And what happens to the silver in Calcutta?'

'Most commonly, bills of exchange are issued; paper money that can be redeemed in England or in India.'

'But what if there isn't enough silver to redeem a bill of exchange?'

Dillon shrugged. 'Then there will be a run on the banks. As you know, there's an embargo on all legitimate trade with China, so no cotton, wool or English piece goods can be exported, and neither can we import tea, silk, rice, porcelain and so on. The silver from the sale of opium is always used to purchase tea, because silver is the only currency the emperor of China will trade in.'

Rhia frowned. 'So China provides our substance and we provide theirs. I expect the black market trade off Lintin Island is thriving.'

'Oh, it is,' Dillon agreed, looking at her intently. 'Then you read the papers, Miss Mahoney.'

'I enjoy that vulgar activity, yes.' Now she had made him smile twice in one night. He took a long draught of porter.

'This is all very dull,' Grace complained, looking bored.

'It isn't though, my love,' Sid assured her. 'It's no different to watching lads play with their marbles in the street. They swap whichever they have too many of, for what they most desire.'

Mr Dillon put down his empty glass. 'A more deadly game than marbles, Sid. One nation is being poisoned by another and the governments of Britain and India have sanctioned it.'

Sid leaned across Grace and lowered his voice to say something to Dillon that Rhia strained to hear.

'Speaking of India, I've only just heard something that might be of interest.'

'Indeed?' Dillon was instantly sober. He stood up, excused himself and beckoned Sid to follow him. They went to stand a short distance away by the fire. Neither Laurence nor Grace took any notice. Laurence refilled his glass and leaned back into the snug contentedly, and Grace became preoccupied with her fingernails.

Rhia strained to hear what Sid and Dillon were discussing, but they had their backs to her and the tavern was noisy. She edged closer to the fire until she could hear their conversation.

'Of course I remember Josiah Blake's accident,' Dillon was saying.

'One of the brokers who has a Quaker client doesn't think it was an accident,' said Sid.

'Who doesn't?' Dillon's tone was sharp and Rhia held her breath.

'The client. And there's a rumour that Blake may have been discovered at something … un-Quakerly – something like opium – and couldn't face the shame.' Sid paused and lowered his voice. 'There's them that say he took his own life.'

'Does your Quaker have a name?'

'The broker wouldn't tell me, so he's either scared or he's been paid, because I've never known him to keep his mouth shut.'

'If you find out who he is, Sid, I'll see to it that you become the favourite of the newspaper investors.'

'You've got yourself a deal, mister.' Sid drained his glass.

Rhia could hardly believe what she'd heard. If both Ryan and Josiah had taken their own lives, did it mean they had both been involved in the opium trade? Was this why the journalist was so interested in Ryan's affairs? She could not bear to think that her uncle had stooped so low. And what about Josiah Blake, with his spotless reputation? It was appalling to think that he, too, should be profiteering from such a filthy trade. Antonia would surely not bear it. She must never find out.

Mr Dillon turned and their eyes met. He raised an eyebrow, she raised one back, and that was that.

Sid retrieved Grace, and Laurence enquired politely after their plans to wed. Mr Dillon turned to Rhia and lowered his voice.

'With regard to your uncle's death, Miss Mahoney. The Yard have interviewed his solicitor and I've learnt that his estate has been frozen pending evidence contrary to suicide.'

'*Contrary* to suicide?'

'There is still a small chance his death was accidental. But this is neither the time nor the place to discuss it. At the very least, we must understand what drove him to it. Are you agreed?'

'Of course.' Rhia almost asked why he cared, and what he really thought of Ryan, but didn't. She was too worried that she might not like what she heard.

He bowed stiffly. 'Then I shall wish you good night and Happy Christmas.'

'And you. Thank you for—' But he was walking away, as bad mannered as ever.

Sid and Grace said goodnight, and Rhia found herself standing beneath the mistletoe with Laurence. He looked at it pointedly and then at her. She laughed, but then his expression became so sombre that she had to look away. When he offered her his arm instead, she was not sure if she felt more disappointed or relieved.

# Cashmere

R hia examined the address on the calling card. The Jerusalem was on Lombard Street. It was not far. The handwriting on the reverse was careful and elegant; definitely not her uncle's, which was sloping and hasty. The Oriental character could mean something or nothing, and the numbers beside it were as puzzling as ever. She needed to do something to keep her mind from the fact that Mr Montgomery hadn't been in touch.

The streets were as damp and glum as they had looked from the morning room at Cloak Lane. When it started to properly rain, Rhia was easily lured into the closest shop, which happened to be Cutbush's Curios. The sign was almost obscured by ivy, which was probably why she'd never noticed it before. Inside, the shop smelt of pipe tobacco and damp and was piled to the rafters with penny-arcade tin drums and sailors' hats, copper pots and old *Pears'* annuals. Mr Cutbush had an oversized moustache, yellowed by tobacco, and an oversized girth. It was a wonder he could move about without toppling any of his precariously stacked whatnots.

The floor above the ground contained merchandise of a more specialised nature; a collector's kingdom come. Here were thimbles and stamps and military regalia and monogrammed goblets and, in a fusty corner, a shelf of antiquated firearms. Rhia felt her heart lurch. How many dealers of antique pistols could there be in London?

Mr Cutbush couldn't remember if he had or hadn't sold any pistols to an Irishman by the name of Ryan Mahoney, but he said that it was peculiar she should enquire, because there had been a Celtic gentleman in asking all manner of questions. 'And quite ghoulish some of them, too,' he added, with a nod that made his jowls wobble like aspic.

Rhia cocked her head at him. 'What do you mean, ghoulish?'

'Well, the likes of, "what sort of wound would such and such a weapon make if it were fired at close range, as opposed to if it were fired at a distance?"'

'And could you answer?'

'Of course, madam. I do not hold any commodities that I don't have a little knowledge of, and it is important to respect the perilous nature of gunpowder.'

'Did the gentleman give you his name?'

'He did not. I would know him again, though; he had a mane of hair and was dressed like a thespian.'

'How long ago was this?'

Mr Cutbush looked puzzled, and then uncertain. 'Well, now you have me. It could have been last week or last July, I'm not much good at remembering such things.'

It sounded as if Mr Dillon had been making enquiries about firearms – but when, and why? Rhia left the curio shop, and was deep in thought when a cart drove through a puddle and threw muddy water up at her. Today she longed to be riding Epona on the headland, where there were no passing vehicles or chimney stacks and no slops raining from upstairs windows. She turned into a shabby lane of weaver's cottages that she judged should come out near Lombard Street. The lane was deserted and bleak. Through a curtainless window, she glimpsed a room almost barren of furnishings. A woman and her skinny brood were huddled together for warmth, all bent over their sewing. In Greystones the weavers were poor, but there were always faggots for a fire and a pot of coddle on the make. There was always someone, like her mother, who cared.

Weaving was once a respectable trade and a profession that could earn a decent wage. If machines were clever enough to make cloth, then how many other trades would they claim? Rhia tried to imagine Spitalfields in the time before the factories, when the French Protestants had run the London silk trade. It was hard to conjure. She'd read that the Huguenots had cultivated a mulberry plantation, since this was all the fussy silk worms would eat. Barely a tree was now to be seen in Spitalfields. Neither the mulberry plants nor the creatures themselves thrived in the climate. Rhia empathised with the silk worm. The penetrating damp had reached her toes, even through her lace-up boots and woollen stockings.

When she came to a junction in the road, she was only a step or two away from Lombard Street and looking forward to a glass of strong coffee. The Jerusalem looked busy from what little she could see of its interior through the fogged glass, but she was not prepared for the atmosphere that greeted her when she entered. This was not at all what she expected. The air was thick with cigar smoke and the smell of men. The confusion of raised voices reminded her of the Dublin pony market. There was barely room to stand, let alone be seated, and she realised her entrance was slowly making an impression. There was not another woman in the room. The Jerusalem was a meeting place, not somewhere warm and dry to enjoy a quiet beverage.

An entire wall was dedicated to the kind of wooden file boxes that one might see at a printer's or stationer's shop, furnished with piles of ledgers. On a long, narrow table beneath were piles of broadsheets, pipe dishes, tin coffee pots and a number of notebooks and pencils. Several sheets of grid-lined paper were pinned on a corkboard close by, though Rhia was not close enough to see the entries inked in their columns. She guessed it had something to do with shipping, since a good number of the men in the room had the salty look of merchant captains. She had seen enough to realise that this was not a place one came to enjoy a harmless cup of coffee. She was beginning to feel self-conscious. She turned to leave as she heard a familiar voice.

'I thought it must be you, Miss Mahoney!' Sid was grinning broadly at her bewilderment. 'I see that you have taken an interest in the exchange!'

'Not in the least. My only interest was in a glass of coffee.'

'Coffee, well you'd best look elsewhere. You will only distract these gentlemen from their business.' Sid seemed hugely entertained that Rhia had come to a coffee house for coffee.

'I tell you what, Miss Mahoney, I'm about done here and then I'm off to visit Gracey. Why not walk with me?' It was a good distance from Cornhill to Regent Street, Rhia had walked it before, but she nodded. Why not? She had nothing better to do. They left and she was relieved to be back in the damp air.

'Is it always so crowded in the Jerusalem?' she asked as they walked back along Cornhill. Sid shook his head.

'Tea and China silk is at a premium – meaning it's scarce and in demand and above the usual market price. There is a lot of selling of small goods going on, to secure ordinary commodities.'

'Ordinary commodities?'

'That's stock that always has a market, no matter how expensive it gets.'

'So it's like chess – minor possessions sacrificed to secure the more powerful?'

'I've never played the game of chess; too clever for me, but that's about it, yes.'

'And what were all the ledgers and folders in the box-shelving?'

'Files. Shipping documents from Bombay, Calcutta, Canton, Sydney, Hobart Town … and all the intermediates – Rio, St Helena and the like. Those files have the arrival and departure dates of every ship, what she's carrying, plus current prices. It's my job to know what's in those. Keeps me on me toes!'

'I should think so.' Rhia remembered the calling card. 'I've another question for you.' She reached into her reticule and extracted the card, turning it over so that Sid could see the characters on the back. 'Do you know what the numbers or the character might mean?'

Sid took the card and squinted at it. 'I've not a darn clue what that squiggle is,' he said, stabbing his finger at the character. 'Chinese I expect. The numbers look to me like coordinates though; that is, an exact place out in the middle of the ocean, but I'm no sailor, Miss Mahoney. I couldn't tell you which bit of ocean it is. Looks like a woman's wrote it though, judging by how neat the hand is.'

Rhia put the card back in her reticule. She'd not considered that it might be a woman's hand. She knew only that the handwriting was not her uncle's. Perhaps he'd had a sweetheart, but why would someone – let alone a woman – write ship's coordinates and a Chinese character on a calling card?

The chimneys of the red-brick mill buildings towered above neglected tenements along Threadneedle Street. The chimneys reminded her of the cigars of the patrons of the Jerusalem. In no time they had walked the length of Cheapside and Sid had pointed out the Mercer's Hall on Ironmonger's Lane, where all the 'gentrified' cloth merchants met. In fact, he said, Mr Montgomery was known as 'king of the mercers'. The City of London, he said, had long been inhabited by financiers and cloth traders, the partnership that had led to merchant banking. 'If only Gracey and I could put together what we know of banking and cloth and do the same,' he joked.

It seemed to take no time at all to reach Regent Street with someone to talk to. When Grace saw Sid in the doorway, she blushed with pleasure. Then she saw Rhia. Her expression changed in an instant. As usual, Sid seemed happily unaware of his fiancée's fluctuating tempers. Perhaps it was for the best. Rhia hovered in the doorway for a moment before she decided against entering the emporium. She waved to Grace and hurried away as though she had somewhere to go.

She dawdled by a clothier's window near Spitalfields, imagining a new dress made from a swathe of India green cashmere. She could not possibly afford to buy the cloth, of course, even if she were to sew it herself. If she didn't find employment soon she would have to spend the last of her money on the passage home, and her goal of returning to Ireland victorious would remain a dream.

When she walked back along the barren street where she'd seen the weavers through the window, Rhia felt ashamed of her desire. No doubt all of these shabby hutches housed families of outworkers, sewing, spinning or weaving around the clock just to make enough for their bread and tea. Yet their profession was at the bosom of the city's prosperity. Ryan had once told her that more factories in the capital were dedicated to the manufacture of cloth than any other industry. The mill owner lived in Hampstead or Ealing and would be lunching on guinea fowl and claret, just as Rhia had at the Montgomerys'.

She almost felt ashamed. She, friend to the Kellys, should never forget that the cloth that has the most ornate finish often has the roughest underside.

# Organza

From All Hallows Eve onwards Londoners acquired a cheerfulness rivalled only by the performance of a pantomime or a hanging. Antonia felt light-hearted as she hurried along with Rhia and Juliette, even though she no longer celebrated Christian festivals. Ceremony and ritual were obstructions between the pious and the divine. Still, how jolly that it was snowing on Christmas Eve, the soft flakes settling on Juliette's black shawl and Rhia's red hood. What a shame that photogenic drawings required stillness; it was not often that Regent Street looked whimsical.

Rhia hadn't wanted to come to the emporium, but Antonia urged her to be adventurous. She pointed out that Mr Montgomery might yet be interested in her designs and that busy men often needed to be reminded of their commitments.

They arrived to find Mr Montgomery (in his shirtsleeves again) with Mr Beckwith behind the counter. A carafe of port wine and some gilt edged glasses sat on the countertop, which was decorated with branches of holly tied with white and gold ribbons. It was all very à la mode and made Antonia feel excessively plain and a little tired. Expensive-looking women glided amongst the displays in unwieldy crinolines. One of them was consulting Grace Elliot about something shimmery in myrtle green.

'Happy Christmas, Mrs Blake. Miss Mahoney.' Mr Montgomery's smile was warm and welcoming and it cheered Antonia instantly. 'Will you take an aperitif?'

'A small one,' she agreed. Why not? It was the season to be a little merry. She glanced at Rhia who looked like she'd sooner leave, but nodded. She had paused at a display near the counter, piled high with rolls of silk organza in the new pastels. Juliette, too, was hanging back, her head bent, not knowing where to look. It would embarrass her to stop with people she thought of as her betters, and this was precisely why Antonia wanted her to join in. If the Lord valued all of his children equally, there was simply no reason why a maid should not take a glass with a mercer.

'Come, Juliette. It is Christmas.'

Juliette took a step forward without lifting her eyes. As she did she knocked against the organza, piled so high that it took only the glance of an elbow to topple it.

'Mercy me! I'm ever so sorry, Mr Montgomery, sir!' Juliette dropped to her knees and tried to pick up one of the rolls, but it was too cumbersome. Rhia and Antonia bent to help her.

In an instant Mr Montgomery was beside them. 'It is no bother at all. Please don't trouble yourselves, ladies.' He pushed up his shirtsleeves and collected two or three of the rolls while Juliette was still on her hands and knees. Antonia stretched out her hand to help her to her feet. 'Come, Juliette, they are too heavy.' When Juliette stood, she was white and shaken and looked terrified. The girl really was an albatross at times. Antonia sighed. Forbearance seemed to have abandoned her, along with humility and modesty. She hoped that it was only grief and that her faith would, one day, be hers again.

Mr Montgomery rearranged the display then rolled down his shirtsleeves. Mr Beckwith poured them each a glass, smiling timidly. Rhia was having a quiet word with Juliette, assuring her that although the organza looked delicate, it was as strong as sailcloth. Rhia was being commendably patient, considering Juliette's unfriendliness and suspicion. Juliette could never before have met someone who looked like a changeling and laughed like a child.

Antonia accepted a glass from Mr Beckwith, but he returned to his ledger and its perfect copperplate entries before she could think of some topic for conversation. She presumed that he had once been a clerk of some kind. She also presumed that Mr Beckwith's fiscal talents were helping to keep the House of Montgomery's doors open during the silver crisis. Mr Montgomery would have an annuity, of course, so it probably wouldn't matter if he was trading at a loss. She knew nothing of his family and it would not do to ask, but his lineage was clearly aristocratic. His breeding was conspicuous in his elocution and manner, as it was in his address. When he came to stand beside Antonia his arm brushed against hers and her heart quickened. She suddenly couldn't think of a thing to say, so she pretended to be interested in a display. Then she caught Rhia looking at the mercer with stony determination and braced herself.

'I wonder if you've had the opportunity to consider my portfolio, Mr Montgomery?' Rhia's tone was cool and calm and Antonia was impressed in spite of herself.

He didn't hesitate. 'I intend to, just as soon as the Christmas trade is behind us.' He paused and glanced over to where Grace was hovering. 'Miss Elliot leaves in February, and I will be looking for an assistant. Would you consider joining us in January with a view to replacing her?'

If he'd simply forgotten about the portfolio, then he had evaded the fact expertly, and Antonia couldn't think less of him for it. His compromise sounded reasonable.

'As a shop girl?'

'An assistant, yes. It would be a starting point, I thought, and while it is quiet, there is room at the back for you to get on with work on our new collection!'

'I will certainly consider it.' Rhia smiled graciously enough, but Antonia could see that she was disappointed. Grace was loitering close by, fussing over the organza display. She looked as unhappy as Rhia about the proposal, and Juliette was biting her cuticles. It was time to leave.

They collected their sack of remnants and waited in the queue at the Piccadilly cabstand. Everywhere Antonia looked, people seemed invigorated by the prospect of the one day in the year when even shopkeepers closed their shutters. She felt envious, which surprised her. Were Josiah here she would barely have noticed the festivities. Which is why she had invited Isaac for Christmas dinner and then, as an after-thought, she'd asked Laurence if his friend Mr Dillon might like to come also.

They were finally the first in line for a hansom and, when they climbed inside they all sank gratefully into the cracked leather seats. Rhia looked preoccupied. Juliette, though no longer quite so drawn, was still biting her nails. A diversion was needed. 'I was thinking earlier about making a photogenic drawing of the street scene,' Antonia said.

'That's a wonderful idea!' Rhia's eyes lit up. 'Is it possible?'

Juliette looked from one to the other of them suspiciously.

'Not unless everyone on the street were standing very still, I'm afraid. A pity. Do you remember the portrait I took of the gentlemen in the garden, Juliette?'

The maid nodded. 'The one that looks like plain paper, you mean?' she mumbled sullenly. It seemed that nothing would shake her from her gloom. Antonia persisted all the same.

She'd once tried to explain the photogenic process to her maid, hoping that she would take an interest; that it might elevate her, but she had only seemed superstitious.

'Yes, but when I expose it, the gentlemen who stood so still in the garden that day will appear on the page.'

'As if by the hand of a ghostly painter,' Rhia added. Juliette threw her a dark look, then shrugged as though she couldn't care less. 'My ma always liked to see a portrait, though we never could afford to have one made.'

'Photogenic drawing has already reached the colonies, so it is possible even your mother has encountered it. Laurence has a colleague in Sydney, and it is immensely popular with the naturalists who are cataloguing the flora there,' Antonia continued. 'In fact, Mr Fox Talbot is a botanist himself.'

Juliette looked fleetingly interested in this, then turned her gaze to the window.

# Lawn

It was a relief to be back home and away from Mrs Blake's chatter about her queer portraits, not to mention all the happy Christmas crowds. The season was ever more popular since they'd banned the rat pits and bear baiting. For once Juliette was glad to have so much work to do. If she didn't occupy her hands soon, her stupid head would probably swell with all the thoughts in it, like something in a freak show. There was much to be done before she and Beth could leave for their three-day holiday. Mrs Blake had insisted on three days, which was kind because one was all that was expected. *And* she was going to cook Christmas dinner herself! Juliette had never seen Mrs Blake cook anything more than a slice of toast.

They scraped the grease off from the stovetop, and rinsed out the oven with vinegar and water, spreading damp tea leaves across the cinders so that the ashes would not settle on the newly clean range. They brushed black lead onto the brass and then rubbed it off with dry leather. When the grates shone, and the fenders and irons, Beth put her plump forearms into a tub of flour up to the elbow in preparation to make beef pudding and Juliette went to the washhouse.

She lit the fire beneath the copper and put the linen on to boil, then put ivory black on the three pairs of sensible boots that were waiting in a row.

The idea wouldn't go away.

It would be a shameless thing to do – was she bold enough? The feeling of it spread through her as she worked, filthy as a cloud of cinders, until it almost choked her. She tried to get the better of it by brushing Mrs Blake's boots harder and harder, but she only became breathless. Finally, she dropped the brush and then the boot and bent over double on her stool, almost gagging to keep from wailing. She took a square of lawn from her apron pocket and stuffed it into her mouth, trying not to make a commotion. Beth and Mrs Blake already thought her insensible. As for the Irish witch, well, who knew what she thought. She could be up to anything with those eyes, black and deep as two hell-holes. Could she *know*? And what she'd said in the cab, about the *ghostly painter* was too awful. She *must* know.

They must *never ever* know about this new idea, though. They would think her wicked and mad, and maybe she was – how could she think such a thing otherwise. Juliette took a big breath, picked up the brush and the boot from the stone floor, and wondered yet again how such a thing could have climbed into her head. Maybe it was 'the light' – that wretched light that Mrs Blake was always on about. For Juliette, light was just a gas lamp, a candle flame, morning creeping through the window, nothing more or less.

She resumed polishing. The idea seemed daring and difficult, but it was the only means of knowing for sure, one way or another.

Juliette lined up the boots, shiny as a row of beetles, and sighed with satisfaction. From tomorrow, she would have three whole days with nothing to do but listen to Beth and her sisters gossiping, and take a walk down to the Serpentine to watch the skaters. She'd need to say extra prayers in church, of course.

Tonight London is white as a snowy owl. I should feel happy, because I've been offered a position, but I feel only disappointed.

It doesn't help to have spent the morning with Juliette who is perpetually gloomy. Mrs Blake says it is because she is without family – her father died when she was young and her mother was transported for petty theft. Myself, I'd wager that Juliette has a guilty secret of her own. She behaves as though she has. She doesn't like me, but I can't say that I'm especially fond of her either.

If not for Laurence I might have become demented with boredom. I don't see much of him, but when he's around the mood is always lighter. He looks at me in a certain way though. I suspect that he might be a little sweet on me. I may even feel the same way, but it is hard to be sure. I am easily flattered, as you know, and probably a little lonely as well. I've no idea how one can distinguish affection from devotion. I am not even sure which part of the body should feel desire, where it is located. Is it to be found in the heart or the head? Or somewhere else entirely.

# Velvet

Antonia sat at the table enjoying the serenity of a clean kitchen. White light glanced off the brass on the range and reflected on the floor, polished so highly that it resembled calm water. Apt, that cleanliness and godliness should be associated.

The kettle was rattling on the range, close to the boil. Tea first, and one of Beth's spiced buns, and then she'd start on Christmas dinner. The goose had been hanging in the larder for three days, which Beth said improved its flavour. Beth had done the real work on the bird the evening before; plucking it and cutting off its neck and feet and then skewering it. Her first task was the onion and sage stuffing, and after that she'd get on with the vegetables and sauces and then the brandy butter for the pudding.

Rhia appeared quietly. She was very good at entering a room without being heard. She was not dressed, and her hair was unbraided. It hung heavily over her shoulders and woollen nightgown. She looked surprised to see someone else abroad.

'Good morning, Antonia. I thought I was the first up. I should have dressed.'

'Good morning, my dear. I woke to light the fires, and thought I'd make sure I've plenty of time to prepare Christmas dinner. It's years since I was on my own in the kitchen.'

'Well you needn't be entirely on your own,' Rhia said with

that insubordinate smile. 'I'm not a terrible cook, only a clumsy one according to my mother.'

Antonia laughed and got up to take the kettle from the range. She poured water into the teapot, feeling Rhia watching her. She wanted to say something, Antonia suspected, but was unsure of its propriety.

'I was thinking about the portrait,' she began. Antonia held her breath. Rhia looked her in the eye. 'You said you'd taken a portrait of several gentlemen in your garden – colleagues of your husband. Was my uncle amongst them?'

Antonia rotated the teapot. She doubted that someone like Rhia was afraid of looking into the faces of the dead. 'Yes,' she said.

'What was the nature of his business with your husband?'

Antonia hesitated. She was still piecing things together from accounts and shipping records. 'The gentlemen in the portrait were planning a joint venture. Mixed-fibre cloths, I believe, even though joint trading is not generally approved in the City. They invested in two clippers, the *Mathilda* and the *Sea Witch*.' Rhia was looking down at her tea, not really listening.

'The portrait. Will you … ?'

'Soon,' said Antonia.

Rhia nodded. 'When I watched the representations coming to life, upstairs, it was a little … eerie.'

'It is an uncanny thing to watch,' Antonia agreed. 'Of course, revealing a latent image by exposing it to light is more delicate.' She felt breathless merely imagining exposing the image. Rhia was watching her closely and with empathy. 'You will know when the time is right,' she said. She reached her hand across the table and touched Antonia's lightly.

The morning passed easily with a companion in the kitchen,

though Rhia had not been jesting about being a clumsy cook. So far she had cut herself with a paring knife and knocked over the apple sauce, and Antonia considered it safer to send her to lay the table.

Laurence came looking for breakfast at half past ten. He was visibly suffering from last evening's revelry, but his natural good cheer prevailed.

'Happy Christmas, Antonia! I don't suppose you've some coffee brewing amongst that collection of pots?'

'I have, but I think you'd better pour it yourself. I'm quite literally up to my elbows, as you can see.' Antonia blew a wisp of hair from her eyes and continued rolling the dough for the gravy dumplings. 'And you could check on the fire in the drawing and dining rooms for me, Laurence. Rhia is in the dining room, and I'm sure she's keeping her eye on it, but you could check all the same.'

Laurence saluted her and then wandered out with a bowl of milky coffee, a Parisian habit apparently. He was clearly taken with Rhia, but whether his affections were returned, or where such an attraction might lead, she could not say.

When the goose was in the oven and the kitchen in order, Antonia felt unreasonably pleased with herself. She wondered how the dining room had fared under Rhia's supervision. The table was laid with the good pink china and Indian silver cutlery, and its centrepiece was a mistletoe wreath and a ring of candles. A little pagan for her taste, but pretty all the same. She glanced at the clock on the mantel. It was later than she had realised, almost midday. She barely had enough time to change and tidy her hair.

The doorbell sounded while Antonia was dressing, and Laurence called out that he would be the Christmas butler. By the time she arrived in the drawing room, Isaac and Mr Dillon were talking by the window and Laurence and Rhia were on the divan looking at photogenic drawings. Laurence was an excellent butler; the fire was dancing and a decanter of claret was unstoppered on the mantelpiece.

Was it her imagination that Isaac and Mr Dillon stopped their conversation too abruptly when she entered? Antonia had the uncomfortable sensation that something was being kept from her. Her immediate thought was that it might be something about Josiah. She shook it off. A woman of faith should feel her husband's loving presence rather than his shadow. It was within her means, by the use of salt and silver nitrate, to see his face. The negative was in the bottom drawer of Josiah's desk, safe in its thick silk wallet. If she kept it thus protected then the latent image would be preserved. As Rhia said, she would know when the time was right.

Isaac and Mr Dillon were standing. She had not seen the journalist since the wake and he had still not visited the barber. He did have a flair for unusual clothing. The fabric of his waistcoat looked positively antique.

'It was gracious of you to invite me, Mrs Blake,' he said. I would probably have spent the day in the basement of the *Globe* with the printers otherwise. I've settled with my conscience by delivering them several bottles of burgundy and a Christmas pudding.'

'Have you no family, Mr Dillon?' Rhia was being bad mannered again. Or did she not like him? She looked positively bewitching in that claret-red velvet. Mr Dillon, to his credit, didn't flinch.

'My brother died recently and my parents are in Snowdonia, which is rather a long way by carriage. They are accustomed to my work habits.'

Antonia took a sip of wine and addressed Isaac's query about the readiness of their cotton shipment for Calcutta. He was eager to sail as soon as *Mathilda* was back from New York. *Sea Witch*, as far as she knew, was still somewhere in Indian waters.

Mr Dillon had turned his back to the room and was looking at the two Madonnas she had recently hung above the mantelpiece.

'I'd thought iconography was disapproved of by an unadorned faith such as yours, Mrs Blake.'

Isaac laughed. 'As long as Antonia does not worship the icons, she is committing no breach of her faith.'

Antonia smiled as best she could. 'They are antiques, Mr Dillon, I admire them for their artistry.' She was privately surprised that he would challenge her faith, and besides, she could not explain something she didn't completely understand herself. All she knew was that these images embodied what Christianity lacked, be that a female divinity, or just equality. She looked at the clock. It was not time to put the potatoes in goose fat. Rhia was still poring over the photogenic drawings on the divan. 'May I see your new pictures, Laurence?'

'They aren't mine. They're from Sydney. From the same chap who gave me the trees.' Laurence chose several images and arranged them in a row on the low table. More trees whose leaves and branches looked too pale to be alive. The light that fell between the straight, narrow trunks was sharp and strong, as though they were the ruined columns of a classical temple. The intensity of the light excited Antonia.

Rhia gave an involuntary shudder as though the picture had exactly the opposite effect on her. 'It looks an unearthly place.'

'A wilderness, by all accounts.' Laurence looked enthralled. 'I hope to visit it myself one day.'

The talk turned to travel and then to commerce and it was soon time for the potatoes. At two o'clock, the goose was finally roasted and glazed and served up sitting in the centre of a bed of mixed greens and caramelised onions. Laurence carved, and Rhia carried the slightly burnt potatoes and honeyed carrots and condiments to the table on platters. Antonia served Bordeaux that she'd found in the cellar. She knew little about wines and spirits and hoped the bottle had not turned.

She took her place beside Mr Dillon, who had taken it upon himself to serve the vegetables. 'I hear that you will be trading in the spring, Mrs Blake?'

'I shall.'

'Have you been to the East?'

'No. I have always kept the home hearth lit. Josiah spent as much time at sea and in Calcutta and Bombay as he spent in London.'

'Am I to understand that your husband was buried in Bombay, madam?' It was a raw question, almost cruelly so, but at least here was someone who was not afraid to speak of the dead. It took more energy to maintain the silence; the unasked.

'I did not intend to cause offence,' he added while she was gathering her thoughts.

'You have not. Josiah was not buried. His body was never recovered.' She sensed that he knew this, so what was his reason for asking?

'No attempt was made to recover him?'

'No one saw the accident, Mr Dillon,' Isaac interjected. He sounded strained.

Mr Dillon frowned. 'If no one saw the accident, then how is it that everyone is certain that it *was* an accident?' The silence at the table was, for a moment, impenetrable.

'It was assumed. The yardarm was broken.' Isaac took a large swallow of wine. His hand was trembling.

Antonia couldn't utter a word.

Isaac regained his composure and put his glass down. 'He was not himself,' he said quietly, 'everyone had noticed it. He must have been standing too close to the aft rigging, which swings around swiftly when the sails are set. He should have known better. One of the crew heard his shout and saw him ...' He glanced at Antonia. She bent her head. 'Saw him go down,' Isaac finished.

When she looked up, Laurence looked as sober as she had ever seen him. 'Were you aware of a letter Josiah wrote to Ryan Mahoney, Isaac?' he asked.

Antonia dropped her fork onto her plate with a clatter. 'What letter?' Her voice sounded uncannily steady.

Laurence's voice almost broke with emotion. 'I'm so sorry, Antonia. I thought telling you would only make things worse. All I know is that there was something in the letter that distressed Ryan.' Laurence sighed heavily. 'He died before he could tell me more and we found nothing at China Wharf.'

Isaac drained half his glass in a swallow. He was normally a slow, careful drinker.

Mr Dillon was watching him. 'You knew nothing of it, Mr Fisher?'

'No.'

Mr Dillon frowned. 'Josiah Blake was, by all accounts, as familiar with the ship as an able seaman, and Ryan knew his pistols like an armourer, yet both of these gentlemen died in accidents that might have killed infinitely less experienced men.'

Rhia, who had said nothing, suddenly tapped her fork on her goblet. The sound rang around the high ceilings and she soon had everyone's attention.

'It is Christmas. There is time enough for dark thoughts on every other day of the year.'

'Well said.' Laurence raised his glass. 'Merry Christmas, all.'

Antonia lifted her glass with some effort and, as crystal tinkled, she caught Rhia's eye. She too had known about the letter. It was a small betrayal, but it felt a betrayal nonetheless.

The conversation turned to the affairs of the City, but Antonia could not focus on it. She thought that she knew Isaac Fisher well, and she had never before now suspected him of not telling the truth.

31 December 1840

There is a sparkling of frost on the roof tiles opposite tonight. I shall take it to be an omen that the new year will likewise sparkle. I have written to Mr Montgomery and agreed to the position of assistant, which is at least a job I know. I can smile at la-di-da ladies who don't deserve my attention, like Mrs Spufford of the pea green décolletage. I suppose I am suited to the post in some ways, having had the experience of St Stephen's Green. I suppose I set my sights too high, that women do not enter a trade so effortlessly.

So I am to spend January and February in the emporium with Grace, who leaves at the end of that month, by which time I should know all there is to know about the difference between Montgomery silk and Mahoney linen.

Your pen is my best companion, Mamo. Sometimes I even think that you are here. I thought I smelt you in Ryan's rooms that day, or at least the lanolin that you used to put in your hair. Were you with us? You once said that you would sooner die than go to London, but since you are already dead perhaps you have reconsidered. I have put the calling card here in my red book, in case it is something important. Maybe one day I will know.

I am walking a tightrope between worlds and I have no idea what to do with myself. Everything seems so uncertain, and I sometimes feel cold to my bones, as if something else terrible were going to happen. It is probably only the after-math of the year's troubles. Or perhaps I will marry after all!

# Linsey

Millbank prison was considered a great achievement by those not incarcerated there. Antonia thought the place unwholesome, being built on marshlands on the banks of the Thames, but she had to admit that it was of superior design to the dark blocks of Newgate.

The various wings of Millbank radiated out from a central watch like a great star, and each long, narrow arm had windows so that day could be distinguished from night. In many other of the prisons Antonia visited, the cells were so dim that it was difficult to tell the difference. Even now, in the middle of February, a little light must provide some relief to those who had been moved to Millbank to await transportation.

Each time she passed through the towering black gates, Antonia was reminded of the compassion and devotion of the indomitable Elizabeth Fry. She was still the shining light of the British Ladies' Society, even though she was now an invalid and rarely in London. Because of Elizabeth, not only Newgate and Millbank, but also Bridewell, Whitecross Street and Coldbath Fields were in excellent order. She had sacrificed her health to ensure that female prisoners were no longer shackled like animals on the long voyages to the colonies. It was her Quaker charities which collected cloth so that the women could make quilts during their months at sea.

Antonia and Juliette were accompanied by a wardress with

muscular forearms along a chill brick corridor towards the
north ward. Their footsteps echoed as though a crowd of
ghosts walked with them. Antonia glanced at Juliette who
wore an unusually stalwart expression. The fact that Juliette
had agreed to come to Millbank at all was something of a
breakthrough. She had only accompanied Antonia to this
prison once before, and had then been gloomy and weepy for
days after. She'd wanted to see the place where her mother
spent the months before she had been transferred to a hulk.
Hulk was an apt name for the great rusting man-o'-wars that
sat in the Thames estuary. They were unfit for use by the navy,
but apparently not unfit for the storage of excess criminals.
Eliza Green was lucky to have escaped a hulk and to be transported instead.

Antonia and Juliette both carried carpet bags containing
items prisoners had requested. Mary Gardner wanted finger-
less gloves for her chilblained hands. She said the endless
sewing made her fingers so numb that she'd all but lost feeling
in them. In the daylight hours the Millbank women were
employed in every industry from common needlework to making brooms, brushes, rugs and mats. Nelly Williams wanted a
copy of the Moses and Son catalogue, though she couldn't read.
She said she liked the pictures of hats and gloves and fancy collars. Should the day never come when she could wear such
showy things herself, then at least she would have had the
pleasure of imagining them. Margaret Dickson had asked for
hair pins, having assured Mrs Blake they were for fixing her
hair, not tinkering a lock. Antonia refrained from asking why
she would bother with such decorative grooming when she sat
on her own all day in a cell.

There were other items in the carpet bags: a wooden comb,
a skein of wool, a paper bag containing a variety of boot but-

tons, wool shawls knitted by one of the Friends, some pretty writing paper for a love note and, of course, Bibles. Antonia was mindful to keep her back straight and her chin lifted as their boots echoed through the dark, winding passages and heavy slate-grey doors. She was here to provide comfort, not to feel intimidated. The doors clanged shut behind them, making Juliette start each time. The ground plan was deceptively simple. In fact, the geometry of the building was impenetrable, a maze even to one who had walked its halls before.

They arrived at the north ward, a structure with steel stairs and a grid of railings connecting all of its three floors. Each floor was visible from every part of the long, narrow corridor of the building and lined with row upon row of identical grey doors. The overall effect was of an enormous aviary whose captive birds were kept in tiny boxes.

They ascended to the second level from the ground, each step they took ringing out on the metal rungs of the stair. At the sound, several wooden rods appeared through the slots in cell doors, the only means by which the women were allowed to catch the attention of the wardress. She appeared not to notice. Antonia could not help but think of Millbank as a fortified limbo. Its one thousand inmates had been transferred here from all over the country as well as from other London prisons.

Margaret Dickson, whose cell was the first they called at, was from Manchester and had been sentenced to seven years for the theft of a trunk of tea from the back of a coach. It was a more impressive crime than much of the petty thieving that resulted in transportation. The warden unclipped a hefty bracelet of keys from her apron and, with a resounding click, the door to Margaret's cell creaked open.

'Look sharp, Dickson, you've a lady visitor.' Juliette's air of servitude was such that she was clearly a subordinate, even though the two women were as plainly clothed as each other. The cell was sparsely furnished. A porcelain tub for washing was fitted with a wooden cover so that it could also be used as a seat; a large earthenware pan sat in one corner, and folded neatly in another was a brown hammock and bedding. A table flap, hinged to the wall, was laid with a tin mug and plate, a wooden spoon and a slate and pencil. Margaret sat on a low stool beneath a small high window, sewing a linsey petticoat which, along with a brown serge pinafore, was the uniform worn by all of the female inmates. Linsey, a blend of linen and wool, was so coarse that even a Quaker would not consider wearing it as an undergarment.

When Margaret saw her visitors, her face lit up . She stood to allow Mrs Blake to sit on her stool and Antonia didn't refuse. There was little else a prisoner could do to be welcoming than offer the only stool in her cell. Juliette perched on the wooden board over the wash basin. The door clanged shut behind them.

'Are you well, Margaret?' It was always the first thing Antonia asked, though the irony of the question was not lost on her. How could anyone be *well* in such a place?

'As well as I can be on cocoa and gruel, Mrs Blake.' Margaret looked less stout, but was otherwise in good spirits. A rapport had developed between the three women the last time Juliette had visited Millbank, since they had all come to London from the north, though all under rather different circumstances.

Margaret chatted away as though she were going to the continent on holiday. She had not yet been told exactly *where* her transport would sail, and she *would* prefer to be sent to the colonies of Bermuda or Gibraltar, since Sydney was an *awful* long way, three months at sea at least.

Antonia listened and glanced quickly at Juliette when Margaret said that she had little hope of ever returning to her family in Manchester once she'd gone. Juliette didn't appear to be listening, though, she was fidgeting with a strand of her shawl and her eyes were darting about the room as though there was something to look at. She seemed on edge, though this was nothing new.

After a time, Antonia rummaged in her bag for the hair pins Margaret had requested and then stood to leave. She expected Juliette to follow, but the maid stayed seated, looking nervous.

'I'd like to stop with Margaret, if you don't mind, Mrs Blake. I'm not sure that we'll see each other again and I'd like to tell her about my ma, in case she gets sent to Sydney town.'

'Of course, Juliette! What a good idea. I'll come and fetch you after I've been to see Nelly, shall I?'

'Yes, please, I hope that's no bother.'

'Don't be silly.' Antonia left, wondering what on earth Juliette could be up to with Margaret. She should not be so suspicious, she should be hopeful. Perhaps the girl was finally reaching out; becoming confident, and that could surely only be a good thing.

Nelly Williams was sweet-faced and flaxen-haired, which was not advantageous in a women's prison. She might as well be deliberately trying to make the others feel ugly. Even here, appearances mattered. Nelly was as excited as a child to receive her catalogue, and Antonia stayed with her, looking at fur mantles and satin slippers. She tried to remember the shades that were being worn on Oxford and Regent Streets because Nelly seemed anxious to know. She felt compelled to point out that the corseted and cosseted were generally unhappy, and that one pretty desire was quickly replaced with another. Nelly said she wouldn't mind being that kind of unhappy.

She left Nelly with her catalogue of fancies, reminded of the scented invitation that had recently arrived from Isabella Montgomery. Isabella's cage was gilded and luxurious, but she was imprisoned nonetheless. For all of his charm and benevolence, her father was typical of his class. Isabella was not allowed an inch of freedom, although she was gasping for it. The invitation, addressed to both Antonia and Rhia, was to Isabella's forthcoming birthday tea, but Antonia didn't think she could bring herself to attend. She would just feel like an old pigeon in an aviary full of coloured birds, all preening and pecking.

Juliette's mood seemed to improve as soon as they left Millbank, and Antonia wondered if she saw the twitch of a secretive smile before they were both forced to cover their noses and mouths with handkerchiefs. The stench was truly awful. 'Perhaps if the night-soil men didn't command a shilling a cesspit, the sewers wouldn't spill over so often,' she observed drily. Sewage was like emotion; it could only be contained to a point before it just burst through its restraints.

Greystones,
County Wicklow

16 February 1841

My dear Rhia,

You must by now have taken up the position at the Montgomery Emporium. I imagine you surrounded by a palette of silk.

My late reply is not for want of will, as you will know, but of time. Annie Kelly and I are spinning all the daylight hours, and at night your father is in need of my company. He is much the same. The physician says that the bones have mended and he can find no reason why he should not walk with a stick. His ailment is, as we know, of the spirit. He won't forgive himself for allowing the ruin of the business, or for letting you leave. He even seems to think that he might have done something to prevent Ryan's death. When he is finally sleeping, I am too weary to write and always, now, consider the cost when the gas lanterns are lit. I may write by tallow, but it is not so true a light. Do not misunderstand me, I don't consider this a hardship, it reminds me to value everything for its worth, as Mamo always said I should. Sometimes I imagine I can hear her voice, reminding me that I was lucky to marry a wealthy man, and of course she is still right.

As to Thomas Kelly, yes he is well and is weaving as deftly as ever. He can produce four yards a day if he works from sunrise to sunset. Thomas and I have been experimenting with worsted. I have been given a sample of merino by an Italian peddler. It is a fine yarn and almost as soft as the wool from the Tibet goat. I have already sold several yards to a Dublin clothier, so we are meeting our needs.

We are all excited that Michael Kelly's sentence will be served by the summer, and that he has somehow managed to raise the money for his passage to Dublin. It will be wonderful to have him home and, of course, the Kellys will be much better off with both looms in use.

I will not hear of you sending banknotes by post, Rhia, you will need your wage in London and you will find plenty to spend it on. We are quite comfortable. Since I know how stubborn you are, let me suggest this. If you have silver to spare then put it in a safe place – not in a bank – and before you spend it, think about how you might wisely invest it in something useful.

From the window I can see the edge of the shale where you used to ride without boots or bonnet, with your hair getting in such a tangle from the salt and the wind. Epona misses you, but I try to take her out every once in a while. Take good care of yourself and do remember to eat sensibly and keep warm.

Your loving mother,
Brigit Mahoney

# Taffeta

Rhia slipped the letter back into her apron pocket. It was always exciting to have word from home and she had put off reading her mother's letter until she could sit with her afternoon tea. She looked around the storeroom with satisfaction. It housed an entire wall of box shelving, piled to the ceiling with rolls and folded bolts of cloth. Rearranging it into some kind of logical order had taken the better part of a month and she was still not finished. This was partly because of the sheer volume of cloth, and partly because of regular interruptions from Grace, who was clearly enjoying being mistress of the shop floor. She found no end of menial tasks for Rhia to do, fetching this or that, or minding the floor while she took her elevenses or ran an errand. It was irritating enough being a minion without Grace enjoying her seniority as much as she did.

Rhia liked the storeroom, though. She never tired of the sight of glossy black satin beside gold devoré or plum brocade against beetle green taffeta. It reminded her a little of the front room at St Stephen's Green. On a bright day like today, the light from the window behind struck the shelving and made the silk velvets shine like jewels.

The back window overlooked a small overgrown courtyard, and against the far wall was a dresser with a mottled mirror and several drawers. In these, Rhia had started to store pots and jars of coloured powders and sable brushes of every thickness. In the centre of the floor was a long trestle table covered partly with bolts of cloth. But in one corner was her red book, and a few squares of card dabbed with the velvety pinks and rich, ruby reds of the damask rose. The designs were firmly a secondary occupation during opening hours at the emporium, but she was determined that she would soon have a collection to present Mr Montgomery with, something to rival anything from Paris. She usually came in early or stayed late so that she had uninterrupted time to work. Today, though, she would be leaving early for Isabella Montgomery's birthday tea. Rhia wasn't particularly looking forward to it, and Grace hadn't been invited. Isabella's tea party seemed just another reason for Grace to feel resentful. Rhia looked at the old ship's clock above the dresser. It was almost time to leave.

She untied her apron and tidied her hair in the mirror, thinking about her mother's cautionary words. She had already taken to stowing guineas in a purse in the bottom of her portmanteau. She was not about to entrust anyone with her precious silver, not after the conversation with Dillon in the Red Lion. Having an income gave her unexpected pleasure. Suddenly, anything was possible.

She was becoming more and more convinced that money was somehow at the root of Ryan's death, whether he had been unprincipled or not. But how could he have lost money if he was trading in opium? Ryan had been a risk-taker, certainly, but would never be described as rash. No doubt he had overextended himself by investing in the joint venture. Mr Dillon presumably knew something about it, since he appeared to know something about most things. Rhia had neither seen nor heard from him since Christmas. He had no reason to call, other than to see Laurence, and Laurence had sailed to New

York more than two weeks ago. The house was quiet without him and Antonia was busier than ever with her forthcoming shipment to India.

Grace was buffing her nails and reading *Sylvia's Home Journal* when Rhia walked through the shop floor, the only way to leave the emporium. They exchanged polite farewells. The end of the month was less than a week away, and then Rhia would be on her own. She already had her own key.

The Montgomery barouche, unexpectedly containing Isabella, pulled up just as Rhia stepped onto the footpath. Isabella looked the parody of a snow queen in her Moscow hat and sable pelisse, with a fur rug across her knees. She was almost breathless with excitement when Rhia stepped up beside her. 'Hello, Miss Mahoney, it seems an absolute age since we've seen each other, and I've come secretly! Father was called to the mercer's hall and Mama said that I might come if I was swift, and that she will receive our guests. But you must not tell. He would be *extremely* cross if he discovered I was out unchaperoned. But it is my birthday and I'll soon be a wife, so I must be free today at least!'

As they passed through Hyde Park, Rhia felt the prickly gaze of side-saddle riders and promenaders carrying lace parasols. Since it was a grey February afternoon, she presumed the parasols were for surveillance. Being inspected for flaws was inevitable. It made Rhia feel like she might have forgotten something essential, and that she had no way of knowing what it was. Isabella on the other hand was perfect for Hyde Park. Everything about her was expensive and modern and she could, and did, hold her head high.

Rhia didn't have a chance to enquire about Isabella's husband-to-be, because her companion hardly drew breath. She was intent on taking an inventory of the guest list. This included the daughters of directors of the Bank of England, a Prussian baroness, an Italian viscount, and sundry earls, lords and dukes. And of course her future husband would be there, though he would be in the parlour with her father and some other gentlemen talking 'business'. He was, she said, 'a shipping magnet'.

'Perhaps he is a magnate?' Rhia suggested, and Isabella agreed that he might be.

As they turned into Belgrave Square, Isabella clutched Rhia's hand, taking her by surprise. 'Oh Miss Mahoney, I wish I were as daring as you! I am so *bored*, especially in the evenings. Papa is always at his club and Mama practically lives in her boudoir. Mama says the servants watch me and report to Papa, but she gets rather muddled so I don't know if it's true. If I had my way I should go out every night to Drury Lane! I know it's risqué, but I have always wanted to have lessons in ballet. Papa should never allow it, he says ballet is vulgar and not at all refined.'

Rhia extracted her hand as gently as she could. She couldn't help liking Isabella, in spite of her chocolate-box existence. 'But you'll soon be married, and you'll probably have children. From what I know of children, you'll never be bored again!'

Isabella sighed. 'Yes, of course. I hope my husband is a kind man.'

'Do you think he is?'

Isabella shrugged 'I don't know. I've only met him once.'

Rhia tried not to show how much this surprised her. It shouldn't. Arranged marriages were common amongst the gentry, and Mr Montgomery would only have his daughter's interest at heart.

'Oh drat!' said Isabella. 'Papa's carriage is here. I'll have to go in the servant's entrance and pretend I've been upstairs.' She jumped to the ground before Rhia could protest and was gone.

The long, circular drive of the Montgomery residence was lined with liveried carriages, sleek landaus, chariots and attendant footmen. Rhia felt her stomach somersault. She had imagined an intimate tea party, not this. Everywhere she looked were domes of pale lemon chiffon and spray embroidery on white organdie and strawberry tulle. A confectionary of fashion. She felt like a plum duff in her purple taffeta coutil. The blend of silk and cotton was her only purchase since starting at the emporium. She had chosen purple to feel brave. The goddess Rhiannon wore a purple cloak.

She stayed in the barouche for a moment to survey the scene and prepare herself. It was just like a page from *Sylvia's Home Journal.* Grace would have loved it. Waists and slippers were pointed, bodices were boned and corsages *en coeur*, crinolines were enormous and flounced, sleeves, if present, were short and tight with a manchette of lace at the elbow.

Rhia stepped to the ground and ascended the imposing stairs as nonchalantly as she could. She felt the eyes of the powdered and thin on her, and saw herself through their eyes: the complexion of a farm worker, Irish cloak (no fur trim), no ringlets. She would have a sip of tea and a bite of cake and then she would develop a headache and leave.

The drawing room was a clutter of crinolines, and there was no sign of Isabella. Prunella Montgomery smiled vaguely at her then patted the divan she was perched on. Rhia sat beside her and Prunella offered a glass of sherry from the decanter at her elbow, presumably her own personal supply. Rhia accepted. Sherry seemed a much better idea than tea.

'Are you enjoying the party, dear?' Prunella asked, hesitating before she said 'dear' as though she'd forgotten Rhia's name. Rhia answered politely that she was, and added that she was also enjoying the emporium. Mrs Montgomery looked confused for a moment and then nodded absently. Rhia could see that she would have to uphold the conversation, so she prattled on about how much she loved being in the storeroom, and how it was like a treasure trove.

Mrs Montgomery raised her eyebrows. Her pale blue eyes had a milky ring around the pupil and there were hollow, bluish shadows beneath them, which no amount of powder could hide. The remnants of beauty were there, but Prunella Montgomery had clearly ceased to care. 'You must get Isabella to show you my collection upstairs, dear,' she said, 'if you think the silks in the emporium are treasures.'

The sherry went down easily under the circumstances, and Mrs Montgomery was soon refilling Rhia's glass along with her own. Her hand was unsteady and the tawny liquid dripped down the outer edge of the glass as she poured.

By the time Rhia had drained her third glass of sherry, she was openly discussing the fate of Mahoney Linen, certain that she was being unsophisticated because her hostess's eyebrows seemed permanently raised. Eventually she realised that they were pencilled on.

When Isabella came into view, her mother called her over. 'You must take your friend up to see the collection, Isabella.'

'Oh yes! You simply must see it, Miss Mahoney.'

Mrs Montgomery took Isabella by the wrist and pulled her close. 'But make sure your father doesn't see you – you know he doesn't like you to neglect your guests.' She took a key from her reticule and pressed it into Isabella's hand.

'We'll take the servant's stair,' Isabella assured her mother, and they exchanged a conspiratorial smile.

Isabella kept hold of Rhia's hand and pulled her along a short corridor off the reception hall where more confections clustered together, their eyes darting to and fro behind watered silk fans.

They hurried up a narrow darkened stair to the second floor landing and Isabella lifted a candelabra from a sideboard and put it down outside one of the doors off the landing so that she could unlock it.

'This is where Mama's cloth is stored,' Isabella said in a whisper.

'Why are you whispering? Are you forbidden here?'

'Oh, no, but the servants are. Mama is very fond of her collection.' Isabella giggled nervously.

'Would your father really be angry if he discovered you had left your guests?'

'Probably, though as I said Mama tends to exaggerate where he's concerned. He means to announce my wedding today you see ...' Isabella trailed off and shrugged as carelessly as she could. 'As you say, it will relieve my boredom. Besides, I shall run away and find employment if I don't like my husband, just as you have!'

Rhia couldn't imagine Isabella surviving for a moment in a world that was not lined with fur and draped in tulle. Surely she must understand that it was her father's money and influence that upholstered her comfortable journey through life.

Isabella opened the door onto an anteroom that must once have been a dressing room. It was furnished only with carved cherry wood trunks. Isabella opened one, and then another, and the dark little room was suddenly transformed. Prunella Montgomery was right. These were treasures. Isabella pulled out length after length of embroidered and appliquéd silk covered in intricate needlework or sewn with tiny pearls. Some were literally weighed down with gemstones. In most, the weave of the fabric was entirely obscured by ornament. The cloth exhaled the scents of foreign lands, which Rhia found as sensuous as the textiles themselves. She exclaimed over each new piece until she felt light-headed. It was soon too much to take in. One of these textiles alone would have stunned her, but an entire room full was overpowering. She could not begin to imagine their value. Isabella had been enjoying her stupefaction, but was suddenly anxious to return before she was missed.

Rhia took a last look around. She had not noticed the hanging on the wall that was twinkling like a galaxy in the candlelight. It was a patchwork of sea-coloured silks, sewn with sapphires and emeralds and peridot. It made Rhia strangely uneasy, giving her the same creeping sensation as the trees in the morning room at Cloak Lane. She was now as eager as Isabella to leave.

On the landing a maid brushed past, and Isabella eyed her suspiciously. She whispered to Rhia. 'That's Hatty the Tattle. We'd better go down the main stair, since she'll know I'm being disobedient if she sees us on the servant's stair.'

Rhia had never known a household so well staffed. There were maids everywhere, plus a butler, a steward and a valet, and who knew how many in the kitchen and stables. It awed her and inspiring awe was no doubt exactly what was intended.

From halfway down the stair, they could see the reception hall below. Mr Montgomery stood right in the middle of the floor, a striking figure in hunting pink and riding boots. He was eyeing their approach whilst talking to Isaac Fisher and to a well-fed, greying gentleman. Isabella's hand reached for Rhia's. 'Oh dear, they've finished earlier than I thought, we should have taken the servant's stair after all.' She sighed stoically. 'Oh well.' Her voice dropped to a whisper as they descended. 'The gentleman with my father is my future husband, Miss Mahoney. Isn't he *old*.' The man wasn't exactly old, but he was easily twice Isabella's age.

Mr Montgomery smiled when they arrived at the bottom of the stairs, but he was thin-lipped with displeasure and the annoyance beneath his words was barely contained.

'I have been looking everywhere for you, Isabella.'

'I was showing Miss Mahoney Mama's collection.'

The gentleman beside her father was beaming. He had a round, pleasant face but looked no more endearing at close quarters. Rhia felt a stab of pity as he offered Isabella his arm. They wandered away, he looking as though he couldn't believe his good fortune in purchasing such a pretty accessory.

Mr Montgomery smiled at Rhia, his ill humour quickly forgotten. Hatty the Tattle hovered with a tray of flutes filled with something pink and fizzing, and Mr Montgomery plucked a glass by the stem for Rhia.

'Are you enjoying the party, Miss Mahoney?'

'Oh, very much,' she lied. She was unbelievably thirsty and emptied half the contents of the flute before she noticed that it was alcoholic. She could feel Isaac's eyes on her, disapproving, she thought. He was standing back politely, within earshot but not noticeably so.

'Marvellous,' said Mr Montgomery. 'I am pleased with your new designs – have I said so?' Before she could answer that he hadn't, he continued, 'We must print one soon. You show great promise.'

'I'm glad to hear it,' Rhia replied. 'I had worried you might think me better suited to the shop floor.' His eyebrows shot up and Rhia almost laughed. No wonder Mrs Montgomery was always sauced – drinking made life so much more enjoyable.

Mr Montgomery smiled to hide his surprise. 'I thought the shop might provide a diversion from the tragedy of your uncle's death.'

Had he only offered her the job as a charitable gesture, then?

Did he genuinely think her designs had great promise, or was this just gentlemanly altruism? She felt emotional about unexpected kindnesses, though she couldn't remember it being of issue a moment ago. She also felt an urgent need to offload her fears. After all, Mr Montgomery had been a colleague of her uncle. 'I suppose you've heard the rumours?' she ventured.

He raised an eyebrow. 'Rumours?'

'That the death of Josiah Blake was not an accident. You don't think … you don't suppose my uncle and Mr Blake might have both been led to take their own lives by the same external force?'

Mr Montgomery looked shocked. Then she caught Isaac's eye – he was glowering. Rhia regretted her words immediately. She suddenly felt sober. 'But I should not have mentioned it, without evidence.'

Mr Montgomery recovered his smile. 'You must voice your fears, of course,' he said placatingly. 'It is the nature of grief. It is perfectly natural to feel distrustful, though I pray your suspicions are ill founded.' He didn't look certain, she thought, and she wondered if everyone else knew more about her uncle's affairs than she.

Mr Montgomery excused himself and, since Isaac had suddenly disappeared, Rhia found her cloak and asked the footman to call a carriage to take her home. She couldn't face saying formal goodbyes and was sure no one would miss her. She had never been very good at parties and was suddenly in urgent need of Beth's ginger loaf cake.

# Embroidery

Rhia lit the spirit lamp and shifted the sheets of cartridge paper scattered across the storeroom table. She had almost two hours before the emporium opened its doors, but the damask rose was going nowhere and she couldn't decide what to do with the indigo either. Both were in need of green.

She had almost covered the entire table in samples by the time she heard Grace arrive. It didn't seem that any time at all had passed, yet it was ten o'clock. She had still not found the elusive shade of green that would not clash with rose or indigo, and she was wary of using too much of her precious powders – they cost a whole shilling for a small pot.

Rhia was putting away her brushes when there was a knock at the half-open door and Isaac Fisher stepped into the store. She had completely forgotten he was coming to collect the remnants for the convict ship committee. Antonia was still busy supervising *Mathilda*'s voyage to Calcutta. Isaac carried a large carpet bag and looked a little strained as they exchanged greetings. Perhaps he, like Rhia, was feeling awkward about her indiscretion at Belgravia.

'Miss Elliot says she would like a word with you on the shop floor,' Isaac said as he put his bag on the trestle table. Rhia could not fathom why Grace could not come and tell her this in person.

In the emporium, Grace was looking smug. 'I've just

remembered that Mr Montgomery said if it's quiet we're to dust the tops of the shelves and I can't find the duster. Do you have it in the storeroom?' Presumably she was hoping that Rhia would offer to dust the shelving.

'I'm sorry, no, I haven't seen it,' Rhia said, all the more annoyed to be interrupted without good cause. Grace wasn't supposed to leave the shop floor unattended, but if she called out Rhia could more or less hear her in the storeroom. Sometimes she thought Grace just liked to have company occasionally, and even Rhia's was better than nothing. Regent Street, like St Stephen's Green, was quiet in February.

Rhia returned to the storeroom irritated, and found Isaac inspecting her work. 'My late wife was a painter,' he said. 'She loved mixing tinctures. I distinctly remember her saying that green has inspired artists more than any other colour.' Isaac looked wistful for a moment. 'What a thing to remember.' He may have been talking to himself.

'It is in every aspect of nature,' Rhia proffered, but Isaac seemed lost in thought and she wasn't sure if he had heard her. She did not yet have the full measure of Isaac Fisher. He was likeable but guarded. Antonia had called him a liberal Quaker, though Rhia wasn't sure exactly what this meant. Presumably he didn't like rules.

'It was apparently the most sought after of recipes,' she added, remembering what the dyer had told her. 'The green dye made from metals corroded parchment, and others disintegrated in the light. Dyers used to dip their cloth first in a vat of yellow tincture made from weld or buckthorn, and then in one of woad blue.' Why did Isaac drop his eyes when she met his gaze? It made her distrust him for a moment.

'Do you know where your green comes from now?' he asked.

'I don't.'

'It is from China,' he said.

'Is that why it is so expensive?'

'It is expensive because it is extracted from the bark of an Oriental tree.' He sighed heavily. 'We are ruining the most inventive race on the earth.' He shook his head as though he were personally responsible. 'I am pleased to see that Jonathan Montgomery had good cause to employ you.'

Rhia felt her colour rise. 'Then you thought he engaged me as an act of charity?'

The Quaker ignored this remark. He looked sombre. 'Even if you have heard rumours about Josiah's death, it would be foolish and dangerous to speak of them. Please do not.'

He picked up the carpet bag, which was now full of remnants, and tipped his hat. 'Good day, Miss Mahoney.' He was gone before she had a chance to retort. What did he mean *dangerous*? Dangerous to her reputation? It was too late for that. And besides, Quakers were supposed to be defenders of free speech. Isaac must know something. He had been on board the *Mathilda* on the day that Josiah Blake died. The thought almost made her shudder. Maybe he knew something about Josiah's death.

The morning passed slowly. Rhia felt restless and troubled after Isaac's visit. She found herself dusting the top of the shelves after all when Grace went to lunch. Then she stood behind the polished walnut counter watching for a certain lightness of step in the women who passed by, for a certain dedication, on a cold February morning, to spending the household allowance on something to ease loneliness or boredom. Two women entered, one dressed in plaid and the other in barber stripe. Their coats were trimmed with musk and their eyes darted around the room. They reeked of cologne as though they had just uncorked an entire perfumery.

They bade Rhia to fetch down one roll after another of the new silk brocades, which were so sleek they slipped across the counter like water. Her shears flashed and clicked until almost a hundred yards had been ordered between them. It was enough to cover four crinolines at a cost that made neither of them flinch.

While Rhia wrapped the cloth in brown paper and tied it up with ribbon, the women discussed an invitation to spend March in an Italian villa. When they eventually left, Rhia felt deflated. Envy? Did she want a husband with a balance at the bankers larger than her capacity to spend? She might once have thought this perfectly reasonable, but she had a taste, now, for being mistress of her own affairs, and she would not easily give it up.

When Grace returned from lunch, Rhia bought a piece of pie from a barrow seller and sat in the storeroom with a cup of tea, looking at her swatches of green. None were right. She needed more moss, less olive. She put the samples away and assessed the tidiness of the shelves. She would have a busy afternoon if she was to finish sorting through all the velvets.

As she stood up there was a sharp rap at her door. Before she could say a word, two gentlemen entered, dressed in the square black hats and dark serge uniforms of the Metropolitan Police. A moment later, Grace appeared behind them, looking as though she had eaten something that disagreed with her.

'Good afternoon, miss,' said the older of the two, though he was still not as old as Rhia was. 'My colleague and I are investigating the theft of a quantity of ...' and here, he took a pad of brown paper from his inner pocket and referred to it, '*a length of embroidered silk* from the Montgomery residence of Belgrave Square. I have here a warrant to search these premises for said goods.'

Rhia was shocked. It seemed somehow worse that there had been a theft at the Montgomerys' when she had only just been there, but surely it was impossible that anything stolen from Belgrave Square would be found here, at the emporium. Were they implying that she might be harbouring stolen property?

'By all means, search the room,' she said briskly, 'but *please* do so neatly and carefully. It has taken me weeks to put it in order.' The senior policeman nodded, and then instructed Grace to begin looking. Grace was clearly in an agony of discomfort. She could not meet Rhia's eye.

Grace removed rolls and folded lengths of cloth from each cubicle. The ship's clock seemed to tick twice as loud to make up for the silence in the room.

It was on one of the higher shelves, which Grace reached only by standing on some low wooden steps, that the embroidery was discovered. Rhia recognised it immediately as the hanging that had disturbed her. Grace put it on the table where the lamp reflected its sea colours onto the walls, like sunlight on water.

Rhia was astonished. She sat down heavily. She didn't understand. In fact, until the two constables stepped forth and stood each at either side of her, she was not even aware that she was to be accused. It was unthinkable.

'Rhia Mahoney, you are forthwith a prisoner of her Majesty Queen Victoria, and will be held in the custody of Her Majesty's prison, Newgate, until such a time as your case may be heard.'

# Crinoline

L ondon disappeared. Perhaps it had only ever been a
photogenic drawing, only the ghost of something real
though sometimes Rhia heard it from her cell – all jovial and
whistling and oblivious to the dark Otherworld that lay behind
the walls of Newgate prison.

She had counted five nights, but she would soon lose count
if she didn't get out of this place. They had not allowed her any
visitors and she did not know any more than she had when she
was first arrested. Nights were an eternity spent on a hard mat
in an open cell, amongst women who bickered and snored and
eyed her gown. They'd steal it from her back while she slept if
they thought they'd get away with it. The pale sheen of her
corinna made her stand out like a gold nugget in a pan full
of earth.

Someone told Rhia that she wouldn't be issued with a prison
uniform until she had been convicted. They didn't realise that
she was innocent and that there had been a miscarriage of justice. Antonia must know by now that she was in Newgate. She
and Mr Montgomery must think her guilty, otherwise they
would have had her released. Each time she had this thought
Rhia felt a wave of sickness, and then all the unanswered questions returned. This was how people went mad. She could see it.

There was ample loneliness and despair within the walls of
Newgate Prison. At night, the living were silent but the dead

were not. To fight it all, Rhia tried everything she could. She tried to feel fortunate (for she would soon be free). She tried, in the absence of paper and ink, writing to Mamo in her head. She even tried smiling, which earned her the threat of a thrashing. Nothing worked. She wasn't safe. Other prisoners had earned their stay in Newgate through poverty or violence or cunning – she could not compete.

Only a stone wall separated the condemned from the gallows of the Old Bailey. A stone wall, only, between life and death. The condemned huddled in a corner of the yard each morning as though they were already reducing the space they occupied on the earth. It terrified Rhia just to look at them. She kept her eyes on the sky in the yard. It was the only time all day that she would see it. She tried to name the blue of the sky but she had forgotten it.

Saying she was innocent was laughable. It hadn't taken long to realise this. If she were to believe what she'd heard in her ward, there were many innocents in here. There was always sewing to do during the day, and this was when the women shared their stories. There were no books in the ward, so telling your story was the next best thing. Above the fireplace, on a sheet of pasteboard, were pinned texts from the scriptures:

*A false witness shall not be unpunished.*
*He that speaketh lies shall perish.*

The messages seemed more futile the more Rhia thought about them, and besides, who here could even read them?

Mary Reardon, who had spent more time in Newgate than she had outside it, was one of the few who had actually spoken to Rhia. Mary told her that the women's ward had once been dismal. It was hard to imagine how the existing ward could be an improvement but according to Mary it was not whitewashed before, and there had been no fire for heat, no mats to sleep on, no pewter bowls to eat from. There was rarely stewed beef then, only gruel and coarse brown bread. Mary was almost toothless and had a bad lisp. It had taken Rhia a while to understand her, but she'd persevered because there was little else to keep occupied with. Mary was beyond the noose and too old to transport. She was presently serving several years for the theft of some buckles from a gentleman's shoes. The shoes weren't on his feet at the time, apparently. This, Rhia supposed, meant that Mary had been in the company of a gentleman in his stockings. She didn't ask for details.

Rhia shivered and pulled the rough wool blanket tighter around her shoulders. It had grown cold, so sunrise was close. According to Mary, she was blessed to have her case heard so quickly. Her arrest had coincided with the next session of the Central Criminal Court, and they only held one session a month. But what if the true thief had yet to be discovered? How did the cloth come to be hidden at the emporium? And how had the constabulary known to look there in the first place? All of these questions would be answered, and she would soon be free. Then she would have Beth draw her a bath with lavender to soothe the fleabites that covered her legs.

After morning gruel in the frigid grey refectory, the women were herded into the yard, but Rhia was led away by a wardress who gripped her elbow as if there was somewhere for her to run to. A few others were also being escorted from the refectory. The sight of the sky made Rhia weep. She was almost free. Even the cramped darkness of the prison van could not dampen her spirits, nor the crowd that had gathered outside the Sessions House to watch the prisoners being led inside.

The benches lining the dark holding cell were already full

when the metal grille clanged behind her. When her eyes adjusted to the dim light the usual hostile, resentful expressions greeted her. She would soon be free of the company of those who considered her privileged because she had no holes in her boots. She'd never before considered that this alone separated her from so many.

The names of her companions were shouted out one by one, along with their crimes as their turn came to leave the cell. Patricia O'Leary, bawdyhouse keeper. Tom Black, forger. Peter Thurn, blackmailer. Harold Jordan, bigamist. Most were thieves of varying calibre. Many were young women. Some looked desperate and frightened, others merely bored.

'Rhiannon Mahoney, thief.' The turnkey's shout echoed along the corridor, repeating her crime as she walked along it. For now she was nothing and no one. Her pale maize gown was soiled and creased and part of its hemline was torn where someone had 'accidentally' stepped on it. Her one consoling possession was the shawl that had been returned to her as she left Newgate. It was barège, a semi-transparent blend of wool and silk. It seemed important to keep track of the names of cloths, it meant she was still the same, still preoccupied with life's colour and texture. She draped it across her tangled hair and crossed it over her shoulders.

She stood in the stall and looked for some sign that she was not alone. The stall was called the dock, perhaps because so many who stood here would be condemned to sail, either from a noose or across the seas. Pasted to the inside of the dock in front of her was another psalm, writ on yellowed paper:

*Ye shall not swear by my name falsely, neither shalt thou profane the name of thy God.*

In the gallery, a sea of faces stared down. Rhia was shocked by the accusation she saw in the eyes of people she didn't know and hadn't injured. She lowered her own eyes. She would walk free today, and they would feel remorse. Tears threatened all the same. She could not bear this, how did anyone. Was there a single person in that room who believed she was innocent?

Rhia made herself lift her head and look at the gallery. She looked straight into the eyes of Mr Dillon and caught her breath. Her heart pitched. He was seated at the far end of the gallery with a notebook and pencil in his hand. He nodded. In that moment, she didn't care if he was here to write something unkind about her. She was just relieved to see a familiar face.

The prosecutor's miserable profession had obviously transformed his features. His lips were thin and mean and, judging by the creases between his brows, he rarely had cause to smile. He probably expected the worst from life, as he did from every wretched soul who stood in the dock. He cleared his throat loudly and the room was silent. He barely raised his eyes from his sheaf of papers as he spoke.

Rhia controlled her dread by imagining that the Sessions House was a theatre and the magistrate a narrator, who introduced, remarked upon and would conclude the play. The prosecutor's role was to ask a certain number of measured questions. As in a theatre, the audience shouted or applauded and generally made its opinion known. The only actor without a part to play – whose words made no significant difference – was the accused.

'Rhiannon Mahoney, you are charged by the Crown and no case has been prepared in your defence.' A clerk stepped forward and whispered in the prosecutor's ear. There was a murmur of speculation from the gallery. The prosecutor nodded briefly and the clerk stepped back. 'I am informed that the counsel for the defence has neglected to arrive at court.' The murmur grew louder, and Rhia looked up at Dillon. He shook his head, his expression dark. The prosecutor banged a small wooden hammer on his stand. 'The charge is the theft of a two yards length of India silk, embroidered with precious stones.' A dramatic gasp rose from the gallery, silenced by the prosecutor's hammer. He turned to Rhia. 'What is your plea?'

'I am not guilty, of course, but I would like to—' A roar of laughter drowned out what she might have said in her own defence. The hammer came down. The laughter shocked Rhia to tears. She didn't bother to wipe them away as they fell. The action would only betray her. The prosecutor did not appear to notice that she had spoken.

'I have here a statement given by the domestic servant Hatty Franklin, which declares, quite clearly, that you were seen visiting the room in which a quantity of precious textiles are stored, at the Montgomery residence in Belgrave Square, on the night of 25 February 1841. Is this correct?'

'It is, but—'

His raised hand silenced her again.

'Is it so that you wore a crinoline on the date aforementioned?'

'Yes, though I must—'

'Please *desist* in attempting to have your will in the courtroom, Miss Mahoney. You are here only to answer the questions I put to you.'

'Is it so, that your Irish family recently suffered the loss of their livelihood?'

Rhia thought that he had placed undue emphasis on the

word *Irish*, but she could not be certain. She nodded. Her hands had started to shake. She gripped them together tightly.

'Yes, it is.' She bowed her head. She no longer bothered trying to hide the tears. Her heart was beating so loud that she could no longer hear the prosecutor's reproaches. When the drone ceased, she looked up. This was what he had been waiting for.

'Miss Mahoney, you have been found guilty by this court of the theft of two yards of embroidered India silk, the property of Mrs Prunella Montgomery. You will henceforth be removed to Millbank prison and will, at a date to be arranged, be transported for seven years to her Majesty's colony of New South Wales.'

She would wake up and find that she was still in Newgate, or Cloak Lane, or St Stephen's Green. Maybe Ryan's death had been a dream too, and the fire. Rhia felt her whole body yield and held onto the edge of the dock. She had just enough sensibility to know that his would be a bad time to faint.

She was led away before she even realised the trial was over, before it had sunk in that she had been found guilty. Not innocent.

Another prison van waited – this time an ominous black windowless coach that looked like a funerary vehicle. As she put her foot on the step, Rhia heard her name spoken and turned to see Dillon talking with one of the guards. He introduced himself as a gentleman of the press and explained that he was covering the trial. He hoped that he might have a quick word, in private, with the prisoner. The guards appeared to recognise him, hesitated, and then allowed him to approach her.

Dillon took her elbow gently, much more gently, it seemed, than she had ever been touched. She wished he would never let her go. He lowered his voice to a whisper.

'I must be brief. Mrs Blake told me that she had arranged your defence. I cannot fathom what has happened, but you can be certain that neither Mrs Blake nor I believe that you are a thief. I didn't expect this outcome. None of us did. I will visit Mr Montgomery personally and start the process of appeal against your sentence immediately, but it is slow. Do not lose hope.' He cast a quick look at the guards, who were becoming impatient. 'We have no more time.'

Rhia nodded. She opened her mouth and hoped that she could speak. 'Mr Dillon, would you please write to—' He was nodding before she finished her sentence.

'I will write to Laurence,' he said briskly.

'No, not to Laurence, to my mother.'

'Yes, of course.' He pulled out his pocket book and a stub of pencil and scribbled the address she gave him. She could not take her eyes from the paper. What she would give just to have something to write on. Either her longing was writ on her face or Mr Dillon could read her mind. He cast a swift glance at the guards and then tore a wad of pages from his notepad. When he shook her hand, he pressed both paper and pencil into it. She pushed them up into her sleeve deftly and they exchanged a small smile. The irony of this act was not lost on either of them. She was behaving like a criminal. Rhia whispered 'thank you' before he strode away purposefully. He looked back and caught her eye just before she was pushed roughly into the dark interior of the van. The resolve in his expression gave her comfort. No matter what distrust she had once felt for him, today he was king of the Otherworld. She had no alternative but to trust him. He was her only hope.

As the door of the prison van closed, Rhia caught a last glimpse of the place she had once thought so brimful of possibility. Already, bright clusters of early daffodils, those messengers of spring, bowed from window boxes along Newgate Street. The forests around Greystones would soon be carpeted in bluebells, and rabbit kittens would hop from their winter burrows. There would be preparations for the spring equinox and a special un-dyed cloth would be spun for the celebrations. Rhia could almost smell the salt on the air as she imagined the seashore, and Thomas Kelly sitting at his loom looking out at the brooding sea. She ached to be in the past, safe from the future. Michael Kelly would be home with his family before she arrived in Sydney. It struck her like a blow. She pulled her mantle across her face and bent her head. If today were a cloth it must be barège. She gazed through its gauzy weave and the straw on the floorboards didn't look quite so slick with filth, or the open curiosity of the other prisoners so invasive. It softened the hostile gaze of the ragged woman seated opposite, who hissed, 'Fancy piece of mutton, aren't ye? Once them prissy locks get shorn off and the fine cloths are gone, thee'll be no better than the rest.'

Everything is grey. The stripes of sky through the small, high window, the linsey prison clothes, the walls, the cloth we sew. Even the food is grey. The world is bled of colour. Could I see myself in a glass, I know that my face would be grey. I feel colourless. I hunger for colour as much as for white bread and jam. Time is measured by the sound of the warden's boots on the steel stair and by the jingle of keys.

I am alone. Once a day we are allowed into the exercise yard, ward by ward. Everyone at Millbank is leaving England. That is why we are here, but I cannot leave. I cannot cross another sea. There are women who have been here for months and months waiting to be assigned to a transport. I pray that Mr Dillon will remember me. I listen to the shadows of prayers of the forgotten, who will not show themselves. I never thought that I would wish for the company of ghosts. I was happy when they left me alone. I remember you saying that spirits are like people and know when they are not welcome.

My hair is gone. It is a prickly crop and I'm over weeping for it as if it were something important. They clipped it off in the refectory (which, by the way, is grey) with great iron shears that looked better suited to cutting through sailcloth. I watched it drift to the flagstones and lie in black coils, dead as my soul, to be swept away and incinerated. The warden said it was a precaution against lice, but it felt like part of my punishment, like the coarse cloth of brown clothing, like this calico apron. If I wish, my prickles can be covered with a cloth cap like a housemaid. My neck is always cold. Who'd have thought that hair afforded so much warmth?

It will be time to go to the yard soon, where I always keep my eyes to the heavens and take full, deep breaths to store air and light, though it never lasts me through all the dark hours. I only ever believe I can get through one more day. Then another. Then another. One after the next. I try to think of colours and cloths and pots of dye. Texture and pattern. But I cannot conjure a palette that isn't dull. I could not write before now, and I only have the paper that Dillon gave me. There is little but the sky that is safe to look at in the yard. I discovered this only after chancing a look at Nora Beck. She is a bully and said that if I gawped at her again she'd give me a beating I'd never forget. It should have frightened me, but in fact I thought it might not be so bad. At least it would make me feel something. Nora is mean, and Agnes, her henchperson, is too. Nora is large, huge in fact, and domineering. It turns the others into cowards. Only one prisoner, Margaret, dares to cross her, and she is nowhere near Nora's physical equal.

I can hear boots on the stairs. I've kept the writing materials inside my undergarments and, thus far, no one has discovered them.

Anon.

# Hessian

Margaret Dickson approached without Rhia noticing. Rhia was looking for flying horses, and angels in the clouds, as she and Thomas had once done. She saw only ships.

'Best get over your miseries, Mahoney.' Margaret had her arms folded across her bosom, and wore an expression that managed to be both stern and teasing. Her hair was a mop of tight ginger curls, so she'd been at Millbank long enough for a few inches of growth. Her skin was so freckled that you could barely see a patch of its true colour. She was plumpish and her eyes were small but sparkly. Margaret nodded towards Nora's group, a dozen or so women standing in a huddle, gossiping and rubbing their hands together against the cold. 'You'll not want *them* thinking you'd be lowering yourself to give them the time of the day?'

'I have no timepiece,' Rhia retorted, and Margaret laughed throatily. 'I knew there'd be a spirit beneath that long face!' She shrugged. 'Not that I care either way, but I'd wager you don't fancy yourself genteel as all that. Most ladies from the trade don't.' She gestured towards the other women and lowered her voice. 'They wouldn't know the difference.'

'Is that what they think – that I fancy myself genteel?'

'What else?'

'How did you know I was from the trade?'

'Word gets around in a prison, Mahoney. You'll see. Besides, I've seen *ladies* of all sorts and I can tell who's who and what's what.' Margaret's expression became earnest. 'To be truthful, I'd a word with Mrs Blake and she asked me to look out for you. It's down to her that you're in this ward, you see. She knows people. Everyone in our ward will be on the same transport. That's the way it works.'

'Mrs Blake was here? When?'

'Two days after you came in, but new prisoners aren't allowed visitors or letters until they've settled a bit. The wailing gives everyone the collywobbles.'

Rhia could have wept. Antonia had been at Millbank. Margaret looked cautiously sympathetic. She shook her head in warning. 'Remember, no wobbles, Mahoney.' She jerked her head at Nora and company. 'They already think you're soft, so you'll need to toughen up, or at least pretend to. Tomorrow's a visiting day and you might have someone in.'

Rhia fought off the emotion. It was always only a breath away. 'How do you know Mrs Blake?'

'Quakers often visit. Saints the lot of 'em, but Mrs Blake especially, with her own troubles and all. She told me her maid has been poorly, though I can't say I'm surprised by it. She's not the full shilling anyway.'

'Juliette?'

'Barmy. Completely. She told me ... but I mustn't say – I promised I wouldn't.' Margaret looked disappointed. Presumably she was keeping some kind of secret for Juliette.

A morsel of gossip was suddenly of huge interest. 'It was something foolish?' she coaxed.

'Oh, *aye*. I'll tell you this much: Juliette gave me something to carry to Sydney, which is where I'm bound for, and if you were to see it, you'd know she was batty.'

Before Rhia could ask any more about Margaret's odd secret, or about Sydney, the clang of the iron bell at the gate to the yard interrupted them and they were rounded up and led back to their cells and their sewing.

By the time there was no light left to sew by, Rhia longed to sleep for ever. In fact, sleep was no friend in this place and she was often wakeful. At least she now knew why she had received no letter from home. Surely by now her mother would have heard from Dillon. What if Brigit was ashamed and couldn't bring herself to write? Rhia put the thought firmly from her mind. If nothing else in the world was true, then she could at least be sure of her mother's love.

Her thoughts turned to Laurence. Even if his advances had been mere flirtations, she still missed him. She might never see him again. He would not think her so desirable now. Her vanity was in tatters, like a bright print left in the weather to fade and tear.

The moon must almost be full, because a pale beam fell across the wooden cover of the washbasin and the shelf above it. In some of Mamo's old stories, the moon was the lantern of the Queen of the Night, whose name varied from story to story, from Anu to Cerridwen, Rhiannon and Cailleach. Rhia thought of Antonia's icons. Mary could also be Queen of the Night. The beam lit the shelf and the only reading material Rhia had seen in weeks, a Bible. She had barely noticed it and had not touched it. If the sighing shadows would not show themselves, then tonight, she decided, she would be Catholic. She reached for the moonlit holy book, before she could think better of it, and opened it randomly. The psalm she read made her close the book just as swiftly:

119:37 *Turn away mine eyes from beholding vanity and quicken thou me in thy way.*

There was no need to look for signs of spirit when they were pushed under your nose. She was not sure if she should feel comforted or reprimanded but for now at least she felt less alone. She slept until the morning bell.

The wardswoman Miss Hayter let herself in to Rhia's cell the next morning. Miss Hayter had shown her the unforgettable kindness of sitting with her on her first night, when Rhia was frightened and almost beside herself with loneliness and homesickness. She did not speak, but sat by the door with some sewing while Rhia sobbed herself to sleep in her hammock.

Miss Hayter was bird-like, plain and quietly spoken but, more than any other warden, she engendered respect amongst the women. Perhaps it was because she was diminutive, so not physically threatening, or because she seemed genuinely concerned for their well-being, or because she appeared to be able to look right through you when she spoke to you. Everyone liked her and wanted to be liked by her, Rhia included.

'You have a visitor, Mahoney.'

Antonia! Rhia almost felt light-hearted as she pulled on her cap and tied her apron strings. Miss Hayter waited quietly, watching with her earnest expression. 'I hear that you are a draughtswoman, Mahoney?' she said.

'I almost was.'

'Perhaps your skill will be useful to you, when we sail.'

'When we sail?'

'Why yes, have you not been told?'

'Told what?' A shiver crept up Rhia's spine.

'The ward has been assigned to the next transport, the

*Rajah*. It is to depart on April the fourth. I myself am to be the matron in charge.'

Rhia opened her mouth, mutely. Miss Hayter was watching her. 'It must seem sudden, but it does happen occasionally. There is a need for literate women in Australia, and particularly for women with a trade.'

'London needs women with a trade too, Miss Hayter, and women who are literate.'

The warden had the grace to look abashed.

'What is today's date?' Rhia whispered.

'It is March the twenty-sixth.'

'Then I have less than two weeks left.'

Miss Hayter nodded. 'There is great opportunity in Sydney, and for one such as yourself—' Rhia didn't hear the rest. She didn't want to hear praise for the colony, she could think only that two weeks wasn't enough time for an appeal to be made. She was not to be saved.

She followed Miss Hayter to the refectory where visitors had been shown. She looked for Antonia among the faces of the free. The people from outside were like brushstrokes of colour – a red scarf, a green hat, blue breeches.

Antonia was not here.

Then she saw Mr Dillon. She supposed he had visited a prison before because he seemed perfectly at ease. He had the good grace not to let his eyes stray to her prison uniform, nor to remark on her appearance. She recalled last night's lesson with some difficulty. His eyes held hers.

'Good morning, Miss Mahoney.'

'Good morning, Mr Dillon.' His face looked different. Though maybe she had never really examined it before. He was somewhere between the beginning and middle of his thirties, she thought, and had a light dusting of freckles on the pale skin of his nose, cheeks and forehead. His hair was as black as her own and tied back with a ribbon. His eyes were a mottle of mossy hazel, like a forest floor. He looked back at her, his eyebrows arched, and retrieved his pocket book from some hidden recess inside his long coat.

'I have word from your mother. I advised her to send any return correspondence to my address. I promised that I would honour its privacy and bring it safely to you. I have fulfilled both promises.' He passed the letter, hidden beneath his hand, across the table towards her and Rhia kept her eyes on his face.

'Is anyone watching?' she whispered as her hand touched his. He cast his eyes about the room and shook his head. He withdrew his hand and Rhia slipped her mother's letter into her apron pocket. A look of co-conspiracy passed between them. 'We are good at this,' she said. He nodded, but his smile quickly disappeared.

'I'll come straight to the point. I've set in motion an appeal to the crown, but it is a lengthy process and could take months. In my opinion, you were targeted to look guilty of this crime, and I'm in the throes of convincing Mr Montgomery of the fact. He says that his wife is certain that you stole the cloth and that you took the key to the storeroom.'

'But I did not! Mrs Montgomery gave the key to Isabella.'

'Prunella Montgomery is not a reliable witness,' Dillon agreed, but the Crown is not interested in that. Your defence was not present at the court, which is an abomination and a matter I've still not been able to get to the bottom of. Mrs Blake engaged one of the best counsels in London, but he will not receive me, nor answer my letters. Mrs Blake herself was going to visit you today, because we've not been allowed to see you before now, but apparently her maid has taken a fit of some kind.' He shook his head. 'It would appear that the maid doesn't want Mrs Blake to see you. At any rate, she will come next time.'

Rhia bent her head. 'Then Juliette will have her way and I will not see her. I have been assigned to a transport that sails to New South Wales on April the fourth. So you see, there is no hope.'

Dillon looked shocked, and then angry. But when he spoke his voice was low and even. 'That is very soon indeed, Miss Mahoney, but there is always hope.'

Rhia stared at her hands, noticing that her fingertips were scoured red from needlework and cold.

'There is something else,' he said quietly. 'I wish that I didn't have to be the one to tell you it.'

What could be worse than this?

'It concerns the death of your uncle.'

Rhia tensed. 'Please be direct, Mr Dillon.'

'Very well. I don't believe Ryan Mahoney's death was accidental.'

'Then you think he took his own life after all?'

'No. I believe he was murdered.'

The bell clanged but Rhia didn't stand.

Mr Dillon stood and bowed as though they were in a drawing room and he was her guest. He said something about Laurence Blake certainly being back in London before the *Rajah* sailed, and something about her belongings being delivered to Millbank, and then he was gone.

She was alone.

## II

# Silver

Behind Me – dips Eternity –
Before me – Immortality –
Myself – the Term between –
Death but the drift of Eastern Gray,
Dissolving into Dawn away,
Before the West begin –

'Tis Miracle before Me – then –
'Tis Miracle behind – between –
A Crescent in the Sea –
With Midnight to the North of Her –
And Midnight to the South of Her –
And Maelstrom – in the Sky

*Emily Dickinson*

# 4 April 1841

A murmur rippled along the procession of rowing boats. The *Rajah* was little more than a dark triangle in the mist, but it was as chilling a sight as a prison van emerging from a London fog. Each creak of the oars brought it closer.

The form of a barque took shape.

The rhythm of the dipping oars gave way to the collision of steely waves against timbers. Above was the mournful cry of gulls. A hush descended as the boats neared the towering hull of the transport.

Further away, through the salty mist, was something even worse, something that made the transport seem like a paper sailing boat by comparison: a dark battalion of leviathans anchored a league away by great chains, each link the size of a carriage wheel.

Hulks.

Finally, something to be grateful for – better to be sent into the unknown than to end up on a prison hulk. A chorus of Hail Marys caught on the wind to be whipped away.

One by one, the rowing boats pulled in to the *Rajah*'s shadow. A rope ladder appeared over the ship's railings, lowered down for the wardens and prisoners to scale the creaking hull to the deck. One by one each woman took her turn and ascended the swinging rope lattice with instructions shouted from above not to look down.

Not that they could help it. The prancing ocean demanded an audience. It might rise up and coil a wave around an unwary ankle. Someone froze midway and was first cajoled and then ordered to keep climbing until finally, tearfully, she crawled up and over the banister at the top.

The rowing boats were eventually empty, and every woman – whether by mettle or by coercion – had reached the deck.

# Hemp

Nelly was still fiercely whispering her Hail Marys as the last of the women assembled on the main deck. Rhia counted each prayer as though it were a rosary bead, until she lost count. There was no chance of freedom now. She looked at the sky, the same sky that stretched above Cloak Lane and Greystones, yet not the same at all. This low, leaden sky was the ceiling of another prison.

In silhouette against it were three masts. Rhia counted the sails. It was something to do. There were six, she thought, though she couldn't be sure because they were furled. She didn't yet want to inspect the rest of the vessel that would carry her away to another world. To the Otherworld. Men hung from the rigging of each mast like monkeys from a tree. She lowered her gaze quickly. They were making her dizzy.

There were too many sailors to keep track of, scurrying about like barefooted clerks. At first, they appeared to be too busy to have noticed the one hundred and fifty women standing on the lilting deck, but close scrutiny revealed this was not the case. The women were each being assessed expertly and craftily. Every time Rhia caught a seaman's eye, it darted away as if his gaze had landed on her by accident rather than by design. The seamen were a motley bunch – some willowy, others brawny, some smooth and youthful, others weathered kegs.

Rhia counted eight penitentiary officers and wardens, all women, standing in a huddle, being addressed by someone who might have been a ship's officer. He was dressed for the town, and although Miss Hayter had mentioned that there were a small number of civilian passenger berths on the *Rajah*, this man seemed to be someone more significant to the ship. He had an air of authority as starched as his sober brown coat. Miss Hayter was listening to him compliantly, as though he were her superior.

Rhia wanted to bend double against the gnawing anxiety, but she pushed her hands deep into the pockets of her apron and focused on keeping her legs rigid against the tilting of the deck. She tried to locate Margaret amongst the women. Her frizz of orange hair was usually easy to spot. She was behind the swarthy Agnes, almost obscured by the sheer volume of Nora. Before Rhia could catch her eye, the huddle of officers and wardens dispersed and the prisoners were arranged into a queue and directed across the main deck and up a short flight of stairs to a smaller, elevated deck which someone called the quarterdeck.

The quarterdeck looked over the rest of the ship, the perfect place to observe the deck below. Rhia had run out of things to count. She took in details, focusing on the minutiae of wood-work and brass, from the banisters, railings and instruments, to the wide oak timbers of the decking. Everything shone and smelt of linseed and wax. It was hard to believe that this gleam-ing vessel was in the charge of men: the ship was as clean and polished as if an army of maids lived on it.

The penitentiary officers and Miss Hayter flanked the rows of women. One of the wardens was reading what looked to be a roll, and kept glancing up to scan their faces. At the opposite end of the deck was a small cluster of men, a few of them in

seafaring costume. The most elderly was a sour-faced clergy-
man. He was talking to the gentleman in the brown coat.
Perhaps the latter was some kind of representative of the courts
– he had the dour air of the prosecutor who had sentenced
Rhia. The captain was easily identified by his battered and old-
fashioned tricorne hat and by the braided epaulettes on his
coat. He had the same ruddy complexion and wispy greying
curls as the Greystones baker, and for this Rhia liked him
immediately. The tall, stern-looking man beside him must be
the ship's surgeon with his pale hands and aura of calm authority. Two young boys in blue serge doublets and ragged breeches
stood a short distance away, casting furtive glances at the
women. Presumably the officer's servants.

Several barefoot seamen started lugging hemp sacks up the
stairs. Many were foreign-looking, their skin anything from
pitch black to pale olive. A few had shaven heads and many had
tattoos on their forearms and wore only canvas breeches held
up with a piece of rope. Rhia was not alone in taking an interest. The other women swivelled their heads to get a better view,
whispering bawdy comments to each other, some even risking
a laugh. There were half-naked men on the *Rajah*. Things were
looking up.

Their appreciation quietened down as their little matron
moved amongst the rows, pausing to have a quiet word with
Nelly who was more distressed than usual. She was the youngest of the women, only seventeen and, Rhia had recently
learned, pregnant. Miss Hayter was holding her hand and
whispering to her reassuringly. The matron was just as strict
and uncompromising as any of the other wardens, but she was
rarely harsh. She had about her the solitary, vaguely disappointed air of a spinster, though her age was difficult to judge.
More than thirty but less than fifty, Rhia thought. She was

plain, in a drab, restrained sort of way, but not plug-ugly like many of the other guards. She wondered if it was requisite that female wardens be mannish and curt, or if they were made so by their profession. Presumably the wardens on the *Rajah* were migrating to Australia. None of them, besides Miss Hayter, looked familiar to Rhia. Perhaps they thought they had a better chance of finding a husband in the colonies where, by all accounts, there was a desperate shortage of females.

Miss Hayter stopped beside Rhia. 'Come and see me after you've been assigned your belongings, Mahoney.'

A glimmer of hope, but Rhia regretted the temptation of optimism instantly. It was too late for salvation. She nodded and turned her head away. She looked at a growing mound of hemp sacks. They probably contained their new uniforms. Still cut of coarse cloth, no doubt. She didn't care to speculate on what other provisions the Quakers deemed necessary for a sea journey that might last anywhere from three to six months.

As soon as all of the sacks had been delivered to the deck, Miss Hayter clapped her hands. 'Collect a bag as I call your name and you will be shown below.'

Rhia waited. The women in her row collected their new belongings and disappeared down the back stairs, each hauling a sack behind. She supposed the stairs led to the lower decks. Nora glared at her as she passed, followed closely by a scowling Agnes. Agnes was always a step behind Nora, and in fawning agreement with her on every matter from the optimum consistency for gruel to the correct number of stitches per yard of linsey. Rhia dropped her head. Not looking Nora in the eye was the best form of protection. Someone brushed past, elbowing her. Rhia looked up quickly. It was Margaret, who winked. It was a small gesture, but a welcome sign of solidarity.

Rhia approached Miss Hayter. She willed herself not to hope. To think of nothing. Not to expect a thing.

'Ah, Mahoney.' Miss Hayter looked pleased about something. 'You are to be assigned to private service for the voyage. There is a botanist travelling to Sydney who has requested a servant. Your name was put forward.'

Rhia didn't know what to say. She had not expected this.

'You must see it as a blessing, Mahoney,' Miss Hayter assured her. 'You'll have a servant's cabin rather than sleeping in steerage with the other women.' The matron lowered her voice. 'It has not escaped our attention that you're unpopular. Confinement often stirs up resentment. It will be better for all if you have separate quarters.'

Rhia wasn't sure about this. She suspected that it was a mixed blessing, but for now she was relieved. But what sort of servant did a botanist require? Was she to be his maid? Was it Miss Hayter who had put her name forward?

'You can collect your things, now,' said the matron briskly. 'Your sack will have your name on it. By the way, I put something into it before we left Millbank, a package that was delivered along with your portmanteau. The gentleman said that Mrs Blake thought you'd like to have it on the voyage.' Miss Hayter looked at her sternly for a moment. 'I don't usually allow this kind of thing, Mahoney, but since you'll have private quarters I see no harm in it.' She looked across the quarterdeck to where the two officer's servants were loitering. 'One of the boys will show you the way.'

Rhia collected her sack, as instructed, and the younger of the two boys approached her with a cocky swagger. He looked ten or eleven, with smooth brown skin and chestnut curls streaked by the sun. 'I'm the midshipman on this tub, but you can call me Albert if you like,' he said and mock-bowed.

Albert was irritatingly cheerful and she couldn't see what he had to be so pleased about.

'Pleased to meet you,' she said warily.

'You don't look too pleased. A lady, are ye?'

Her laugh sounded bitter, even to her own ears. 'Would I be here if I were a lady?'

He shrugged. 'You talk different to the rest of the cargo.' He gestured with this thumb downwards. 'Got a name?'

'I have.'

'Let's have it then.'

'Mahoney.'

'*Mahoney?* Hmm.'

Rhia looked at Albert suspiciously. He seemed a little too savvy for his years. 'I suppose you've been on other prison ships?'

'Aye, but not this 'un. She's been in the dry docks up Aberdeen. She's clean as a whistle, now. Last transport I was on, the bilge had a stink to wake the dead. They used to be much worse, though – prison ships, that is. The likes of you weren't allowed on the deck and there were shackles and scores who perished.'

Rhia shivered at the blandness of his tone, as though the death of convicts was barely notable. 'Then we'll be allowed on deck?'

'I 'spect so. There's laws now, y'see. The men don't like it, but I don't mind.'

'The sailors you mean?'

'*Seamen.* They don't mind lookin' you over, or havin' you in their hammock, but they don't want you in the way on deck.'

'What is the bilge?' she asked, as if she cared.

'Never mind, ye'll see. They said you're to stay in your cabin till you're called to the mess.'

'The mess?' Was this to be her first task? How much mess could a botanist make in his first hours onboard?

'Aye, that's where the lot of 'em sleep and where ye'll get your supper and such. It's ten or a dozen together, that's the usual way. The passengers board later and the captain don't like them to see the prisoners, so you're to keep out of sight.'

They had descended two flights of slippery stairs and were now on a lower deck where a narrow passageway led around a built-in area of the ship. The passenger deck, Rhia guessed.

'Here's yours,' Albert said. They were outside a low, narrow door at the aft end of the deck. Rhia held her breath and clutched her sack as she stepped inside. The 'cabin' was little more than a cupboard, smaller than her cell at Millbank. It was windowless, and it took her a moment to adjust to the low light. There was space enough for a hammock and a shelf, and there were two iron hooks on the only narrow strip of wall. It smelt of damp rope.

Albert was still grinning when she caught his eye, but there was something that might have been pity beneath his affected chirpiness. In this virtually friendless existence, even the sympathy of a free-spirited boy was welcome. Rhia attempted to smile back but the muscles of her face were frozen with emotion.

'You've only to take a step or two,' he said, 'and ye can look at the sea and the sky and ye'll not find *that* in London!' Presumably Albert thought this might be of some comfort to her. How could he know that the sea was the last thing she'd look at to feel comforted. When he was gone, she leant against the naked timbers of the wall, and let all pretence dissolve.

She took off her cap, and put it on the shelf as carefully as if she was arranging a lace doily. The emotion rushed at her without warning. It took her legs first, weakening her knees.

She slid down the wall until she was crouching and put her head in her hands. She tried to think of reasons to be grateful. She was not on a prison hulk, she was not sentenced to death, she was not ill, she was not pregnant. But the tide would not be stopped. It claimed her and she sobbed until she was emptied out and her body was limp.

When the emotion had passed, the only thing to look at, besides her tears on the floorboards, was the lumpy canvas sack beside her. Rhia wiped her eyes on her apron and untied the length of cord that fastened it. She leaned closer to read what was embroidered onto the hem along the neck of the sack. It was a reminder that this was a benevolent offering from *The Convict Ship Committee of the British Society of Ladies.* She would have wept some more but she was spent.

At the top of the sack was a flat, square package wrapped in brown paper. This must be the parcel received for her at Millbank, presumably delivered by Dillon. She unwrapped it. Her red book and, fastened to its spine with a ribbon, Mamo's pen and a small silver key. It took her a moment to realise that this was the key to her portmanteau. She put the book gently on the shelf. She was not so alone after all. The next item was, predictably, a Bible. She placed this to one side. She may never dare to open another Bible. She removed a hessian apron, and then another of black cotton; a black cotton cap; a comb; two stay laces; a knife and fork; a ball of string. Next was a hessian bag for linen and a smaller one containing pins, needles and sewing cotton in black, white, red and blue. There were two balls of black worsted and multiple hanks of coloured thread. There were darning needles, a bodkin, a thimble and a pair of scissors.

The rest of the sack was filled with patchwork pieces – the scrap cloth and remains that Antonia and her Friends had been collecting from tailors and clothiers and mercers, including the Montgomery emporium. Rhia managed a small, wry smile. Who would have thought that she would be the beneficiary of Quaker prison reform.

She folded her aprons and cap onto the shelf, and arranged the other items next to them. She would save the pleasure of inspecting weaves and prints for another time since there was nothing else to look forward to. Her limbs felt heavy, and her heart empty, but she was composed. She had weathered her first storm.

It occurred to Rhia that there was no point in sitting on the floor when there was a perfectly good hammock to lie in. She climbed into it with some difficulty and pulled a blanket over herself. It smelt mildewed and was rough on her skin, but if she closed her eyes she could just imagine the feel of cambric sheets and soft eider quilts.

If today were a cloth it would be sailcloth.

# Twill

The rapping knocked through the dream of a hammock swinging above a pit of sea serpents. It was a half-waking dream, but Rhia was still relieved to put her feet on the solid timber floor. Then the floor moved. She kept her legs braced and leaned across to open the door. It was the other boy, the steward. He was gangly and hunched and seemed shy and unsure of himself. He was two or three years older than Albert, she judged, but had none of the midshipman's pluck. He held his dirty wool cap in his hands, agitating it as he spoke.

'You're wanted in the passenger saloon.'

Rhia followed the steward along the timber railings towards the prow for almost the entire length of the lower passenger deck, and then up a short flight of stairs, marvelling at his steady gait. The light had improved, and the hulks were visible. They only looked more sinister for their visibility, and a very real reason to feel grateful. Beyond, the shore of Woolwich where a tangle of vessels was moored – tall-masted merchant-men, pretty little sloops with brightly painted prows. Rhia quickly looked away from land and freedom.

The passenger saloon was an airy, spacious room, with windows all along one side and freshly lacquered woodwork. There were oil paintings of ships and palm-fringed islands on the walls and an upholstered divan at either end with a mahogany occasional table bolted to the floor nearby. It was like a drawing room and a dining room combined. A slight, fair-haired man stood with his back to her, inspecting one of the paintings. The botanist, presumably. The steward had already disappeared.

The man turned. His skin was as delicate as porcelain and his face characterless, though not unpleasant. He was, she judged, much the same age as she was, which surprised her. She'd expected someone older. He had an air of downtrodden respectability that suited his vocation. His morning coat was of good quality twill, but worn and old-fashioned. A naturalist needed a patron if his vocation was to become a profession. Though perhaps Mr Reeve had found himself one, to be under-taking such a long voyage? He was inspecting her, as well. He took a deep breath before he spoke, as if to steady his nerves.

'Miss Mahoney?'

'Mr Reeve?' He nodded. He was struggling to know what to say, and Rhia didn't feel like helping. She might have, once. She waited. She had all the time on God's earth. Except that she was no longer on the earth, she remembered, she was in Manannán's realm now.

'I hope we can work well together,' he managed finally, lamely.

Rhia almost laughed at the absurdity of the situation. She supposed she would have to rescue him after all. 'What sort of work do you do, Mr Reeve?'

He laughed nervously. 'Of course. Foolish of me. I have a ... sizable collection of preserved flora – herbs, seed pods et cetera, et cetera – that I am cataloguing. I intend to establish a research provision in Sydney, to study the plant life of the Antipodes and compare it with that of the Continent.'

When he spoke of his work and his ambition he was almost engaging and Rhia didn't have to feign interest. 'It must be exciting, making botanical discoveries. But I still don't understand why you need my assistance.'

'You were recommended.' He coughed self-consciously, as though to play down the admission. Could it have been Antonia who requested that she be assigned to private service on the *Rajah*? Maybe it didn't matter who had recommended her.

Mr Reeve hurried on. 'I'm told you will be required to undertake sewing duties with the other women. Shall we devise a schedule – if this is suitable?'

Rhia snorted before she could stop herself. 'You're forgetting that I am a prisoner, Mr Reeve. I must do as I am told.'

He looked perplexed, but he nodded. 'Very well. I will confer with Miss Hayter. Um, you are … dismissed.'

Rhia dug her fingernails into the palms of her hands as she walked back along the rocking leeway to her cabin. She had *asked* for that. She was a prisoner *and* a servant, and her self-respect had already failed her. It had happened so naturally. If she wasn't careful her spirit would be snuffed out entirely. Ironic that she'd so recently thought she didn't know who she was any more. At least she had established that Mr Reeve did not understand irony. She would be more cautious in the future.

She experimented with a wide gait until she reached her cabin. Each footfall touched the deck before she expected it. It made her sick to think that, in more ways than one, the Otherworld was rising up to meet her. She cast a furtive look to the sea. It was dove grey and as smooth as silk. The cloth that she had named the morning after the fire. If this was the reason that Mamo had sent her away then it served her right for listening to a ghost.

The sails had been unfurled. Rhia counted them. Five were square and rigged to the main and mizzen masts, and one was small and triangular; rigged aft. She barely noticed the two hurrying seamen who brushed past her, though the funk of sweat and damp canvas lingered after them. She felt the rigging shudder and then the rhythmic rocking motion of the great hull. They were hauling anchor.

She hurried, as best she could, back to her hutch. When she was safely in her hammock, she fixed her gaze on the ceiling. She would not, she *could* not watch the shoreline disappear, and with it all of her hopes. No one and nothing could save her now.

*You must save yourself.*

How could she save herself? She closed her eyes and saw her own wretched form, huddled and swaying in the hammock. She saw the entire ship, sails set and masts as straight and tall as watchtowers.

*The watchtowers are places between the world of men and the Otherworld. Wild honey drips from the forest's trees, and there are endless stocks of mead and wine. No illness comes from across the seas, nor death nor pain nor sad decline.*

Rhia sat up, her heart pounding. The hammock was swinging wildly. She looked around. It was not Mamo's voice, it was her own… Was it little Rhia the fey that she kept sensing, with some message from the past?

Rhia reached into the pocket of her apron and closed her hand over the fold of paper there. She had read the letter Dillon had delivered many times now and always kept it in her pocket. She unfolded it carefully.

20 March 1841

My dear,

I am in haste to catch the last post so I must be brief. I have longed to come to you, but your father is so frail. Lately he thinks he sees Mamo at night in her long johns and old shawl. He says that she is not pleased to have him in her cottage. I have told him again and again that Mamo has been dead years, and that if she were going to show herself to anyone then it would be to you. When you were wee, you believed that you could travel between the Otherworld and the world of men, just like the Rhiannon of the stories. Mamo always said that this was why you were afraid of the sea – that within it you saw the reflection of your true self.

I am comforted only by the certainty of your innocence and the belief that it will be proven. Mr Dillon has explained to me the circumstances of your arrest. He seems genuinely concerned for your welfare, and this also is a comfort. I hope that I may one day meet him.

The world will spill her sorrows time and time again. Mamo would say that it is in ourselves, not in the church, that we find what is Holy. In this, she and I did not always agree, but you are a woman now and can decide for yourself. You are always in my heart.

I will always be,
Your loving mother,

Brigit Mahoney

Rhia folded the letter carefully and put it back in her pocket. She took her book from the shelf that she could reach without leaving the hammock, and untied the ribbon around her silver pen. The little key to her trunk was still fastened to it with a tight knot. The ribbon was long enough to tie around her neck so that the key was hidden by her underclothing. The cartridge of the pen was full of ink, she could tell by its weight. She looked at the delicate engravings on its shank, the looping pattern of the three-way knot. This symbol stood for all that was holy, if you believed in the old stories. The knot was the three fates: past, present and future. It stood for the trinity of spirit, mind and physical body long before the trinity of Father, Son and Holy Spirit was conceived. It represented the three phases of the moon, by which the tides – of oceans and of women – were measured. It was, some said, the triple goddess.

The red book felt thicker than it should. A piece of cloth had become lodged in its pages. Rhia removed the fold and opened it out, staring at it in confusion. It was her chintz, the sampler that Thomas had woven for her. The square of patterned linen lay like a window to a place where there were brilliant birds and flowering, curling branches bright with berries.

19 April 1841

Albert assures me that he's never known anyone to die of seasickness, which surprises me. The simple engineering of the knotted and looped ropes that suspend the hammock offsets the tilt of the keel, so as the ship rolls across the waves, the hammock remains stable. More or less. The stomach does not. Albert says the sickness is something to do with the balance between my belly and the belly of the ship. He delivers my ration of three pints of fresh water every morning (without spilling a drop, he says) and his is almost the only face I've seen, besides Miss Hayter, who looks in every day and gives me arrowroot biscuits and ginger cordial, the ship's surgeon's remedy for nausea. Miss Hayter tells me that half of the women below and most of the wardens are incapacitated, so it has been impossible to begin any kind of regimen. She seems disappointed. If there's one thing I've come to realise about her character, it is her love of order and routine. She is perfectly suited to her profession.

As to my daily ration of water, I may choose either to drink it or wash in it. Albert advises drinking it, since there is plenty of seawater for washing. He says that the sickness *should* run its course before we arrive in Brazil, though he's known some who've passed the time between Woolwich and Rio bent double over the railings. No sea legs at all, apparently. It is, by his account, a four week voyage to Rio, so we must be almost halfway there already. I am better today, but it has still taken the better part of an hour to write this, and it is crooked and the ink has run.

I'd best be sparing with ink, I've no idea how or when I might obtain more.

# Knots

Albert rapped on her door whilst Rhia was gingerly placing one foot in front of another and holding onto the wall.

'If you're up and about, Mahoney, your matron says you're to come up on deck. I'll wait for you, if you want.'

At least illness had provided refuge from the others, and from Mr Reeve. Rhia groaned as she pulled a stiff black calico cap over her cropped hair, and tied the dour black apron around her uniform. The coarse blend of wool and flax irritated her skin more than usual, but it was warm. Not, of course, in the same way as the soft stroke of cashmere petticoats against silk stockings. It seemed that she'd been cold for ever. In Millbank, the damp from the river stone seeped into everything; air, clothing and bones. Her clothing was heavy with the perennial moisture of Manannán's domain. Now they were due south, at least the temperature should improve, if nothing else.

Albert was his usual chirpy self. He'd been feeding her morsels of gossip to keep her mind from her miseries. She'd heard of the first tryst, between a galley hand and a convict, and knew that the preacher, Reverend Boswell, had a bad case of flatus. Or as Albert called it, 'tooting'. Albert said he'd never heard anything like it, and that he'd had the bad luck to be downwind more than once. There was, according to Albert, a passenger who went on the deck early in the morning to lay pieces of parchment in the sun.

'He's not right in the head, that's what I reckon,' Albert said, pointing out a coil of rope on the deck so that Rhia wouldn't trip over it. Then he stood still, looking over the sea. 'Will you look at that, Mahoney,' he said, pointing out across the waves. She followed the line of his finger, and saw a loop of silver, and then another, and a line of large fins carving through the waves. 'That'll be porpoises,' said Albert. 'You don't normally see them in this latitude, they're usually closer to the South Americas. They've come 'specially to say hello, I s'pose.'

This made Rhia smile. 'Well after all,' she said without thinking, 'Rhiannon was the wife of Manannán, and queen of the sea.'

Albert looked at her as if she was speaking Greek. 'Manna-who?'

'The king of the sea.'

'You mean Triton.'

'The same.'

Albert looked at her suspiciously. 'Then who's Rena—?'

'Rhiannon. I was named for her.'

Albert frowned. 'What's her game?'

'She could restore the dead to life and lull the living to death.'

Albert let out a low whistle and looked at Rhia suspiciously. Then, as though he thought better of standing so close to the deck railings with her, he set off hastily along the side of the ship he called leeward. Rhia followed gingerly, keeping her gait wide and her gaze anywhere but on those capering waves.

The assembly for morning prayer was small, fewer than fifty prisoners and no passengers. Albert paused before they reached the top of the last, short flight of stairs before the quarterdeck. 'Rev Tooting says he's returning to his flock in the colony, so I suppose he's got some merino.' Rhia laughed aloud.

Albert looked surprised, either because he'd never heard her laugh or because he hadn't been joking. He shook his head. 'Never known there to be a preacher on board a transport.' He added, 'Captain says it's a good omen.'

Albert left Rhia to climb the last few stairs on her own, and she felt his absence acutely. He had succeeded in lightening her heart. She took her place at the back of the ragged assembly. The sour smell of sickness hung in the air. She probably reeked of it herself. Reverend Boswell droned his lesson, a sermon on deliverance from sin and damnation. She wondered if the deliverance of a shipload of sinners to the colonies counted as redemption.

Rhia soon lost interest in the sermon and edged a little closer to the brass railings of the quarterdeck so that she could see more of the main deck. There was ceaseless activity. A command was passed from the bow of the ship to the mate or the bosun – she was not sure which – and then to a sailor who scurried up the rigging and adjusted a sail. The bosun kept his eye to the sails, to judge any change in the direction of the wind, Rhia supposed. She looked up, following his gaze. It was astonishing that these men could read the wind and the sea so that a ship could travel, at speed, to the farthest reaches of the earth. For a moment she felt a sense of wonder, rather than horror, at the thought of what she was undertaking.

When the sermon was over, Rhia did her best to fall in with the others as they filed behind a warden on their way back to the mess. They descended four short flights of stairs, through two lower decks and past dark, musty recesses 'tween decks. Their destination was a hatch in the floor of the lower passenger deck, from which the tip of a ladder protruded.

Before she even put her boot on the top rung of the ladder, Rhia smelt the stale air below. On a passenger vessel, the orlop was assigned to those travelling at the cheapest rate, along with livestock, luggage and provisions. On a merchantman such as the *Rajah*, it was also the part of the ship that would be used for transporting cargo. On this occasion, human cargo.

She descended into the dark, airless space below feeling increasingly fortunate to have her hutch. More reason to feel grateful. Her eyes slowly became accustomed to the dim interior of the hull. Eventually she could make out that the length of the ship's lower chamber was divided up into partitions by sailcloth. She glimpsed two other messes and could now see two rows of six hammocks hanging from the great struts of oak that supported the deck above. A long table, with benches at either side, was bolted to the floor in between.

Several of the hammocks looked like large brown cocoons which occasionally issued a moan. The odour of sickness was almost overwhelming in this stuffy, confined space. On the table sat pewter bowls, a cast iron pot and a plate of hard, dry biscuits. The stale smell and the sight of food did nothing for the delicate balance between Rhia's belly and that of the ship.

Most of the women who had attended prayer passed through the first mess to one of the identical chambers running the length of the orlop. A few stayed and sat at the table in the first mess. Rhia didn't know what to do, so she stood back from the ladder, against a small patch of bare timber hull, and waited to see what would happen next.

'You might as well stay in this mess, Mahoney,' said the warden irritably when she noticed Rhia. The woman was skinny and beak-nosed and enjoyed being in charge. Amongst the half-dozen women who were now around the table, Rhia recognized Nell, Agnes and Jane. She sat beside Jane, who was tall and angular and stooped a little. She was habitually gloomy and silent but, if provoked, could conjure an impressive tantrum.

'Mahoney,' barked Beak Nose, with her sinewy arms crossed over her flat chest, 'sit at the table. You'll eat your meals here in Mess One, and there'll be instruction for you all from your mess captain this morning.' At least she would not have to venture any further into the belly of the ship. It was bad enough here, even with the hatch open.

No one at the table spoke to her, which was probably because of Agnes. Agnes was the only prisoner Rhia knew of who had darker skin than her own. She prayed that Nora was not in one of the brown cocoons.

Rhia's stomach protested at the mere sight of the sticky gruel. She slipped some of the hard, soda biscuits into her apron pocket. Afterwards, two women cleared the pewter utensils into a pail, and helped each other hoist it up the ladder to the deck. The others took out their sewing. Beak Nose lit a lantern, which illuminated the dim corners of the mess, but barely made it less gloomy. Rhia had never much liked the slick smell of lamp oil and wick but now she inhaled it as though it were tea rose.

She cast her eyes around warily. The chamber was neat, with a hook beside each hammock and a low shelf to fold belongings onto. She scanned the hammocks for clues about their inhabitants, and thought she saw a frizz of orange hair poking out of one. It could be Margaret.

The women were talking amongst themselves with the ease that comes from sharing every waking hour. Rhia listened silently. As usual, she felt that she was trespassing amongst those who had earned their sentences through poverty or cunning. She hoped that she was as invisible as she felt, but she knew she wasn't because she sensed Jane's eyes on her intermittently. She felt awkward and miserable sitting with nothing to do and no one to talk to.

A sharp jab in her ribs from Jane's bony finger made her jump. She slipped a piece of patchwork onto Rhia's lap and put a needle and thread on the table in front of her. When Rhia stole a look at her, Jane was innocently absorbed in her own needlework.

Agnes was retelling the tale of her arrest. Everyone had heard it before, but it acquired more vibrancy at each telling. Today, the constable who had pursued Agnes to the St Giles brothel, finding her dressed only in her stays and bloomers, was far more handsome than at the last telling, and she more saucy.

'So I hid the banknotes – the ones I took from *herself*, and I put them in my garter,' she said. Rhia was sure Agnes had hidden the stolen banknotes in her corsage last time, rather than in her stockings, but no one seemed to care. She was a natural storyteller with her Gypsy ancestry, and she made them laugh. The Mess had already formed a sisterhood. She had felt less alone in her hutch.

Miss Hayter's sturdy black boots and brown wool stockings appeared through the hatch and descended the ladder. When she had found her balance after a tilt of the floor, she looked around, her eyes resting on Rhia.

'Fetch your sewing things, Mahoney,' she said briskly. 'Now that enough of you are on your feet, we will start working on a quilt together.'

Rhia felt light-hearted at the prospect of a few moments alone in the light and air. She climbed to the deck wondering how she would ever survive weeks and months of this. In prison there had always at least been the idea of freedom, with the horses' hooves on the cobbles of Newgate Street, or the sounds of river traffic drifting across the water at Millbank. Here there was only ocean and sky.

And Mr Reeve.

The botanist was standing at the deck rail not far from her cabin door, gazing across corrugations of steely water. Rhia came as close as she dared to the railings and noticed that he held a pocketbook. He was intent on sketching something, a sea bird perhaps, but he looked frustrated. When he saw her he snapped the book shut quickly.

'Miss Mahoney. I am pleased to see that you are improved.'

'You weren't ill yourself?'

He shook his head. 'I'm not afflicted. I was, at first. I spent much of a voyage to the Greek Islands in my bunk.'

Rhia gestured to his pocketbook. 'Were you drawing?' He shook his head and looked embarrassed. 'Only scribbling. I am a poor illustrator – a calamity in my profession.'

'I suppose it is,' she agreed. 'I am expected below. I must ...'

'Of course. Yes. Ah, Miss Hayter has agreed to release you after lunch each day. I will be in the passenger saloon at one o'clock.'

'Is that where we will be working?' She was relieved. She had feared they might be alone together in his cabin.

'The captain has agreed to assign an empty cabin. I am travelling with rather a large number of samples, you see.'

Rhia's heart sank, but she was not going to make the mistake of waiting to be dismissed again. 'I will see you at one o'clock.' She hurried away.

In her cabin, she collected her sewing bag and as many patchwork pieces as would fit in her apron pocket. She wondered which half of the day she would come to dread more, mornings in the orlop or afternoons with Mr Reeve. She hoped, at least, to catch sight of Margaret soon.

Below, two more women had joined the sewing circle. One of them was Nora. Rhia braced herself, but Nora was still too ill to cast even a withering look at her. In fact, she had to be commended for even getting to the table.

Miss Hayter cleared her throat and straightened her back as though she were addressing a regiment rather than a few women only an arm's reach away. 'We are blessed that, by the good grace and hard work of the ladies of the Convict Ship Society, there will be no idle hands on this voyage. In two weeks' time, if the wind stays behind us, the *Rajah* will put into the harbour of Rio de Janeiro, in the Portuguese kingdom of Brazil.' She said this as though it were a great privilege to visit another kingdom on a prison ship.

'Any quilt finished in time will be sold in the São Sebastiao market in Rio, and the proceeds will be returned to the mess who sewed it. I hasten to add that these wages will be kept in trust, to avoid ... loss during the voyage. You will be supervised daily in groups, on the quarterdeck, so that you have fresh air and sufficient light to sew by.'

It was then ascertained whom amongst them were the most skilled needlewomen. Of the eight now at the table, both Jane and Nell had been seamstresses, Nora, surprisingly, a stay maker, Agnes a bonnet maker, and someone else a muslin sewer.

Miss Hayter proceeded to reel off a list of rules. No woman was allowed on deck without permission; there would be no gambling and no selling of clothes or other possessions; there would be weekly assignations from each mess to collect provisions from the galley and a daily rota for washing dishes and utensils. Each woman must attend to her own laundry and under *no circumstance* must fresh water be used for this purpose. Seawater was perfectly adequate and available in abundance (as though they needed reminding). Finally, each woman was expected to conduct herself in a quiet, orderly and respectful manner, and a list of dissenters would be kept by the surgeon superintendent, and delivered to the governor's office when they arrived in Sydney.

The daily routine formed another set of commandments. At daylight, roll up and stow hammocks and bedclothes. At half past six, clean the water closets, decks and messes – only then would they be issued their daily allowance of drinking water, along with a ration of biscuits. Then, the surgeon would visit any who were ill. Breakfast was at eight a.m., followed by more cleaning. Then it was time to sew. In fair weather the sewing would take place on the quarterdeck, otherwise, below. There was a specific time for the issue of the allowance of lime juice against scurvy, and a time for a healthful dose of wine. ('Hally-bloody-lujah,' said Agnes under her breath.) Tuesdays and Fridays were laundry days. Wednesday was for bathing. In seawater. After eight-thirty p.m. they were forbidden to talk or make noise of any kind.

The morning saw neat hems sewn around patchwork pieces in poor light. Lunch was a stew of salted beef with hanks of coarse bread. Nora still hadn't uttered a word. She sat scowling at her sewing, a film of sweat on her face and neck. She was, happily, still too unwell to be her usual tyrannical self.

Rhia's afternoon with Mr Reeve drew closer with every stitch. Being a servant, she supposed that she should not have an opinion about anything. She supposed she was capable of not having an opinion. The only thing that comforted her was the knowledge that he, like she, had no idea what to make of the arrangement.

After lunch Rhia almost navigated the route to the passenger saloon without getting lost. She found herself at the neck of a dark, narrow passageway when she thought she should be at a flight of stairs 'tween decks. The passageway smelt of boiled cabbage, so presumably she was close to the galley. She felt unreasonably pleased with herself when she finally stumbled across the passenger saloon's small white door. Should she knock or just enter? While she hesitated, a cabin door opened further along the passenger deck and a man started walking towards her. She recognised him as the man in the brown coat towards whom Miss Hayter had seemed so deferential. His appearance wasn't noteworthy, but for his tallow-wax complexion and bland expression, but he did appear to be taking as much interest in her as she was in him, and he now looked displeased. 'Have you permission to be on an upper deck?' he said officiously.

'Are you an officer of this ship?' she retorted, without thinking.

'I am the agent of her majesty's government on this ship. My name is Mr Wardell.'

'It isn't enough that we are lackeys to prison guards and ship's officers? Are we also under the command of Whitehall?' It might have been wise to at least appear to be humbled. She would quickly be on the governor's blacklist at this rate. Mr Wardell's expression barely changed, apart from the elevation of an eyebrow.

'Your name?'

'Mahoney. I am assigned to private service. I have an appointment with Mr Reeve in the saloon.'

'Very well. Carry on.' Wardell opened the door of the saloon and went in himself, not bothering to allow her in first, or even hold the door.

Two ladies sat on one of the divans sipping on steaming glasses. They were dressed in pretty travelling costumes and white lace gloves. Rhia could smell hot chocolate and sweet pastry and it made her mouth water. She must be recovering. She'd give anything for a slice of Beth's ginger loaf. The ladies looked through her. She *was* invisible after all.

Rhia scanned the few small clusters of gentlemen standing and seated around tables, talking and smoking cigars, before she saw Mr Reeve. He had his back to her and was hunched over a table in the corner of the room. Beside him, and also with his back to Rhia, was a tall, rumpled man with untidy, dark blond hair. Her heart jolted painfully. He reminded her of Laurence Blake.

The man turned.

The world stood still.

It was Laurence. Rhia opened her mouth and then closed it again quickly. She made herself keep walking, through a coil of cigar smoke, past a silver platter of dainty sandwiches. She didn't know what else to do. Laurence had been expecting her. His expression said that she should give nothing away. Somehow, she managed to cross the room, keeping her eyes carefully averted from his face.

Mr Reeve nodded to her indifferently, as though he were experimenting with his authority. 'Good afternoon, miss. Mr Blake and I were just discussing the very subtle differences between these specimens. Mr Blake is a professional of photogenic drawing.' Mr Reeve was a little flushed and seemed excited to be in Laurence's company. Perhaps his passion for his work was matched by that for the status and respectability it could bring him.

Rhia tried to focus on the neat line of dried leaves laid out on the table. Behind them was a small tower of wooden receptacles, each as shallow as a cigar box. She was only inches from Laurence and she could feel his eyes on her. She could not imagine how she must appear to him. She had not seen herself in a glass for so long that she had forgotten what she had looked like with hair, let alone without it.

Finally, Laurence spoke. 'Do you notice any difference in

the leaves, Miss Mahoney? I can't for the life of me see it.' She detected one of his teasing undertones, but Mr Reeve would be impervious to it. She looked hard at the row of fragile, grey-brown specimens, forcing herself to concentrate. 'There is a difference in the vein pattern,' she almost whispered, hardly trusting her voice.

Mr Reeve chuckled, obviously pleased. 'I can see that you are favourably appointed! It takes a power of observation to see such a thing.' What blarney. It was not such a clever thing at all to notice common differences in the infrastructure of leaves.

Rhia allowed herself the smallest of smiles, not because she had pleased the botanist with her powers of observation, but because she was not alone after all.

It is early, barely light. The air cloys. It is too warm for linsey, but no other uniform is provided. I sleep in my chemise. Last night I almost removed it, but I cannot lock my cabin door. Miss Hayter says she will purchase cotton in Rio so we can sew summer dresses. Presumably she has an allowance from Whitehall for such things.

I suppose it was foolish to imagine that Laurence might discover my quarters. How could he without drawing attention to himself? Besides, he would assume that I'm in the orlop with the others. I don't dare try and find his cabin. I hear that Mr Wardell is on the prowl because Agnes was caught meeting the galley hand, her sweetheart, two nights ago. She was only cautioned, but if it happens again she'll be whipped before the entire ship.

The captain has made a small, unoccupied cabin on the lower deck available to Mr Reeve. It has a good-sized writing table, upon which he spreads his notebooks and his callow drawings. I don't much like being in an airless cabin with Mr Reeve, who stares at me when he thinks I am occupied, but the passenger saloon reminds me too much of freedom. The passengers are entirely unaware of their privileges, just as I once was. I was dismissive of the petty vanities of society, yet now I desire nothing more.

Today will pass under this monotonous regime and then another day and another. I try not to look at the sea but, as you might guess, that is something of an impossibility. So far Manannán has been kind, there have been no real storms, although there is occasionally rough weather and items regularly fall off the shelf in my cabin and off the table in the mess. Maybe today I will see my friend Margaret on her feet. It is a blessing to have her in my mess, but it seems she is to be the last to recover her health for she has not yet left her hammock.

# Patchwork

O utside, the sky was an intense blue behind the white sails. *Name the colour.*

Rhia spun around, but the deck was deserted. It was the pesky voice again, as if she didn't have troubles enough.

'Ultramarine,' she said, sighing. She knew what the voice was doing, making her take note of things she had once loved and cherished. 'Ultramarine, a rare blue, once as expensive as gold,' she added, hoping no one was listening to her talking to herself. She remembered something else. In Latin, *ultramarinus* meant 'beyond the sea', a reference to the origin of the lapis lazuli from which ultramarine was made. When they took Michael Kelly away, they took him to 'parts beyond the seas'. She and Thomas had discussed it, because when they were children they had believed that the Otherworld lay *beyond the seas*. Now here she was, going to a place forested with unearthly white trees and inhabited by criminals and other dangerous creatures. Worse still, Michael would have left Sydney by the time she arrived.

When she reached the orlop hatch, Rhia performed her morning ritual, just as she used to do in the yard at Millbank. She filled her eyes with sky and her lungs with clear air before she put her foot on the top rung of the ladder.

She had thus far avoided a proper scrap with Nora and Agnes because there was always a warden at hand, but she could feel their animosity building. The last time Nora was on dish duty she had tipped Rhia's uneaten breakfast gruel into her lap. An accident, she insisted with an evil grin. Rhia didn't react immediately. She chose to sit, calm and silent, with the sticky slop soaking through her clothing. She could see that it displeased Nora intensely. When Nora disappeared up the ladder with the dish pail, and while nobody was looking, Rhia removed her apron and tipped the gruel into Nora's hammock. She was still waiting for a counter attack.

This morning, Agnes was in the middle of one of her brothel tales when Rhia sat down. Nora and Agnes exchanged looks, and Rhia could tell from the way Agnes's eyes narrowed that she was in a mood. She was probably in a sulk over not seeing her sweetheart. She gave Rhia a toxic look but barely faltered in her narration.

'The landlady at this establishment, Madam *Mahoney,* fancied herself *class,* and a cut above the dirty streetwalkers, but she was a slut who'd have it with a donkey if it'd pay her a ha'penny.' It raised a laugh and Rhia kept her head bent low over her breakfast.

'Don't be a bitch, Agnes.' It was Margaret. 'She's done you no harm.' Margaret was still in her hammock, but her pale face was propped over its edge, and when she caught Rhia's eye she winked before groaning and rolling over. A moment later, though, she was sitting on the edge of the hammock, her legs dangling, looking at the floor as if she was wondering if she could make it that far.

Everyone was watching as Margaret stood up, grabbing the shelf by her bed to steady herself. 'Sweet Jesus, my legs are made of rubber.'

'Don't blaspheme, Dickson,' snapped Jane, who had recently become excessively pious.

It took Margaret several minutes to reach the breakfast table. She stumbled twice, but shooed Nelly away when she tried to help. Margaret ate nothing, but made a show of being cheerful. She could no longer be described as plump, and there was a whitish tinge to her lips. Sleeping in the airless belly of the ship was unhealthful enough without the sickness on top of it. The surgeon, Mr Donovan, said that Margaret had something else, something besides seasickness, but he didn't say exactly what it was. Maybe he didn't know.

The temperature and the stink increased at the same rate. One hundred and fifty bodies at one end of the orlop, livestock at the other, and the once-mysterious *bilge* saw to it. Bilge was an appropriate name for the lowest, internal part of the hull, and Rhia had soon discovered its function. Everything from the cook's waste and the overflow from water closets to pomade and cosmetics sloshed around underneath the orlop.

Once the morning's chores were done, Rhia waited with Margaret until everyone had climbed the ladder. Margaret's gait was halting and careful as she adjusted to being upright in a moving world. When they reached the top of the ladder, she stood for a moment, squinting in the white light glancing off the sea. She had a firm hold on Rhia's arm.

'I've always said the rich were fools with their money, and here's the proof. Imagine taking to the sea for enjoyment or to recover from infirmity!'

Rhia laughed. 'I've missed you, Margaret.'

'Oh, I know,' Margaret retorted. 'I've got ears. I know what they get up to and I've been after the strength to give Agnes a slap for weeks. Someone's got to. She's got the curse, though, and it always makes her worse. I'll wait a day or two.' There had been ongoing complaints about the effects of washing laundry in seawater. Cloth became stiff with dried salt, and caused chafing. Almost all the women, Rhia included, had had their courses by now and needed to wash their cloths. They had suffered the consequences. Few in the orlop bothered to spare others their private discomforts. Everything was a topic for conversation. It passed the time.

On the quarterdeck, each mess sat in a sewing circle under an awning of sailcloth. Little piles of patchwork were scattered about within reach. Several quilts were now under way. The late April sun seemed overly bright. There had been complaints about the sunlight at first. It hurt their eyes after so long in the dark.

Rhia felt light-hearted to have someone to talk to. Until now her interaction with the other prisoners was limited to an occasional smile or a wary 'hello' from Jane. Jane especially liked to roll her eyes at Rhia when Georgina, her arch-rival, said something foolish. This happened fairly frequently because Georgina, a squat Liverpudlian, wasn't the brightest button in the tin.

Margaret spent the morning poring over pieces of cloth, pocketing a delicate muslin that reminded her of a once-treasured dress. She was not the first. If a piece was especially pretty or considered to be of value, it would be surreptitiously folded into an apron pocket and no one would say a word. Nelly wept when she saw some white gabardine, saying it looked like it was from a bride's dress, and she'd never be a bride. Who'd have her?

The morning wore on and Rhia listened to the talk. She was piecing together the lives her companions had led before becoming prisoners. Jane had been in love, Georgina had lost a child and Agnes had left two wee sons behind in the workhouse. The only real difference between them and Rhia was that she had been blessed with good fortune. It made her an outsider here in the same way as any of these women would have been had they come to St Stephen's Green or entered the Montgomery Emporium. What was the ruin of Mahoney Linen against the loss of babes, or taking a beating every night, which is what happened to Nelly. Until she killed her sweetheart. Nelly hardly looked capable of killing a fly, let alone a man. He'd waggled the kitchen knife at her so she hit him over the head with the lid of the stew pot. And that was that. The only thing that had kept her from the noose was pregnancy.

Thieving was not always the result of having fallen from the Lord's grace, as Reverend Tooting liked to think, but of desperation. Or vanity. Georgina had stolen a pair of boots from her mistress, Jane had hidden a length of ribbon from the market in her apron, Susan had taken a veil and a pair of gloves from a clothier's. Agnes and Nora had both become professional thieves because they couldn't make a decent living from needlework. Sarah stole a shawl from her mistress. It seemed perfectly reasonable that a woman who worked all day making pretty things she could not afford to wear herself, might easily be tempted to steal from someone who had finery to spare.

Tales of loss and violence, as well as tales of love, were told as the squares and triangles of cloth became long strips of patchwork. They might have been stitching together scraps of their old lives and making something of them. The talk was just as often hopeful as despairing. Georgina said she'd heard that they were in need of alehouses in Sydney and that she fancied the trade because her grandmother had been a brewer, and that growing hops was easy. Jane retorted that she hadn't the wits for the brewing trade. Agnes planned to run a brothel.

Rhia wondered if she was the only one of them who was leaving behind the best part of her life.

The talk turned to one of the young deck hands that had

shimmied up the main mast as though it were no more than the trunk of an apple tree. While the others were laughing at some remark of Nora's about the bulge in his breeches, Margaret lowered her voice and leaned close to Rhia.

'Do you remember I told you that I was carrying something for Mrs Blake's ding-dong maid?' The conspiratorial note in Margaret's voice made Rhia immediately alert.

'Of course I remember.' In fact, she had almost forgotten. Presumably Margaret had changed her mind about keeping Juliette's secret.

'What would you say if I told you it was nothing more than a plain sheet of parchment?' she whispered.

'Is it?'

Margaret shrugged. 'Not according to Juliette, though how she thinks a plain sheet of parchment hides a portrait, I can't imagine! I've been thinking about the promise I made to keep this flapdoodle to myself, but now I think that I'm only wasting my time with it. I mean, what are the Quaker ladies in Sydney going to think when I give them such a thing?'

Rhia frowned. The parchment could only be a photogenic negative. 'But why does Juliette want the Quakers to have it?'

'To pass on to her mother.'

'Then Juliette's mother is in Sydney?'

'Aye,' said Margaret. 'She's been there more than ten years. What if you were to send such a thing to your mam? It'd break her heart to receive a page with nought on it.'

Rhia was still trying to piece things together. 'She didn't write her mother a letter, then?'

'She can't write. Brought up in the workhouse, poor fool. But I should never have taken it, so I'm as big a fool myself.'

What on earth was Juliette up to? 'May I see it?' Rhia said.

Margaret shrugged. 'I don't see why not. At least then I'll not have to make the decision by myself. I'll show you after supper.' She looked up at the sun. 'Almost dinnertime, and then you'll be off to see the boss. Do you suppose Botany Bay's full of botanists?'

The thought made Rhia smile. 'I sincerely hope not. It's hard to imagine that there's much there in the way of botany. I don't know what Mr Reeve expects to find – I've seen a picture of Sydney, it looks a colourless place.'

Margaret shrugged. 'I don't mind.' She gestured to the strips of patchwork that coiled around them. 'That's the most colour I've seen in two years and it's making my eyes hurt.'

When they went below for lunch, Margaret went straight to her hammock saying she was worn out by all the sunshine. Rhia did her best to eat whatever preserved meat the cook had seen fit to serve up as stew, and left as soon as possible.

Mr Reeve's workroom was on the upper deck, close by his cabin. When she entered, he was bent over his desk, his small wire spectacles crooked on the bridge of his nose. The cabin, which he said was too small, had a bunk and was four times the size of her hutch. It also had considerably more shelves. Both the bunk and shelves were stacked with his little wooden boxes.

'Good afternoon, Mahoney.' He had picked up the habit of calling her this from Miss Hayter and seemed to be enjoying it. He didn't look up from his study of an enormous Latin botanical. 'Just carry on where we left off yesterday.'

They rarely needed to speak, beyond the cursory, which suited Rhia well. It was her job to refer to his annotated drawings, which told her into which family or category a specimen fell, and then to label a compartment in a box for it. It was extremely useful that she recognised many of the more common plants and herbs from *Culpeper's*. She only occasionally managed to match foreign medicinal herbs to Mr Reeve's terrible drawings. She sometimes had to ask him to confirm that the specimen she was looking at was the same plant he had illustrated.

She did much of her work kneeling on the rough wooden floor, bent over spiky seed pods and wands of feathery, paper-thin leaves. Today, there were dried Michaela's daisies from America and there was frangipani from Tahiti, as well as henbane and burdock and feverfew. She found it easier to work on the floor, now, and to feel the swelling and falling of the waves beneath her. She did not trust the furniture. She'd been thrown from her bench in the orlop too many times, everyone had. By the end of an afternoon with Mr Reeve, her knees were always cramped and her back aching.

After an hour or so she straightened and stretched. She caught him watching her again. He looked back down at his book, quickly. She knew he must wonder about her crime and her past, but she doubted that he would ever have the nerve to ask her outright.

'You seem to know a lot about botanicals, Mahoney.'

She shrugged. 'I like to find patterns in nature, and I like to know the name of what I'm looking at.'

'But to what ends? What use could such knowledge possibly be to ...'

'To a woman?'

'Well, yes. Yes indeed!'

'I don't mean to shock you, Mr Reeve, but the female mind is capable of more than counting stitches and weaning babes.'

'I don't expect that you are a conventional woman, Mahoney.'

'Thank Christ for that!' She had Mamo to thank, really. Mr

Reeve looked shocked, which was gratifying. It silenced him for the rest of the afternoon.

Rhia usually had a few minutes to spare before she was due in the mess for supper. There was a secluded corner in a 'tween decks cranny where, through a vent called a scuttle, she could see part of the main deck and a narrow strip of ocean. It was manageable, this much sea. As they held their course south, there were more daylight hours, and she began to notice how the seascape she had thought so monotonous was, in fact, constantly changing. Sometimes it looked as dirty and lifeless as the Liffey on a winter's day, and at others like a giant look-ing-glass reflecting the sky and the clouds. On some days its curves and frills were seductive, and on others there were ridges of water, serrated and menacing. The sea had a mean glint today, so after her first sighting Rhia did not look at it again. In the stories of Manannán, ships that disappeared in storms drifted to the enchanted or haunted islands of the Otherworld.

Rhia turned her back on Manannán and saw Albert's frayed breeches emerge through a hatch to the upper deck. She called to him as loud as she dared. He jumped from the stairs to the deck, lightly, and was in front of her, beaming, in a moment.

'I see you've found my hideaway, Mahoney.'

'Yours! I thought it was my hideaway.'

'Ye'll see that me tobacco tin's here.' Albert reached into a dark knot in the timbers and pulled it out. 'Like a smoke?'

'Another time. I'll be late.' She hesitated, even though she'd made her decision. 'Albert. I've a favour to ask.'

He shrugged. 'Let's 'ave it.'

'Do you know the passenger Laurence Blake?'

'With the haystack?' He gestured to his hair. 'The one who puts parchment out on deck in the sun?'

'That's almost certainly him. Would you give him a message from me?'

Albert's smile broadened. She knew what he was thinking.

'Tell Mr Blake where my cabin is.'

His eyes filled with mischief.

'You needn't think it's anything – there is nothing – I mean, Mr Blake is a friend. As it happens, I knew him before I was – I knew him in London. I need to speak with him. It's important.'

'Sure it is,' Albert said, his grin widening. Rhia didn't care what he thought. Albert mock-bowed, and swaggered away, whistling.

# Valetine

Jane and Georgina were laying the table, sullenly, the clang of pewter bowls being slammed down signalled that all was not well between them. Georgina was scowling and periodically scratching her hair beneath her cap. The two had almost come to blows on the quarterdeck over head lice.

'It only takes one itching head to send the little beasties stomping through every scalp,' Jane was saying, so if you don't drown them in vinegar I'll tip a bottle over you with pleasure. Otherwise I'll ask Matron to shave your head.' Georgina burst into tears and threw herself onto her hammock.

Supper was dried biscuits, pea soup and suet pudding. Already the fresh food was being used sparingly, and they were still ten days off Rio. Albert said they would take on fresh water, fruit and meat, rum, tobacco and Portuguese wine – all the essential stocks – when they docked.

The best thing about supper was not the gritty suet pudding, which occasionally had a little molasses in it, but the ration of wine. It was the cheapest, the roughest imaginable, and was served in a dented pewter tankard, but it may as well have been the best claret in the world. It shortened the shadows and sweetened tempers.

After supper two lanterns were lit and placed at either end of the table, in order that the women could sit and read the scriptures. No one was allowed to light a lantern or a taper without a warden present, and – as yet – no one yet had broken this rule. There was no means of knowing what punishment dissenters could expect to face. However, it was known that Agnes was a whisker away from a flogging. There were irons chained to the timbers in a certain dark corner where the bilge water leaked into a cupboard of a cell, large enough only for a person to crouch in. The wardens' favourite threat was being added to the surgeon superintendent's list. Nobody had a clue who was on the list, or what offences were considered suitably grave to deserve being listed. How would the theft of two tapers, a flint and some matches be looked upon? Rhia had slipped them into her apron pocket whilst a quarrel was in progress. She was a convicted thief, so what difference did it make?

Margaret beckoned to Rhia from her hammock while the others were mending, reading from their Bibles, or checking each other for lice. She passed Rhia a flat, silk wallet, which she slipped into the pocket of her apron. This done, Margaret made a great show of a piece of valetine, a blue figured silk that she'd discovered in her sack. It was not large, perhaps half a yard squared, but it was a pretty find and they agreed that it was too fine a piece for a quilt and should be put aside for 'later', to make a purse or a reticule.

Rhia trod the leeward passageway timidly when it was time to return to her hutch. The sea was rising high and falling heavily, and the deck felt greasy beneath her boots. The moon was as full and luminous as a giant pearl behind the masts. She'd not noticed it waxing. She had stopped believing that the Queen of the Night gave a damn what happened to her. The best she and her moon lantern could do for Rhia now was to help her safely back to her cabin. The moonlight cast silver shadows on every cresting wave. As she turned away, one reared up like a horse on its back legs and showered her with icy water. She had not seen it coming and it shook her to the core. Manannán be damned.

Rhia took off her boots and practically crawled back to her cabin. When she closed the door she leaned against it and shut her eyes. When she opened them she was looking at a small white square on the floor. She picked it up and lit a taper. *Laurence Blake, Photogenic Drawing, 64 Cloak Lane, the City of London.* On the back were the words: *Tonight, ten o'clock.*

Rhia lay on her hammock and stared into the dense dark, determined to stay awake. She must keep her mind where her boots were, as Annie Kelly was fond of saying. If you let your mind wander into regrets, you would fall backwards, and if you let it loose on imaginings, it was hurtling forwards without you. What was there for her in the present? Only the hollow feeling that she had failed. Why else would she be here? A gentle tap on her door made Rhia sit up, disoriented. Was it already ten o'clock? She scrambled from the hammock to her feet, finding her cap. Her hair had grown a little, but washing it in a bucket of saltwater could not be enhancing it. She opened the door. It was Laurence.

They stood looking at each other. He stepped into her cabin and Rhia closed the door. In the dark, he embraced her as though it were the most natural thing in the world. His lips touched hers so lightly that she couldn't be sure that he'd actually kissed her; that she was in the arms of someone who gave a damn what happened to her.

Rhia turned away to hide her confusion and to wipe her tears on her apron. She fumbled in her pocket for a taper and matches. Once the taper was lit, she felt awkward and self-conscious. There was only a yard of floor between them.

'This is a long way from Cloak Lane,' said Laurence.

'It is,' she agreed.

'Antonia would approve of your new Quaker colours, but you've grown thin.'

'The food is awful. Someone should complain. I miss Beth's ginger loaf terribly.' Laurence was looking at her with an expression she couldn't decipher.

'It's very good timing that you should visit this evening,' she said quickly. 'I've something to show you.' She took the parchment from its wallet.

Laurence needed to take only one step to examine it more closely. She held the taper over it. To her, it looked like a piece of cartridge paper with a sheen like polished cotton.

Laurence looked perplexed. 'Where on earth did you get a photogenic negative?'

'I thought that was what it was.'

'It looks as though it has already been exposed, though it is difficult to say for certain in this light.'

'I can't remember what that means.'

'When a negative image has been "burnt" into the chemicals the parchment is treated with, it acquires a certain ghostly image, a little like a watermark.'

'I hadn't noticed.'

'Your eye is not trained to see it. Where did you get this?'

Rhia told him what Margaret had told her, and he shook his head. His face looked eerie in the flickering candlelight. 'This is extremely odd, Rhia.' She liked hearing her name. She had been Mahoney for so long. 'Did your friend Margaret say nothing else?' he asked.

'She knows something, but she won't tell me what it is. She is supposed to be keeping a secret for Juliette.'

The creak of a deck timber outside made them both freeze.

Rhia held her breath. In a moment there was a sound like a footfall, towards the aft stairwell.

She whispered, 'Do you think someone saw you?'

Laurence shook his head. 'I was careful. But I don't want to make things worse for you.'

She shrugged. 'How could things be worse? Tell me, quickly, how you come to be on board.'

'Dillon told me the name of your ship, of course. I was fortunate that there was still a berth available – though there was a good chance of it, the transports are not popular passenger vessels. Besides, I told you I wanted to see Australia, the light has always drawn me. But I had a much more important reason to travel at such short notice.' Laurence took her hand. She wanted him to comfort her, but she didn't know to what degree. She had thought that she wanted Thomas, all those years ago and that desire came only with true love. It seemed unlikely, now, considering the nightly assignations between prisoners and crew.

Laurence squeezed her hand and let it go. 'May I take the negative until tomorrow? I'd rather like to see it by daylight. I'll have Albert return it.'

'Of course.'

He kissed her again, and left.

Rhia lay in her hammock, awake, for a long time. Her uncertainty disturbed her. She had great affection for Laurence. He made her laugh and she felt safe. Perhaps this was enough?

# Balzarine

Antonia gazed into the dim recess where a row of sober grey and brown linen hung. *As limp as my own humility,* she thought. Once, rows of taffeta and silk organza whispered to her, cloths with names – *Andalusian* and *Ariel*. Once, her shawls were as fine as cobwebs, not dull and sturdy. She chose her newest linen, recalling the name the draper had given to the colour: *London Smoke*. Apt.

She made herself reflect, as she dressed, on the purpose of plainness. An unadorned costume was dismissive of fashion and of class. Without finery one was the equal of another, no matter how rich one's purse. Josiah had even used the singular 'thou' rather than the plural 'you' that many Londoners found quaint and eccentric. He said the latter was a sign of flattery because 'you' was once used to address a superior, as a signifier of title and hierarchy. Antonia thought it a little outmoded, and could not bring herself to alter her speech. She was altered enough.

She smoothed her hair with a wooden comb and knotted it at the nape of her neck, then descended the stairs thoughtfully, her hand slipping over the polished banister. How could her anticipation of Mr Montgomery's visit mingle so easily with her memories of Josiah? What if her ideology were no stronger than her impulses? Josiah had guided her to the inward. Every day without him was a test of her courage. Without him there were no gentle words of guidance, no eyes filled with kindness, no loving embrace.

The kitchen was reassuringly warm. Beth always lit the range at daylight. The porridge was already cooked and steaming on the table in its cast iron pot. It was the best porridge Antonia had ever tasted. She had watched Beth make it once – a knob of butter, a pinch of salt and a measure of cream made all the difference. Josiah professed to prefer plain food, so when he had praised Beth for her porridge, Antonia merely smiled.

The house was too quiet without Laurence and Rhia. She now made a habit of sharing the first meal of the day with Beth and Juliette, telling herself that she wanted to feel as their equal when in fact she was just lonely. She simply did not know how to reconcile the idea of equality with the fact that she was a mistress with domestic servants. Of course, she provided employment and the household was the closest thing Juliette had to a family. The tangled feelings of protectiveness and irritation were, no doubt, maternal. Antonia had not been given anyone else to watch over.

This morning, as usual, they discussed which household chores needed special attention, the first being the furniture. The dining table and carved-back chairs looked brittle and were in need of furniture paste. Beth looked perplexed.

'Do you mean linseed and vinegar, Mrs Blake?'

'No. My mother had a recipe for preserving English walnut. Beeswax, white wax, curd soap and turpentine. It softens the wood and protects it.'

Beth sighed and ladled a second large helping of porridge into her bowl. 'Very well.'

Antonia smiled. Beth liked to have something to be long-suffering over. 'The morning room needs dusting before our guest arrives, Juliette,' she continued. 'A goose's wing should reach into the lofty corners, and the velvet pile will need sweeping with the hard whisk brush.' Juliette nodded but remained silent and hunched. At least she seemed less melancholy now that spring sunshine, rather than drizzle, glanced off the window panes. The exertion would do her good. Antonia suspected that her recurring infirmity was merely habitual gloom. The physician had described it in much the same way physicians tended to describe most feminine ailments. 'A nervous disorder, Mrs Blake. Give her laudanum and keep the curtains drawn to prevent over-stimulation.' As soon as he had gone, Antonia opened the curtains and windows wide. Juliette's real ailment was her secret. Considering the turn she'd taken when Antonia said she wanted to visit Rhia, it must have something to do with her mother, who was in Millbank before she was transported. Rhia's incarceration had merely tipped the balance. Either that, or Juliette knew something about Rhia's arrest.

After breakfast Antonia went to Josiah's office. She no longer needed to take deep, steadying breaths before entering. She thanked Josiah, silently and often, for his fastidious business acumen. She was now familiar with the last season's consignments and accounts, and could model this season's on them. There was only the matter of payment to the crew of *Mathilda* that she needed to discuss with Mr Montgomery, since it was not clear why certain of the Manx sailors had been paid more than others. She supposed there was some hierarchy of skill or experience that she knew nothing of. The mystery of why the *Mathilda* had not been signed out of the Calcutta dry dock remained unanswered. The document she had given Ryan had never been returned to her. But she must not think of that. She would never know the truth.

She had been corresponding with Mr Montgomery, as well

as with Mr Dillon, on the matter of Rhia's repeal, which was partly why Jonathan Montgomery was calling this morning. The joint venture was a secondary reason for his visit. He was well connected, and seemed to have associates in the legal profession, perhaps even in the court. He was not convinced, though, that there had been a miscarriage of justice.

The doorknocker sounded, and made Antonia's heart pound. She rose and straightened her skirts. Linen crushed all too easily when it was not blended with silk or wool. She walked the length of the hallway more slowly than she wanted to, her heart still thudding. She put her hand to the crucifix beneath her bodice.

'Please bring us some coffee, Juliette dear,' she called out as she passed the dining room where both girls were rubbing the table top with flannel.

Mr Montgomery was as immaculate as usual. His frockcoat was of some finely twilled wool, Italian no doubt, and his silk cravat was lemon yellow. He was as crisp as the spring sunshine, and entirely at ease. Antonia felt herself soften as she stepped aside to let him in. It had happened again. Without a thought or any warning, her body was yielding to him.

'Good morning, Mr Montgomery. Are you well?'

'Very well, Mrs Blake.'

'Allow me to take your hat and cane.'

The morning room smelt of linseed and roses. Juliette had arranged several stems carefully in a blue bowl on the table. She was a thoughtful girl, in spite of her shortcomings. 'You will be comfortable on the Chesterfield,' she said. 'Will you have coffee?'

He said that he would and flicked his coat-tails before he sat. His smile was warm and easy, his long legs gracefully crossed. Antonia perched on the edge of a straight-backed chair and smoothed her skirt again. She cleared her throat. 'Tell me, do you believe that Rhia Mahoney is innocent?'

He ran his fingers through his iron-grey hair thoughtfully. 'I have spoken again to my maid, Hatty, and she insists that she saw Miss Mahoney with the silk. My wife says that she did not trust Miss Mahoney from the first. It is an impossible situation. I have spoken with the prosecutor, who says that the case against seemed irrefutable.'

'But surely Hatty was mistaken – perhaps she was lying, covering for someone else? And then there is the mystery of the absent defence.'

He looked affronted. 'I can assure you that all members of my household staff are of good character.' He frowned. 'As to the counsel, I simply do not know what to think. I have written to him myself but he has been on the Continent all winter.'

'But Rhia's good character and her family's reputation must account for something!'

'One would think so, but the family has fallen on hard times, which worked against her. Be assured that I am doing everything in my power to have her sentence repealed on the grounds of good character. Do not concern yourself unduly, Antonia.'

He had never used her first name before but he did it so naturally now – as if to suggest they were familiars, as if it was an established fact. He smiled kindly, but she thought she saw a flicker of doubt in his eyes. Perhaps he wondered if she was entirely sensible in believing Rhia Mahoney innocent.

'Tell me more about your photogenic drawing,' he said. 'I confess that I'm a little mesmerised by it. I understand that it is still too soon to experiment with …' He shook his head. 'It still seems impossible that we have lost two of our company.'

Antonia bowed her head. There were creases in her linen

skirts, in spite of her care. She remembered the conversation at Christmas, about Josiah's letter to Ryan Mahoney. It had presumably been a business concern. She pushed her shoulders down and straightened her back. 'The portrait is on my mind,' she said.

He was leaning towards her as though her every word mattered to him.

She felt her breath become shallow at his attention. 'It needs only to be soaked in a salt solution and brushed with silver nitrate to make it light sensitive. I can show you the negative, if you would like.'

'Yes, why not!'

Antonia bustled to Josiah's office, relieved to be away from Jonathan Montgomery's magnetism and excited to be discussing photogenic drawing with someone besides Juliette. She so missed Laurence, but Rhia needed him. She only hoped that that his feelings for her were not misguided.

She opened the lower drawer of the desk. It was empty. The wallet had been here last time she looked, but when was that? It must be months ago. Could she have moved it and forgotten? Surely not. She looked in the other drawers. Nothing. She must have left it somewhere else, or Juliette had tidied it away.

She looked into the dining room where Beth was now polishing alone, her cheeks crimson. 'Where is Juliette, Beth?'

'She's taken one of her queer turns. I've made the coffee, though. It's just brewing. Shall I fetch it for you?'

'Never mind, Beth, I can get it myself.' Beth looked relieved. She didn't like serving *genteels*, it made her nervous.

Mr Montgomery was where she had left him. Antonia explained that she had misplaced the negative and he smiled and shrugged. She poured steaming coffee into two of her pretty Moroccan glasses. 'The *Mathilda* has set sail?' she asked.

He nodded. 'Isaac and Francis left with the shipment yesterday. The remaining cotton is on its way to Manchester.'

'Then we are agreed that we will try the wool and cotton blend first? I know that Ryan was impressed with the quality of Australian merino.'

'The yarn is high quality, but the Parramatta cloth that is woven in the colony is still low grade.'

The conversation turned to business. Mr Montgomery suggested that they might try balzarine, a blend of half-cotton, half-worsted. The wool could be Australian merino. What did she think? Antonia agreed that it could. Australia was no longer merely an idea. By the summer, Rhia and Laurence would both be there, and the *Mathilda* would be in Calcutta. Without Josiah.

When her guest took his leave, Antonia went in search of Juliette. She found her in her room at the top of the house. 'Is something the matter, Juliette?'

Juliette turned over in her narrow bed so that she was facing the wall. She didn't speak. This silent gloom was at least preferable to the weeping gloom. Antonia closed the door quietly. She would ask about the negative later.

Rhia,

The negative contains a latent image, but it is impossible to know if it is intact without exposure. I have the necessary apparatus, but the process requires strong light. I'd best not expose it on the deck as I do my other images! There is sufficient light in the middle of the afternoon in my cabin. Of course we must have the permission of Margaret before we attempt a representation. Assure her that the process will not affect the negative, which can be used several times. Let's bide our time. I will formulate a plan.

I saw Mr Wardell was patrolling the lower deck last night. Perhaps it was he who passed by your cabin?

Affectionately,
Laurence

You would not know from Mr Reeve's drawings that *Matricaria recutita* and *Chicorium intybus* are strains of camomile and chicory. I am starting to think that I should offer to do the drawings myself. Would he be insulted? Do I care? He has been uncharacteristically quiet lately, and I feel him watching me more and more. He is becoming brazen and will occasionally ask me something that is not related to our work, something of Dublin or the trade. Any lingering courtesy or respect for me is long gone but I, too, take more liberties with politeness now. I asked him something about a Jamaican tobacco leaf and I could hardly believe it when his reply was that my uncle's death must have been unnerving. How much does he know about me? I put the Jamaican tobacco leaf away slowly, taking as much time over it as I could. I kept my attention on the patterns in the leaf, trying to gather my wits. I thought *Nicotiana tabacum* is a more melodic name than *tobacco*. Mr Reeve is hoping that he might discover wild tobacco, you see, or a relative to it, in Australia. If the weed were suitable to the soil and climate of the colony, it would be a significant discovery. It would also be lucrative. He is equally enthusiastic about the mercenary and the botanical. It is not entirely what I would expect from a naturalist, but Mr Reeve is also a social climber. I can tell by the way he boasts about the important people he knows in London. It means nothing to me, I have not heard of any of them. He is foolish and impressionable. As for the commercial merits of the tobacco plant, I remember that you used the solution of tobacco leaves soaked in water as an insect repellent one wet summer, when the mosquitoes were insatiable. According to the stories circulating below, there are insects in Australia that are larger and more poisonous than those in the jungles of the South Americas. The place sounds more lethal with every new thing I learn.

I had to answer Mr Reeve so I told him that, yes, my uncle's death *was* unnerving. I felt like saying that the rosehip he'd drawn was almost unrecognisable. Such a simple thing to render, yet he manages to make it ugly and clumsy.

He said that it must be painful to speak of it, and that he had lost a family member himself recently, and that it was an unexpected death, like my uncle's. I couldn't keep pretending. I asked how he knew about Ryan. 'I am not at liberty to say,' he said airily, but he still looked at me as if I might divulge some confidence. He wants me to trust him and like him, yet he has no idea how to be likeable.

I decided that I was under no obligation to answer his questions and told him that the leaves of the rosehip were wrong. He sighed heavily, as though he was disappointed in me, and put his spectacles back on, saying he was at my disposal, should I need to talk! He is the last person in whom I would confide. He is becoming bold and nosy. However, I enjoy the cataloguing work. It is interesting, and it is the only contact I have with any form of artistry. It is like a long draught of cool water when I am parched with thirst.

I have not unfolded the chintz again, nor picked up the precious pencil that Mr Dillon gave me after my trial. I don't have the heart to draw and my ink is running low.

Now there is daylight beneath my door. Another day.

# Gabardine

Albert was waiting in the cranny 'tween decks, looking at the main deck through the scuttle. It was his lookout post. 'Mornin' Mahoney. I've a message from your fancy man. Says he's got a plan to get you away from the weed tomorrow.' That was Albert's nickname for the botanist. 'Think one of them will wed you?'

Rhia rolled her eyes. 'I'm not the type men wed. I wasn't before, so it's even less likely that I would be now, wouldn't you think?'

'Wouldn't be so sure. Quickest way to freedom in Sydney. You'll see,' said Albert. 'Besides, you're not half bad-looking.'

Rhia laughed and ruffled his hair, which surprised them both.

Below, Margaret was sitting on the edge of her hammock, her feet dangling. She looked awful, but she smiled when Rhia appeared. She had made it as far as this twice in the past week, but as soon as she put her feet on the floor and stood up, it all went bad. Everyone was watching. The mess united in few things, but everyone wanted Margaret back on her feet. She kept the peace and was relentlessly cheerful.

As usual, Jane and Georgina weren't talking. From their hissing exchange at breakfast, it was now clear that they had both been bedding the sailor they'd had the disagreement about. Roughly half the women were now with seamen. Danger and disobedience broke the monotony and it was what they were used to anyway. Mr Wardell, in his signature brown gabardine, couldn't be everywhere at once, so the odds for getting away with it weren't bad.

Margaret put one foot on the floor and groaned. No one breathed a word. 'For pity's sake stop gawping, I'm not a sideshow! Mahoney, help me out of this wretched thing.'

Margaret made it to the table to a round of applause. She wasn't alone in refusing the gruel. It was thinner every morning, just like the pea soup had ever fewer peas floating in salty broth. The floor tilted suddenly, and everyone put their hands on their bowl. Only one was upended, but Jane jumped out of the way just in time. They were getting better at the swift reflex. No one had worn the contents of a bowl for days. Margaret laughed. 'Look at us all, sitting round holding onto our measly supper. What a sight! Heaven must be a place where the land is as still as a preacher's prick.'

Jane tut-tutted.

Nora picked up her bowl with her beefy hands and put it to her lips. She took a loud slurp and then wiped her mouth with her hand. 'Heaven is full of mutton with dumplings,' she said.

Agnes added, 'Suet pudding with rabbit in gravy.'

'And fat strawberries with yellow cream,' Sarah said with a hungry look, 'and cider made from red apples.'

'Manchester apples,' added Margaret, then looked like she was going to throw up. 'I'd sooner be in any other prison than on this wretched ship – Bridewell included.'

'Is Bridewell worse than Newgate?' Rhia asked, tentatively.

Margaret opened her mouth to reply, but Jane was shaking her head emphatically. 'Coventry's the worst,' she said. 'I was there a year, the first time. Bigger rodents than the river rats at Millbank.' She was looking at Rhia strangely. 'I've been in a few prisons, and I've met plenty who say they didn't do the crime. But I can see that you're no thief, Mahoney.'

There was a stunned silence for a minute. Rhia could only think of the matches and taper she'd stolen. Finally Nora snorted. 'Bollocks. Oxford Street's swarming with ladies who thieve. Mahoney's just as guilty as anyone here.'

'Pull your horns in, Nora,' snapped Margaret.

A few spooned in their soup silently and others left the table to lie in their hammocks or sew. Nora cursed under her breath at Margaret but let the matter lie. Rhia pushed her bowl away and caught Margaret's eye. It felt like a small victory.

The temperature seemed to rise more each day. The awning on the quarterdeck barely made a difference, it could not protect them from the motionless air. Even lifting a copper needle took effort, and languor irritated everyone. Their clothes were stifling. Tempers frayed. No one wore boots now. It was too hot, and besides, the feel of the timbers beneath your feet made it easier to stay upright when the sea was rough.

The women in Rhia's mess were hemming their second quilt for the Rio market. They would be there any day. It made Rhia ache to think of land. There would be buds on the hawthorn and sweet william at Greystones, and the dusky smell of tea rose would be clinging to the arbour in the kitchen garden. Her mother might be bent over her little bushes of thyme or sage, her skirts catching on the spiked rosemary branches. If Mamo were there she would be with her precious sheep. Could sheep see the dead?

Margaret interrupted this pastoral vision, 'What a fine turn the ladies in grey have done us. Most of these,' she jerked her head at the circle of needlewomen, 'have never earned an honest penny, and here we are labouring together peaceably.'

'More or less peaceably,' Rhia agreed, since Jane and

Georgina were scowling at each other from opposite ends of the awning. No one was particularly cheerful this morning, which could be the heat or the curse with its knack for re-arranging itself so that everyone was waspish at the same time.

There was no point in trying to have a quiet word with Margaret until the gossip started, or a half-naked sailor came into sight. Rhia looked back to her own sewing. The geometric black and red she was stitching must be from a theatrical costumer. It had a boldness that she'd not seen before. On either side of it were patterns that looked so familiar they might have been old Mahoney prints. She had once spent hours watching the rotary printer at the Dublin factory tattooing a length of virgin linen with new mineral dyes. Colourfast dyes had been in use for years now but, back then, the gleaming machines had thrilled Rhia. She had been just as caught up as everyone in the great excitement of the modern. Now it was hard not to blame the modern for the fate of these women.

They were laughing at something Nora said about Miss Hayter's new hairstyle. It was true that their matron was taking particular care with her appearance lately. Was it possible she had a sailor herself? It seemed a good moment to tell Margaret about Laurence, and about the negative.

Margaret's eyes widened. 'Your gentleman friend can do as he pleases with the thing, so long as I have it back when we arrive in Sydney. Devil sweep me, I don't know what to be more surprised about!' Margaret suddenly put her hand to her mouth. She looked as though she had just remembered something unpleasant.

'*What*, Margaret?'

'I can't keep the rest of the secret now, can I?' she said, *sotto voce*. 'It's bound to be more nonsense, of course.' She looked undecided, then she sighed. 'Juliette told me why she wanted to send the thing to her mother.'

Rhia waited, hardly breathing, while Margaret chewed her lip and grappled with her conscience. Finally she shook her head and looked back to her sewing. She had decided against confiding after all.

After lunch, as Rhia was preparing to leave, Margaret pulled her aside. 'If I tell you I'll have broken my oath, and I'm trying to be good. I promised Mrs Blake. But then I'm already a sinner, so what difference does it make? I'll think on it.'

# Upholstery

M r Reeve was in shirtsleeves, half his buttons undone. He had removed his waistcoat and was holding the bridge of his spectacles with a finger to keep them from slipping down the bridge of his nose while he read from a botany journal. His hair was sticking to his forehead. 'I say, this is interesting, Mahoney!'

Rhia looked up from puzzling over some drawing at whose identity she could not even hazard a guess. Perspiration trickled beneath her clothes, and her undergarments were damp. She couldn't bear to have her cap on and had finally ceased to care what state her hair was in. 'Mm,' she said, hardly bothering to sound interested.

'It says here that they've found *phormium tenax* in New South Wales! I don't suppose you know what that is.'

'Flax,' said Rhia, feeling pleased when he looked disappointed.

'You're always surprising me, Mahoney. But here is something that might surprise you. The naturalist Henry Watson says here that he has seen many *specimens* in Sydney.' Mr Reeve laughed quietly at this. 'And I quote. "On this occasion, I had an opportunity of seeing a specimen of the best society in the colony, and I looked in vain for any mark by which I could distinguish it from any refined or genteel company in England. The equipages were fashionable, the ladies were in general pretty and elegantly attired, and the gentlemen equally unexceptional in their dress and attire. Here, in a very pleasing garden, I saw the gigantic lily, said to be the chief floral ornament of the Australian wilderness."'

Mr Reeve looked pleased, but Rhia couldn't tell if it was the prospect of ladies who were in general pretty and elegantly attired, or the gigantic lily that excited him so much.

There was a tap on the door. It was Albert. He handed Mr Reeve a piece of notepaper, winking at Rhia as the botanist frowned and read. Albert stepped out of view of the open door, but Rhia guessed that he was within earshot.

Mr Reeve looked irritated when he folded the note, creasing it sharply and deliberately.

'Mr Blake has received Mr Wardell's permission to have your assistance this afternoon, Mahoney. He did mention his intent at breakfast yesterday, but I assumed he'd have the courtesy to inform me before this. *Apparently* you are the only person on this ship with the necessary skill. I was unaware that you were also versed in photogenic drawing, Mahoney. You *are* full of surprises.'

Rhia tried not to show that she too had been unaware of her expertise. 'Only a little. I – I lodged with someone in London who had a calotype studio.' Mr Reeve looked perplexed, his pale eyes blinking rapidly. He mopped his face with a handkerchief. He was not sure whether to be suspicious or not.

'Strange that Mr Blake should know of it when I did not,' he said, almost sulkily. 'I plan to use photogenic drawing in my own work one day, you know.' They both knew that photogenic drawing was a wealthy man's pursuit, which accounted for the botanist's dejected expression.

'I suppose I *must* release you.' He sighed heavily to make it clear how much it would inconvenience him. 'I thought you were to be *my* assistant.' His petulance might have been laughable were it not so irritating.

'I've not always been a prisoner, Mr Reeve. Not so long ago, I was a Catholic merchant's daughter and lived in a large house in Dublin with servants. It would have been scandalous that I be left alone in a cabin with either you or Mr Blake.' She stood to leave and realised that she wasn't wearing her cap. She didn't want Laurence to see her hair. As she bent to pick it up, her mother's letter fell from her apron pocket to the floor at his feet. Without hesitation, Mr Reeve picked it up and started to unfold it. He had gone too far. Rhia snatched it back from him.

'You have no right!'

He looked stunned, and then his face reddened. He shrugged and turned away.

'We all carry mementos of those we hold dear,' he mumbled, bent over his table with his back to her. She hoped he was ashamed. What could have made him behave in such a way? Perhaps he thought it was a love letter, but even so it was none of his business.

Outside, Albert was smoking. He gave her a curious look. He'd probably heard everything. She followed him along a narrow, low-ceilinged corridor beyond their snug 'tween decks. Albert was singing softly. *'In Dublin's fair city, where the girls are so pretty, I first laid my eyes on Rhiannon Mahoney …'*

She felt tears gathering in the corners of her eyes. 'I am grateful, Albert. I'll find some means of repaying you.'

'No need. Mr Blake already has.' He jingled some coins in his pocket and grinned. 'Pay attention,' he added, 'this is the *secret* way to the passenger deck,' he chuckled, 'in case ye ever need to get there secretly.' He led her down a dark passageway that looked vaguely familiar. She had almost come this way once when she was lost.

The only part of the narrow, weaving passageway that contained signs of life was an open door, from which issued dim gaslight and the smell of roasting fowl. The galley. It was no meal for the prisoner's table being prepared. The only meat Rhia had tasted for weeks was stewed beef, ropey and without flavour. She peered into the galley as they passed, and glimpsed the bone-thin back of a man in an enormous dirty apron that almost wrapped around him twice. He wore a Chinaman's close-fitting cap and his long, stringy plait reached to his waist. Rhia had no time to take in more of the galley than that it was dim and steamy and not particularly clean. The stoop of the cook's thin back made him look unwell.

They reached the end of the passageway and climbed a short flight of steps to the passenger deck. Albert delivered her to the door of Laurence's cabin, smirked cheekily and disappeared.

Laurence opened the door as though he had been standing on the other side waiting. Rhia stepped inside. The cabin felt spacious, though it was not much bigger than Mr Reeve's. Light funnelled through a narrow window and fell across a writing table. The window was filled with sea and sky. On the table was a lacquered stationery box and something that looked like a small book press, though between its two wooden plates was a piece of glass. Beside it was the wallet that held the negative.

Rhia looked around. There was a built-in bed with wainscoting and an upholstered armchair. A patterned rug covered the floor, soft beneath her bare feet. The chair looked luxurious; the linen clean. These were things that had once seemed ordinary, that she once might not even have noticed. She no longer belonged in a room like this and felt uncomfortable.

Laurence didn't seem to notice. He took a step closer and held both her hands. 'Rhia.'

She held her breath.

'To see you like this ...'

She looked away and tried to be flippant. 'Do I look so awful?'

'No! Well, you've looked better,' he said. Rhia was relieved to see his humour return. She didn't recognise this sombre Laurence who seemed on the verge of declaring his love at any moment. 'I'd place my life in Dillon's hands,' he continued, 'but I hope that he is wrong.'

'Wrong?'

'I hope that your being here has nothing to do with Ryan's death.'

She had long since given up trying to understand what the connection could possibly be. 'What do you mean, Laurence?'

Laurence looked regretful immediately. 'Dillon said nothing to you?' She shook her head. He frowned. 'I shouldn't have told you. Christ knows you have troubles enough.'

How could her arrest be connected to Ryan's death? It made no sense. If Mr Dillon was in search of a scandal then perhaps she been too hasty in trusting him.

Laurence took the negative from the wallet. He opened the stationery box and removed a piece of paper that looked almost identical. He placed the plain paper on top of the negative and then fixed both beneath the glass. He removed the wooden plate from the top of the press so that the sunlight was falling directly onto the glass.

'It will take approximately fifteen minutes. For goodness sake sit down, Rhia, you look as though you're about to fall over. I keep a spirit lamp and coffee pot in my washroom, would you care for a glass?'

She smiled. The thought alone revived her.

'I'll take that to be a yes,' he said. He disappeared through a panelled door behind her.

Rhia perched on the chair, allowing the soft upholstery and the lilting blue and green through the window to soothe her. She was still smiling. Coffee, a friend and a comfortable chair. It seemed the most extraordinary luxury.

The paper beneath the press was changing colour.

Laurence returned and placed a steaming glass in her hand. His fingers brushed hers, but she did not thrill at it. She wished she had. She inhaled the sharp fragrance rising from the glass. Laurence turned away to check on the transfer and beckoned her over.

Beneath the glass, a shadowy outline was forming in shades of brown. Some of the gradations were almost purple, while others had a reddish tinge. The image became sharper by the moment. A group of men stood on a lawn before a stone wall and plentiful ivy. It was the garden at Cloak Lane. She stood perfectly still in case she disturbed the spell that sunlight was working on salt and silver. More detail appeared. The shine of a patent shoe, the grain of cloth, the bristle of whiskers. Rhia leaned closer, completely transfixed. The tableau was almost complete. She recognised four of the five men: Ryan, Mr Montgomery, Mr Beckwith and Isaac Fisher. The fifth man, another Quaker, identifiable by his flat, wide-brimmed hat and collarless coat, could only be Josiah Blake. He had a round, kind face and, unlike the others, he was gazing into the lens with an intensity that made Rhia feel that she was prying. Of the five men, two were dead.

Laurence was nodding as if he understood something. 'This is the portrait Antonia took last summer,' he said. 'She couldn't bring herself to transfer the image, to see Josiah.' Laurence faltered. It was strange for him, too, to look at Josiah. Just as it was for her to see her uncle.

She could not take her eyes from Ryan. He was smiling, his eyes laughing and his cravat tied rakishly. Mr Montgomery looked dashing, his posture elegant and erect and his face relaxed. Mr Beckwith was stooped and awkward but he had straightened his necktie and smoothed his hair. Isaac Fisher looked as inscrutable as always.

'I am stunned,' she said finally. 'I suppose I should give it to Margaret so that she can keep it with the negative. I assume Juliette wanted her mother to see the portrait for some reason. Do you think Antonia gave it to Juliette, though?'

Laurence shook his head. 'I cannot believe she would, though I suppose she might have decided that she couldn't ever face seeing Josiah. It is impossible to know.'

'It doesn't make sense,' Rhia agreed.

Laurence shrugged. 'The maid has always been … unpredictable. Though I'd be curious to know her reasoning, if there is any. You take the negative for now, and once I've fixed the image I'll have Albert deliver the portrait to you.'

Rhia nodded. 'Is it four o'clock yet?' Laurence pulled a timepiece from the pocket of his waistcoat.

'Almost.' He lifted the glass plate and removed the negative gently. He replaced it in its wallet and gave it to Rhia. When it was safely in her apron pocket, he took her hand again.

'Rhia,' he began hesitantly, 'you know, there is a way I could help.' She knew what he was going to say. Could she marry Laurence? Was she a fool if she didn't? It seemed, in many ways, to be the only thing to do. She was fond of Laurence; they were friends. Perhaps the rest would come. She needed to think. 'I must go. I'll be in trouble.' She left before he could say anything else.

In the mess, Margaret was at the table comforting a tearful Nelly, whose girth was now as round as a butter churn. Miss Hayter was settling a dispute over whose turn it was to take the pail up to the deck. Rhia beckoned to Margaret when Nelly went to her hammock to continue weeping. Margaret listened silently to her description of the portrait, but looked increasingly distressed.

'Throw me from the mason's cliff,' she said finally. 'What if the maid was being truthful! Margaret closed her eyes for a moment, then opened them and looked at Rhia squarely. 'I shouldn't tell you, but I can't keep it a secret now, can I? Juliette thinks that one of the men in the picture is a murderer.'

# Cross stitch

Rhia lay in her hammock, pushing her hand against the wall to make it swing. It helped her to think. *If* her arrest was connected to Ryan's death, then presumably someone wanted her out of London. Why, she did not know, nor why Juliette thought that one of the men in the portrait was a murderer, nor what her mother in Sydney might have to do with it. *Which* man did she think was a killer, and *who* had he killed? Possibly one of the dead men was the murderer and his own death an act of retribution. The more she thought, the more confused she became. She needed to talk to Laurence. But what if he asked her to marry him? It was a risk she'd have to take.

At least now she knew that her answer must be no.

She slipped from her cabin. The deck was silent and the moon huge. The ocean looked as black as pitch and she shivered as she remembered another part of the story of Manannán and Rhiannon. Manannán only allowed the lost land to rise from beyond the sea every seven years. Seven years was the length of her sentence.

She encountered no one as she crept along the back passageway Albert had shown her, but as she neared the galley the shadow of a man lengthened into the passageway. The cook had almost collided with her before she had time to retreat. He muttered something in his own language before he lifted his lantern and looked at Rhia.

'You a prisoner, huh?'

She nodded, wondering if he would report her. The face illuminated by the lantern was gaunt and listless; his eyes strangely vacant. She had seen sailors in the port of Dublin that looked like this, who came in on the junks from Hong Kong or Canton. Nell the Fryer called China 'the kingdom of the walking dead'. The spell of opium made it impossible for them to inhabit either the world of the living or that of the dead. Rhia waited for the cook to say something else, but he didn't. He wore a faded, colourless tunic and wide-legged trousers and no shoes. On one skinny forearm was a small tattoo of a Chinese character. The character looked familiar. At his waist sagged a leather belt from which hung several canvas scabbards, and from them protruded the smooth wooden hilts of his cooking knives, too precious to leave unattended. After a moment of scrutiny, he turned his back on Rhia and disappeared.

Just as Rhia was silently congratulating herself on finding her way to the passenger deck, a figure blocked the deck in front of her. Another lantern was lifted and this time Mr Wardell's face was illuminated. He didn't look pleased. He peered at her for a moment before he recognised her.

'Mahoney. You know that it is forbidden for prisoners to leave their quarters without permission.'

Rhia thought quickly. 'Yes, I know, but Margaret Dickson has taken ill and needs the surgeon. I was looking for the infirmary.'

Mr Wardell's eyes narrowed. 'The infirmary is on the starboard side. I'll fetch the surgeon myself. Please return to your cabin.' Rhia did as she was told. She would not be able to see Laurence, and Margaret would probably deny that she had sent for help, but there was nothing to be done.

Rhia returned to her hammock, but sleep was impossible.

She sat up and lit a taper, then reached for her book. She found the calling card from Ryan's room and examined the Chinese symbol. She knew though, before she even looked at it closely, that the character she had seen on the cook's forearm was the same as the one on the reverse of the card. She put it back into the book and took out her pen.

1 May 1841

I remember from your stories that Manannán can conjure storms powerful enough to sink ships, and that he can carry mortals safely to his island. If it is Manannán that I am afraid of, then why am I named after his consort? Is something to be learnt from these infernal stories? I am overtired.

The door opened, flooding the cabin with the rosy light of early morning. Laurence stood smiling at her. He must have known she'd been looking for him. Rhia sat up. 'I wanted to talk to you,' she said.

'I thought so,' he said.

'One of the men in the portrait is a murderer.'

'Ah.'

'Is that all you can say!'

'Rhia. I wanted to help you, but I don't know how I can, now.'

'It doesn't matter. I'm not sure that I love you anyway.'

'I had wondered …' He disappeared and the door closed. Rhia lay down again. At least she didn't have to make a decision now.

Margaret was not in her hammock: so she'd played along with the infirmary story after all. Rhia was rostered with Nora to take all the bedding onto the poop deck, above the quarterdeck, where the blankets were shaken out and aired once a week. Nora scowled when she realised that her companion was to be Rhia. She swung a sackful of bedding at her, almost bowling her over, then hauled her own bundle onto her broad shoulder as if it were a bag of feathers. They climbed the ladder without a word.

On the quarterdeck, half a dozen of the youngest seamen were on their knees in a line, tarring and caulking the timbers and quietly singing a shanty, alternating a solo and chorus. The language bore similarities to Irish, so it was probably Welsh or Manx. A cauldron of pitch was smoking on a huge brazier. The pitch, Albert said, kept the cracks between the decking sealed. The endless washing down of the timbers that Rhia had at first thought uncharacteristically clean and fastidious, also had a purpose. It kept the wood from shrinking in the equatorial heat. When the sea was calm 'ventilations' – variously called scuttles and ports – were opened in the hull so that the warm air could circulate throughout and dry out any parts that were damp and musty. Describing the area below decks as damp and musty was kind. It was, at best, rancid.

Several of the deck hands paused to watch Rhia and Nora pass, their eyes riveted to Nora's imposing bosom. The singing stopped and a remark was made about cannon balls. A low laugh tripped along the line of boys. They had chosen the wrong woman. Nora dropped her sack on the deck and put her ham hands on her vast hips.

'I don't suppose you little sods have seen the glories beneath a woman's petticoats, but if you've not the guts to look her in the eye, you'll get nowhere near her bloomers.' It wasn't entirely true, but an impressive sermon all the same. Nora tossed her head and picked up her bundle, walking straight across the decking that was being caulked, so the boys had to move out of her way.

When they reached the ladder to the poop deck, Rhia was laughing. She stole a glance at Nora who was also laughing. Their eyes met and, for the first time, Nora didn't scowl at her. As they came to the top of the ladder and were at eye level with the upper deck, they heard low voices. Captain Ferguson and Miss Hayter were embracing. Someone coughed close by and they hastily pulled apart and retreated.

Albert poked his head out from behind a coil of rope. Nora sighed. 'Is there no peace from bloody sailors? Go on, Mahoney, go see what the little squint wants.'

Albert was sitting with his back resting against the rope, whittling at a piece of wood with a short-bladed dagger.

'Mornin', Mahoney.' Albert looked smug. 'I expect ye'll be wanting to get a message to your sweetheart?'

'I do need to speak with him, as it happens. Would you see if he could visit me? Perhaps tonight?'

Albert grinned and kept whittling. 'Could do.'

'Albert, do you know if Margaret Dickson is in the infirmary?'

'Aye. They took her in last night. Groaning and carrying on, she was.' Albert shook his head. 'I heard Mr Donovan say she's got acute something-or-other and he's tried castor oil, chalk mixture and sulphate of something-or-other.'

'That's very informative.'

Albert grinned. 'I'll go see your fancy man now. He likes to be up early – something to do with the light.' He tipped his cap and disappeared down the hatch.

Before they had shaken out even half of the bedding, there was a burst of shouting, as if a squall was approaching. They leant over the railing to look down onto the quarterdeck where the sailors who had been caulking were standing in a huddle listening to something that James, the gangly ship's boy was telling them. In another moment James appeared on the poop deck. He looked frightened.

'You're to return to the mess immediately, captain's orders.'

'So now the captain's ordering us about too,' Nora muttered sullenly. They stuffed the blankets back in their sacks and heaved them down the ladders and steps to the orlop.

There was a hum of excitement as more and more women returned below from various early morning chores. A rumour was spreading that there would be no prayer service, which made it feel like a holiday, until Miss Hayter came below and the hatch was closed from above.

'What's all the fuss about, Matron?' asked Agnes, as they collected around the table. No one seemed to know anything, not even someone who had been keeping company with the captain.

'You're all to be confined below for the day,' Miss Hayter said calmly. 'All that I can tell you is that a crime has been committed. Mr Wardell, Mr Donovan and Captain Ferguson are conducting enquiries.'

A moment later the hatch opened again and a pair of bare feet appeared, descending the ladder slowly, followed by a dirty hem. Margaret smiled wanly as she arrived at the bottom of the ladder, but wouldn't look Rhia in the eye.

'Are you a suspect, Dickson?' asked Jane.

'Suppose so. I'm just happy to be away from Mr Donovan's stinking potions.'

They took out their last few strips of patchwork, even though the light was poor. They were only days off Rio, and the final quilt was almost completed.

Margaret looked like she wanted to get back into her hammock, but she stayed at the table with the others. 'I've had an idea,' she said mysteriously, and paused tantalisingly for effect.

'Come on, Dickson,' snapped Nora, 'let's have it.'

'In time, in my own sweet time. What I'm thinking is, since we've all benefited from the charity of the ladies in grey, why don't we do something to show our appreciation?'

'Oh yes,' breathed Nelly. 'But what?'

'A quilt, but not a coverlet like the ones for Rio, a pretty one that they could hang somewhere, with writing on it, saying how much we're grateful for their efforts.'

There was a chorus of approval.

'That's a fine idea, Dickson,' said Miss Hayter. 'I could even ask the governor's wife to put it on the next ship back to London.'

'Ask her to have it delivered to Mrs Blake,' said Margaret, 'she runs the Convict Ship committee. She visited many of us at Millbank.'

Miss Hayter nodded her approval. 'I know Mrs Blake. We'll start on it today. It would take our minds off ... other things.'

'I could start on the cross stitch,' offered Margaret, 'if we were allowed a lamp or two, Matron.' The lamp oil was running low so it was now against the rules to light lanterns by daylight, but it may as well be night with the hatch closed.

'Yes, Dickson, good point. You can't be expected to stay down here all day in the dark.'

A few women started looked through their patchwork pieces for the pretty scraps they had been saving. Agnes remained sitting with her arms crossed, glowering, and both Georgina and Sarah had returned to their hammocks.

'So this quilt isn't for selling?' Agnes snapped.

'That's right,' Margaret retorted. 'It's a *gift*.'

'Well, that's a foolish idea if ever I heard one,' grumbled Agnes. 'What's the point in that?'

Miss Hayter said she thought it might do to make a fancy border for the dedication in broderie perse, a type of appliqué made from cutting out a pattern from upholstery chintz and stitching it into place.

'Has anyone chintz?' she asked. If anyone had chintz, they were keeping quiet about it. It was expensive cloth and might do nicely, one day, to make into a throw for the back of an armchair, or to pretty up a cushion.

Rhia couldn't bear for her chintz to be cut up and sewn into a quilt to be sent back to England.

'We'll need to think carefully about the design before we start,' said Miss Hayter.

'What if it were a medallion design,' Rhia suggested tentatively, 'concentric rows.'

Agnes rolled her eyes. 'Oh shut your trap, Mahoney.' She frowned. 'What's *concentric* anyway?'

'Stripes in a circle, you fool,' hissed Nora.

Miss Hayter was nodding. 'Good, Mahoney. Splendid. If each of you sews one band, then we would have ten strips.'

They passed the time till lunch choosing prints and colours, and whatever was going on above decks was temporarily forgotten. This new quilt was going home. It had meaning.

They agreed that the strips of patchwork would radiate out from the central panel that bore Margaret's dedication, like a medallion. Two of the strips would be much wider than the others and backed with plain linen and appliquéd with a simple flower motif with each petal sewn from a printed cloth. One of these wider panels would surround the centrepiece and the other would form the outer edge of the quilt.

Rhia took her patchwork and sat beside Margaret at the end of the table. At close quarters, Margaret looked tenser than she seemed at first. She was sewing so quickly that she had almost stitched an entire letter before Rhia remembered that she had the negative in her apron pocket. She nudged Margaret with her elbow and passed it, beneath the table.

'By the way,' she whispered. 'Thank you for the favour, Margaret, I hoped that you would understand.'

'What favour. Understand what?'

'I needed to have some reason for being on deck, so I said I was looking for the infirmary, and that you were ill.'

'I've no idea what you're on about. I *was* ill. I went to the infirmary just after you left the mess last night.'

If Margaret were already in the infirmary when Rhia encountered Mr Wardell, he would know she had lied.

Margaret bent her head over her stitching and whispered, 'Albert fetched me from the infirmary, to say I was to be sent below. He was in a state.' She drew in her breath. 'Someone's had the graveyard clay.'

'What?'

'*Perished.*'

Rhia stared at her.

Margaret looked back with wide eyes.

'Who?' Rhia whispered.

Margaret looked down at her sewing, then she dropped it on the table and put her hand over her eyes.

'*Who*, Margaret!'

'It's your friend,' she said. 'Albert found him in his cabin this morning with a knife stuck in his neck.'

# Canvas

Michael glanced around him. The small tenancy he'd acquired when Frank croaked it in the brick pit looked different. The letter changed everything.

The young guard who'd dragged Frank away by the boots had rolled his eyes and given an exasperated sigh, as though the poor bastard had died to be obstructive. Michael recalled how he'd clenched his fist, a twitch away from taking a swing. But the boy was only copying his superiors, and the death of a convict was considered an inconvenience. Frank had been five years in the dank coalmines in Newcastle, north of Sydney, before that, so his lungs were like creaking bellows before he went down the brick pit.

Newcastle was on the Hunter, and Michael had written a piece on how Newcastle was originally called Coal Harbour, on account of a rich black seam that was discovered there. An ill-planned (and unsuccessful) Irish rebellion that originated in Castle Hill, near Parramatta, meant that a good many Irish were sent down the coalmines, and the name New Castle stuck. More recently, the riches of the Hunter valley were the cedar trees: the *Governor's* cedar. The cedar forests were quickly vanishing, from what Michael had heard, in order that all government buildings were panelled, floored and furnished with the stuff. It seemed an unbecoming fate for a tree as majestic and ancient as a cedar – trodden on by men in patent shoe leather.

Frank knew he wasn't ever going to make it home. He told Michael where he kept the key to this place a few days before he died. It was an attic at the top of the ironmonger's at the north end of George Street. Luxuries like a single lodging were rare, even amongst the convicts assigned to private service. Most shared digs in the slums in Glebe, on the western reaches of the city. Glebe was a filthy hole – no sewage, no clean water and more bodies to a room than a doss house in the rookeries. It was not the kind of place to make a man mindful of his humanity.

The room was sparsely furnished, with a canvas cot against one wall and a crate for a table at the window. On the crate was a spirit lamp and a pile of pamphlets. Near the window were a few hooks nailed to the bare tongue-and-groove walls. It was all Michael needed or wanted. It had never been home but it was a refuge. He could walk away from here with his belongings in a wheat sack and not look back once.

Michael looked back to the piece of paper in his hand that changed everything. It was still there. It was real. It was a thing of beauty. It bore a crimson stamp that read, *HR Queen Victoria's Governor of New South Wales.* His Ticket of Leave. Many considered this slip of paper to represent a transition from slavery to poverty, but Michael had no intention of becoming a lackey to the self-appointed gentry of New South Wales. He was going home and he didn't even have to work his passage. He had the fifty pounds for his fare, and more besides. All the years of running his one-man press in Maggie's basement would be paying him in the only currency he valued: freedom.

He smiled as he buttoned his breeches and splashed water on his face from the bucket in the corner. He laced his boots and all the while he thought of Annie. The same sun that was turning its baking glaze from the colonists would be warming the sand at the bottom of his garden at home.

Home.

He walked down George Street as if a tail wind was licking at his heels, coaxing him to trip a jig. He smiled to Dan the draper, who tipped his hat and smiled back.

'Don't suppose you know anyone looking for lodgings do you, Mister Kelly? I've got a couple of nice clean rooms upstairs if you do. Tuppence a bed a night.'

'I'm not, Dan. I'm going home. I'll be sure to put the word out, though.'

'Going home, eh? Well I'll be blowed, that's not something you hear every day. I've got some fine merino in. Soft as silk. Should come take a look.'

'I'll do that. I'm bound for Dublin and they say there's more call for wool than linen these days.'

'You're a lucky man, Michael Kelly.'

'Aye.' Michael's smile broadened as he continued on his way, enjoying the unfamiliar feeling of being lucky.

Oscar was sitting on the wrong side of the bar with his lunch, a pint of stout, and the usual rabble were lined up either side. Michael felt an unexpected bolt of emotion. He'd miss the company of these hard-drinking dissidents.

'Afternoon, Mick,' said Oscar. A chorus of greetings, variously slurred, drowned out Oscar's Kilkenny lilt.

'Afternoon, gents. The usual when you're ready, Oscar.'

Once they'd completed the ritual of remarking on the taste of the brew and someone had blamed the lime, Michael set his jar of stout down on a barrel and packed his pipe.

'Penny for 'em.' Will O'Shea had shuffled over to inspect the contents of Michael's tobacco tin. Michael pushed it towards him and shrugged.

'Not worth a penny, Will.'

'Heard from your lad?'

'Not in a few weeks – should be something from him on the next transport.'

'Anything goin' on?' Will wasn't much interested in everyday goings on; he was asking after Ireland.

'Just the usual. Hungry lads up against the weight of the Crown.'

Will shrugged. 'Been the same for a hundred years. Used to think I could change it too, it's the fool in me.'

'If fools are the only men who think it's worth fighting for, then fools are heroes.'

'And heroes are fools. So are colonists for that matter. Any man who would build a city without a treasury has to be.' Even pickled, Will was good for a yarn.

Michael frowned. It was a strange thing to say out of the blue. 'Now that always gets me. How did anyone trade?'

'Tobacco, boots, rum, everything was currency, wasn't it? If you could write a letter or do sums then you could trade. Of course, once the foreign merchants and military started stopping in the harbour, all manner of coinage was in use: ducats, rupees, Spanish dollars, Dutch guilders and so on. It was all taken out of circulation years ago.' Will's eyes narrowed for a moment, as though he was trying to decide about something. 'What a coincidence we should be having this conversation.' But there were no coincidences with Will, and besides, he was the one doing the talking.

Michael tried not to appear too interested. 'Why's that?'

'Well, I heard a rumour.' He said no more. It was clear what he was after.

'Is it worth a pint?' asked Michael.

'Oh, aye.' Will grinned. Once a jar of stout was in front of him and he'd helped himself to more tobacco, he leaned across the barrel and lowered his voice.

'One of the boys at the Sydney Herald is involved in some ... *personal* business, with the wife of the governor's secretary.'

'You don't say?' Michael took a drag on his smoke, watching Will carefully.

'Aye. And she told him – under strictest confidence of *course*,' Will paused to smirk, secrets being only another form of currency.

'Of course,' Michael agreed.

'She told him that the vault at Government House, where they stored the old currency, was busted open. All that foreign silver's gone.'

'Is that right? When?'

'Oh, some time ago.'

Michael nodded slowly. 'Then there could be some very busy coiners, down the Rocks.'

'That's what I thought,' Will agreed.

'Have you told anyone else?'

'No reason to.'

'Well if you find a reason, would you let me know?' Will agreed that he would, and Michael stood up and drained his stout. He needed to walk.

At the end of George Street the hard glitter of the Pacific stretched out until it hit the wall of the horizon. He was going home, he could afford to be reflective, to be impressed by the achievement of this fledgling city now more than thirty thousand strong. The lattice of streets that traced across the elevated sandstone had once seemed prohibitively foreign, but now the grid was as familiar as the hatched creases on the palm of his hand.

He'd write something about it tonight, in his last pamphlet, about how there was little reminiscent of England or Ireland here, including the promise of reform. The pretensions of class were cast off like a rotten garment, unfit for clothing an Australian. Three generations could now arguably call themselves Australian, but what did the Originals think of that? It reminded Michael that he hadn't seen Jarrah in a while.

Jarrah's people were a different type of prisoner; they were under house arrest. Sydney's slums leaked filth into their hallowed dirt, which was surely the equivalent of emptying the night soil into St Patrick's cathedral. This entire continent was the temple of its people, just as Ireland had once been.

They shut us in the orlop for two days, which means it is three days since Laurence died. Surely he cannot be dead when I can still hear his voice and feel the warmth of his hand? How will Antonia bear it? We are anchored in São Sebastião, Rio, and I must find a way to send a letter. I am waiting for someone to say that it was all a terrible mistake; to receive a note from Laurence.

An extra hammock was hung for me in the mess, which caused a minor riot because Agnes didn't want to sleep anywhere near me, and Jane wouldn't swap places with Agnes because then she'd be next to Georgina. And to complicate matters more, no one is brave enough to admit that they didn't want to be too close to Nora, because her snoring is ear-splitting and probably keeps the pigs and chickens at the other end awake. At breakfast yesterday Agnes threatened Jane with a beating for snoring, even though everyone knew it was Nora. Jane took it out on Georgina, of course. She called her a lardy twit for thinking Australia was off the west coast of Wales. Margaret has been so quiet that it worries me. She worked on her cross-stitch all the time we were below, with her head bent so that no one could see her face. I think she feels more poorly than she will admit. And of course, she knows what happened to Laurence. No one else below does, as far as I know. Miss Hayter must, especially if she is the captain's sweetheart. I wonder if she shares his bed?

Nelly has been annoying everyone because she is so tearful, and the stink and the heat make her ill. I've no idea how many months gone she is now, but her belly is rising like baker's dough.

This morning, just as Georgina took a swing at Jane, we heard a shout above, and then those sweet words: *Land ahead!*

Miss Hayter came below with the other wardens. Our little matron was flushed with excitement that we were at the mouth of the harbour of Rio de Janeiro. Nora made one of her snorting noises and said, 'What sort of name is that for a country?' But you could tell she was as pleased as anyone. Miss Hayter had to shout to make herself heard above the cheer that went up, and when we learned that we were to be allowed up on deck, there was a scramble for the ladder.

The light was as sharp as knives on deck after two days in the dark, and the air was so fresh that it was like an elixir. Everyone crowded at the railings on the quarterdeck. At first sight, the distant buildings and trees and the masts of foreign vessels seemed so perfect that they might have been a painting. A landform on the water's edge is like a beast at the gateway to a bountiful land. I can see why the medieval sailors believed Brazil to be Manannán's Lost Land. But then, they'd didn't ever make it as far as Australia. After a month at sea I have almost forgotten the smells of the earth. I am still noticing the changes on the air. It is like a perfumery; citrus and a faint, woody scent and a honeyed blossom that I don't recognise.

The thrill of being moored in a busy harbour does not disguise the fact that the mood of the crew has changed. The scant few that are still on the ship. I've noticed two dark-skinned men that I don't recognise. They are burly – not built for shimmying up a mast, and it is doubtful that they are seamen. I think they are hired guards from Rio. I have no idea how Laurence's death is being treated by the ships' officers and Mr Wardell. I haven't seen Albert yet. He must be ashore.

It is damn unfair that the free world should be so breath-takingly beautiful when we are on this floating hoosegow. That's what Margaret calls the ship, though I have no idea what it means. The turtles are like small islands floating sleepily in green water, and don't appear to be disturbed even by the occasional excitable porpoise. The porpoises seem so pleased with themselves and their acrobatics and they, above all else, make me pine for freedom.

So now I have seen the coastline of Brazil, but not in the way that I once imagined I would visit a foreign land. At the edges of the inlet is a crescent of pale sand, scooped around a fringed shoreline. Church spires and pretty white bunga-lows are a reminder of comfort and safety. Dark-eyed children in painted rowing boats float around us and are warned repeatedly by the bosun's mate not to climb on board to sell their bananas and lemons. Across the water float har-monies of church bells and laughter and some kind of night songbird.

There are new rules, of course, while we are in the har-bour. Anyone on deck is to be under guard at all times, whether they are airing the bedding, sewing or emptying the water closets. I have been told that Mr Reeve will not need me until we set sail. As far as I know, none of the women have been questioned about Laurence's death. Surely we would be the first to be under suspicion? Besides, Mr Wardell saw me outside Laurence's cabin on the night of his death. Does this mean there is another suspect?

Miss Hayter returned from the Rio market this after-noon in a new straw bonnet and with hundreds of yards of ugly cotton with which we are to sew new clothes. She said at supper that there is a piece of silver for each of us. All the quilts have been sold. The money, apparently, will be kept in trust. She seems to think that it will only encourage gambling. Having spent two full days below, I've noted that a nip of rum is the price for a comb, and an orange is worth a silver thimble.

The quilt for the Quakers is taking shape. There was nothing else to do but sew for two days below. The flowers and birds of my chintz would be perfect to cut out and appliqué onto the centrepiece. If I want to contribute in a meaningful way to the quilt, then I should offer it up for the broderie perse. I have benefited from Antonia's kindness more than any.

I sometimes wonder if you are here, but I don't suppose you are. It sounds as if you are too busy making my father miserable. It was madness to imagine that you could have made this happen to me, but even when I did think so, and I hated you for it, I felt less alone. You could not say, now, that I am spoilt and idle!

# Chintz

In the morning, Albert was leaning over the aft railings with a barnacle scraper, filing off the clinging grey shells that were making the ship resemble a giant crustacean.

'Evening, Mahoney.' He smiled his crooked grin, but it lacked substance. His hair was clumped together in blades as though he had been swimming in the sea and his feet were sandy. For a moment they stood looking at each other. It had to be said, but neither was willing.

'I have not seen you since ...' Rhia began.

'No, not since then.' Albert's shoulders slumped. He looked around covertly. He beckoned to her, and sidled into a hold where a mound of sailcloth was stored. 'I've been doing some extra listening,' he said. 'Seems the poop deck is where anyone who wants a private word goes. Wardell told the Captain he saw you on the deck that night.'

Rhia nodded. She had expected it. 'Maybe I'll be accused.'

'They don't think it was you. Wardell saw someone else creeping about but he didn't get a good look. Too dark.' He looked her hard in the eye. 'I saw someone too.'

'Who?!'

Albert looked at his feet. 'I couldn't say. Too dark.'

'But I *saw* Laurence! He came to my cabin early in the morning.'

Albert shook his head. 'He couldn't have. Surgeon says he

died around midnight – he can tell by the body or something.'

She seemed to have lost the knack for distinguishing between the living and the dead. Albert was looking at her strangely.

'I'm so sorry, Albert, I'm the one who sent you to Laurence's cabin that morning.'

He shrugged. 'I'd have gone anyway. I took him his water pail sometimes. I liked him.'

'What happened? How?' Rhia was still trying to remember what Laurence had said, besides the fact that he couldn't marry her. At least now she knew why.

'Letter opener,' Albert said. 'Surgeon reckons he got woken up by someone creeping about in his cabin – unless he was expecting someone and let them in. He was in his nightshirt … there was blood.' Albert was trying not to cry; they both were. Rhia remembered the portrait. 'Did you notice – was there a photogenic drawing on his table?'

'A what?'

'A photogenic drawing – like a painting of a group of men.'

'Oh, that. I saw it when I took him the salt.'

'The salt?'

'The day before. I couldn't think why he'd want a bowl of salt, so he showed me the picture. It wasn't there when I found him. I know it wasn't there because I looked around, to see how it might have happened.' He was still struggling to be brave, this boy with a man's life. He looked down at his feet again and ran his big toe along a crack in the decking, but Rhia had already seen the tears. 'I never understood it,' he said. 'Painting with light, he called it. Too clever for me.'

Rhia barely heard him. 'Maybe whoever killed him has taken the portrait.'

'Who'd want it?'

She shook her head. Who on the *Rajah*, besides Margaret, even knew about the portrait, let alone wanted it? 'Albert, can you get into Laurence's cabin?'

He shrugged. 'If I wanted to.' It was clear that he didn't.

'If the portrait hasn't been stolen, then it must be in the cabin somewhere. If you find it—'

'If I find it, it's yours.'

'There's something else.'

'You're not easily pleased, are you, Mahoney?'

'If I were, I wouldn't be on this cursed ship. I need to send a letter. Is it possible before we sail?'

'We sail tomorrow. I've leave to go ashore tonight. Is that letter writ?'

'It is.' She'd used paper from her red book and the envelope that Laurence slipped beneath her door. Her precious fountain pen was near emptied of ink, but the letter was in her apron pocket. She gave it to Albert. 'Be sure the postmaster uses sealing wax,' she said. 'Albert, I'll pay you for this as soon as … soon.'

Albert rolled his eyes. 'I've already bought myself a cutlass and I've coin to spare.'

'How long will it take the post to reach London?'

'Depends. Usually three weeks by clipper.' He turned to go, but there was something else Rhia needed to know. 'Albert, is he … ?'

'He's in the ice chest in the infirmary. Surgeon wanted to take a good look, so he'd know how it happened. They were going to take him ashore, but the port authority wouldn't have it.'

'But what will happen?'

'He'll be buried at sea, soon as we're out of the harbour.'

\*

Agnes started it by insisting that a madman was picking off the passengers one by one. She said there had been three deaths already, which was why they'd all been confined below, and reckoned that he'd be coming for one of them next. Georgina had heard that a gentleman had his throat slit for a purse full of silver, but they'd caught the killer and thrown him in a dungeon in Rio. Someone else judged that the cook looked the sort to be going about sticking knives in people. Rhia had the same thought – besides, the cook had the best selection of knives. It was generally agreed that at least one person had got it in the neck from a madman, but debate about the finer details, and whether or not the killer was still aboard, was tireless.

On the third morning out of São Sebastião, the air hung heavy with humidity and apprehension. There were no wardens in the mess, so Margaret sat in her hammock with her bowl of gruel, which she wasn't even eating. Rhia had the chintz in her apron pocket to show to Margaret before she made a final decision. She had not yet reached Margaret when the women's idle chatter stopped abruptly and the table fell silent. Instantly she knew – things were about to get messy.

Georgina was slurping her gruel as loudly as she could because she knew that this, above all else, irritated Jane. Jane glared at her dangerously. Nora grinned happily, enjoying the tension, and the others were eating warily, waiting. Jane finally hurled her spoon at Georgina, hitting her on the bridge of the nose.

'Bitch!' Georgina shrieked. She stood up, leaned over the table and upended her bowl onto Jane's head. The gluey stuff coated Jane's short hair and slid down her neck. She cursed, all godly pretensions forgotten, and hurled her bowl towards Georgina, but hit Agnes who lurched at Jane and toppled her off her bench. They rolled around the floor, tearing at each other's clothes, screaming and pulling each other's hair. No one attempted to pull them apart.

When Miss Hayter arrived Nora was urging them on with cheers and Nelly was wailing. The others, including Rhia and Margaret, were watching. There was nothing else to do. Miss Hayter barked orders like a military commander, and the two were eventually separated.

When they were all at the table again, Jane dabbed a long scratch on her cheek and Agnes hoisted her bosom back into her underclothing. Miss Hayter cleared her throat. 'Get out your sewing, girls,' she said calmly, as if nothing had happened. 'Has anyone thought about our centrepiece?'

This decided Rhia. She took the chintz from her pocket and unfolded it without saying a word, and spread it out on the table.

Miss Hayter looked surprised. 'A lovely piece, Mahoney. Was it in your bag?'

'No. It is mine.'

Jane was leaning over the chintz, tracing her long finger along the wing of a bird. 'It *is* fine,' she breathed. 'As even a weave as I've seen.'

'Yours, Mahoney?' Miss Hayter frowned. 'Then you brought it with you?'

Rhia nodded. 'It is my own design.'

Agnes scoffed. 'Don't lie, Mahoney!'

'That's *quality*, that is,' breathed Nelly.

Miss Hayter interjected firmly. 'Did you not know, Agnes, that Mahoney worked in the trade and is a print designer?'

She turned to Rhia. 'Was this a design for the House of Montgomery?'

'No. I wasn't really a designer. I only hoped to be. It is a picture of ... it's from stories my grandmother once ...' She trailed off, confused by the emotion she felt. She must not weep.

There was awestruck silence as the women crowded around. Rhia caught Margaret's eye. She was grinning like a proud mother. Everyone was leaning over the chintz now, examining every inch. 'Them birds are lovely,' cooed Nelly. 'I once seen some like that in Covent Garden, in a wire cage.' There was general agreement that it was a real piece of work and that Rhia was clever as.

'It is quite perfect for the broderie perse, Mahoney, *perfect*.' Miss Hayter was shaking her head. 'It does seem a shame to cut it up, though. Are you sure?'

Rhia nodded. 'It doesn't matter. I don't want it.' She had never expected to feel that she belonged amongst these women. She hadn't even known that she wanted to.

Every seaman who passed by the awning on the quarterdeck was inspected for signs of villainy as well as for the usual attributes. It had been established that the murderer would be dangerous-looking and acting suspiciously, but there was endless disagreement over how these characteristics manifested. Agnes's current favourite was a Spaniard with a wayward eye and an uneven gait. 'He's got to be a madman,' she whispered.

'Not all killers are madmen,' reasoned Sarah. 'Nelly isn't. My Harry wasn't when he took the shovel to the rent collector.'

'But only a madman would kill for no reason,' said Agnes authoritatively.

'I thought you said the killer stole a purse full of silver,' Nora snapped.

'I never did. It was Jane said it.'

'I did not say so,' Jane retorted.

'But,' Agnes continued, 'if there *was* a purse full of silver just sitting there because the man whose silver it was had got it in the neck, then I would have had it, and so would you.'

Nora threw her sewing down in disgust. 'Don't be a bloody fool, Agnes. He's not got into the man's cabin and killed him *then* seen the silver. It makes no sense.'

Rhia pricked her finger with a needle and bit her lip to keep from crying out. Margaret shot her a look. If Laurence's killer *was* on the boat, and if they wanted the portrait enough to kill for it, then surely they might come for her. Maybe they still would. At present the cook still seemed the most likely culprit. Perhaps he was a paid killer? It was difficult to imagine what personal motives he might have. Money, probably.

The dispute continued all morning whilst they stitched as carefully as if they were mending their dreams. This undertaking had brought them together like nothing else, in spite of the bickering, and today Rhia felt included.

Later, she found Mr Reeve gloating over some cartridge paper and brown ink he'd bought in Rio. 'A superior colour, don't you think, Mahoney?' He was looking at her over the rims of his spectacles, showing her how he had wasted his new ink on another poor rendering. The illustration was of some plant he had seen ashore, but it looked more like a broom head. 'I must say I'm rather taken with the colour of this ink. I wonder what plant it is derived from.'

'Sepia is made from the secretions of cuttlefish,' Rhia said, enjoying his raised eyebrows. 'When they are afraid,' she added for good measure. If humans secreted ink when they were frightened, the ship would be awash in it by now.

'How knowledgeable, Mahoney. It is no wonder you are unmarried.' He laughed as though this were wit of the highest order. She turned back to the specimens spread on the floor and they worked in silence. After a while the botanist threw down his pencil in disgust.

'I cannot draw this blasted foliage,' he complained. His frustration with his own lack of skill usually manifested as heavy sighing and the occasional crumpling of paper, but he wanted his records completed before they reached Sydney and he was starting to lag behind. He was as slow an illustrator as he was a poor one.

Rhia tried not to smile. 'Perhaps I could help?'

He looked suspicious. 'You can *draw* as well, Mahoney?'

'I am told that I can.'

He sighed. 'Very well. Show me what you can do.'

She took a sheet of his new cartridge paper, running her hand over its smooth surface before she marked it. It was of more use for wrapping up gunpowder than it was to Mr Reeve. She dipped the steel nib of his antiquated fountain pen into the inkbottle slowly, savouring the feeling of its weight between her fingers. She traced the outline of the glossy leaf that lay on the table, then the veins, almost effortlessly. It looked like a camellia leaf but was four times the size. When she looked up, Mr Reeve was watching with undisguised envy.

'You have a steady hand, given the circumstances.'

'The circumstances?'

'Well, given the situation, you know, the news of our friend Mr Blake.' He was looking at her suspiciously. He probably thought she had something to do with it. After all, she had visited Laurence just before his murder. And in Mr Reeve's eyes, she was a convicted criminal. She wanted to shout at him that Laurence Blake was not *his* friend, but her friend. He was on the boat because of *her* and now he was dead. But she must not shout and she must not confide, even though a grudging camaraderie seemed to be developing between them. 'It is a shame the ship's officers have not bothered to inform us of the progress of their enquiry,' was all she said, hoping that she sounded unconcerned.

'But they have. There was a passenger meeting in the saloon on the evening before we sailed from São Sebastião.'

Rhia grimaced. 'Of course. It would not be considered necessary to inform those of us who have not paid for our passage,' she said sardonically. Just as they had not been invited to Laurence's burial. Albert had told her about it. As usual, irony was lost on Mr Reeve. He only blinked at her and looked a little confused.

'It has been discovered that Mr Blake was fleeing London after a business enterprise collapsed,' he said, 'and that he was in debt to such an amount that his creditors hunted him down and killed him. I hear that he booked his passage in haste.'

Rhia felt like slapping him. 'And how did these creditors know of his whereabouts?'

The botanist shrugged as though it should not be considered important. He was looking at what she had been drawing on his precious cartridge paper. Inside the leaf, where there should have been a lattice of veins, was a triple knot. She was as surprised as Mr Reeve, but she rather liked the way it filled the leaf.

*Don't forget me, I am Cerridwen, guardian of the cauldron of inspiration.*

How could she forget the muse who had so cruelly deserted her, and who persisted in reminding her of all that she had lost?

# Threads

Today, every wharf at Circular Quay had a foreign vessel cabled to it. The paved esplanade at the sand's reach was, as usual, rowdy with fishmongers and foreigners. Everyone in Sydney was a foreigner, of course, but an order of ascendancy prevailed – a result of the farcical notion of British superiority. The quay excited Michael more than any other part of the city. The strip of beach reminded him of his seafaring youth, and now it contained the promise of home. It was his past and his future. It was also where the postmaster's office was situated.

There was a letter from Thomas in two parts. The page on top was dated later than the second page. It was brief and, judging by the scrawl, had been written in haste.

18 March 1841

We've just had word. Rhia Mahoney is in prison. They say she is a thief, but no one here believes it and I know you will not either. She is to be sent to New South Wales. This may not reach you in time. Perhaps you will already be on your way home.

Michael reread the postscript in disbelief: he was not mistaken, yet it did not seem possible. Rhia Mahoney a thief? She'd always been a mischief, and he had not seen her in more than seven years, but still. He rolled up a smoke, lost in thought, before he read the letter proper. It was about wool, mostly. Thomas said he'd asked Brigit Mahoney, and yes, she was interested in merino from Sydney. Other news though, was sobering.

Sean O'Leary fell by a landlord's firearm last Sunday, leaving his Mary a widow and two wee lads.

Mam sends her love and wishes every day that she had learnt to read and write.

Freedom,
Thomas

Michael folded the thick, coarse paper slowly and deliberately and threw his fag end into the sand, grinding it in with the heel of his boot. Calvin would know which transports were due in.

The Port Authority office was awash with towers of black-spined books and scrolls. It seemed unfeasible that a mind as sharp as Calvin's could function in such a messy place. A young sergeant was sitting at a table with his back to the door scribbling away strenuously. Calvin was at his desk, frowning over a pile of paper. He looked up.

'Afternoon, Michael.' His tone said he didn't like Michael's chances of getting his attention.

'Cal.' Michael nodded. 'Mind if I use your yard to smoke?' Michael shot him a look and Calvin nodded.

'Give me a minute.'

Michael left the bungalow via the verandah at the back. Beyond, there was a log and a patch of sand. All around, the spiky grass trees rustled with life; with birds big enough to make a shrub move, and reptiles the size of dogs.

He sat on the log and rolled two. It helped him to think. In Thomas's previous letter, he'd said Rhia was lodging with a widowed Quaker in London who was in the cloth trade. A Quaker *widow*. He shook his head. He was being foolish.

Calvin appeared and Michael handed him a roll-up. The policeman took a deep draw and closed his eyes for a minute, then looked sidelong at Michael. 'What's going on?'

'I had a tip about a robbery at Government bloody House. You know anything about that?'

'Nope. When?'

'Not too recent.' Michael frowned. 'So they've kept the constabulary out of it. That makes it more interesting.'

Calvin shrugged. 'Cagey lot. Some guv's obviously got a personal interest. What got flogged?'

'Silver. Foreign coin.'

'Well, well. Things might be starting to make some sense.'

'Are they?' It didn't make sense to Michael. He remembered Thomas's letter. 'By the way, did you say the dead Quaker in Bombay was a cloth trader?'

'That's right.'

'Heard any more about him?'

Calvin shook his head. 'Sodding sailor's disappeared. He's probably gone bush. Might need to get Jarrah after him. You think there's a connection?'

'No. Maybe. I don't know.'

'Well that's concise.'

Michael shrugged. 'Just a feeling. But if there's a coining racket on, then I might have something else for you. I'd sooner make my own enquiries. It's not the small-fry forgers that interest me, it's their master. By the way, have you seen any Cape and Orient ships in the harbour? *Medusa*, *Raven*, *Empress* ... can't think of any others just now.'

'Any reason?'

'The shipping company is owned by the Crown bankers.'

'So?'

'They take delivery of all the silver from the opium trade – once it's laundered through the Calcutta exchange.'

'I'm not following you, Michael. What's opium got to do with a counterfeiting operation?'

'I'm not sure yet, but the bank's filthy. Always has been. Their last mercantile was the slave trade. Their Cape and Orient fleet are for hire to any pirate who'll pay. I'll wager that there's Cape and Orient clippers coming through Sydney with silver bound directly to Barings, no questions asked.'

'I think you're getting in a bit deep, mate.'

Michael shrugged. 'Is there a transport due?'

Calvin nodded. 'The *Rajah*. Any time now.'

'Would you let me know if there's a Rhia Mahoney on board?'

'Passenger or prisoner?'

'Prisoner.'

'A friend?'

'Of my boy. I'm starting to get an itch … there's a connection, but I can't for the bloody life of me figure it out.'

Calvin threw his fag end into a rusting bucket and got to his feet. 'If there's one thing you've a knack for, it's pulling the threads together.'

'I'm a weaver.'

'Weaver, publisher, sailor, zealot. What else?'

'A bloody genius, if I'm right about this.'

The Rocks had been quiet such a long time now that Michael was starting to wonder if he'd missed the action. There was always some kind of caper going on at the Rocks, always someone on the make, so why was his gut telling him this was any different?

He stared at the back of the bungalow. The timbers were bleached grey and the roofing iron was rusting up. There was a parakeet sitting on the guttering, like a jewel in the dirt. Maybe he wasn't going home just yet. He wasn't going anywhere until the *Rajah* docked.

# Sailcloth

A ntonia scanned the columns of June's ledger, concentrating as best as she could on figures. Hundreds of yards of balzarine had been despatched to New York, Milan, Amsterdam and Berlin. There was no French buyer yet, but Mr Montgomery had assured her that by the spring, a walking dress cut from their new cloth would be Paris fashion. The perfect blend of wool and cotton would be in every mercer's catalogue, in *Pears* and in *Sylvia's Home Journal*: 'Warm enough for March, light enough for July.' Antonia took a deep breath. She had done it. She had talked about it, and studied Josiah's methodology, and she had thought about little else, and finally she had put her self-doubt and her grief aside. And now death again, sidling up to her, taking her heart piece by piece. Josiah had not lived to suffer the loss of Ryan Mahoney, for which she had been grateful. But it was a blessing he had not lived to suffer the loss of his beloved Laurence, too. She thanked the Lord. Rhia's letter had arrived three days ago, and it had taken Antonia this long to merely believe it true. No one else knew yet.

Mr Dillon was to call at eleven. Antonia looked at the old ship's clock above the wainscoting. Soon. Could she tell him? What would they talk about if she couldn't? She could engage him in conversation about his column and defend the industrialists, the *capitalists*, he was so bent on maligning. The very word was an insult to anyone who strived to protect tradition in industry, to make work for idle hands. She could point out that there was nothing to be gained from nostalgia over the days when fibres had been spun and woven by hand. Did Mr Dillon even understand that most machine-made cloth was of superior quality? Surely he, a commerce writer, knew that a mechanised loom produced a more uniform weave. Linen alone benefited from being hand-spun. Of course, Mahoney Linen had not survived the revolution of the machine, which was – indirectly – why Rhia was aboard that maligned ship. And why Laurence was dead. But who was she to try to unravel the spindle of the fates?

Antonia forced her attention back to the ledger. It was a small comfort that all was in order with the business, and that her colleagues were experienced and principled men. Josiah would never have associated with them otherwise. The old Isaac was struggling back. He had simply ceased to care after his wife's death, and now Antonia had an intimate under-standing of how it felt to have little left to live for. Isaac kept his troubles quiet, but she and Josiah had known. The Quaker congregation did not take kindly to a Friend who could not manage his finances. What was bad for the business of one, reflected on the reputation of all. Isaac arranged the hire of clippers and the shipping of cotton to India. He was a master of the logistics and mechanics of shipping. With Mr Beckwith's talent for money, Mr Montgomery's flare for retail and Ryan and Josiah's trading expertise, the joint enterprise must have seemed the perfect company. The company in her portrait. Rhia had *seen* the portrait.

Laurence had transferred the negative on the *Rajah*. She could not fathom how had it come to be on the ship and in his possession. Had he taken it in error, thinking it was his? He could not have ... The bell cord along the wainscoting pulled. Antonia laid down her pen. She stood and straightened her plain collar and smoothed her hair, as if this could prepare her to tell a man that his best friend was dead.

Juliette was at the front door before her. It opened and the hallway was flooded with sunlight. Antonia could not see Mr Dillon's features, only his silhouette, like a photogram. It seemed apt, since she had not yet the measure of this man who was a symmetry of brooding and wit. She knew him from his *London Globe* writings, but hardly at all from his company. She smiled as naturally as she could. 'Thank you for calling at such short notice, Mr Dillon. I know you are busy.'

Juliette slipped away.

'Could you bring us tea please, Juliette,' Antonia called after her.

Mr Dillon stepped into the hall and to one side, so that the light fell across his face. He was striking, in a mildly untidy way. He wore his black hair tied back, as usual, though a strand or two had fallen loose. His clothes were worn carelessly, though his waistcoat was embroidered with colourful stitching. His heeled boots were covered in dust.

'I'm frequently in the City,' he said.

He followed her into the morning room but ignored her invitation to be seated. She was grateful for the amber walls, today. She needed light. He stood by the window instead, and she stood across the room by the Chesterfield. He seemed preoccupied, but then he usually did.

'I have grave news,' she began, and he looked at her sharply. He sensed it. He turned back to the window and tapped his fingers on the sill. Antonia felt her hand quiver as she smoothed her hair. 'Laurence has – is – he has been ...' She sat down clumsily. 'He has died. Murdered.'

Juliette was standing in the doorway. She must have heard because she was leaning against the doorframe, white as lime. Mr Dillon was quiet for so long that Antonia wondered if he had heard her. He didn't turn to speak. 'How can you know this?' There was an accusing edge to his voice.

'I have a letter. From Rhia. From São Sebastião.'

Mr Dillon turned. His guard was down. He was laid bare. He was devastated.

'Will you not be seated, Mr Dillon?' Antonia said. Her voice seemed to echo around the room as though they were in a mausoleum. He sat opposite her.

'Perhaps you will fetch us that tea, Juliette?' said Antonia. The maid did not appear to have heard. 'Juliette!'

Juliette crept away.

Mr Dillon leaned towards her, and his gaze was as sharp as knives. 'Tell me what you know,' he said.

'Almost nothing. On the day he died, he transferred a photogenic image. It was a portrait that I exposed in my garden last summer. The negative had gone missing. I cannot understand.' She shook her head. 'Is it possible that whomever killed him stole the negative from me and now has the portrait?'

'Whom is this a portrait of?'

'Josiah, Ryan, Mr Beckwith, Mr Montgomery and Isaac.'

Dillon was shaking his head. He looked bewildered.

'What does it mean?' she whispered.

'Who has the negative now?' he asked.

She shook her head. 'Rhia did not say. She wrote the letter in haste.'

Juliette entered with a tray. The cups rattled against the saucers precariously as she lowered it to the table between them. Antonia suspected the maid was about to have another of her turns and she did have not the patience. If she had not love and patience, then her faith was of no use at all. It seemed of little use, lately.

# Stitchery

Juliette put the tray on the table, her hands were so unsteady that it was a blessing nothing had broken. She supposed Mrs Blake still didn't know, since she was not paying her any attention. It had to be the work of the Irish witch that the negative had been made into a portrait. That was not supposed to happen, not *before* it reached Sydney. It was just her miserable luck, and now her mother would never see it and Juliette would never know if it was *him*. But – Mr Blake, murdered! She supposed it was her fault, since she had some curse on her that caused people to die.

'Juliette!'

Juliette had hardly noticed that the tea was spilling all over her hand, or that it was scorching hot. There wasn't much in the cup, but the saucer was full of tea. She put the pot down. It was only a matter of time before Mrs Blake found out what she had done. Maybe Mr Dillon already knew – he seemed the type to know everything, and who'd ever heard of a newspaperman who could keep a secret?

'Juliette.'

'Yes, Mrs Blake?'

'Is something wrong?'

She nodded. He might as well hear it too, and then he could judge for himself if she was wicked. She felt light-headed. Let them judge her. She was done with secrets.

'Juliette?' Mrs Blake prompted her. 'Is it to do with Rhia?'

'No. Yes. Oh, I don't know!' Black calico ballooned around her and her knees hit the floorboards with a crack. The man was by her side like he'd flown there, his hand beneath her elbow. She was surprised by the lightness of his touch. Maybe he was a witch too. He was Welsh, after all. Their eyes met and she wondered if he knew.

She was propelled to the Chesterfield but refused a cup of tea. She'd couldn't tell them everything. She could not tell them she had stolen the negative – that she wanted her mother to see him, to identify him and tell the world that he was an evil man.

'It's to do with my pa.'

'He died, didn't he, in a dispute of some kind?' Mrs Blake sounded so weary. Juliette only felt worse.

'I was only wee, seven or eight. A young man who called himself John Hannam came to take his apprenticeship at our loom. He was a quiet sort, he never said much, but he knew how to talk nice. He was a quick learner, Pa said he was a clever one. He slept in the barn at night and worked all day, and he was on the town whenever he had a day off, up to no good.'

They were both listening quietly. Mr Dillon had narrowed his eyes, as though he thought she was saying something important. She noticed the fancy stitchery on his waistcoat.

'Pa found a pile of banknotes hidden in the barn and asked John Hannam about it. Pa said he didn't want a thief to cross his threshold. John Hannam turned nasty, said it was his business.' The memory still turned her cold and made her anxious. It was as if she was back in their little cottage on the day everything turned bad. 'He took the fire poker and struck Pa in the head then threw it across the room in a temper. It landed half in the fire. I was there, behind the loom, but they didn't see me. John

Hannam walked away, just like that. I ran to the window to make sure he'd gone. He went to the barn and came out with a pistol. Pa couldn't get up. I took the poker and waited at the door. When John Hannam walked in I struck at him on his forearm twice. I left a black burn, like a brand, the shape of a V. It would have left a scar. He shot Pa then he looked at me and I think he was wondering if he should kill me too. I wish he had.'

Mrs Blake's fingers were at her lips. The Welshman was watching her closely.

'John Hannam was never arrested?' he said.

'No, sir. He came from another county. The constabulary stopped looking for him after a few days, that's the way it usually happens. Ma never stopped, though. She went to all the weaver's taverns and found out that John Hannam had a friend he always drank with who was good with his letters. We found out after that the two of them had a racket going with banknotes. I'm not sure what sort of fiddling they did exactly. The constable reckoned their type had different names for different days of the week and that Hannam probably wasn't his real name.'

'And why did they think a man like John Hannam would want to be a weaver's apprentice?'

'They – the constabulary – said he might have wanted to learn the trade for his own reasons, or maybe he just wanted to look the respectable type.'

Mr Dillon nodded as though this made good sense. 'Your mother was transported, wasn't she?' Juliette nodded. He probably thought she was lying because her mother was a thief.

Mrs Blake stood up. 'The tea will be stewed,' she said, as though this were the most important thing in the world.

Juliette jumped up but almost fell over. Mrs Blake pushed her back down firmly.

'I'll make another pot myself. I need to think.'

When she'd gone, Mr Dillon was still looking at her with those pitch black eyes.

'Is there something else, that you'd rather Mrs Blake didn't know?'

'Yes, sir. I only *think*, though. I can't be certain, so I can't say.'

'That … ?'

'That one of them killed my pa.'

'One of whom?'

He was going to make her say it! 'One of the men in the picture, in the *negative*. My ma would know, if she could see him again. She'd recognise him. I was too young to remember for sure.'

He was nodding. 'You took the negative, then? Because you think one of the men in the portrait is Hannam? But how did it get onto the ship?'

'Margaret.'

'Who?'

'I visit the prisons with Mrs Blake. Margaret was in Millbank.'

'And are you prepared to tell me which of the respectable gentlemen traders in the portrait might be John Hannam?'

'It wouldn't be right. It was a long time ago. I was only wee. I couldn't. Not until I'm certain.'

Mrs Blake came in with the teapot. She looked like she might spill it as well if she tried to pour.

Juliette got to her feet. She didn't belong here, sitting as though she were one of them. Nor could she answer any more questions. In the hallway she stopped and listened to their quiet conversation. Mr Dillon said the news about Laurence was a blow and that he could not think straight. He said they must talk about Rhia, and Mrs Blake agreed that they must. She said the letter from Rio had only renewed her determination to have the little witch proven innocent. Of course, Mrs Blake would never call Rhia that. Much as Juliette disliked the Irish strumpet, even she didn't think that Rhia Mahoney deserved to be sent away for ever.

Mr Dillon asked Mrs Blake to call on him soon in his offices, and she said that she would.

It is too sultry to do anything much but sit in the shade of the sailcloth on the quarterdeck. Today a small breeze blew a path through the stifling air and cleared my head to write. I ran out of ink not long after São Sebastião, so I refilled my pen with Mr Reeve's sepia. I have become rather a good thief, as it happens. I decided that I should write a letter to Michael Kelly, just in case he is still in Sydney.

The only respite since Rio came when we dropped anchor off the Cape of Good Hope, but that was weeks ago. Fresh water and new provisions were loaded, including a small herd of goats, but there was little to be seen from the deck but a rocky shoreline and a row of huts.

The orlop is noxious and Nora is in such a black mood that no one will go near her. Agnes says it's Nelly's baby that's making Nora irritable. *Irritable!* Agnes confided that Nora lost three babes in five years, before they were weaned. Two to cholera and the other to the pox. It goes some way to explaining why she is such a harridan. Nelly's little girl was born in the night more than two weeks ago. Nelly didn't want Mr Donovan there, and from what I can gather, the entire mess partook in the delivery. I have no regret that I was absent. Margaret says she bellowed like a caged bear. But when I came for breakfast in the morning, there was Nelly, proud as a peacock, with the tiniest, pinkest little person wrapped up beside her in her hammock. It made me weep. I've no idea why. Her name is Pearl.

Margaret has been in the infirmary again, which seems commonplace now. She is no better and she is no worse. She says she just needs to get off this bucket onto solid earth. She managed to escape Mr Donovan's potions for long enough to come and see me last night, though.

Mr Reeve pretends at being my friend and I am pretending as well, just to have someone to talk to. Yesterday, though, I talked too much and regret it. I am now the illustrator of his botanical archive, which has become considerably more accurate since he laid down his pen. He has alluded that I might be of some use to him as an assistant when we arrive in Sydney, but he would have to pay for my upkeep if I were to continue in private service and I can tell that he is not pleased about this. I'd wager that he could not afford it, and I still wonder how he found the means to pay for his passage. I have gathered that his father is dead and that his mother takes in mending, so it could not be family money.

Yesterday I woke from a terrible dream in which Mr Dillon blamed me for Laurence's death. I felt miserable about it all day and still do. When I took the glass stopper from the pot of sepia, a few drops fell on the clean cartridge paper. It was a minor catastrophe, but I wept all the same. Mr Reeve was at loss over such inconvenient behaviour. He offered a handkerchief and asked if there was something I wanted to talk about. I've no idea what came over me, because I told him everything – that I was acquainted with Laurence, and about the photogenic drawing and how it disappeared. He asked, quite rightly, what could be so important about this portrait that someone would kill for it? 'The idea is perfectly insensible,' he said. He managed to say this in such a way that he might have been talking about the death of a dung beetle.

Of course, I didn't disclose the last piece of the puzzle –

that the portrait supposedly identifies a murderer. What if someone should think it was Ryan? The more I think about it, though, the more I wonder if Juliette is just all worked up over nothing. Mr Reeve seems fascinated by the idea of the portrait and suggested that the men might have a common enemy, and asked me if I could think of any other reason why someone might steal such a thing. I eventually lost my patience and told him I had been dwelling on little else for weeks, and that no I still couldn't think of any reason. He is probably hoping to solve the mystery himself, but he is simply not clever enough.

Albert says we are travelling north now, along the eastern coastline of Australia, and that we are within a week of Sydney Cove if the wind stays behind us. Sometimes you can see the shadow of land on the horizon, but now the thought of leaving the ship is as daunting as was the thought of boarding it. I am sick of the sight of needlework. We are sewing shirts, now. Before that we made ourselves summer gowns. They are shapeless and ugly, made of cheap brown cotton, but cooler than linsey. The quilt for the Quakers is finished. It is larger than any of the coverlets that were sold in Rio, measuring more than one hundred and twenty inches across its longest side. At its centre is a square of broderie perse that I cut, so carefully, from my precious chintz and arranged in a spray of bright birds and blossoms. My herringbone stitch is now as swift and neat as anyone's. No doubt I might find work as a needlewoman when I am free, not that I'd want it.

When I am free.

Freedom no longer even haunts my dreams. I am a prisoner, by day and by night. I am so listless that even Manannán has ceased to provoke me. My greatest fear now is that I might become so miserable that I cease to see colours and patterns altogether.

The quilt is to be presented to the wife of the Governor of New South Wales, who is a great admirer of Elizabeth Fry and prison reform. We hope that she will take responsibility for sending it back to London where it will be presented to the ladies of the Convict Ship Committee. Miss Hayter has agreed that it should be delivered to Antonia Blake, as a representative of the charity, on behalf of all of the women of the *Rajah*. The dedication is complete. Margaret has been working on it from the infirmary. Her cross-stitch (which she says is so perfect because she is always cross) graces the lower, outer border of the quilt. Last night she escaped Mr Donovan for long enough to come and tell me that she has found the perfect hiding place for the negative, and that I mustn't worry because it is safe. It is peculiar that she should feel it necessary to come and tell me this and as I said to her, I wish she had come to my cabin before now. We both know that it is too risky, though, with Wardell on the prowl. She looked better for taking the air and I think she might finally be growing strong again.

I suppose I must make the effort to rise. There has been more noise than usual on the lower deck this morning; perhaps a storm is brewing. A storm would be welcome, to interrupt the boredom and lethargy of these long, still days.

# Herringbone

A foreign vessel was the cause of the commotion on deck, visible in the distance off to the north. It was odd to see an interruption to the endless, vacant miles of ocean. Rhia thought no more about it until she saw it again from the quarterdeck after breakfast. The ship drew closer through the morning until its outline was distinguishable. It was a junk.

'Chinese,' said Agnes, knowingly. 'Seen one on the Thames.'

The wind dropped and the vessel barely drew nearer throughout the day.

In the afternoon, as Rhia was preparing to leave Mr Reeve, there was shouting and the pounding of feet outside. A moment later the steward, James, opened the door. 'Captain says everyone's to stay in their cabins.'

Mr Reeve jumped like a frightened rabbit and bumped his head on a shelf. 'Whatever's going on?'

'Chinamen', said James. 'Might be pirates. They probably think we're carrying opium or sterling.'

'*Pirates!* But why would they think that?' asked Mr Reeve, his voice close to a squeak.

The steward looked at Mr Reeve as though he'd no clue about anything, which was a fair assessment. 'Well, we're this side of India and we're a barque, sir, and we're due north. We could be on our way to Lintin Island.'

Mr Reeve was pale to his gills. 'Then they'll realise they are mistaken soon enough,' he said without much confidence. Rhia couldn't help feeling a small thrill. Perhaps they'd not make it to Sydney Cove after all! Could it be worse to be a prisoner of a pirate than of the Crown?

'Might be too late by then,' said the steward dramatically, and hastened away to do whatever an officer's servant does to defend his ship against Chinese pirates.

Being confined indefinitely with the botanist was out of the question. 'I think it would be best if I went below with the others,' Rhia said as soon as the steward left.

'I think you should stay. It might be dangerous, Mahoney.' He buttoned his frayed tweed waistcoat in spite of the heat, as though it might afford him some protection. He didn't want to be on his own.

'I think it would be best if I went,' she said, already halfway out the door. She had no intention of going below. She crept along the dark passageways that Albert had shown her, until she was at the cranny 'tween decks. There was a view of the prow part of the main deck through the scuttle in the timberwork. Orders were shouted down the line from the captain to the ship's boys. On the gun deck at the prow, half a dozen barrels of black steel were levelled at the approaching ship – its red sails now easily distinguishable. Rhia had seen plenty of these bamboo-masted ships in the port of Dublin, trading porcelain and figured silk. Orders continued to be shouted down the line of barefoot sailors. Cutlasses and pistols had appeared, stuck into belts and cummerbunds. To all appearances, the crew were expecting trouble.

'Well, well, it's Mahoney, turned ship's lookout.' Rhia jumped. It was Albert. 'Shouldn't you be on deck?' she whispered.

He shrugged. 'I'm short-sighted, so it's no good my trying to make a mark with a pistol. I'll fight if they come on board.'

Albert patted his belt, and she saw his new cutlass glinting there. 'Give us a look through the scuttle,' he said.

Rhia stepped aside so he could see the deck.

'What do you think?' she asked, suddenly feeling less certain about being the prisoner of pirates. 'What would they want with a ship of prisoners?'

'They won't know it's a prison ship. They'll be after bounty. There's a busy shipping route between Calcutta, Canton and Sydney. Sometimes silver goes through Sydney before it gets to Calcutta, if it's a clipper or a barque carrying rice or tea or whatever. There's all manner of dealing goes on in the open sea.'

'You mean criminal dealings?'

Albert grinned. He was doing his best to look brave, but she could see he was worried. 'Most traders run rackets of some kind or other – even if it's only not paying all their port taxes.' He turned his attention back to the scuttle.

'What's happening?'

'You don't have to whisper – no one can hear us. The cook's on deck and he's talking to one of the Chinamen who's come up to the side in a rowing boat.'

'What's he saying?'

'I don't know, he's talking Chinaman.' Albert was silent for a long moment.

Rhia remembered something she'd been wanting to ask him. 'Albert?'

'Mm.'

'Do you know what the Cook's tattoo means?'

'I asked him myself,' Albert said after another long silence. He would not take his eye from the scuttle.

'And?'

'He used to be a silversmith and he says it's to remind him that there's more to life than a stinking galley.'

'But what does the symbol mean?'

'Silver.'

'What's happening now?'

'If ye'd stop asking me questions I might be able to— ah.'

'What!' Rhia wanted to push him out of the way so she could see for herself.

'They've brought the body up on deck. That's the one thing that'll ward 'em off. It's a bad omen to any seaman, English or Chinaman, if a woman dies on a ship. Now there's two Chinamen on deck and the bosun has his hand on his pistol. They're looking at the body. Aye, that's done it, they can't get off our deck fast enough now!'

Cailleach had been busy. 'A woman? Who has died?'

Albert looked at her strangely, and Rhia knew the answer before he told her.

'Dickson,' he said. 'Two days ago.'

Margaret.

The afternoon dragged, and so did supper in the orlop. Everyone knew now, and the mood was dark. Just as Rhia was wondering if they would be allowed to attend Margaret's burial, a warden came below and herded them all up the ladder for an 'evening service'.

The sea was as smooth as silk and there was barely a wisp of wind. It was still baking hot, even with the sun sinking into the dark water. Reverend Boswell stood at the prow, his hair damp beneath his flat preacher's hat. His congregation was divided into three parts. The women, barefoot in their black aprons and cloth caps, stood at the back with their heads bent. This deference owed as much to the final piercing rays of the sun as to the solemnity of the occasion. The passengers, half a dozen ladies and the same number of sweating husbands in Sunday broadcloth, were as far away from them as they could be. The crew comprised another huddle, restless and resentful. The Lord was encroaching on their domain. Behind them on the deck was a long, body-shaped cylinder of sailcloth.

Boswell mopped his brow. 'Lord have mercy on the soul of the sinner Margaret Dickson.' A gust of wind lifted up his hat and spun it away into the silken sea. For a moment the preacher looked too startled to speak, but he recovered, and shot a withering look at the women. The laughter was contagious and no one was attempting to hide it. Margaret clearly didn't take kindly to being called a sinner.

Her body had been sewn into the sailcloth and was now raised onto the shoulders of four sailors. A plank of wood rested on the deck rail, held in place by four more. Margaret was laid on it. Her bier was tilted until she spun into the sea like a spent cocoon. She disappeared instantly into Manannán's vault.

# III

# Wool

The gum has no shade,
And the wattle no fruit;
The parrot don't warble
In trolls like the flute;
The cockatoo cooeth
Not much like a dove,
Yet fear not to ride
To my station my love.
Four hundred miles off
Is the goal of our way,
It is done in a week
At but sixty a day.
The plains are all dusty,
The creeks are all dried,
'Tis the fairest of weather
To bring home my bride.
The blue vault of heaven
Shall curtain thy form,
One side of the Gum tree
The moonbeam must warm;
The whizzing mosquito
Shall dance o'er thy head,
And the goanna shall squat
At the foot of thy bed;
The brave laughing jackass
Shall sing thee to sleep,
And the snake o'er thy slumbers
His vigils shall keep.
Then sleep, lady, sleep
Without dreaming of pain,
Till the frost of the morning
Shall wake thee again

*Robert Lowe*

# Fur

The cold sea swirled at Rhia's ankles. The sodden weight of her hem was all that anchored her as they waded to the shore from the *Rajah*'s rowing boats. Her legs felt like they might buckle at any time. They were sea legs, now.

The sunset was a wildfire behind those strange trees. The tallest, whitest trees she had ever seen. Smooth branches and pale trunks glared in the half-light. The air was a choir of sighs and screeches, and the long grass beyond the sand rustled with unseen creatures.

Rhia could hear Nelly praying behind her, little Pearl tied to her front in a shawl. Nelly expected natives to be waiting for them in the trees, ready to run them through with spears and stew them in a vat. Ahead, Jane, who had put her foot down on something sharp in the water, was limping painfully. More than half the women, including Nora and Agnes, had reached the shore. There was something that weighted the air here, something beyond their experience. It had coiled itself around Rhia as soon as her bare feet were drawn down in the soft suck of brown sand. This place felt old. Old. The Wicklow Hills, by comparison, might have sprouted from the earth last spring.

At the edges of Manannán's kingdom is the land where all earthly souls seek to enter. Each time a wave curls onto its shore, another spirit is granted entry.

Rhia forced her attention onto what she could see. The harbour front was a hundred yards away to the north, lit with gaslamps and braziers. There were two clippers moored at the quay, and at least three more anchored a mile or so out to sea. The sound of men's voices was tossed about on the waves along with the snatch of a shanty and the creaking of willow as crates were unloaded onto the sand. There were low timber buildings, *bungalows* Albert had called them in Rio, along the seafront. To the south were towering cliffs and dark, jagged rocks and, she presumed, a hundred more coves like this one. The smells of wood smoke and livestock mingled with the scent of Mr Reeve's uncharted flora.

There was nothing here to remind her of home.

They were herded towards a strip of beach deserted but for a band of soldiers in dusty coats. The soldiers eyed them as they stumbled from the sea. Did they expect someone to try and run into the dark thicket beyond the sand? As if any of these frightened, exhausted women would. Better to face another prison than those ghostly trees and the beasts that inhabited them.

By the light of the soldier's lanterns they marched along a path through the grass and the underbrush and between the trees to a dusty road. The forest was not as dense as it had looked from the beach, but the trees were as unearthly. They had sparse, silver foliage, and the bark hung from their trunks in strips, as though they were shedding skin. Like snakes. Something thumped close by, making the underbrush quiver and the ground vibrate. Were there bears in Australia? Nelly had taken out her rosary beads.

The soldiers didn't seem to be paying the bear any attention. They were assessing the herd of women and made no attempt to pretend otherwise. Why would they? They were female livestock who may as well be fettered, and no longer the sole property of the Crown. They were appraised as they walked, presumably to see who had limbs strong enough for tilling soil and who might still yield a brood.

Rhia kept her eyes to the road, concentrating on not stumbling on the motionless ground, vaguely noticing how the pale dust clung to her wet feet. She swallowed the bitterness that rose in her throat as she remembered her dream of sovereignty. What a time to think of it. Sovereignty be damned. Agnes said that the best way to get out of the female factory was to find a husband. She knew this because her paramour on the *Rajah* had taken two such wives. No one had seen fit to ask what had happened to them. Sailors, soldiers and free settlers could all take convicts for wives.

Rhia felt something prod her in the ribs. She looked up into the dirty face of a boy barely old enough to shave. He had a stick of some kind and he was tapping it against his hand. He looked her over as he had probably seen a superior do. His eyes lingered on her chest. She folded her arms. He looked at her face last, and she was ready. She hissed one of Mamo's best curses at him, as though she knew the kind of witchcraft that Juliette had suspected her of. He looked away. He was not that brave after all. She noticed that Nelly had attracted the attention of a young soldier with a kinder face. He offered her a drink from a little flask hooked to his belt. He said something to her, and in response Nelly pulled the shawl aside proudly so that he could see Pearl.

A mile or so along the dirt track, there were suddenly fewer trees and wider streets and, at first, rough-hewn bungalows. Further still was red brick and new masonry and even a gaslamp or two. They were being watched with idle curiosity by children playing at the side of the road and men smoking on steps and women standing on verandahs with infants on their hips. Their expressions said that they had seen many such processions. Rhia kept from catching the eye of any of them. She didn't want to see either sympathy or indifference.

They passed partly constructed walls and timber frames and then elegant structures of honey-coloured stone as the street widened. They passed a large green with new grass and rose-bushes planted around its perimeter and a paved path through the middle, lined with seedling trees. Here was a nation in its infancy and Rhia almost wished that she gave a damn.

They were heading for somewhere called the Barracks, this much they knew. In the morning, most of them would be taken to the female factory at a place called Parramatta. Rhia had clearly not been assigned to private service, in spite of Mr Reeve's assurance that he had requested her as his servant. She knew he could not afford a servant. He would not have thought to pay her the respect of calling her his assistant.

The Barracks lay opposite the green. It rose above tall, exterior walls and had a paved courtyard. Its external geometry was stern but elegant. Inside, though, it rivalled Newgate for neglect. The dividing walls were unfinished slabs of pine, and the floor was stamped earth and mildewed straw. It was fitting accommodation for livestock. Rhia wanted only to lie in a hammock or on a mat, or even on a wooden pallet. If she could close her eyes, maybe the ringing in her ears would stop and the earth would be still.

The soldiers divided them between two large, open cells. There were no hammocks or mats, only more straw, and there was not enough room on the floor for sixty women to lie down. There was a scuffle for a piece of wall to lean against, but only one half-hearted cuff fight. No one had the energy. They sat and listened to someone retching in another cell.

'That's not a good sign,' said Jane.

'Think it's the food?' Georgina whispered.

'Shut your ugly mug,' Jane hissed.

Once they had settled, a beefy turnkey with a beard like a Jew peered in through the iron bars.

'Don't think this lot will give us any trouble,' he called over his shoulder to someone Rhia couldn't see. He unlocked the grille and dragged in a vat and a bulging sack. The vat was full of thin, salty broth and the sack was crammed with unleavened bread and tin bowls. They ate hungrily in spite of the forewarning. It was something to do.

Rhia closed her eyes. It was growing cold. She would not think of home. She would not think of her family. She would not think of the bathroom at Cloak Lane. She would not remember the dead. She would never think of freedom again, she decided. She sat with her back to the splintered wood, feeling the cold seep into her, and thought of … nothing.

She dozed fitfully, being woken time and again by a raging desire to scratch her itchy skin, or by Nora's growling snore. In the small hours it seemed that everyone in the cell was awake, and that morale had reached its lowest. Jane was weeping again and each time she sniffed, Nora kicked her, which only made her sobs louder. There were bugs in the straw, so small they couldn't be seen, and they left itching welts on the warmest, softest areas of flesh.

At sunrise, Agnes passed around some hard arrowroot biscuits, broken into pieces, which she'd smuggled from the ship in her apron. They were stale and tasteless, but the gesture was one of solidarity. They had come this far together, and they had survived.

'How about a story, Agnes?' said someone.

'Not a hope. I've none in me.' She sighed. 'It's this place, it's so uncanny quiet.' It was. But it wasn't the prison that weighted the air; it was a quiet that rose up from the earth like a silent requiem.

When a thin stream of daylight slid through a small high window they were roused by the turnkey, who was sleepy and cantankerous and herded them outside to a line of covered wagons. Rhia's wagon was full even before she stepped up, and three more women were shoved in after her before the canvas was fastened with rope and buckles. It jolted off on a rumbling, shaking ride. Nothing to look at but the others' miserable faces. She supposed she looked much the same, with dark rings under her eyes and straw in her hair and the blades of her shoulders visible through the dirty material of her gown.

The journey was short, and before long they were unloaded onto a grassy bank. Even the grass was foreign. It was thick and springy and a little sharp beneath their feet. And then there was the river, like nothing Rhia had ever seen. It dwarfed the distant rows of pale stone and painted timber. It flowed into the harbour from the west, cutting through the landscape as though it was hurrying somewhere important. The waiting barge, tethered to a rickety pier, was like a flat-bottomed freight boat with one large sail. Freight, livestock, it was all the same. At its helm was a withered seaman wearing an over-large military coat with a dirty kerchief tied around his head.

No one spoke. The landscape seemed hallowed, somehow; more than a church – the immensity of the sky above, the smooth dark water with mist smoking above it, and the jungle of silver eucalypts on either bank. From these, periodically, rose flocks of brilliantly coloured parakeets and enormous white birds with yellow crests.

Birds of jewel colour.

Rhia was numb with cold but even so she felt a low, visceral fear of the green-brown water and its flanking forest. It couldn't be real. She had, finally, reached the Otherworld.

The July sun was strong and sharp and eventually warmed them a little. Rhia judged that at least one hundred of the *Rajah* women were in the barge, sitting on the long side-benches or on the floor, dumbstruck by the mazarine sky. She saw her own uneasiness reflected wherever she looked. Were there beasts in the forest, or in the water? What were those noises they kept hearing, the same as last night – the thumping through the trees and that high-pitched cry that sounded so uncannily like human laughter? 'Natives,' said Nelly between clenched teeth and Hail Marys. She was certain she'd end up in a pot before they reached Parramatta. Her soldier was on the barge, though.

The sun rose and they were issued with more of the unleavened bread to stop the gripe of hunger. Another hour passed, or more, before someone screamed. It was so shrill a sound that a great mantle of birds rose from the trees, shrieking in chorus. There was a man on the shore, standing between two white tree trunks, but he was not white. He was as black as polished leather. Dressed in a cloak of patchwork fur and, it appeared, little else, he didn't move a whisker. He watched with solemn disinterest as they passed. His rod-straight pose and the stoic rills of his face made Rhia wonder, fleetingly, if he might actually be a statue. His face was the mask of time itself, yet there was something hauntingly familiar about him. Perhaps it was the presence of this man's people that she had felt the moment she stepped onto their land. The barge passed by slowly but he didn't move or follow them with his eyes.

When the sun was high above, they chugged over to a cleared part of the shore where there was an inn of sorts. It was an unpainted bungalow with a dangerously leaning verandah.

It proved to be little more than a rum shop, and the only fare to be had, besides rum, was something the lubricated inn-keeper called kangaroo pie. This was a stew served inside a wedge of the same tasteless bread they had been eating since they arrived. The innkeeper called it 'damper', even though it was as dry as the ashes it was baked in. They sat around the dugout fire on logs, eating their kangaroo pie. The meat was, apparently, 'wild and to be found hereabouts'. The innkeeper might be described in the same way.

There was no tarrying after they had eaten. They returned to the barge, just as the thumping noise started up again, sounding closer than ever. Then something that looked noth-ing like a bear jumped out in front of their trudging queue. It was gone in a bouncing grey blur that raised a shriek from several women and, again, from a canopy full of birds. When the creature and its noise disappeared, the slightly crazed laughter of the innkeeper could still be heard.

'That there's a kangaroo,' he called, between splutters.

'Well,' spat Nora, with a toss of her head. 'It's nought but a monstrous-large hare with the tail of an overgrown rat.'

Rhia laughed from relief and nerves and because the crea-ture was either the largest rat or the strangest-looking hare she'd ever seen. She could tell Nora had been as shaken as any of them, but she still had her mettle. This, too, was a relief. Rhia didn't know what she'd do if Nora lost her spite. While there was still one amongst them who couldn't be broken, they could survive anything. The laughter spread quickly and by the time they reached the barge they were all as merry as if they'd been at the rum.

The wind was behind them all afternoon and they knew that they had reached their destination when a high stone wall rose up in place of the tree line. It seemed to run for ever along the riverbank. The wall was grey and foreboding and almost made Rhia wish she could remember a prayer.

It could only be a prison.

Disembodied voices floated across the water, presumably from the unseen township of Parramatta. They pulled into a pier near some towering, blacked iron gates and Rhia caught Nora's eye. To her astonishment, Nora winked and leaned towards her. 'It won't be for ever,' she said. 'And whatever you do, Mahoney, don't let 'em see you're afraid.'

I'm losing count of the weeks, but shall never forget the first night. We were gathered together on the spiky lawn at twilight, surrounded by the silhouettes of eucalypts. That's what the strange trees here are called. They are like sentinels at the edge of the world. That night, the superintendent told us that there are three classes of women here at the House of Female Correction, otherwise known as the female factory. The classes are Crime, General and Merit. The *Rajah* women are firmly 'Crime', and we've had our heads shorn again as a mark of this. It was not as bad as that first time at Millbank, but I had only just started to feel less like a hedgehog. I can't fathom how men put up with prickles on their chins, it is like sleeping on a pincushion.

As to the class system, General class inmates are girls who've returned pregnant after being assigned to service. There are a significant number of them. Merit class have managed six months of good behaviour and can leave the grounds, though they must be back by nightfall. If you are Crime, you work all hours. We are the machines in the factory and we are the servants of the ruling class of turnkeys and wardens.

The superintendent is a heavy-jawed harpy, much like her counterparts in Newgate and Millbank. I realise now how lucky we were to have Miss Hayter on the *Rajah* (and by the way, Albert told me that she and Captain Ferguson are engaged to be married!). I suppose the superintendent has a name and a mother, but it is hard to imagine it. She presides over a number of outbuildings including stores for wool and flax and places for bleaching cloth.

It took me some time to notice it, but the female factory is not unattractive to look at, for a place so miserable. It is three-storeys of sandstone with a clock tower and cupola and an oak-shingled roof. The upper windows are lead glazed and those below are barred, of course, but still lead-lights. There's a kitchen and bake house, a spinning room and dungeon-like privies. It is in the privies that all manner of illicit activity takes place, from rum smuggling to trysts with soldiers and, I hear, between women, too.

Inside the main building, the entire ground level is a refectory lined with long, narrow tables and benches, and the floor is paved with slabs of a pale timber called stringy bark. The sleeping quarters, where I am now, are nothing new. By the light of the tallow (the first one I've managed to steal) you can just see that the floor is covered with bodies. We sleep on bedrolls that we fold up in the morning, and are so close to each other that if you venture an incautious leg out in the night you can easily start a scuffle. Some of the women have collected scraps of fleece and piled them together to sleep on, but it's dirty and flea-ridden and I prefer the hard floor and blankets, though they are made from the roughest wool you can imagine. It is spun here at the factory, and it is a coarse tweed that is, not surprisingly, called Parramatta cloth. I've heard that it is being exported to England, but I cannot see it making much of an impact – it makes your spun wool seem as soft as silk by comparison, Mamo.

The warden who is assigned to the spinning room is not unfriendly and is finally answering my questions, now that she sees that I can still spin as fast while she's talking quietly to me. I've learnt that the only market for Parramatta cloth in Australia is for prison clothing. I suppose much of the population of Sydney is clothed in it, then. It is heavy, brown and dowdy, of course, but it is warm. It is winter in Australia while it is summer in Ireland, which still confounds me. I am always cold.

We were set to work the day after we arrived spinning the fleece that comes from the sheep stations north of Sydney. The settlers are paid in cloth, and around four pounds of fleece yields a yard of cloth, so there's not much in it for them once they've paid the surplus of one pound to the government for the cost of manufacture. The Crown is making money from our labour! And this is called free trade.

There are other officers who aren't as friendly as the spinning-room warden. Nora has now been sent three times to do hard labour in the grounds, for no more than a sideways stare and a grumble. There is no satisfaction in grumbling when you are made to break stones and dig the hard earth as penance. We are denied tea and sugar for minor offences, and I've gone without for my blessed interestedness, otherwise known as asking questions of the wrong warden.

The spinning room is dim and airless with a smoky fire at one end. There are several women I know working there – Jane and Nelly and Agnes, and Nora when she isn't being punished. Pearl is always close by Nelly in a willow cradle that someone gave her, and the baby is growing fat and sweet in spite of the misery around her. Nelly's soldier has applied to make her his wife. I hope she can leave before Pearl grows out of her cradle.

The women who cannot spin pick the bracken and dags from the fleece, or card the spun wool. The yarn is woven somewhere else in Parramatta, by male convicts on manual looms. Weaving is considered to be men's work, even here, as though the simple mechanism of a loom is beyond female comprehension.

There are no mills to provide the power for mechanised looms here. It seems that there are precious few in the entire colony. I occasionally think of what Ryan said to me the night he died, when he came to my room. I thought then that it was a dream. He said it was up to me to send a shipload of Australian wool to my mother. Well, here am I spinning the stuff, but I'm damned if I can see how this gets me any closer to shipping it. The oily feel of the fleece and the action of twirling the yarn between my fingertips onto the spindle is such a familiar action that I cannot keep my thoughts from Greystones. I've given up on trying to banish thoughts of home because it is only in imagination and memory that I feel alive. My body is always either cold or tired or hungry. I can conjure all sorts of things now. A meal of porter, coddle and soda bread with Annie Kelly's yellow butter and blackberries with thick cream. Sometimes I can almost feel the cloth that I once wore and, very rarely, I catch a glimmer of a pattern in my mind's eye, as though it were dancing just out of reach.

One last thing and then I must sleep, because the bell rings at daybreak and we have only minutes to be ready and at breakfast in the refectory. It is too miserable to be sent to the spinning room hungry as well as cold. The female factory has other functions, besides the spinning of coarse wool. It is a wife market, too, because free men can select a wife from amongst the convict women. None are obliged to leave with their suitors, thank Christ, but I hear that most do, just to be rid of the place.

Agnes has discovered a roaring trade in buttock and twang and, since she means to run her own place when she's free, she is keen to have some experience of an Australian brothel. Prostitution is the only means to afford a life outside of the factory, if you have no other skill, and the reason for the number of inmates who return pregnant. Many of the women who are allowed outside the grounds use their leisure time earning a bit extra at their second job. I hear there were several established brothels in Parramatta. I have considered the possibility myself, but am too unskilled.

28 July 1841

I have met a real Australian now, though I wouldn't tell anyone but you. I'm certain that it was the same gentleman we saw from the Parramatta River the day we arrived, and now I know why he seemed familiar. I've seen him before. I saw him first in the photogenic drawing at Cloak Lane. He was the figure amongst the trees. I swear that it was he. I would say this to none but you.

He was standing behind an enormous old tree when we were sent to collect firewood after supper in the grounds. If he hadn't moved, then I would have thought him part of the tree, because his limbs and his fur cape blended so well into the bark in the twilight. It was as if he was waiting for me. A foolish notion, I know. I would have made a sound, but he put a finger to his lips. He greeted me in English, of sorts, and asked me my name and the name of my ship. If he *was* real, rather than a shadow, then I can't imagine how he got into the grounds, so I suppose he was a spirit of some kind. This place is swarming with them.

Our property is locked up in one of the stores, to be returned to us when we receive either a ticket of leave, or an offer of marriage. It was easier than I expected to get to my trunk. There are no firm rules against inspecting your own property, and I've had my eye on the soldier who guards the stores, and I made sure that he also had his eye on me. The stores are large sheds, made of rough, untreated timber with a corrugated iron roof. The guard is no more than a pimply youth who wears his serge tunic with so much pride that I can tell he's not yet had reason to think ill of his profession.

I smiled at him last time I was collecting firewood and then I decided to try something. I walked right up to him and asked him if I could see if my trunk was safe. It was almost that easy. He wanted a kiss, of course. I gave him a good kiss on the lips, but he must have thought he could have more, and his hand wandered until I had to slap it away. He was disappointed but, thankfully, kept his part of the bargain. The building is the size of a barn and is stacked from top to bottom with the sorriest collection of luggage you've ever seen. There are cracks between and across the wall timbers and a dusty lattice of sunlight fell like a net of light across walls stacked with the belongings of the displaced.

There is an alphabetical system of sorts in place, so we knew where to search, and narrowed it down to looking for a brown card label with my name on it. My old trunk looked shamefully handsome amongst threadbare sacks and patched-up carpet bags and wicker baskets. The soldier pulled it across the floor towards me, and I felt afraid to open it, as though it were Pandora's box. It is too much a reminder of the past.

The boy had the good grace to go and wait by the door while I took the little key from around my neck and fitted it into the padlock. At first it wouldn't turn in the lock because it was so rusted up from the sea crossing. But with enough fiddling it sprang open. Inside were the chattels of a forgotten life. I hardly dared touch the pretty gowns and shawls, stays, petticoats, hats, boots and stockings. They belong to someone feminine, refined, not to me with my red raw hands and flea-bitten ankles. Who packed my belongings so carefully and lovingly? It could only have been Antonia. I touched my paints and my ink as though they were lost treasure, and then I saw something else I'd forgotten; the purse where I kept the few guineas I had saved. It felt heavier. The guard was smoking and not paying me any attention, so I opened the clasp. I counted at least seventy sovereigns in silver. More than I ever earned.

# Parramatta Cloth

Jarrah was standing just out of reach of the light from the lantern on George Street, looking pleased with himself. Michael shook his head. 'You actually *found* her?'

Jarrah shrugged and smiled, his teeth as white as lamps. 'She found me, boss, behind a grandfather tree, then the wombat woman shouted at her.'

'She got in strife, then?'

Jarrah nodded. 'That's a bad place.'

'Damn right. I don't know how you got so good at finding people. It's quite a talent.'

Jarrah shrugged. 'Too much noise here,' he jabbed his bony finger at Michael's head, 'means you don't hear this,' he said, poking his belly. 'Dangerous. You still got that knife?'

'Of course,' Michael said. The knife was in his boot and he didn't go anywhere without it. Jarrah had made it for him. He'd seen a big shark or two in his time, but he had no idea how Jarrah got hold of the tooth of one. It must have been a beast, by the size of the tooth. Michael used to wonder what it was about white men that interested Jarrah enough to work for the constabulary, but then Calvin told him how they'd met. Jarrah was only a boy when his parents were hunted and shot by some young constables who thought the life of a black man was as worthless as their own souls. When Calvin found out what had happened, he had the killers tried for a different unsolved murder and they were returned to London to rot in Newgate or face the gallows. Rough justice was what most people got here.

Jarrah turned to go. In a blink he would dissolve into the shadows.

'So I'll see you by the lagoon at dawn?' Michael called into the dark.

'Yes, boss. I'll be there.' Jarrah's grin flashed before he disappeared completely, and Michael continued on his way to the Rocks. He and Jarrah had a little errand to run for Calvin, tracking the missing sailor who knew something about the dead Quaker.

Maggie seemed pleased that he'd decided to 'stay a spell' even though she didn't believe it was just to print one more pamphlet. She knew him too well to ask questions, though. The less she knew, the better for everyone, and she wouldn't even lose her rent when Michael eventually left. The Stanhope was to be taken over by a Belfast penny-a-liner who'd had a desk at the *Sydney Herald* briefly, before he'd written something cynical about the governor and the cedar trade.

'Evenin', Michael.' Maggie had her feet up on the kitchen table and was smoking a cigarillo and reading a copy of *Pears'*. She imported them for entertainment and loved to tut-tut and shake her head over London frivolity. But at the same time she was examining every detail with deep curiosity; more than was necessary for a woman with such little use for clothing. The slippery cloth of her house gown was hanging either side of her legs, showing her pink stockings and white thighs. Michael couldn't always command his gaze. His eyes had their own interests.

'Evening, Maggie. What news?'

'Oh, I've something you'll like.'

'That right?'

One of the girls wandered in wearing only stays and frilly bloomers. She poured a cup of stewed tea from the iron kettle, and winked at Michael suggestively before she left. He sighed heavily. 'I'm not a fucking saint,' he called after her, but she just giggled and wagged her arse at him.

'It's finally picked up down at the junction,' said Maggie. 'One of the Smith boys was in seeing Fran, full of rum and talk, and said he needed extra because they'd soon be working all the nights God made and he wouldn't see a cunny for that long.'

'How long?'

'Well, Michael, for a boy that age, a week might seem like he's being a saint, whereas for you, it's taken years.'

'That's amusing, Maggie. And thanks for the tip.'

'That's not all. There's someone been asking after you down at the quay.'

Michael was immediately alert. 'Who?'

'A ship's boy, according to my man. His name's Albert and he came in on a transport called *Rajah*.'

Michael stood up. 'That's something needs attending to directly. I'll be back before you close your shutters – I've some work to do downstairs.'

Maggie shook her head and tut-tutted. 'I'll leave the back door on the latch. Be careful, would you?'


The Portcullis at Circular Quay was the most popular of the seafront taverns because it was the first to refill its casks with Jamaican when a ship came in from the South Americas. Michael still habitually stayed clear of the public houses along the quay which had once reminded him too much of freedom.

The room was dim, with too few lanterns hanging from the

rafters. It smelt as rank as any place full of seafaring men, in spite of the rum fumes and tobacco. Michael ordered a jar, then packed his pipe and settled in to listen to the talk. There were several barefoot lads in canvas breeches behind him, proud of their adventures on various trading craft and transports, and someone was boasting about an encounter with Chinese pirates. The *Rajah* was the only vessel Michael knew of that had recently had a run-in with a junk. He sauntered over.

'Evening, lads.'

'Evenin' to you,' said the only boy brave enough to speak. The others looked as though they expected trouble.

'Which of you lads came in on the *Rajah*?'

'James here was the steward,' said the boy.

Michael turned his attention to an older, sunburnt lad who looked worried. 'I hear there was some trouble on your transport?'

'That's right, but we saw to it,' he said with false bravado.

'I'm not talking about the pirates, I'm talking about the murder.'

The boy looked frightened. 'I wouldn't know anything about that.'

'Do you know where I can find the ship's mate, Albert?'

'He's a wharfie. He'll be at the last pier. There's a clipper put in from Ceylon.'

Michael left the tavern and walked along the quay. The yellow gaslight lent the activity along the wharves an eerie, jaundiced rhythm. There was only one other ship in, besides the one at the end of the quay, but there were still navvies heaving sacks and crates about, and a herd of merino getting in the way of everything.

At the last pier was a pretty clipper with Oriental characters painted around her prow. It looked as though she was all but unloaded, since a huddle of young wharfies were sitting on the edge of the pier, dangling their legs above the inky, lapping sea and smoking. Michael approached them. 'Any of you boys called Albert?'

The smallest narrowed his eyes and looked Michael over. 'What's it to you?'

'My name's Michael Kelly. Will you take a walk with me?' Albert was on his feet instantly and, without a backward glance at his scruffy colleagues, fell into step with Michael to the end of the pier and down onto the sand.

When they were out of earshot, Albert squinted at Michael with the same half-suspicious scrutiny. 'You a friend of Mahoney?'

'If you mean Rhia, then yes, I used to work for her family back home.'

Albert nodded. 'That's what she told me. She's gone upriver to Parramatta.'

'Aye, I know that. I heard you've been asking after me.'

Albert hesitated. 'I've a letter for you.'

'A letter? Well I'll be blowed. I suppose it's at your lodgings?'

Albert shook his head. 'Wouldn't be safe there, would it?' He reached deep into the inside pocket of his too-big sailor's coat and pulled out a piece of cartridge paper, folded into a small square and tied with a piece of string. He handed it to Michael solemnly. Michael untied the string and unfolded the paper. She had a pretty hand, he thought. Unusual ink, though. You didn't see much sepia. Michael always used black for the press.

Dear Mr Kelly,

I asked Albert to try and find you, and to destroy this if he doesn't. I am guessing that you know of my uncle's death and of my situation – Thomas told me that he writes to you regularly. I will not waste precious paper trying to convince you of my innocence.

A man was murdered on the *Rajah*. Perhaps you have heard. His name was Laurence Blake and he was the cousin by marriage of Antonia Blake, the kind Quaker with whom I lodged in London. Laurence was a photogenic portraitist, and before he died he made a portrait of five gentlemen. The gentlemen did not sit for Laurence himself, and I will not go into the complicated means by which he obtained the negative of the portrait, but it was intended to reach a woman by the name of Eliza Green, the mother of Mrs Blake's maid, Juliette. According to Juliette (who, I admit, is a little batty) one of the gentlemen in the portrait is a murderer, and only her mother can identify him. I have no idea why, and realise as I write this how unlikely it all sounds. As far as I know, Eliza Green is currently employed as a housekeeper on a sheep station somewhere called Rose Hill.

When Laurence died, the portrait disappeared from his cabin. The negative was in the safe keeping of Margaret, one of the *Rajah* convicts, and that too is gone. Margaret herself died before we reached Sydney and before I could discover where she hid the negative. I fear she might have kept it about her person, and took it with her to her watery grave. The disappearance of the portrait is a mystery that may or may not be connected to Laurence's death. Because the *Rajah* was close to the port of Rio at the time, it is possible that he was killed for his money, since his purse was also stolen. Perhaps the killer thought the portrait was of some value, since photogenic drawings are still very rare. Without it, we will never know if one of the five men really is a murderer, or if Juliette's nerves have created a phantom. Two of the gentlemen in the portrait were my uncle Ryan and Mrs Blake's husband, Josiah. It leaves only three alive.

I was assigned to a botanist as his servant throughout the voyage. His name is Mr Reeve, and he seems to me largely sensible, if dull and irritating. As you see, I am still as intolerant as I ever was. In fact, I am worse. I have confided some of the above to Mr Reeve in the hope that he might be able to help. Perhaps he has discovered something else?

I hope that we meet again one day.

Rhiannon Mahoney


Michael reread the letter while Albert waited, restlessly kicking the sand and smoking. He folded it and put it in his pocket, shaking his head.

'Well, what did she say?' Albert coaxed impatiently.

'You haven't read it?'

'Course I haven't bloody read it.'

Of course he hadn't. He couldn't read. 'She was telling me about a murder and a certain portrait and a certain botanist.'

'Reeve.' Albert looked like he'd smelt something rotten.

'You don't like him?'

'He pretends to be a gentleman but you can tell he isn't.'

'You know a lot, Master Albert.'

'It's how I get by.'

'Aye, and me.' Michael grinned. The boy would be all right. 'Is there any other reason you don't like this Mr Reeve?'

Albert looked uncertain for a moment, then he shrugged. 'I thought I saw him snooping around on the night Mr Blake got it in the neck, and if he wasn't so weak-kneed I'd say he might have done the killing himself.'

Michael looked at him sharply.

'Did you tell any of the ship's officers this?'

'Course I did. I told Wardell, the Whitehall guv.' Albert looked down at his bare feet and kicked some sand. 'Wardell said it would take someone strong and clever, and that that ruled out Reeve. He told me to stop nosing around and stirring up trouble.'

'And did you tell Rhia?'

Albert shook his head. 'She had enough troubles, losing her friend.'

'Was Laurence Blake her sweetheart, then?'

Albert shrugged again. 'She said he wasn't.'

'And do you know where this Mr Reeve is now?'

'I heard he's got lodgings in the bachelor rooms on Elizabeth Street.' Albert looked at his feet again. 'If you see her will you tell her I was asking after her?'

'Sure I will.' Michael stretched out his hand and Albert took it, shaking it firmly. The boy turned away and walked back along the sand. He reminded Michael of someone. It took him a minute, then he realised – he reminded him of his younger self.

# Worsted

A ntonia ascended the last few stone steps of the *London Globe* building feeling increasingly nervous. She was convinced that Mr Dillon's invitation was not a courtesy. He was not a courteous man.

Still, it was a relief to leave Fleet Street behind. There had been a fracas outside the Parcel Delivery Office because a wagon had tipped coming through the archway of Temple Bar. A lone constable was grappling with a band of enterprising urchins who were helping themselves to the parcels.

Inside, the reception hall was not the hushed sanctuary Antonia had imagined. Corridors seemed to run in every direction, and messenger boys and clerks flew past at speed with arms full of type-trays or paper, or commodious ledgers. Studious-looking men with woolly side-whiskers and cheroots gathered in huddles at the necks of the corridors. Everyone had an air of self-importance and a sense of urgency.

Antonia perched on the edge of a bench and smoothed her skirts. She had not worn twilled wool since before her marriage. She found that it cheered her, after all, to surrender to small vanities.

'Good morning, Mrs Blake.' Antonia jumped. Mr Dillon was smiling. His cutaway coat was a little dramatic and his long hair was tied back. He looked more like a poet than a newspaperman.

He lowered his voice. 'In this building the walls are always listening, but there is somewhere quiet, close by.'

Antonia stood, relieved to be leaving so quickly. 'Then lead the way.'

The press of Fleet Street swept them up immediately, past the tempting window displays of bookbinders, stationers and dealers in all commodities from escritoires and repositories to fancy inkwells and old-fashioned quills. Antonia averted her eyes from the seduction of a patent account book.

Mr Dillon was striding without a sideways glance but he seemed to sense her mood. 'Fleet Street can be a vexation to the spirit,' he said. 'Do you object to entering a church, Mrs Blake?'

'Is that where you are taking me?'

'It seems appropriate. The order that built this church had interests in common with your own.' They were walking through Temple Bar. He could only be referring to one church. 'I know little about the Templars,' she said warily. He looked surprised.

'Weren't they also persecuted because of their independence and their wealth? I hear that this church was a depository bank and a residence for visiting kings, as well as a place of worship. That sounds very Quakerly to me! There is something pleasingly practical and unholy about the place,' he finished, with a sideways look at her to see if she was convinced.

Antonia smiled. 'Then I can enter with conscience.'

Mr Dillon nodded. 'I can see some of the logic in your faith, Mrs Blake. I suppose it is not easily … impressed by ritual and decoration. But isn't there innocent pleasure to be had from the vainglorious that is not a distraction from godliness?'

Antonia sighed. How could he know that this was precisely what preoccupied her? 'It isn't possible to ignore the material world, Mr Dillon, especially not for my gender. The female eye seeks out detail and harmony. Quakerism is more a journey inwards than a display of outward devotion.'

'But you are displaying your own brand of devotion by the very plainness of your dress, and by your code of conduct.' He was a terrier. He would not let something alone until it was in shreds.

'We cannot avoid appearances,' she said, carefully. 'Even if one turns away from the looking-glass, one's reflection is always to be seen in others.' How well she knew it.

He looked thoughtful as they entered at the great medieval doors. The circular nave at the end of the long chancel was almost deserted. The gothic widows of its turret were positioned so that the stone flags and the vaulted arches and marble pillars were lit to their best advantage. Of course, the elegant symmetry was cleverly designed to evoke reverence, but she felt soothed just the same.

Mr Dillon led her to a carved stone bench in a private gallery off the nave, and they sat quietly for a moment before he spoke. 'I've brought you here, where it is peaceful, because what I have to say is … difficult.'

Antonia braced herself. 'More ill tidings?'

'It has taken some time to unearth the paperwork at the Jerusalem, but I have evidence that Isaac Fisher and Ryan Mahoney were the signatories on the hire of the barque *Mathilda* on at least two occasions, between Calcutta and Lintin Island. The purpose of both voyages was to ship several hundred caskets of opium resin.'

Antonia's heart felt like lead. It did not seem possible. He dropped his voice. 'What I propose is conjecture only. I have no evidence. You may recall that last Christmas Isaac denied knowledge of a letter written by your late husband?'

'Yes,' Antonia whispered, afraid of what he would suggest.

'I suspected at the time that he was lying. If he wasn't, then he was certainly concealing something. It is *possible*, Mrs Blake, that Isaac thinks your husband's letter incriminates him. If so, he might also believe that Ryan told both Rhia and Laurence what was in the letter. He may have decided that it was safer to have Rhia out of the way. And you told me yourself that Isaac helped Laurence to secure a last-minute berth on the *Rajah*. It would not be unfeasible to arrange for Laurence to be killed on the ship. The port of Rio is full of mercenaries for hire, if the price is right.'

Antonia's head was spinning. What treachery would this man suggest next? 'Isaac could not arrange for the deaths of three innocent men, you do not know him!'

'I want to be wrong, Mrs Blake. I hope with all my heart that I am. But we both know that Isaac Fisher is in financial trouble, which will make him unpopular with the Quakers and, if he is excommunicated from your faith, it would mean his certain ruin as a trader, wouldn't it?'

'Yes, but ...' Antonia could think of no defence for Isaac but that she simply could not believe him to be a criminal. He was a liberal, yes, but surely not so much that he would stoop to an immoral trade. If Isaac and Ryan had been profiting from the sale of opium then what had they to show for it? Where was the money? 'I simply cannot believe it, not until I have seen Josiah's letter myself.'

Dillon nodded. 'Of course. The letter.' He looked like he was weighing something up. Was he deciding what to tell her? He hesitated; then he frowned. 'I have discovered its whereabouts. I managed to make myself enough of a nuisance to Ryan's solicitor. As I explained to him, I merely wanted his help with a piece I'm writing on one of the oldest brothels in St Giles, knowing as I do that he is familiar with the establishment. He quickly admitted that there is a letter that bears the stamp of the postmaster of Bombay in his vault along with Ryan's will.'

Antonia held her breath. 'Will he allow it?'

'He cannot break the law, and neither can we. Ryan's papers may not be released until a magistrate's signature testifies that the death was not a case of self-murder. I appealed against that decree, on the grounds of insufficient evidence. I expect Rhia's pardon will have reached Sydney by now,' he added, perhaps in an attempt to cheer her. 'The mail clippers travel much faster than the passenger transports.' He paused. 'As to the other matter …' he trailed off as if he'd had second thoughts about what he was going to say.

'The other matter?'

'How is your maid?'

'She has calmed down. She has always been troubled.'

'I am intrigued by her case and have posted a notice which is to be circulated to all the newspaper's regional offices. I have suggested that, should a certain twenty-year-old forging racket in Manchester be dug up, it could warrant an inch or two in the national paper. That's enough to have many a penny-a-liner looking through the piles of yellowed newsprint in basements.'

Antonia sat with her hands clasped, willing herself to be soothed by the cool air and rarefied light in the nave. She was not soothed, she was anxious and confused. 'Why should you care, Mr Dillon?'

He looked surprised, then thoughtful. 'I suppose I have an appetite for justice. It makes me an unpopular dinner guest. My brother was killed by lies. He died alone in an opium den in Canton. And now Laurence. People who don't deserve to die. You must be careful not to reveal either what you know or what you suspect, Mrs Blake. I'm merely investigating a hunch.

I have other hunches as well, but I'd prefer to keep these to myself for the moment. Tell me, when is Mr Fisher due to return from India?'

'The *Mathilda* is expected in January.'

'Later than you anticipated?'

'Yes. They are detained in Calcutta.' Antonia put her hand to her mouth. Perhaps they were detained because either *Mathilda* or *Sea Witch* was somewhere between Calcutta and Lintin Island! She looked at Mr Dillon. 'Do you think we should tell Mr Montgomery? The clippers are jointly owned.'

'Absolutely not. I insist, Mrs Blake, that this is not to be discussed with *anyone*.'

Antonia shook her head. She still couldn't believe it. 'I shall pray for courage,' she said.

'If that will help, Mrs Blake, then that is what you must do.'

# Tweed

Elizabeth Street, with its scenic view across Hyde Park, was not a part of town that Michael frequented. It was gentrified, inhabited by solicitors, physicians and clergymen, and held little interest for him. Elizabeth Street was the perfect address for someone he already disliked.

Mr Reeve's room was easily found. It was in a two-storey timber house with a sign on the gate that read *Rooms available for respectable gentlemen*. On the other side of the glass-panelled front door stretched a long, narrow corridor, along which were several closed doors. On a dresser was a row of letterboxes labelled neatly with room numbers and tenants' names.

The man looked a little startled when he opened the door to his unannounced visitor. He also looked as spineless as Albert had made him out to be. He was dressed in shirtsleeves and a rather shabby tweed waistcoat and breeches, but he had the air of someone who thought he was important. He was, at a glance, a man with aspirations.

'Good evening,' he said to Michael, with a discernible quaver. 'I was not expecting a caller.'

'My name's Kelly. I'm an acquaintance of Rhia Mahoney. May I come in?'

Mr Reeve looked like he might close the door in Michael's face, so he took the precaution of placing a boot inside the doorframe. 'I won't take much of your time, I've only a question or two for you and then I'll be on my way.'

A flicker of fear lit the young man's characterless face before it was disguised by a stiff, unnatural smile. 'Of course, Mr Kelly. Come in.'

The room was not large. It was furnished with a pine bed and a small table. On the table was an enormous book and half a glass of claret. There was a fire in the grate. Piled up on the floor, and on top of a portmanteau against the wall, were a great number of cigar boxes.

Michael had no interest in putting this man at ease. He may as well just get to the point and see what happened. 'I've reason to believe that you stole a portrait from the cabin of Laurence Blake.'

Mr Reeve was clearly afraid now. He began sweating in spite of the chill in the building. These timber frames were built for long, hot summers rather than short cold winters. He hid his fear reasonably well with arrogance. 'What business is it of yours?'

Michael took a step closer to where the man was standing with his back to the fire. He was not planning on losing his temper, but there was no harm in showing that he had one. 'The thing is, I've made it my business to protect the interests of the Mahoneys. They're *friends*. But that notion probably isn't familiar to you. Now, why don't you go and get that portrait, so I can have a look at it?'

Something in his tone seemed to strike a chord. Reeve cast one last resentful look at Michael before he went to the table and removed a stiff piece of parchment from one of the back leaves of the book. He returned slowly, keeping the image against his chest. Michael held out his hand, but the botanist was staring at him, his eyes darting around with a look of wild indecision. Michael stepped closer, within striking distance. He felt his fist clench, that reflex. He unclenched it. 'I'll only say this once. Hand it over, or I'll have it my way.'

With a final grimace, Reeve held out the parchment, but just as Michael thought he would relinquish it, he threw it into the fire. It turned the flames blue and green and then it was only a twist of ash. The last expression on the botanist's face, before Michael's fist connected with his jaw, was of smug complicity. The blow sent him sprawling backwards onto the floor. Michael didn't look at him again. He left the room, closing the door quietly behind him.

As he walked along the edge of Hyde Park, he cursed with frustration for allowing it to happen. Then, with some effort, put the incident firmly from his mind. No point in ruining an otherwise fine evening. He noticed how the pearly crescent of the moon hung behind the row of seedling Norfolk pines. He noticed how neatly the flowerbeds were dug where the rose bushes had been planted, incongruously, amongst ferns and spiky native shrubs. As if you could tame this land. He'd only returned from the bush with Jarrah that morning, and he was looking forward to a draught of stout and a meal that didn't still have its fur on.

Should he tell Calvin about the missing sailor first, or about an unconscious botanist lying in a bachelor room on Elizabeth Street? Either way it was time to give the Port Authority an update. Calvin would either be at the White Horse on Pitt Street or with a lady friend. The establishment Calvin preferred wasn't called a brothel; it was a *Gentleman's Club*, and the prostitutes were a cut above Maggie's girls. Even Maggie would admit it. They were cleaner, better dressed and more discreet. They were also more expensive.

It was early yet. Cal was probably still at the tavern.

The White Horse was where the wigs and uniforms of Sydney took their drink, and there wasn't a dusty boot or a dirty fingernail in sight. Sure enough, Cal was settled in a snug with an ale and a broadsheet. Michael got himself a jar and sat down opposite him. 'Evening, Calvin.'

'Michael.'

'It's a shame to disturb you when you're off duty.'

'I'm never off duty.'

Michael nodded. It was true. He told the policeman about the remote squatter's hut where they'd found evidence of a camp, and how Jarrah pointed out the flattened kikuyu grass and the tracks in the dust; signs that a drover had come through with a herd of cattle. Jarrah probably could have told Michael how many cattle exactly, had he wanted to know. Calvin's man had camped in the hut for a few nights and then, when opportunity called, had gone off with an overlander. Chances were he wouldn't get anywhere near as far as the northern plains before he realised droving was no life for a sailor. He'd be back, and Calvin would be waiting for him.

'That isn't all,' Michael said, when he'd completed his report and taken a long draught. 'I wonder if you'd make some enquiries about a passenger on the *Rajah* for me.'

'The transport the Mahoney woman came in on? Would this have anything to do with the death I told you about on that transport?'

'Aye. I might just be going quietly doolally, but I've got a hunch there's a connection between the Quaker who died in Bombay, the murder on the *Rajah*, and Rhia Mahoney.'

'I hope you aren't going to tell me she's in on it, Michael.'

'Not a chance.'

'That's good, because she's been pardoned.'

'Jesus. What? Are you sure?'

'Sure I'm sure. I was at the governor's office today handing over all my paperwork and I saw her name on the list.'

'Well I'll be damned. This just gets curiouser all the time. I don't suppose there's a chance you could get your hands on that document; speed things up a little?'

'Of course I can, Michael. There's no point wearing a hat like a toy soldier if you can't bend the rules a little now and then.' He lifted his glass. 'Cheers. Here's to freeing the bloody Irish.'

Michael grinned and lifted his own. 'Aye. Cheers.'

# Alpaca

Rhia didn't recognise the man in the visitor's cell. She supposed he was shopping for a wife. The lines etched into his face and the Parramatta shirting placed him as a convict, or an ex-convict.

When he smiled she knew him instantly.

'You've grown up,' Michael Kelly said, 'though you looked better with your hair.' The sight of Michael Kelly, here at the ends of the earth, was a joy as fathomless as all of the oceans she had crossed, something beyond all the months of fear and loneliness. She reached across the table and took his hands in hers. Michael's hands were rough and sunburnt brown, and he gripped her as if she might try and get away.

As if she would.

She held back her tears, and she could see that he was doing the same.

'I've something for you.' He reached into a pocket inside his waistcoat and laid a thick, brown envelope on the table. Rhia picked it up, her hands shaking so much that she wondered if she could even open it. She turned it over. The wax seal was scarlet. She peered at it, trying to make out the insignia.

'That is the seal of the Governor of New South Wales,' said Michael quietly. This meant nothing to Rhia. She looked to the superintendent, who stood with her arms crossed and her eyebrows raised.

'Now, we don't see one of them often,' the superintendent grunted, but her voice had a less aggressive quality. Usually the woman talked in a low growl, as though she was some kind of sheep hound. Now she just shrugged. 'You'd better open it, hadn't you, Mahoney?'

Rhia broke the seal. The document was brief, only a few lines. It made her crumple. Michael made no attempt to interfere with her messy weeping except to give her his handkerchief and tell her it was clean. The superintendent remained silent, in spite of the noise.

'I hope those are happy tears,' Michael said when she quietened enough for him to get a word in.

Rhia laughed and the sound startled her. When had she last laughed? She looked at the single page in front of her, at the one sentence that mattered: *This ticket of leave is granted to the prisoner of Her Majesty, Rhiannon Mahoney.* There was a date, *4 October 1841*, that meant nothing to her – could be tomorrow, or long weeks ago, she had lost track. She blinked and straightened her back, feeling freedom surge up her spine and into her limbs.

'But why are you delivering my pardon, Mr Kelly?' There were any number of things she could have asked him. Why he was still in Australia, how he knew where to find her, what on earth she should do now. She was full of questions, but too light-headed to care much about answers.

'Let's just say I know someone.'

Rhia was trying to comprehend what the document in her hands actually meant. 'Then whoever committed the crime I was accused of has confessed?'

Michael laughed mirthlessly. 'What a fine thing, to hear that someone still expects the best from people, even after spending the better half of a year in the company of prisoners.'

'I've spent the better part of a year in very good company,

and I've learnt a thing or two.' Neither of these things had occurred to Rhia before this moment, and she suddenly felt like weeping all over again.

'I can see that, but we're taking up the good superintendent's valuable time. I don't expect you've much in the way of goods and chattels?'

'A trunk in the lock-up.'

'A trunk! You're travelling in style then. There's a barge departing Parramatta at sunset that will have us in Sydney just after sun-up tomorrow.'

The first leg of her journey towards freedom. It must be a dream.

Taking her leave from the female factory took little time. In the cold spinning room, Jane was immediately tearful and Georgina pretended to be happy for her. Rhia had not expected to feel any sadness in leaving, but these women had become like family, and suddenly, they no longer had anything in common, and they all knew it. They probably thought she would forget them. As if she would.

Nora and Agnes were in the kitchen garden with a dozen or so others, in their thick brown aprons, breaking the hard earth as penance for their unbreakable spirits. Nora straightened up when she saw Rhia. She stood still, resting on her spade, in defiance of the warden at the other end of the patch. 'Didn't I tell you, Mahoney, that it wouldn't be for ever? You've got our blessing, hasn't she, Agnes?' Agnes nodded, but she wasn't brave enough to stop digging. 'We always knew you weren't a thief,' she said, with her sly grin.

'Well thanks for nothing, then,' said Rhia with a small laugh. She wouldn't cry. She hadn't ever dared to cry in front of Nora and she wasn't about to start now.

'Give my love to damp and dreary London and don't forget us,' was all Nora had time to say before the warden bore down on them, scowling at Rhia and giving Nora a shove in the ribs to get her back to work. Nora winked at her and went back to digging and humming to herself cheerfully, making the warden stew all the more.

In the sleeping quarters, Rhia collected her red book from beneath her bedroll and walked, without a backward look, from the last place in which she would ever dream of freedom.

In the superintendent's office, where she had to sign something, she listened inattentively to passionless words of caution and advice. The world was full of temptation and sin and Rhia was being given a second chance. She turned away while the superintendent was still sermonising, and walked out the door.

Michael collected her at the gates in a cart that had her trunk tied with a rope in the back. They drove through Parramatta on a wide dusty road with bungalows either side and horses tethered to verandahs. The town had the vaguely desolate air of a place that was waiting to be noticed, or to be called home.

'There's an inn this side of town where you can bathe and change,' Michael said after they'd gone a mile or two in silence. 'I don't expect you'll be wanting to wear that fine uniform any longer than necessary.'

'No, I don't,' Rhia agreed. The thought of taking off the coarse cloth and never putting it on again made her want to dance a jig. There was so much to say and, at the same time, nothing. There was plenty of time for talking.

The inn was whitewashed stone, low and long, with a neat drive and a canopy of tall, purple flowering trees behind.

'Jacaranda,' Michael said, smiling at her wide-eyed gaze. 'That's what the Originals called them. First sign that summer's on the way. I sure won't be missing the summers here. I'll tip my hat to the damp and the cold and the fog from now until the end of my days.'

'It's a long time you've been here.'

'Aye, it's a long time.'

If the innkeeper's wife thought it unusual that someone with a shorn head and convict's clothes should want a room for the afternoon, she didn't show it, not after Michael had paid her. She bustled around in a spartan room with a fireplace, bare floorboards and an iron bed that felt to Rhia like a queen's chamber. She put a copper hipbath by the fire and poured in kettle after kettle until it was full of warm water, then threw in a handful of eucalypt leaves and left Rhia to bathe.

The bath was large enough to sit in with her knees pulled up. The warm water slipped over her limbs like silk. She still couldn't believe that she had woken this morning in prison and was now bathing in scented water. She didn't step out of it until the water was cold and her teeth chattering.

She lay on the bed, simply, indulgently, because she could. It was not a soft bed, but it smelt of sunlight and linen. Her trunk sat in the middle of the floor. She hardly dared to open it, dress in something that was not the colour of dirt, pretend to be someone that she knew she would never be again.

She edged towards the trunk slowly and lifted the lid. Before, when there was no chance of wearing the clothes that lay within, it had been safe to look. She removed the gown that lay closest to the top, her green alpaca. She was a stranger to every detail of freedom, and suddenly the idea of being faced with a choice scared her. She rummaged around for a shawl, stockings and boots, hardly caring if they matched, hardly remembering that, once, the minutiae was meticulously chosen and coordinated. She dressed slowly, half remembering, half forgetting the downy feel of a cashmere petticoat against her legs, silk stockings sliding through her fingers, the soft leather of calfskin.

She could hear Michael Kelly outside, presumably talking to the innkeeper on the verandah. The hallway was timber from floor to ceiling and ran the length of the building. Halfway along it stood a mirrored dresser. She could not remember the last time she had seen her own face. It was in another life. She knew she should walk past the glass without looking.

But she couldn't.

She turned towards the glass slowly. A startled creature stared back. Could this face be her own? Her skin was darker by a shade, and her spiky hair made her look boyish. Her face was narrower and her eyes seemed larger. Her dress looked too big. She leaned closer. The skin beneath her eyes looked bruised. She turned away. She had seen enough.

When Michael saw her, clean and in her own clothes, he looked surprised. Presumably she now looked more like a woman. She didn't feel it.

'I've asked for a meal,' he said. 'You could use some meat by the look of you. They've only emu and kangaroo, though. Closest thing you'll get to pheasant or rabbit.'

'Emu is a bird?'

'Aye, a big one.'

Rhia didn't care what she ate, she didn't care about anything except that she could sit on the steps looking out at gum trees without feeling like their alabaster trunks were the bars of her prison. The sky had turned indigo. The land was alive. She didn't belong here. The spirits of this place wished only to be left alone.

The innkeeper served some kind of home-made ale and they drank a toast to freedom and to Ireland. Michael wanted to know some things, so she told him everything she could think of; what had happened in London, what had happened on the transport.

'I visited your Mr Reeve in Sydney,' he said when she paused and took a sip from her cup. The home-brew was strong and sharp and you could taste the sun and the eucalypt and the red dirt in it. 'He's a liar,' Michael added, then proceeded to tell her why. Rhia's head started to spin. The very idea that Mr Reeve was part of it seemed a remote possibility. She couldn't understand it. Michael wanted to know everything she could think of about the botanist, the things they'd spoken of, his behaviour towards her, his reaction to Laurence's death. When he told her what had happened to the portrait, her heart sank.

'How will Eliza Green be able to tell us if one of the men is a murderer if the portrait is destroyed?'

'I thought there was a template somewhere?' Michael said. 'Isn't it like a stereograph, this uncanny portraiture?'

Rhia shook her head. 'The negative is made of paper and it was lost.'

Michael looked thoughtful. 'I say we pay this Eliza a visit. The sheep station where she works is this side of Sydney.' He looked at her plate, pleased to see that she had made short work of her meat. 'It's almost time to go,' he said.

The passenger barge to Sydney was more comfortable and less crowded than the one that was used for ferrying prisoners upriver. Rhia had room to stretch out on an upholstered bench, though she didn't believe she would sleep a wink on a night such as this. She had never seen so many stars, and the lantern of the Queen of the Night was full and luminous.

# Lace

A river had borne her away at sunrise, and now a new sunrise and another river would carry her back home. It could only be Dillon who was responsible for her pardon. She didn't expect that he would ever forgive her. If she hadn't been on the *Rajah*, Laurence would be alive.

Rhia sat up and looked around for Michael. He was sitting where he'd been last night, at the aft of the barge where he could keep an eye on things. He had acquired a wary edge that she didn't remember in the old Michael Kelly. He was changed, like her. He saw her stir and came to join her.

'I've had a word with the captain,' he said, 'and he's agreed to let us off at the Rose Hill jetty, a few miles upriver of Sydney. He'll deliver your trunk to the Port Authority. It will be safe there.'

Rhia nodded. 'I wonder what Eliza will think of her daughter's ideas.'

'What do you think of them?'

What did she think? Juliette belonged to another life. 'I think she's less than sensible and more than a little odd. But I suppose there's always a chance that she's right.'

'Ah yes, the men in the portrait.' Michael was squinting at the tree line as though trying to piece something together. 'There's Ryan and the Quaker Josiah Blake, and what about the three who are still alive?'

'Mr Montgomery is the Regent Street mercer I worked for, then there's his associate Mr Beckwith, and another Quaker trader, Isaac Fisher. Isaac is a friend of the Blakes.'

Michael nodded as he sat filling his pipe and looking out over the green water. Some slim silvery fish were leaping into the air a short distance from the boat. 'Do you know anything about the nature of their common business? Michael asked, lighting a cigarette.

'They own two ships. The Blakes and Isaac buy American cotton and have it spun in English mills and then woven, dyed and printed in India. Mr Montgomery buys silk from China and France, and Ryan, as you know, was an importer and exporter, not only of Mahoney Linen, but many other cloths. He supplied several London mercers, including the Montgomery Emporium.'

Rhia watched Michael register all of this, but she couldn't tell what he was thinking. 'I heard about Josiah Blake's death,' he said, 'and I heard that he knew something he shouldn't have and that he was killed for it.'

Rhia remembered the conversation she had heard between Sid and Dillon at the Red Lion. 'Could he have been shipping opium?'

Michael shrugged. 'He could have been.'

Rhia remembered something else. 'My uncle received a letter from Josiah Blake, sent from Bombay before he died. The letter could not be found, but Mr Dillon seems to think it important.'

'Who is Mr Dillon?'

'A journalist. A friend of Laurence's. He thinks Ryan was involved in the China trade.'

'Ryan? Opium?' Michael looked doubtful.

Rhia nodded, relieved that he didn't believe it either. 'But how did you know about Josiah Blake?'

'The shipping news isn't always printed. Plenty of sailors who work in Calcutta and Bombay come through Sydney. Bad news travels farthest and fastest.'

The barge was slowing and heading for a jetty almost hidden by mangroves. The tangle of submerged trees was home to an entire flock of crimson and blue parakeets, of jewel colour.

Michael stood up. 'I reckon this is our stop.'

He held out his hand to help Rhia onto the jetty, but she leapt from the shallow hull without needing to take it. The rocking of a craft on the water no longer destabilised her, and neither did the unknown depths beneath it. She now knew depths more worthy of fear.

They walked cautiously along the sagging timbers of the jetty. There was a clearing, and behind it towered the trees, the colour of clean silver. Michael sat down on a fallen trunk as though he was waiting for somebody. Rhia sat beside him. The wild land rang with sound; a concerto of birdsong and trilling cicadas and rustling, scuttling creatures. There was a familiar thumping close by and, as usual, Rhia jumped. She might have acquired sea legs but she couldn't get used to kangaroos. In amongst the misty green of the eucalypts were clusters of brick red and golden yellow. She registered the colours and patterns and stored them away. Something had begun to stir in her. Perhaps Cerridwen was feeling more generous.

'What are we waiting for?' she asked Michael

'A friend,' he said. Rhia thought he was joking. It was hard to tell. Michael had always been dry, but now he was dry as dust. She asked him the names of the red and yellow trees. 'Waratah and wattle,' he said.

Colour was returning.

When a man materialised from the trees, Rhia recognised him. This time, though, he was dressed in breeches and braces and a too-small shirt, without boots or stockings. His calves were long and thin, though ridged with muscle, and his bare feet looked like dusty shoe leather.

'Morning, boss.' The shining black face grinned from ear to ear as though he was enjoying a private joke.

'Morning, Jarrah. You'll have met Rhia Mahoney.' Jarrah nodded at her, still grinning.

'So,' said Michael, 'how far is this place?'

'Not far, boss. Follow me.'

Jarrah walked through the dry underbrush, as though he was following an invisible path. He seemed to flow through the land soundlessly, almost without touching it; the low hanging branches and spiky shrubs barely moved as he passed.

Rhia picked up her skirts and did her best to keep up. Her cumbersome clothing seemed a little ridiculous in these conditions. She didn't especially mind the prickle of heat though, nor the insects that swarmed around her face. She could have walked all day, now she was free to.

Michael stopped abruptly in front of her and she almost collided with him. In front of him, Jarrah stood unmoving, his hand held up to signal that they should be still. At first Rhia wondered why he didn't just step over the branch lying on the ground in front of him, but then the branch curled and slid sideways. It was a brown snake. Jarrah moved so quickly that she couldn't say how he suddenly came to be holding the tail of a four-foot snake, and cracking its head to the ground as though it were a whip. In another moment he had it draped around his neck. 'That fella nearly got me,' he chuckled over his shoulder as he started walking again. 'Now he's breakfast.'

They came to the edge of the forest and a vast acreage of cleared land. At the end of a winding drive was a long, low, stone bungalow surrounded by an elegant verandah with pretty iron railings. Lace curtains stirred between open doors. The cleared land was fenced for miles around and hundreds of sheep were grazing in the fields beyond. No wonder the graziers of Australia could produce such fine merino – the conditions here were perfect and the land just went on and on. Rhia had heard that this continent was the size of Europe and, looking at the endless sky, she believed it could be true.

They stepped from the cover of the trees, but Jarrah stayed, collecting bark and twigs to make a fire so that he could cook his snake. He said he'd keep some for them in the ashes, and Rhia said that she wasn't very hungry.

They didn't get far along the drive before two mongrel dogs came hurtling towards them as though they were escaped sheep. A moment later a thin, anxious-looking woman appeared on the verandah, wiping her hands on her apron. She had to be Juliette's mother, the resemblance was unmistakeable.

'Good morning to you!' Michael called. 'We're looking for Eliza Green.'

'That's my name,' the woman replied, looking even more apprehensive.

'You've no need to worry, Mrs Green. We've word of your daughter.'

'Juliette!' Eliza clutched the railing as though her legs might not hold her. 'You'd better come in,' she managed finally. 'They've gone into the town, so I can make you a cup of tea. Have you had your breakfast? The young lady looks hungry.'

She bustled them into a large, airy room and then fussed away again.

'A grazier is a wealthy man in New South Wales,' Michael observed in his driest tone as they perched on the edge of upholstered chairs. He ran his hand along the smooth, polished wood. 'That's cedar. Governor's wood.'

Rhia supposed this was a drawing room. It was furnished in the gleaming red wood, with Oriental rugs covering wide, glossy floorboards. A pretty pianoforte stood in a corner and oil paintings of the English countryside covered the walls.

Eliza returned with a pot of tea, a flat loaf and some fresh butter. It looked a more appetising breakfast than Jarrah's snake. Eliza picked up the teapot but her hand was unsteady, so Rhia took it from her and poured them each a cup, glancing at Michael. 'I think we should tell Mrs Green why we're here.'

He nodded.

Rhia explained, as best she could, what a photogenic drawing was and what had brought them to Rose Hill. Even to her ears it sounded like blarney. Eliza picked imaginary flecks from her apron and then destroyed a piece of bread with her fingers. When it was reduced to a pile of crumbs, she clasped her hands together.

Rhia waited until Eliza looked ready before she spoke again. 'Do you know why Juliette might have thought one of the men was a murderer, Mrs Green?'

Eliza looked a little dazed. It was a lot to take in. 'I know only one man who's been murdered, and that was my husband,' she said finally.

Rhia and Michael let this settle on a respectful silence.

'And what happened to him?' Michael asked quietly.

She told them how she had been widowed, violently, and had become so impoverished that hunger drove her to steal food. As if that were not enough, she'd been caught, tried and sent away from her child.

Michael was shaking his head. 'Can you think of any reason why Juliette might think one of the men in the portrait killed her father?'

'Only if she'd recognised him. But she was only wee.'

'But she must have a strong suspicion, to want you to see it,' Michael pressed.

'Oh, I'd know John Hannam all right. I went looking for him myself. But men like that are cunning, there's no end to what they'll do. He's trampled on my heart and left his filthy mark.'

Michael was nodding, but looking through the doors and out across the fields of sheep. 'Mrs Green,' he said finally, 'what would you say if I told you there's a clipper leaving Sydney for London in two weeks and you could have a ticket home?'

'I'd say you have no idea what a maidservant earns, Mr Kelly.'

'What I'm saying, Mrs Green, is that I've a job as ship's carpenter on that clipper so I've no need to pay my own way. I've reason to believe you'll be needed as a witness and I'm willing to pay your passage to London. You see, I was thinking I'd be needing to buy this young lady's fare, but she tells me she has money of her own.'

Eliza more or less hurtled across the floor and threw her arms around Michael. She was laughing and then she was weeping and then she seemed to be doing both at once.

Michael winked at Rhia. 'I'd say she's agreed.'

'Yes,' said Rhia, 'I'd say so.'

20 October 1841

We walked all day, from Rose Hill to George Street, and tonight I will sleep in a real bed. It is narrow and hard and this room is plain, but it smells of sunshine and feels like a palace. This is the home of a draper and his wife. They're friends of Michael Kelly and they're kind people.

Michael is quieter than I remember, but being a prisoner makes you quiet. His Aboriginal friend, though, is the lord of silence. He doesn't even make a sound when he treads on the dry underbrush of the eucalypt forest. I don't expect he knew what to make of me any more than I did of him. He heard me asking Michael about the names of flowers and plants, and would occasionally point to something and tell me what it was called, though I'm not sure if it was in his language or not. The laughing bird is a kookaburra, the huge white parakeet with a yellow crest is a cockatoo and the lizard the size of a crocodile is a goanna. Michael says there are crocodiles too, but they're further north. I hope he's right about that.

I feel like an interloper in the world of the free, just as I once did in the world of the convicted. I don't think I quite believe it yet, and I don't seem to be the person I once was. I cannot even remember who or what I was. Perhaps this is just what you intended. I don't think it was entirely necessary that I sail halfway around the earth on a stinking ship to be changed, but I take your point. I am not exactly heroic when even the sound of a passing cart makes me edgy. I have lost my armour against the world. I will find it again, though I expect it will take a little time.

Tonight we dined on mutton and potatoes, and we talked about wool. I can afford to invest in a small amount of merino, just as Ryan said I should. I put it to Michael immediately, so at least I am still impulsive! He looked surprised and then doubtful and then, thankfully, thoughtful. He said he'd been thinking of sending some wool to Dublin himself but he hadn't expected to find a business partner. I could tell he was thinking that he hadn't expected to find one who was a woman, either. I hadn't expected it myself, but it suddenly seems perfectly sensible. This is what I have come here to do. It must have been Antonia who put the money in my purse. I will repay her when our ship comes in. And now I will go to bed. In a bed.

# Straw

Who would have thought he'd feel such pride in showing someone from home around Sydney? Michael was pleased as punch when Rhia exclaimed over the elegantly carved stone edifices of Government House, and the fine turret of St Philip's church. Gone was the bitterness of the early years when he'd seen how labouring men were expendable. The pain and fury of it had led to his pamphlet, and countless angry essays about the false gods of commerce that the colonists had hewn from the sandstone cliffs. He'd paid his dues to the real cost of nationhood, to the butchery and the heartbreak of the forgotten.

He pointed out loan and investment companies, the library, the offices of the Australian Gas Light Company and the Australian Sugar Company, the literary and scientific societies, the School of Arts and the new museum. Rhia was shaking her head by the time they were back on George Street.

'I'd no idea that an architect could earn a living in Australia,' she said.

Michael laughed. 'The principle architect was transported for forgery. The change in his circumstances turned out well for him. He'd never have designed so many important public buildings if he'd stayed in Bristol.'

Rhia had her eye on the shop windows as they passed saddlers, tea dealers and druggists and, closer to the quay, ship chandlers and sail makers. She stopped at a milliner to look at the bonnets behind the panelled window. She turned with a raised eyebrow and a look that Michael recognised. She was, after all, a woman.

There had always been something about Rhia Mahoney, Michael reflected as she disappeared through the milliner's doorway. She had the old woman's eyes, the grandmother – as dark as pitch and somehow a little unnatural, as if they could see beyond the visible. Michael took out his tobacco tin and watched the street. A cart and dray swung past, piled high with bales of merino. There had been a lot of talk of wool, and Rhia was right, it was time to start shipping. The loss of liberty did strange things to you. It made you hungry for life.

She emerged from the milliner with her ragged head hidden beneath a new straw hat – not a bonnet, a hat, with a flat crown and a broad rim. 'It looks well on you,' he said, and meant it. It shaded her face and gave her the look of a pioneer. They were almost outside Dan's. 'I'll not stop,' he said, 'I've some business this evening.' She'd not asked about his business, though he could tell she was curious. She put her hand into her reticule and pulled out a crumpled calling card and handed it to him. 'The Chinese character on the back stands for silver,' she said, 'but I don't know where the coordinates are. Do you?'

Michael looked at the card. 'That's just off shore,' he said, 'a bit north but not far at all. Where did this come from?'

'I found it on the floor at China Wharf the day Ryan died. That lovely copperplate isn't his handwriting, though.' She raised that eyebrow again to make her point. 'Good night then,' she said. But she wanted to say something more. She looked at him almost shyly, and then down at her hands. 'How is Thomas?'

'In good health, still sensible, and hard-working too, from what I can gather. But you'd want to know about the condition of his heart, being a woman, and I can't tell you about that.'

'I'm only asking as a friend.'

'Aye, I know that. I might even have known it before the two of you did, without wanting to sound too clever. You're not made from moulds that fit together, are you. There's much to be said for a friendship that has outlasted romance. I sometimes wonder if ...' He couldn't say it. Seven years was a long time to be away. People changed. Rhia was looking right into him with her sloe-black eyes, as if she could see it.

'They must have been lonely years,' she said.

'I made a life for myself, and that's just what you'll do when you get home. Maybe it's this place. You can't just give up because you've found yourself at the farthest reaches of the earth. The people here – colonists, settlers, prisoners – all want the same thing: freedom.' Rhia was watching him intently, and Michael laughed. 'I'd best get off my soapbox and get on with my business.'

'Well,' she said, 'when next we meet I hope to have the price for a clipper full of merino to Dublin. Godspeed, Mr Kelly.'

'Aye, Godspeed.' He watched her walk into the drapery before he set off. She moved slowly and carefully, like an old lady. He didn't think she was ready to ship wool just yet. He took another look at the calling card and put it in his pocked thoughtfully.

Maggie's girls hadn't seen any of the Smiths for months now, and one of Calvin's night patrols had reported some unusual goings-on in one of the small inlets off the cove. As if that wasn't enough, Jarrah had finally tracked down the rigger who knew something about Josiah Blake's death. He'd got as far north as the Hunter River, a good seventy miles, which was impressive for a sailor on horseback.

Calvin was sitting on the verandah with his boots on the rails, smoking. It was the posture he liked to take as the gas lanterns were lit at Circular Quay. He was still hugely entertained by the notion of gaslight. It was also the best time of the day to watch the shop girls on their way to the quay and, after all, women were as much a glowing mystery as gas. Of course, gas was a natural phenomenon, and women were another thing altogether with that unknown quality which could soften your heart or harden your cock. Calvin had never married. No woman could or should put up with being of less importance than a policeman's work. The map of Calvin's heart was his work. He was in love with his strip of sand and docks and maritime industry, and devoted to keeping it running as smooth as oil.

Calvin leaned forward instinctively when a timber creaked, his hand reaching towards the boot where he kept his pistol. He had the natural uneasiness of one who kept the law in a lawless land, but he wasn't usually so twitchy.

'It's only me, Cal.'

'Michael. Ready for the show?'

'You think they'll be shipping soon?'

'Any time now. I've got boys keeping watch on the beach. There's a clipper anchored outside of the harbour's reach; just beyond the sights of my telescope. But I know a fisherman who likes to throw his net out in the deep water, and he tells me she's called *Sea Witch*. I've got men on the beach tonight so you and I can have a chat with the sailor who went droving.'

'Well, I can tell you exactly where I think you'll find your clipper,' said Michael and handed Calvin the calling card.

'The Jerusalem Coffee House?'

'Turn the card over, man.'

'Ah,' said the policeman. 'What's the squiggle?'

'Chinese character for silver.'

'Ah.'

They walked to the barracks, smoking and talking about who should, and should not, be on the cricket team. There was a big match soon between the constabulary and the military.

The boy was younger than Michael had imagined, which accounted for his lack of judgement in sailing back into Sydney Cove when Calvin had warned him against it. He was sitting in the corner of his cell with his head bent sulkily. He barely looked up when the two men entered.

'Evening, son,' said Calvin cheerfully. 'I've brought an associate along to see if we can't, between us, get you out of here.' The sailor looked up quickly, his expression fleetingly hopeful before he narrowed his eyes suspiciously.

'Why'd ye care?'

'I don't care especially, but I need some information. If I say I'll let you go once I've heard what I want to, then that's what I'll do because I'm a man of my word. But if you walk free today, I don't want to see you again. Ever. I mean it this time.'

The prisoner looked at his hands. 'Well I still don't know nothin'.'

'That's not what I heard. I heard you told someone that the Quaker who fell off the *Mathilda* was up to no good.'

'No, that's not what I said.' He bit his lip and stopped himself before he gave any more away.

'Then you did say *something*?'

Silence. Calvin turned to Michael. 'You know, I told this boy that if he came back to my patch he'd be in a rope cravat when he left again. Am I a man of my word, Michael?'

'Aye, you are, Calvin.' Michael looked at the youth. He could see that he was scared out of his wits, and not just of the gallows. 'If you tell us what you know, we'll have the master of this coining operation so swiftly he'll not have time to come after you for ratting.' He watched the boy's eyes widen with surprise.

'How'd you know about the coining?'

'By the end of this week there won't be a coiner left in the Rocks, and the only crew on the *Sea Witch* will be soldiers. Now, you can either talk or not, it's your life, son.'

This seemed to decide him. He took a deep, resigned breath. 'I seen the Quaker gent in the Calcutta bazaar, but I thought he was the other one, the one that was hiring crew to go up to Lintin Island. I needed the work, see. So I told him I was as good a rigger as any. He looked at me peculiar, like he didn't know what I was on about, so I said I knew that he, being a Quaker, shouldn't exactly be filling clippers full of black gold and I hoped he didn't mind my coming to him. The problem was, see, that no one seemed to know anything much about that charter, since most of the crew were Indian and the craft, *Mathilda*, was supposedly signed off to the dry dock.'

Michael frowned. This didn't entirely make sense to him. 'So the *Mathilda* was making an undocumented run to Lintin Island.'

The boy nodded.

'You said you thought the Quaker was the *other one*?'

'Well, I made a mistake, see. I was told it was the Quaker who came in on the *Mathilda* who was in charge of the run to Lintin Island, but two flat-hats came in on *Mathilda* – and he was the wrong one. Which accounts for why he looked at me so strange.'

'Then why was Josiah Blake, the Quaker gentleman you spoke to, killed?'

'He started asking questions. He went to the dry dock and asked to see the register and found out that the *Mathilda* was never there when she was supposed to be.'

'And what about the coining, did Josiah know about that, too?'

'I might have let on something about it.'

Michael was beginning to wonder how the so-called criminal before him was ever going to make a career of it. 'You *might* have?'

'Well, it was confusing, see. I only realised what was going on when I got to Sydney. The *Mathilda* sails from Calcutta to Lintin Island with opium, collects silver and then, instead of going directly back to Calcutta, to the exchange, she sails south into the open sea where she meets with the *Sea Witch*, who's left Sydney with counterfeit—'

'So the counterfeit silver is exchanged for the real silver at sea, and the forged coins are absorbed into the Calcutta exchange, while the *Sea Witch*, with her cargo of real silver, sails for London?'

'That's it.'

'And the master of this crime is a Quaker?'

'I wouldn't know for sure. It's the ship's captain that's in charge at sea. I've never known a Quaker to go to Lintin Island.'

Michael looked at Calvin. 'I believe that gentleman's name is Isaac Fisher,' he said.

The policeman was frowning. 'Of course, it is always possible that he doesn't even know his opium charter is collecting counterfeit on its return voyage.'

'I hadn't thought of that,' Michael admitted. 'I do know, though, that the *Mathilda* and the *Sea Witch* are the joint property of a collective of London cloth traders.'

'So how do we narrow down who chartered the Sydney leg?'

Michael looked at him. 'Two of them are dead, including Josiah Blake.'

'How interesting.' Calvin looked back to the boy. 'So, we've established that the cloth trade isn't profitable enough for a certain trader and that Mick the Fence is the boss of a coining racket in Sydney?'

'Wasn't *me* told you 'bout Mick being the boss!'

'Then he is?'

'Bollocks. Aye.'

Calvin took his watch from his coat pocket. 'It's getting late. You can stay in tonight, and tomorrow I'm putting you on the first vessel that hauls anchor and you can work your passage to wherever she's sailing.'

As soon as they were outside, Calvin looked sidelong at Michael. 'You didn't tell me this was Mick the Fence's operation'.

'I wasn't entirely sure myself until just recently.'

Calvin grinned slyly. 'I knew it anyway. I wouldn't be doing my job if I didn't, would I? I've got a watch at the Hare and Hound on the junction road. You can see Mick's from one of the upstairs rooms.'

Michael shook his head. 'I thought Mick was too clever to use his own place for business. They'd be in a basement if he is, though, and his is one of the few in the Rocks. If they're melting down old coin and casting plaster moulds, they're probably forging guineas – copper on the inside, silver-plated. No point in wasting time on shillings, they wouldn't make mercantile princes wealthy enough, or give punters a leg up.'

Calvin was listening keenly and nodding. 'Speaking of punters, I've had a word with a man by the name of Wardell, the government agent on the *Rajah*. He says he's looking into the story the ship's boy told you, about seeing the botanist on

427

deck the night of the killing. He also said he'd find out when Reeve's passage was booked and by whom. It's unlikely he's come so far from home without a benefactor.'

'Now that's of interest,' Michael said, 'because I was just going to ask if you'd care to pay a call to Mr Reeve. I've a matter to discuss with him that I think you'd find interesting.'

'Is that so?'

'Aye,' said Michael.

The light is as dazzling as the sky is cloudless and the temperature constant. This place is the opposite of Ireland in every way. The seasons are reversed, and the south wind colder than the north. Instead of fog and damp, the air is dry and translucent. The poisonous breath of industry has not yet touched it. It is spring but already as warm as our Irish summer. I expect the light and warmth account, in part, for the geniality of people. I spent this morning with Joan, the draper's wife, who laughed approvingly when I cursed over spilt tea and then offered me a cigarillo after breakfast. I took one, but I've still some practising to do before I master smoking.

I bothered Joan with questions all morning, because this place seems so full of contradictions. It is a modern nation in the making, and at the same time an ancient one being ruined. The Originals, as Michael Kelly calls them, are nowhere to be seen. Had I not met Jarrah, I might not have known they were here but for the spirits amongst the trees, watching the foolish empire builders from the shadows. Now I know why the trees seem so ghostly. There are bone-chilling stories about the killings, and when I hear of the murderous behaviour of the English and the Irish, I feel ashamed to tread here.

Joan says that oranges can be grown in New South Wales, that she plucked one herself, early in the morning, with the dew still fresh on it. She says she has fat green peas on her table for ten months of the year and that her linen will dry in an hour. But she also has a spider the size of a fob watch in her pantry, and thieving possums climb in through open windows and help themselves to any food left unattended.

In just three days we will be sailing, and there is plenty to keep me busy. Dan and Joan have found the best priced merino in New South Wales, and I'm gathering stamina to supervise the shipment. Joan says that she will help and that I must not try and do too much too soon. Whenever I feel daunted I think of Antonia. It is faith that makes the difference, be it faith in some deity or an inner light, or in oneself.

I can't say I'm looking forward to another sea voyage so soon, but it will bear no resemblance to my outward passage. I've an entire season's patterns crowding my thoughts after my long walk, and I intend to fill a book with them before I reach London. If Mr Montgomery won't buy them for a good price, then they will become the first prints for Mahoney Wool.

Convention be damned.

# Houndstooth

Reeve was at least smart enough not to close the door on Calvin and Michael. He still had a purple bruise on his left cheekbone where Michael's fist had connected with it.

'Good evening, Mr Reeve,' said Cal cheerfully.

The botanist merely scowled and turned his back on them, returning to whatever he had been doing. When they followed him into the room he was at his table, scribbling in a book with agitated strokes, his head hung like a sulky child.

'Just a courtesy call,' continued Cal, 'to update you on my enquiry into your suspected criminal activities. I've had a conversation with a Mr Wardell. You might remember that he was the Government agent on board the *Rajah*. He seemed to think that you were in the vicinity of Laurence Blake's cabin on the night he was murdered.'

That had Reeve's attention. He looked up, worried.

'Furthermore,' the policeman continued, sitting himself down in the chair opposite the botanist, 'he tells me that your passage was paid for with a bankers draft.'

Michael had not known this. He glanced sharply at Calvin who gave him an affirmative nod. The policeman had been doing some snooping around. That was his job, after all. 'Anything you'd like to add, Michael?' Calvin asked.

Michael was thinking fast. 'There is. I'm wondering if whoever paid your passage also paid you to keep an eye on Rhia

431

Mahoney. I wonder if you were supposed to discover what, if anything, she knew about the death of Josiah Blake. Maybe you thought Rhia had something, a letter perhaps, that your boss wanted. You thought that she'd given it to Laurence Blake for safe keeping. You entered his cabin while he slept, hoping to find it and unwittingly – or witlessly – woke him. He might have grabbed you, you might have picked up the letter knife, intending only to threaten him, not to murder him. Either way, you panicked and killed him.' Michael was thinking aloud, piecing together all the little details Rhia had told him. 'Maybe it wasn't an accident, because if word got out that you'd been snooping in a respectable passenger's cabin, your hopes of station and wealth would have been instantly dashed. You searched his cabin and found the portrait and recognised one of the men in it.' Michael hadn't taken his eyes from Reeve, whose own eyes just grew wider and more startled. The open drafting book displayed poorly executed drawings of indigenous flora.

'Of course I have a patron,' Reeve said finally, 'it is essential and normal in my profession. But his identity is a private matter and what you are accusing me of is utter twaddle.' He didn't sound convincing, or convinced.

Calvin nodded slowly. '*Twaddle?* You'd prefer to move into the barracks, then, than to give us a name? It must be rather a large boodle you stand to lose. You might find, eventually, that freedom is worth more.'

'I've found it priceless myself over the years,' Michael agreed.

Reeve looked as if he might retch. 'You've not a scrap of evidence and I have nothing more to say.'

'I don't need evidence to arrest a man in Sydney, Mr Reeve. And I'll guarantee you'll have more to say, once you've seen your new accommodation. The idea of a lenient sentence might seem more appealing in a few days. That's what we offer here in return for a confession, for *names*. We make our own rules here. Think about that.'

Cal went to the doorway and called out to the two young constables who were waiting in the hallway. Michael watched Reeve. It was clear that he *was* thinking about it, because he had picked up his pencil and was scribbling so hard on his drafting paper that he tore a hole clear through it. When Calvin's boys walked in – and they *were* boys – eager to have something to do to pass the time, Reeve threw down his pencil, looking piteously sorry for himself.

'We'll leave you with your escort, then,' said Calvin. 'Don't worry about strapping his hands, lads, I saw you loading your pistols out in the hallway.'

As they walked back to Macquarie Street, past the Barracks, Calvin shook his head. 'He's someone's lackey and he's expecting to be saved, I'm certain of it. I'll hold him on suspicion of murder for a while, until I can coax a confession out of him. It might not take so long before he starts missing his gentlemanly pretensions.'

Michael nodded. He needed a drink. 'You lot are busy at the moment, aren't you? Are they still keeping a watch on Mick's?'

'They are. I'm not planning on getting too involved, though it's supposed to be my night off. There's half a dozen armed men in an upstairs room at the Hare and Hound and my sergeant's got more boys at the harbour. They've been waiting around all week and they're getting restless. It's all got to go off soon, unless they've managed to sneak past under our noses. We've even managed to borrow some of the governor's soldiers.'

'It wouldn't hurt to have a jar at the Hare and Hound, would it?' Michael asked.

Calvin gave a long-suffering sigh, but Michael could tell he didn't mind the idea.

The Hare and Hound, at the Rocks, was only a street away from Mick the Fence's pine-board bungalow. They went in the side entrance of the tavern and straight upstairs to one of the front rooms. There were four men sitting at the table eating and smoking, and two at the windows, from where they had a reasonable view of the approach to Mick's. Calvin had a quiet word with the two on watch before he and Michael left them to it.

The tavern downstairs was as ill lit and dingy as any public house in the Rocks, and the ale coming out of the barrel looked too thin. Rum was a much safer bet. They found a corner where Calvin's uniform wouldn't create too much interest and settled to wait.

Michael had been avoiding telling the policeman exactly how imminent his departure was, but he couldn't just leave without saying goodbye. He'd thought about it, of course. He hated goodbyes, and besides Maggie, Calvin was the closest thing to a friend he had in Sydney. Once they were on their second measure of rum he decided it was time.

'I've got a passage as ship's carpenter on the next one out.'

'Is that right?' Calvin was silent for a moment. 'Well I'll be bloody damned.'

'Aye.'

Calvin opened his mouth to say something else, but one of the men from upstairs sidled over to them and jerked his head in the direction of the road.

It was on.

They threw their smokes into the tin on the table and got to their feet silently. Calvin took his pistol from his boot and stuck it in his belt. 'There's just nothing like a good raid,' he said. 'You're welcome to join in, Michael. Think of it as a parting gift.'

Michael shrugged. 'Why not? I should have remembered that you don't have nights off.'

Three or four of the Port Authority constables were already under the shadowy overhang of Mick's front verandah. It took a few minutes for the others to assemble, noiselessly, outside the rickety bungalow. The building was of an almost identical layout to Maggie's, Michael noted, which was convenient, since he knew where the entrance to the basement would be.

It was agreed that an advance party of four men – Calvin, Michael and the two brawniest constables – would attempt to enter the building quiet as snakes, and spring a surprise on whatever was taking place in the basement. The other half a dozen men were to join them on a signal from Calvin, and were told to keep their firearms in their belts unless otherwise instructed. There had been trouble, recently, with trigger-happy boys who thought a smoking pistol was an accessory to their authority.

The operation ran smoothly. Mick's basement was rigged out like a subterranean kitchen; a fire roared in the deep stone recess that had clearly been excavated for the purpose, and a crucible hung from an iron hook above the flames. The room was thick with smoke and fumes. Around the hearth stood several characters Michael recognised, including those three fools the Smith brothers. Their faces wore expressions ranging from incomprehension to alarm.

On a long bench against the wall were an array of files and other tools for removing silver, the shavings of which would be melted in the crucible. Some large brass scales sat on a spindle-legged table along with moulds and stamps. There too sat Mick the Fence. He was dressed for town, his ginger hair and whiskers oiled and his houndstooth frock coat clean. He didn't make a move. He knew the game was up. Several large tea chests, nailed shut, sat close to the bottom of the stairs, presumably waiting to be transported to the harbour.

'Evening, gents,' boomed Calvin merrily, as he and his men spoiled what looked like a well-run operation. There was a flurry of activity as the Smiths and another of the coiners tried to get past Michael, who was standing at the bottom of the stairs. He managed to detain two of them, one by the collar and another with a well-aimed fist. The other two made it almost to the top of the stairs before they met some constables descending. After an energetic scuffle, a good deal of cursing, a broken arm and two bleeding noses (one coiner, one constable), the job was done. Mick was still sitting, his houndstooth still immaculate.

One of the tea chests was prised open. It was brimful of shiny new guineas of such a grade that Michael let out a low, impressed whistle. 'Your boss in London is going to be very unhappy. That's fine coining all right.'

'Thank you, gracious sir,' said Mick, with a mock bow. He stood and took off his coat and folded it neatly. He'd been in the barracks before and he liked his threads too much to see them ruined. He had the quiet confidence of someone who knew the law as if he'd written it himself. He, like the botanist, thought his boss would get him off.

In the wee hours, Michael and Calvin sat with their boots resting on the verandah rails at the Port Authority, smoking. They'd just had a report that a small army of men from the George Street station had boarded the *Sea Witch*. Calvin poured another measure of his emergency rum into a tin mug and handed it to Michael. 'We may as well finish the bottle now,' he said. 'As I was saying, I'll be bloody sorry to see you go.'

'I wish I could say I'll be sorry to leave, but you know I won't.' Michael raised his mug and clinked it against Calvin's. 'But here's to you, the finest chief constable of the Port Authority Sydney has seen.'

'I'm the only chief constable of the Port Authority Sydney has seen.'

'Aye. You're the best hands down then. Well, here's to you having as much of a lark on your night off next year.'

'I'll drink to that.'

The two men sat together beneath the dark, deep arc of the sky, listening to the waves crashing on the Antipodean shore; lost in their own thoughts.

Michael was thinking about Annie. Would she still want him, after all this time?

It is taking an age to navigate the Thames. Michael says the captain expected us to be at the dock an hour ago. He and Eliza are on the deck, in spite of the cold, seeing the sights, but I feel easier looking through the window of the saloon. This is a different place to that which, ten months ago, I thought I was leaving for ever, because *I* am not the same. The sky is still dove grey. The river still as brown as cocoa. The tower and the bridge are monuments of civilisation, but I am less in awe.

The voyage was uneventful. I expected the seasickness, and I half expected Manannán to show me white mares in the sea and for the moonrise to bring ghosts, but the sea and the moon were only the sea and the moon. My red book is filled with patterns, which accounts for why I have not put pen to paper to write before now. There has been little to say. The passage was mercifully uneventful. No death, no pirates and no cuff fights in the orlop.

There were few women at all on board besides Mrs Green and two spinster sisters. The sisters sailed to Van Diemen's Land some years ago in the hope of securing husbands, but finding none to fit their requirements, or so they say, they sailed on to Sydney. They are neither young nor comely as far as I can tell, though they insist that they had no shortage of admirers, either in Hobart or Sydney. Mrs Green struck up a friendship with them even before we left Circular Quay, when it was discovered that all three shared a passion for crochet. They have, between them, filled a wicker hamper with cotton doilies and collars.

For myself, I could barely finish a design quickly enough before another hurried from my pencil. I still have the same little pencil that Mr Dillon gave me that day, but I use it sparingly. I can't say why I have kept it. My new designs have a different essence. Even I can see it. The patterns are sharper and, when I open my paintbox, the colours I mix are strong and full of light. I've designed repeat patterns of jacaranda, wattle and waratah as well as orange blossom and winter rose. I think they will look very fine in wool.

I've seen little of Michael for the entire thirteen weeks at sea. He was kept busy on repairs. He told me that the ship's hull had not been properly dried out in some years. The shipping line between London and Sydney has become so busy that the hold was in urgent need of new timbers to replace old rotting ones. We have talked, though. Michael has told me what happened in Sydney before we left and what he knows and what he suspects. As for the counterfeiting, I am stunned by the boldness of it. Opium *and* counterfeit! I still cannot believe that Ryan was involved in such a swindle, though perhaps that is because I don't want to believe that I have known so little about my own uncle. And Isaac, in spite of his moods, did not seem a man who would take advantage of another's weakness. But now that the seed of doubt has been planted, I keep remembering things. For instance, Isaac overheard my conversation with Mr Montgomery at Isabella's birthday tea; he also came to the emporium on the morning of the day that I was arrested, and was alone in the storeroom for a time. He could have put the cloth there, and then told the constabulary. Of course, almost everyone I know has, at some time, been under suspicion in my mind – Grace and Isabella and Mr Montgomery. And Mr Dillon of course. It is hard to trust anyone when you have been betrayed.

439

We have progressed a little further now, past paddle steamboats and wherries and into one of the congested canals that lead to the docks of the London Pool. This, I am informed, is the oldest port along the river. It seems impossible that any craft in the queue of river traffic will find a place to unload goods and passengers. There are three-masted barques and cargo vessels and barges in a queue in front of us. There is such a donnybrook of shouting and activity on the docks that Circular Quay in Sydney seems like a millpond. I'd best put away my pen now, since we'll soon be docking. My heart is clattering like a tin drum.

# Crochet

By the time she came up on deck, Rhia had realised that she no longer desired anything of London. She would pay her respects to Mrs Blake and call on Mr Montgomery to resolve the matter of the stolen cloth, and then arrange her passage to Dublin.

Michael was leaning on the rails staring upriver. He had his scant belongings in a small canvas sack and the broad brim of his rabbit-felt hat pulled down low over his eyes. He was travelling as light as a sailor. It didn't look as if there was much that he'd wanted to salvage from his former life. Eliza Green was sitting on her trunk watching the acrobatics above. The riggers shimmied up the masts and pulled ropes and hoists to and fro, collapsing each section of sailcloth into a scalloped fold and tying it to a yardarm or mast.

They had decided that they would, all three, call unannounced at Cloak Lane. Eliza had done little but loop yarn around a hooked needle and talk about Juliette for weeks. But now, facing a reunion that she had never believed could happen, she was silent and nervous. Rhia couldn't begin to imagine how she must feel,

It took another two hours before they were in a carriage amidst the noonday crowds of Cheapside and Cornhill. It didn't seem real. Michael was studiously ignoring the ballyhoo and reading a broadsheet he'd bought from a paperboy at the docks. Eliza was in a frenzy of crocheting. It still intrigued

Rhia that she could weave such a delicate a web with her little wooden hook without even looking at her hands. The congestion along Cornhill was worse than usual. They'd come to a halt between a coal cart and a fishmonger. The latter was closest, and the funk of the catch outranked the oily smell of coal and the stink of manure.

They set off again, Michael's gaze now fixed on the street. His expression might have been aloofness or indifference. There were many means of hiding emotion, though, and this was his. Rhia wondered if he too was thinking of Greystones. They were so close to home now. She cast a sidelong look at Eliza, who had put her crochet away and was fidgeting with the ends of her new plaid shawl. Eliza had admired it in a clothier's window on George Street. She had pranced about like a young girl when Rhia bought it for her.

When the carriage stopped again, it was outside the Blake terrace on Cloak Lane.

'We're here,' Rhia said. No one moved. Rhia looked from Michael to Eliza. 'I wonder if I should speak with Mrs Blake first?' Michael nodded in agreement and Eliza managed a squeak, her hands to her cheeks.

Rhia stood for a moment, looking at the cast iron beast with a ring through its nose, before she lifted it to knock. She remembered how nervous she'd felt, standing here with Ryan, little more than a year ago. Would she encounter the ghost of her former self within? She knocked.

Antonia opened the door. She didn't recognise Rhia immediately, and then she looked astonished and embraced her fiercely.

'Sweet lord! Is it you?' She stood back and looked at Rhia, and Rhia looked at her. Antonia was wearing worsted, and it was blue. A dark, sensible blue, but blue all the same.

'Welcome home,' Antonia said, but Rhia didn't say that she was not home yet.

'I am not alone,' she said, instead. She explained, as quickly and concisely as she could, how Juliette's mother came to be waiting in the carriage at the bottom of the steps to see her daughter, and who Michael Kelly was.

Neither Rhia, Michael nor Mrs Blake witnessed the reunion between mother and daughter. It was agreed that Eliza should make herself comfortable in the drawing room whilst Antonia did her best to prepare Juliette for the event.

When Antonia joined Rhia and Michael in the kitchen, where Beth was fussing about worrying over how to make the lunch stretch to feed so many, they all looked at her expectantly. Antonia smiled.

'I couldn't help stopping for a moment outside the door to make sure that all was well,' she began.

Rhia nodded impatiently. 'Did you hear anything?'

'I heard Juliette laugh. I don't believe I've heard her laugh before.' Antonia wiped away a tear, although she was smiling. 'They both began talking at once and continued talking over each other.' She looked at Rhia and then at Michael. 'Well,' she said, clearly lost for words. The kettle on the range was hissing insistently, so she busied herself preparing a pot of tea. 'I hope you will agree to be my guest, Mr Kelly,' she said. 'The house has been empty too long.' She put the teapot and cups on the table. 'I shall send word to Mr Dillon and Mr Montgomery. They must know immediately of your safe return, Rhia. Mr Dillon petitioned ceaselessly for your pardon.'

Rhia felt her heart lurch at the mention of Dillon. She would have to look him in the eye, even though he must hate her. She wondered if Antonia, too, blamed her for Laurence's death. Nothing in her expression or manner suggested it. She was forgiving by nature though. Dillon was not. He would have no interest in her company without Laurence to mediate. He would think her ugly, with her hair only just long enough for pins and her thin, brown limbs. But why should she care what he thought of her?

Antonia and Michael had spent little time on formalities; Michael wanted to know where Isaac was, and Antonia didn't even seem surprised.

'Your return to London has coincided with that of the *Mathilda*,' she said. 'It docked only days ago. Isaac has been in India since the summer.'

'That's a long time,' Michael remarked casually, though Rhia knew what he was thinking.

'Yes,' Antonia agreed. 'It is a long time.' She smoothed her forehead with the tips of her fingers. 'Mr Dillon seems to think...' She hesitated.

'That your friend Isaac Fisher has been dabbling in the China trade?' Michael's voice was, characteristically, lacking emotion. If you didn't know him, you might think that he didn't care.

'Then you know.' Antonia seemed relieved.

Rhia wondered what manner of cloth this day would weave.

'Rhia and I put our heads together and figured a few things out,' said Michael, 'and I'll warrant you know a thing or two as well, by now. Your Mr Dillon also, by the sounds of it. So why don't we wait until we're all met, share what we know, and see where it leads. It's something of a puzzle, at present.'

'It's more a quilt,' Rhia said, thinking aloud. Today was not just one cloth alone. Its pieces now needed putting together.

'The quilt!' said Antonia. 'I had almost forgotten. I took delivery of the *Rajah* quilt last month, and when I saw the appliqué I knew that the chintz was yours, Rhia. It very nearly brought me to tears. I was sorry that your beautiful chintz had been cut up but, and this is most strange, when I saw it I knew that you were all right … that everything would be all right. I received a letter from the governor's wife, on behalf of all the needlewomen, saying it was made as a gift for the Quakers of the British Ladies Society.'

'Then the quilt is here, in the house?' It hardly seemed possible that it had crossed the seas twice and made it back to London before Rhia herself.

'It is. And soon I will show you.'

The talk turned to other things. Antonia asked Michael about his family. She had asked nothing of Sydney, Rhia noted, not from either of them. She would hear it all one day.

'Would you like a ginger loaf for your tea, Miss Mahoney?' asked Beth when she could get a word in.

'Would I! The thought of your ginger loaf is all that has kept me from despair, Beth.'

# Broadcloth

R hia woke in the afternoon in the bed with ivory curtains and arabesques. She dressed slowly in a gown that had been hanging in the wardrobe since the last time she was in this room. It was Japanese rose: a rich, deep pink with none of the hard lustre of mineral dye. The cloth caressed her, but she did not feel unworthy of it, now. She pinned her hair as best she could with only a hand glass, and then slipped her feet into slippers, as though she were dressing in someone else's finery. She walked slowly down the wide, polished stairs. It was only hours since she had arrived in London for the second time. Another life had begun.

Voices drifted out from the morning room.

Michael was almost unrecognisable, standing against the mantelpiece dressed in a clean shirt and breeches. He'd shaved and oiled his hair. He was smoking and talking to Mr Dillon. Dillon's back was to the door. He was warming his hands over the fire, his black hair reaching his shoulders. He turned as Rhia came in and bowed politely, and as he did Rhia became aware of the unsteadiness of her legs. It was nothing to do with him, only the swaying of the solid earth because her legs were still at sea.

'It is good to see you back in London, Miss Mahoney.'

It is good to be here.' She examined his face. She could see no trace of anger or accusation. She could think of nothing at all to say. It seemed that she no longer knew how to be polite. Some would argue that she never had.

Antonia coughed delicately. She was sitting on the Chesterfield with her needlework. For a moment it had seemed to Rhia that she was alone in the room with Dillon. Antonia smiled at her. 'You look well in that colour. Now that we're all here, I'll help Beth with the tea. I've accommodated Juliette and her mother in a guesthouse in Cornhill where they can continue their reunion privately.'

Antonia left for the kitchen, and Mr Dillon and Michael continued their conversation. Michael was saying he'd come to the conclusion there was no such thing as free trade, that everything had its cost. They had much in common, Rhia thought. They were both personally affronted by corruption, and their weapon of choice was a pen not a pistol (though Michael possessed another weapon besides – she'd seen its hilt sticking out of his boot).

She'd not yet dared to look at the photogenic drawing on the wall. The trees. She edged her gaze towards it cautiously. It looked different now. Maybe because it no longer had the power to frighten her: she had made her peace by facing her fear.

Antonia returned with a tea tray and they sat around the table, Mr Dillon opposite Rhia. She might not be frightened of shadows and spirits any more, but she was having trouble looking at him. It was merely something new to overcome. She looked him straight in the eye and thought she saw something she hadn't seen before, something softer, a silent enquiry. It didn't make her feel weak, like some paragon of femininity in a penny romance. Rather, she felt as though she were inhabiting her own skin for the very first time. Dillon looked away, leaving Rhia wondering if he was not indifferent to her after all.

He glanced around the table, though when his eyes met Rhia's again they were guarded. 'We know that Isaac Fisher and Ryan Mahoney were using the *Mathilda* to trade opium, and that she and her sister ship, *Sea Witch*, were engaged in a counterfeiting operation. Do you think it's possible, Mr Kelly, that they were chartered by separate parties?'

'Aye,' Michael agreed, 'most merchant ships are for hire when they are not otherwise engaged.'

'So,' Dillon pressed, '*Mathilda* left Lintin Island with a cargo of silver, and sailed into Pacific waters just east of Sydney Cove where the silver was to be transferred onto the *Sea Witch*, in return for a hull full of counterfeit coin?'

Michael nodded, and Dillon's proposal settled silently. He looked at Rhia. 'Will you tell Mrs Blake about the negative?'

Antonia looked at Rhia expectantly, and Rhia explained, as delicately as she could, how the negative came to be on the *Rajah*, how the portrait was made, and how it was then destroyed.

Antonia was shaking her head. 'No wonder ...' She trailed off, no doubt thinking about Juliette's peculiar behaviour. She took a sip of tea, looking at Dillon. 'You knew, didn't you, the day you came to visit – the day Juliette told us about her father?'

He nodded. 'Forgive me, but I saw no point in telling you. It would only have made things awkward between you and your maid.'

Antonia looked confused. 'But the negative has not been destroyed?' She was looking at Rhia almost pleadingly.

'It has been lost. Probably destroyed. I'm so sorry, Antonia.'

Antonia shook her head, bewildered.

'I think I'd like to see something of this photogenic drawing,' Michael remarked. 'I can't get the measure of it.' He was trying to soften the blow, Rhia thought, and she liked him all the better for it.

'Then you shall,' Antonia assured him.

'But first,' he said, 'I should tell you about the evening I visited the botanist Mr Reeve, and about Mick the Fence who got arrested for counterfeiting.'

By the time they left Sydney, Michael said, more than a dozen arrests had been made, including the captain of the *Sea Witch*. The captain said he didn't know anything except that an agent in Calcutta chartered the clipper and that whomever paid for the charter would not easily be traced. 'There are plenty of merchants who do not wish to be associated with the opium trade,' Michael said. 'Twenty thousand pounds' worth of counterfeit silver guineas was returned to the governor's office, from whence the coin was stolen in the first place. It'll probably be sold as alloy and used to line another few buildings with cedar,' he observed drily. 'Hard to know who's the bigger crook, the coiner or the government of New South Wales.'

'No ringmaster was named?' Dillon asked.

Michael shook his head. 'Aye. And it wouldn't surprise me if Mick himself doesn't know his master's name. There's bound to be an in-between to protect the boss. Besides, Mick the Fence will never talk: he's a professional and it would be bad for business. All he said on the matter was that, seeing as there was a silver shortage, he and his men were doing the Crown a service in supplying freshly minted coins.'

Antonia was tapping her fingers on the table in an agitated rhythm. 'I simply find it inconceivable that Isaac is trading in opium, let alone in counterfeit. Yes, I do know that Quaker ships carried slaves, so there's no need to remind me of it, but *this* ... I can hardly believe that I could have misjudged his character so wildly, and for so long. Thank God Josiah did not live to see this day.'

'I think we must give Isaac the opportunity to defend himself,' interjected Dillon.

'Yes, we must,' she agreed. 'I shall invite him to do so.'

'Montgomery and Beckwith should also be here,' said Dillon.

'Very well,' said Antonia. 'And you and Mr Kelly, of course.'

'I would have it no other way,' he replied.

'Nor I,' added Michael. 'There was a letter, wasn't there, Mrs Blake, written by your husband?'

'There was,' she agreed, 'Mr Dillon has located it.'

Michael frowned to hear that Ryan Mahoney's solicitor would not release the letter until a magistrate ruled that the death was not self-murder. 'Is that so?' he said quietly. 'Well, perhaps you could leave that one to me.'

Antonia stood up. 'Mr Kelly, would you still like to see a demonstration of photogenic drawing?'

'I would.'

They left the room. Rhia was certain that Antonia had deliberately left her alone with Mr Dillon. The silence increased, with nothing but the hiss of wood sap from the fire to interrupt it. Rhia stole a glance, wondering if he cared as little as he seemed to that they were sitting opposite each other with nothing to say. He seemed preoccupied.

'I have a feeling,' he said finally, 'that Mrs Blake's maid may have been the key all along.'

'Then you believe that one of the men in the portrait is a murderer?'

'I have no doubt of it. I've been waiting for some archive newsprint on forging rackets operating around Manchester at the time of Mr Green's murder.'

'And?'

'And I've received my response, but let's keep that between us for now.'

'Then you think John Hannam is connected to the Sydney counterfeiting?'

'I think there's a decent chance of it, yes.'

They lapsed into silence again. Rhia let her eyes rest somewhere safe; on his coat. 'Are you wearing English broadcloth?' she asked. He laughed, and she felt the stiffness in her shoulders ease.

'I believe it is Welsh, like your name. When I was young the people in my village believed that Rhiannon appeared to her followers riding a white horse.'

'Yes, she did. And a purple cloak.'

Dillon looked at her with the same softness she'd seen before, then he turned to the fire. 'Michael tells me you and he have a common interest in Australian wool?'

'Our first shipment should arrive in Dublin shortly.'

'And do you intend to be there to meet it, Miss Mahoney?'

'I do.'

'Then London is not the place for you, after all?'

It was the question she had asked herself that morning, as they sailed past spires and steeples and beneath London Bridge. The sight of the city had made her ache for Greystones. Only one more expanse of water, the Irish Sea, now separated her from home. She shrugged. She longed for the shale and the hills, and to see her mother, and even her father, but she was not sure that she'd want to stay. 'There was a time when I wanted nothing more than to see London and to travel to foreign lands, and now I have, though not in the way I imagined,' she added, laughing. 'I'm more settled, but that isn't to say I would be content to pass the remainder of my days in an Irish village.'

'You might find that the solution lies in your work, Miss Mahoney. I have always found it so. You are an artist, but you seem to also enjoy the liveliness of the trade.'

He had noticed something about her that she had hardly known herself. Before she could think better of it, she was telling him of her desire to return home with a profession.

'Desire is one vehicle for the truth,' he mused with a half smile.

She looked at him with mock-horror. 'But you are encouraging a woman to have a profession!'

Dillon wasn't smiling any more, he was looking at her; into her, with intense earnest. 'You've already had the courage to defy convention,' he said, 'I liked it in you from the first, and I know that Laurence was in awe of that quality in you. He was very fond of you, as you must know.' His voice faltered and he stood up and walked to the fire, half turning away from her. Rhia took the opportunity to inspect every line of his profile – his straight nose and long forehead, the colour of his skin, the black hair. He suddenly seemed so familiar a friend, yet she hardly knew him.

'I can't pretend that I had no knowledge of Mr Blake's feelings,' she said carefully, 'but my sentiments were not ... in accord with his.'

'I had wondered.' He hesitated. 'Laurence was my friend, and I would not say this if he—'

'If he were alive?'

'Yes.'

'What? What would you not say?'

'That I loved you from the first.'

# Quilt

Beth tapped lightly on the bedroom door and entered with a basketful of kindling as Antonia was sealing the envelopes ready for the butcher's boy. He was swifter than the morning post, and always happy to earn a farthing or two extra.

'Lovely fresh morning, madam.'

'It is, Beth. Have our guests risen?'

'Oh Mr Kelly's been up since dawn – says it's always been that way with him. He hasn't had any breakfast though, just wanted a pot of tea.'

'And Rhia?'

'I heard her moving about as I passed by. I'll just build your fire before I put on the porridge.'

'Never mind, Beth, you've enough to do with Juliette away. I can dress without the fire.' She gave Beth the envelopes for the boy; one for Isaac and one for Jonathan Montgomery.

Antonia washed her face in lemon water, dressed in her worsted and pinned her hair. Both guests were in the morning room when she arrived, sitting at the table by the front window, which was laid for breakfast. Michael stood when she entered.

'Good morning, Mrs Blake.'

'And to you both,' she said. 'I hope you slept well?'

'Yes, thank you,' said Michael. He didn't look as though

he'd slept well. How odd and unfamiliar this must all be to him. To be in London after years as a prisoner, to know that he was so close to seeing his wife and son. He must have wanted to sail straight to Dublin from Sydney. But as Mr Dillon had said, they had business in common, and Michael Kelly didn't strike her as the kind of man that would leave business unfinished.

'I didn't sleep a wink,' said Rhia. 'Probably because the floor wasn't moving.'

Or perhaps because of Mr Dillon, Antonia thought. She sat and Rhia poured her coffee. They spoke of wool. She thought it an excellent venture and said so. 'In fact,' she added, 'should you require an agent in London, I would be delighted to join you.'

Beth cleared their bowls and Michael complimented her, saying that her porridge had to be the best he'd ever tasted, even though he'd not had any in years.

'Then there's no porridge in Sydney?' Beth looked scandalised.

'Oats are fed to horses in Sydney, and people eat toast because wheat is cheap.' Michael stood up and put on his broad-brimmed hat. 'I've some business this morning, Mrs Blake, and then I'll be meeting Dillon somewhere called the Red Lion. Thank you again for your hospitality.'

'But you'll come back here, Mr Kelly?'

'Aye, of course.'

Rhia told Michael where the Red Lion was, and he took his leave.

Antonia looked at her once-lodger. It was not only that she was without her lovely long hair, she was changed in a way that was hard to define. 'We've not really had time to speak, have we?' she said. 'I simply cannot begin to imagine ...' She faltered.

'I have prayed for you,' she said. It was inadequate. Anything would be.

Rhia looked down at her hands. 'Well then it was your prayers as well as your money that brought me home.'

'What do you mean?' It was an odd thing to say.

'I found the money you put in my purse. Without it I would never have been able to pay for my passage, or buy the merino.'

'But I didn't put any money in your purse, though I saw it in your portmanteau when I packed your things.' They were both silent, considering this. Rhia looked confused. 'Then who?'

'It could only have been Mr Dillon,' Antonia said. 'It was he who collected your trunk and brought it to Millbank. If I'd thought of it I would certainly have stowed some money for you, but I was so shocked.'

'Of course. And I didn't expect it. But I can hardly believe that Mr Dillon … it was so generous.'

'He thinks very highly of you,' said Antonia. Anyone could see it. 'I cannot imagine how you've kept body and soul together,' she added.

Rhia smiled. 'Through the stories my grandmother used to tell me. It was she who named me.'

'I see,' Antonia said, although she didn't.

'Rhiannon was cursed and falsely accused and exiled. She was only released from the curse by her own suffering and by the help of Manannán, god of the sea.'

It seemed an apt fairytale, Antonia thought. No different, in some ways, to the Christian stories of magic potions and the dead returning to life. She didn't know what to say, so she changed the subject. 'There is something you must see.'

The quilt was in the camphor wood chest against the wall. Antonia brought it back to the table.

Rhia eyed the bundle of patchwork warily, as though

memories might tumble out of it. She touched it lightly. 'It was Margaret who asked that it be presented to you, and it was she who composed and embroidered the dedication.'

Antonia spread the quilt across the back of the Chesterfield, which it could easily have covered twice, and examined Margaret's cross-stitch.

> To the Ladies of the Convict Ship Committee. This quilt worked by the convicts of the ship *Rajah* during their voyage is presented as a testimony of the gratitude with which they remember their exertions for their welfare while in England and during their passage and also as proof that they have not neglected the Ladies kind admonitions of being industrious. June 1841.

Antonia leaned closer. The central panel, stitched with the dedication, was unyielding. Something was fortifying the pocket between the stitching and its lining. She had noticed it before, and suspected that the embroidery card had been left in. Rhia noticed it as well. Behind the dedication, instead of plain linen, was a square of blue valetine silk.

'Margaret's favourite piece of cloth,' Rhia said. 'I recognise it. She said she was going to keep it and make it into a purse. They looked at each other and Antonia wondered if they were having the same thought. Along one edge of the valetine, the stitching was tacked rather than sewn prettily and neatly as it was on the other three sides.

Antonia fetched her embroidery scissors and, her hands unsteady, snipped the loose stitching away. In the pocket was a stiff piece of parchment. Another disappointment would be too much.

'My hands are shaking, Rhia, you do it,' she said.

'It is the negative,' said Rhia. 'I recognise it.'

'There is no guarantee that it will still make a representation,' said Antonia. Her heart was thumping. 'The sun is strong this morning. The kitchen would be best, at this hour.'

She hurried from the room to find her apparatus. She didn't know what she was more afraid of: seeing Josiah's face again or that Isaac might be identified as a killer. Rhia followed her upstairs to the studio and then back to the kitchen. They did not speak. They were both preoccupied with the urgency of the undertaking.

Beth was polishing the silver on the kitchen table. She looked mystified as Antonia set up her frame on the bench-top under the window. She laid a clean sheet of treated parchment onto the negative, then clamped them together and positioned the frame so that the sunlight streamed across it.

There was nothing anyone could do. She could not bear to watch. Rhia took her by the elbow, gently. 'Beth might be pleased to have help polishing the silver.'

'Yes, quite,' Antonia agreed, hardly hearing her.

Beth looked horrified. 'Oh, there's no need!'

Rhia laughed. 'I've put my hand to dirtier tasks than cleaning silver, Beth.'

They took turns dipping their flannels into the foul smelling brew. It was her mother's recipe, Beth said, when Rhia wrinkled her nose, made from flour of sulphur and boiled onions. They polished candlesticks and salt cellars and cake forks, and Antonia took the watch from her pocket every two or three minutes.

When it was time, she put down her cloth and smoothed her hair, and then her skirts, before she approached the little wooden frame on the bench top.

A portrait had materialised: an almost perfect image, as

though it had been penned in sepia. Five men stood in Antonia's garden, just as they had almost two years ago. There was Josiah, looking straight at her. Her heart lurched, but she felt only relief. His image had not been spirited away. It was there all the time, waiting for the sun to reveal it. She could feel his gaze again.

Standing beside Josiah was Isaac, looking a little stiff and uncomfortable, and on his other side, Mr Montgomery wore a bemused expression but looked as handsome and elegant as ever. On one end of the row of men was Mr Beckwith, his head bent shyly so that his eyes were shaded. At the other end was Ryan Mahoney, attempting to preserve his rakish smile for the interminable time the exposure had taken.

Antonia unscrewed the bolts that held the frame in place and laid the photogenic drawing carefully on the bench top. The chord above the wainscoting yanked and the bell in the kitchen clanged making them all jump, then laugh nervously. 'Who can that be?' Antonia looked at the clock. It was only ten o'clock. 'I'll go, Beth.'

Isaac Fisher stood on the doorstep, hat in hands, the crisp morning light behind him. Even with his face in shadow it was clear that he was ill at ease. 'I came immediately, Antonia. There seemed some urgency in your letter.'

'Isaac!' She didn't know what to say to him. She should have thought this through. She had expected him to call later in the afternoon, if at all. 'Come in. We're in the kitchen. Rhia is here. Her ship put in yesterday.' She scrutinised his face as she took his hat. Surely he wouldn't want Rhia in London? He looked surprised, of course, and then he smiled wanly. He looked tired.

'That is good news.'

'Yes.'

Isaac followed Antonia down the hallway. She felt light-headed, as if she was only loosely anchored to the ground. Some part of her was becoming detached, observing the scene from a distance. It was out of her hands now. Now she must simply speak the truth.

If Rhia felt anxious at the sight of Isaac, she didn't show it. She smiled and said how nice it was to see him, and then she helped Beth clear the silver from the table. Beth hurried away as soon as she could, sensing there would soon be more 'goings on' in her kitchen.

Isaac surveyed the room in his usual unhurried way. He had probably never been in the Cloak Lane kitchen before. His eyes came to rest on the bench where the still portrait lay in the sunlight. He moved towards it slowly and deliberately. Antonia watched him, hardly breathing. Rhia was standing, holding the back of a chair. Their eyes met and Rhia raised an eyebrow. Antonia straightened her back. 'Isaac, there is something we must discuss. I ... I have heard ...' She faltered. The truth was not easily spoken after all.

Isaac was looking at the portrait. He seemed dazed. 'Extraordinary,' he muttered.

'Is it true,' said Rhia boldly, 'that you and my uncle were trading in opium?'

He turned slowly. He didn't look surprised. He shook his head, but not in denial. In shame?

'It is true,' he said. 'But I have achieved my purpose now. You need not tell me, Antonia, that I am not worthy of the Society of Friends. It has been as much a convenience as anything, to continue to be a Quaker. It has not been in my heart since Louisa died.'

Antonia was deflated. She had wanted, desperately, to be proven wrong. 'Quaker or no, it is an immoral trade. I had thought more of you.'

'Well you need not. It is a narrow view that you hold, but I understand it well enough.'

His tone angered her. 'Then was it worth it, for the profit?'

'Who can say? But the money has been well spent and I have done what I had to.'

'How can you say such a thing! To think of the damage your trading has done in China and in India.'

Isaac sighed. 'Antonia. Keep your bonnet on. I have, these past years, visited many villages in India where the weavers do not have land to grow crops because there are fields of poppies instead of rice. There is no simple solution in a modern economy that relies on the produce of other economies. This is the new world. The British government would never place itself at the mercy of a nation as sophisticated and impenetrable as China, they simply would not tolerate it. They are far too narrow-minded. This nation's unprecedented consumption of commodities – tea, mostly – has left our silver stocks depleted. The only way to fill the vaults of British banks is to encourage opium use in China.'

'I do understand the economics, Isaac. What I don't understand is that you seem to think it perfectly reasonable.'

'My lovely Antonia. Allow me to finish. With the profit made, I have purchased back land that will feed Indian families. This was what Ryan and I planned together, and it was necessary to tell Jonathan because he is part-owner in *Mathilda* and *Sea Witch*. I didn't tell Josiah, of course, because the knowledge would have compromised his Quaker oath. He was, as you well know, an unyielding moralist. I am the first to admit that it is a filthy trade, but I have now used it against itself and I am content. I can only hope that Ryan is resting in peace too.'

Antonia was speechless.

Rhia's voice was unsteady. 'Then the money has been spent charitably.'

'Of course.'

'And the counterfeiting?'

Isaac looked at her sharply. 'Counterfeiting?'

'You must know that the *Mathilda* made a voyage from Lintin Island into Pacific waters to meet the *Sea Witch*? The silver from Lintin Island was to be exchanged for guineas that were illegally coined in Sydney.'

If Isaac was guilty, then it was a performance worthy of Drury Lane. He looked puzzled, his eyes darting about the room as if he was trying to piece the story together. He was in no hurry to tell them what he was thinking. Antonia held her breath. She looked at Rhia, who looked impatient. Isaac finally nodded slowly.

'I have never been to Lintin Island. I was busy in Calcutta, arranging land deeds and so on. Everything takes a very long time in India. Mr Beckwith accompanied the shipment for me. It was purely a business arrangement; I paid him for his time and good management. I can see now why there was a delay in returning to Calcutta, and why the captain was such a cagey old salt.' He shook his head. 'I can see it now.'

The bell chord yanked again. Beth called out from the front of the house that she'd see to it, and arrived a moment later with a note for Antonia from Mr Montgomery. He regretted that he would not be able to call that afternoon as requested. He and Mr Beckwith had an important engagement.

Antonia folded the page. She frowned as something occurred to her. 'But Isaac, if you weren't aware of the counterfeiting operation, then surely Mr Beckwith was!'

'He must know something about it,' Isaac agreed. 'I'll speak to him and to Montgomery about it as a matter of urgency. Our clippers are not for charter to anyone who'll pay. It is bad enough that they've carried opium.'

Isaac looked at the portrait again. 'I see that you found your missing negative. You must be pleased, Antonia.'

'That is another matter entirely,' Antonia said. She looked at Rhia, who seemed to know exactly what she was thinking.

'Tell me the address of the guest house in Cornhill,' Rhia said, 'and I'll go and fetch Eliza.'

# Felt

Rhia ran all the way to Cornhill, holding her chambertine skirts up from the puddles of melting snow. By the time she reached the lodgings where the Greens were accommodated, her hair had lost its pins and she'd attracted plenty of curious looks.

Eliza and Juliette were in the landlady's tidy front room, talking so intently by the fire that they didn't notice her at first. They seemed at ease in each other's company. Juliette looked wary as soon as she saw Rhia. 'What is it?' she said, avoiding Rhia's eyes. Juliette hadn't looked her in the eye since she'd caught her talking to photogenic gum trees in the middle of the night.

'Would you come to Cloak Lane? There is something you must see, Mrs Green.' Both women were immediately on edge; you could see it in their hands. They had the same nervous, fluttering gestures.

Rhia tried to keep the talk going as they walked briskly back to Cloak Lane. She measured her footsteps as best she could so as not to feed the anxiety they all felt. She asked Eliza what she thought she'd do, now that she was in London.

'Mrs Blake says I should be selling my collars and doilies at Petticoat Lane, and she needs a housekeeper, as well. She says she wants to spend more time with the trade.'

Rhia laughed. 'I'm pleased to hear it. She is very good at finding employment for women.' Eliza just shook her head as though she still couldn't believe the way her life had turned around.

Antonia must have been waiting in the hallway for she opened the door the instant they knocked. She ushered them into the morning room and dismissed Eliza's protestations about sitting on the Chesterfield. Isaac was at the table, bent over the morning issue of the *Globe*. He might have been reading, but Rhia doubted it. The portrait was next to the broadsheet. Antonia picked it up as though it were made of glass and then sat down beside Eliza, holding it against her chest so that the picture was hidden.

'Eliza. There is something ...' Antonia faltered. 'I would like you to look at this.' She hesitated and then lay the portrait upon her lap.

Eliza gazed at it, frowning. It took her a minute to understand what she was looking at. But Juliette knew exactly what it was. Her hand went to her mouth and her eyes darted to Rhia suspiciously, as though this must be her doing.

'Do you recognise any of these men?' Antonia prodded gently.

Eliza didn't seem to have heard; she was still trying to comprehend the portrait.

Juliette looked at Antonia, wide-eyed. 'I don't understand.' She had seen not one ghost but two: Josiah Blake and Ryan Mahoney.

'I know what you did, Juliette,' Antonia said quietly, 'and why. But you see, the negative found its way back to me anyway. Who would have thought it?' She shrugged as though it was nothing more than a mildly interesting event.

Eliza yelped and threw the portrait onto the floor as though it had bitten her.

'That's him, that's John Hannam all right,' she croaked. She put her hand to her throat as if something had grabbed at it.

Antonia picked the portrait up. 'Which one is John Hannam?' Everyone was silent, watching Eliza.

Eliza stabbed her finger at Mr Montgomery. Rhia felt a chill. No one spoke. It must be a mistake. She looked around. Juliette didn't look surprised, of course. Isaac was nodding as though he had already suspected as much, and Antonia was clearly devastated.

'But that simply isn't possible, Eliza. Mr Montgomery is a respectable man. A wealthy man, from a good family.'

'Do you know anything about Jonathan Montgomery's family, Antonia?' Isaac asked.

'No. But I assumed …' She trailed off. 'Do you?'

'No,' said Isaac. 'I, also, assumed. Respectability only needs wealth to defend it these days.'

Rhia couldn't stand still a moment longer. She needed air. She needed to think. It could not be possible that Mr Montgomery was behind the deaths of Josiah and Ryan. She stood up. 'Mr Dillon and Michael Kelly are meeting in Covent Garden,' she said. 'I'll find them.'

'Take my chaise,' Isaac offered.

'I'd sooner take one of your horses, if I may. I'd be faster.'

'Very well. I'll unhitch the mare.'

Isaac left to do this while Rhia fetched her cloak. By the time she reached the footpath, he'd put a bridle and reins on one of his pretty greys.

'I don't have a saddle,' he said as he handed her the reins.

'I don't have need of one,' she replied. Isaac held the mare still while she mounted.

She rode through Cornhill, easily manoeuvring past slow-moving carriages. On Threadneedle Street, a queue had formed behind a brewer's cart that was unloading tuns at a tavern. She rode past, barely noticing the shocked expressions of ladies in hansom cabs as they stared at her skirts hitched up around her knees. You'd think they'd never seen a leg. It was cold. She wished she'd thought to put on her longer boots and a riding skirt instead. She pulled her hood lower over her face against the frigid air.

The road beyond Cheapside looked clearer, so she pressed her heels into the mare's flanks. They almost reached a canter along Newgate Street. She didn't look at the prison, not once. She wondered if someone within those grey walls was listening to the hooves on the cobbles, as she once had. She said a prayer. It came out so naturally that she barely noticed.

At Holborn the thoroughfare was congested again, and Rhia wondered if any of the side streets to the south cut through to Drury Lane. She saw three grey doves, sitting on the wrought iron curl of a street lamp on the corner of an alleyway. She took a chance.

If Mr Montgomery was indeed John Hannam then they needed evidence. It would do no good to accuse him otherwise. She had a feeling, though, that this was precisely what Dillon and Michael were up to. It would have been easy enough for Mr Montgomery to take the embroidery from his wife's collection and put it into the emporium. And he only needed to pay his maid, or threaten her, to get her to lie. He must have suspected that Rhia knew something. She remembered the afternoon of Isabella's tea party. She'd said something. She couldn't remember what exactly, she'd been quite drunk, but it was something about being suspicious of Josiah's and Ryan's death. Mr Montgomery knew that she'd been with Isabella, seeing the collection. It would have been easy to convince his wife.

Rhia nudged the mare along the narrow passage towards the Covent Garden market square. Rows of hackney carriages queued around its periphery, their drivers smoking or talking in huddles beside a brazier, stamping their feet to stay warm.

'Lovely set of pegs, miss,' one of the drivers remarked as she passed.

'Thank you,' she said. She rode straight across the square and through a laneway clogged with barrows. She arrived at the Red Lion at the same time as Dillon, who was hurrying along from the opposite direction. The collar of his long coat was up around his ears and his breath was a puff of mist around him. Rhia dropped her hood back as they drew closer and he laughed when he recognised her.

'I've been waiting to see Rhiannon on her mare,' he said, 'but isn't your cloak the wrong colour?'

'I've news.'

'Ah.' He took the reins. 'There's a stable at the back, I'll tie her up. Mr Kelly's probably inside.'

Michael Kelly was in a snug, smoking and reading a trade journal. He looked out of place, Rhia thought, with his sunburnt skin, felt hat and stockman's boots. They had spoken of Greystones at breakfast, before Antonia arrived, and for the first time Rhia saw his raw longing to be home. There were tears in his eyes when he spoke of Annie. There had been no time to send a letter from Sydney that would reach home before they did. No one in Greystones knew that she and Michael Kelly were in London. Michael looked up as Dillon arrived with a jug of porter.

'I've news,' said Michael.

'That's all of us, then,' Dillon said. 'You first,' he added, looking at Rhia.

She described what had happened that morning, and when she named Mr Montgomery Dillon slammed his hand down on the table making her jump. 'I knew it!' he said, shaking his head in disgust. 'I knew it. I didn't want to jump to conclusions, but I should have. Well, we've evidence now.'

'We have,' said Michael. 'I paid a visit to Ryan's solicitor this morning.' He drew a sealed envelope from his waistcoat pocket. 'But it isn't mine to open.' He handed it to Rhia

'Not now,' she said. 'We should be on our way.'

'Aye,' said Michael, draining his glass. 'I'll find us a cab.'

'Rhiannon is on horseback,' said Dillon, glancing at her with a half-smile as he used her full name. 'I'd like to recruit Sid if we're going to pay Montgomery a visit, so let's you and I stop at the Jerusalem on the way.' He looked at Rhia and raised an eyebrow. If she had been in any doubt, before, about her feelings for him, she was no longer. She had no idea how one came back to earth from this soaring weightless feeling.

She rode hard and reached Cloak Lane before Dillon and Michael.

Juliette opened the door and shocked Rhia by attempting a smile. In the morning room, Eliza sat crocheting while Isaac was pacing. They all looked up at her expectantly.

'They're coming. They'll be here soon,' she said.

Antonia said something about people wanting lunch and disappeared, obviously needing to keep busy with something.

Michael, Dillon and Sid arrived.

No one seemed to want the curried salmon sandwiches Beth had prepared, and Rhia couldn't even eat ginger cake though she took a bite just to keep Beth happy. For a time there were several conversations taking place at once. Sid shook Rhia's hand so hard that it made her shoulder ache. 'You look well, Miss Mahoney,' he said, beaming.

'That's a lie!' She laughed.

'It is, but I'm pleased to see you all the same.'

Michael raised his voice until everyone was listening. 'I've paid a visit to Ryan Mahoney's solicitor, and persuaded him to hand over a letter that Josiah Blake posted to Ryan.'

'How ever were you able to convince him?' Antonia asked.

'I'd rather not say, Mrs Blake.' Michael turned to Rhia who took the envelope from her cloak pocket. She broke the seal. Inside was another envelope, already opened. The address on this was China Wharf and it bore the stamp of the Bombay postmaster. Inside this was a single leaf of parchment.

Rhia unfolded it and read Josiah's letter aloud.

Arabian Sea
March 1840

My dear Mahoney,

My pen is slipping in my damp grasp and the mirth of the ocean is rattling my inkpot. The closeness of the air is stifling, but not so much as my fear. It has grown since I stumbled on the opium sheds in Calcutta and was mistaken for Isaac.

It might be only fear that makes the shadows follow me, scorning my good sense. I have prayed like a condemned man as we navigated the east India shore and through the Strait of Ceylon. But the feeling of danger has only grown and now I am unable to distinguish between the shadow of a mast and that of a man. The crew from Calcutta are neither men I recognise nor trust, so I keep to my cabin, seeking only the company of my goodly companions.

Before we left Calcutta I sought out the sailor who apprehended me thinking that I was Isaac. I found him in a tavern, drunk. But instead of telling me more about the *Mathilda* being chartered to Lintin Island, he was rambling about two ships meeting in the open sea. He assured me that he could tell me no more or I'd certainly have the law after him.

Our friend Isaac has seen fit to trade outside of the law of Emperor Tao-kuang and in defiance of the Quaker ethic. Perhaps you knew this? The trade may not be illegal in England, but it is immoral. The emperor's trade law is farcical of course. It is not honoured by the merchants of Jardine Matheson and the East India Company, and indeed the Queen herself seems content to ignore a reasonable request in order to expand her empire. If this is the new world, then I prefer the old.

I had a private word with Mr Beckwith last night, and he seemed distressed. He promised me that he would investigate, and I told him that I would write to you so that you might make discreet enquiries from London. The Jerusalem should have a record of charters with signatories. If there is a criminal in our company, and it is neither you nor I, and it is not Isaac, then it can only be Jonathan Montgomery. I hope I have not overly distressed poor Mr Beckwith whom, I now realise, must also have come to this conclusion.

As you know, we are often in Calcutta for up to eight weeks so that we might travel to the indigo dyers and wood block printers in remote villages. The ship's crew is usually entirely different for each passage, sailors being itinerant and not inclined to wait in port, idle, when they could be at sea earning a wage. Calcutta is a busy sea port with a sizeable ship building yard. It was my mistaken belief that *Mathilda* was in the dry dock during our last stay. It was a convenient misapprehension, and Isaac was not then obliged to tell me an untruth.

I entreat you to make your own enquiries, Mahoney, and I beg you to be cautious. I admit that I always felt curious to know more of Jonathan's past, which he has kept private. One does not wish to pry. Perhaps he has other crimes to hide.

I hope to be returned safely to you, and that this foreboding that I have is no more than cowardice. But should any ill befall me, please take care of my beloved Antonia. I need convey no message of my affections to her, she can be in no doubt of my devotion.

I remain your steadfast and loyal friend,

Josiah Blake

Rhia folded the page and returned it to its envelope. Antonia was weeping. Dillon held out his hand for the letter. 'It will be needed as evidence,' he said quietly. Rhia gave it to him and their fingers brushed against each other. It was a light touch only, but its current spread through her.

Dillon waited for Antonia to compose herself, and then said, 'I promise I will take good care of the letter, Mrs Blake. Your husband was wrong about one thing only. Mr Beckwith would not have been shocked to hear that Jonathan Montgomery, once John Hannam, is a criminal. He is not only Montgomery's associate but also his accomplice. How else could Montgomery have discovered that Ryan had the letter? Josiah told Beckwith he was writing to Ryan. It could only have been Beckwith who killed both Josiah and Ryan.'

The room was silent as everyone considered this. Shy, retiring Mr Beckwith, a killer?

'When I met Ryan,' Dillon continued, 'it was because I was investigating London merchants who were trading with China. I knew he was hiding something from me. I was curious about his firearms, and he assured me that his interest was antiquarian, and that he didn't even know how to fire one. Furthermore, he said that he kept no bullets. I saw no reason to disbelieve him, and I still do not. If he were to take his own life, it would have had to be premeditated, not something he did in a moment of despair.'

'Then it was not his own pistol that shot him?' Rhia heard her voice as though from afar.

Dillon shook his head. 'It was not. The shot was taken from a greater distance than an arm's reach. It was a simple matter for Mr Beckwith to arrive with his own firearm, and then to place Ryan's in his hand once he was dead. It is easy enough to dust gunpowder residue around the barrel of the gun so that it appears to have been fired.'

Antonia, now composed, was looking around the room. 'Where is Juliette?'

Juliette stepped forward from the shadow of the doorway.

'When did you suspect Mr Montgomery?' Antonia asked.

'And how?' Rhia added.

'It was the day I came to the emporium with you,' she said breathlessly. 'He rolled up his shirtsleeves when I knocked that organza to the floor. I saw a scar the shape of the burn that I left on John Hannam's arm before he killed my father. And then I just knew that it was he – there was something about him. I couldn't say what, but I *knew*.'

Juliette didn't bother to hide her tears, and now Eliza was weeping as well and dabbing her eyes with her crochet.

'I think I know what John Hannam was up to when your father found the banknotes hidden in the barn, Juliette,' said Dillon. 'I've acquired some old newsprint from around Manchester. There was a racket that made the papers, involving forged banknotes being exchanged for coin. Each exchange took place in a different part of the city and at a different bank.

More than three thousand pounds was extorted in and around Manchester over two years.'

This, Dillon argued, was the means by which John Hannam had transformed himself into Jonathan Montgomery, a little-known cloth magnate from an aristocratic northern family. It was an easy task to seduce London society; it only took money, which allowed one to marry into more money. No doubt Prunella had been hoodwinked like everyone else, charmed by the art of manners and the attentions of a handsome man. Then there was Francis Beckwith's beautiful copperplate. Rhia had thought it ill-suited to his character, but it was well suited to a forger. She should have suspected him immediately she saw the handwriting on Jerusalem calling card.

Rhia looked at Dillon. He and Michael were making preparations to leave, as though an unspoken message had passed between them. And it was not just a room full of weeping women that was calling them away.

Sid noticed too. 'I'm coming,' he said.

'And I,' Isaac added. Antonia was still holding onto his arm. He looked at her kindly. 'If you'll be all right on your own?'

'Heavens!' she said indignantly, 'I have a business and a household to run. I don't have time to swoon.'

Isaac smiled and his face changed. He was looking at Antonia with such tenderness that Rhia looked away. Why had she not noticed it before?

'We could do with the extra men,' Michael agreed.

Dylan nodded. 'I'll take Isaac's chaise and call at the Westminster station on the way to Regent Street. I imagine they'll spare a couple of constables if I ask nicely. They like to have something to wave their truncheons at.'

'Montgomery could be at Belgravia,' Sid said.

'I'm coming with you,' Rhia said, preparing to stand her

ground. She caught Dillon's eye. He opened his mouth to protest, hesitated and then nodded. Michael looked at her sharply and she returned the look. He shrugged. 'I'm not going to argue with you, I can see there's no point. I suppose it's your right to accuse the man who did that to your hair.'

'Off we go then!' Sid rubbed his hands together, and then buttoned up his waistcoat and straightened his cap as if he was off to the music hall.

# Leather

It was agreed, en route, that Sid would go into the House of Montgomery on his own first, to see if Mr Montgomery was there. Rhia wouldn't set foot in the place without good cause, and as far as she was concerned no cause was good enough. She didn't much care to see Grace, either.

The Regent Street hackney stand was just outside the emporium and fate and fortune were riding with them because a carriage pulled away just as they arrived. Sid disappeared into the emporium, and Rhia watched from the carriage while Michael and Isaac stood on the footpath outside. Michael looked like he'd stepped out of another time, with his thick linen shirt and rough wool breeches. He leant on a lamp-post smoking and watching the bustle of the street. Isaac stood talking to him. They made an unlikely pair, the Quaker and the dissenter. They barely attracted a curious glance, though, amongst Londoners.

Ladies went in and came out. Rhia saw a ghost of herself entering through the same door in her red cloak a lifetime ago. She hardly knew that Rhia now. She had thought herself so fine and worldly.

Sid came out after a few minutes and they climbed back into the carriage. 'Grace says her boss is at Belgrave Square,' he said. 'But we'd best wait for Mr Dillon before we set off.' They waited, each lost in their own thoughts.

'Grace decided to stay at the emporium, then?' Rhia asked Sid.

'That's right. She said she saw no reason why she shouldn't keep her position just because we were being married. I wonder who might have put that idea into her head, Miss Mahoney?'

All around the sanctuary of their carriage, London jostled and shouted and hurried as though this were just any other day. It could take some time for Mr Dillon to arrive if the roads were this busy all the way from Westminster. Everywhere Rhia looked, now, she saw the ghosts of parts of her; young women in crinoline cages in awe of the fancy shops, as though this place might magically turn them into someone other than who they were. She no longer felt in awe of the capital, she might be *in* it, but she was not *of* it. She could almost hear Mamo, chuckling, at her shoulder.

Isaac's chaise stopped beside them, accompanied by two constables on horseback. Mr Dillon sat on the hammercloth holding the reins. His hair was loose and he was wearing a shallow-brimmed black hat and his leather coat. He looked like he was ready for anything. After a short conference they agreed on their plan and set off again.

All the way to Belgravia, Rhia felt her anger building as she thought about Mr Montgomery, the man she had wanted to impress. The man whom she had admired. To think that she had even felt grateful to him! She wondered if he had offered her a position to find out exactly what she knew. He had probably never intended to use her designs.

They stopped beside a copse of trees a short distance from the Montgomery residence. The policemen would wait at the gates until they were called for. As agreed, Rhia and Isaac climbed the cold marble steps to the front entrance as though they were simply paying a visit. At the imposing black doors that could hide anything, they stood still for a moment and looked at each other. Isaac smiled. Although he looked strained, he also seemed liberated; as though he, too, had been freed. They waited until Dillon, Michael and Sid had disappeared around the side of the building towards the servants' and tradesmen's entrance, then Isaac nodded.

Rhia lifted the heavy brass knocker.

The butler opened the door, a squat man with a dour expression and depressed air. 'Yes,' he said.

'We are here to see Jonathan Montgomery,' said Isaac.

'I'm afraid the Montgomerys are dining, sir.'

Isaac nodded unsympathetically. 'I suggest you interrupt their luncheon, then. Perhaps you could show us straight to the dining room?'

'That is out of the question,' the butler replied blandly.

'I see,' Isaac replied. 'There are two constables waiting on the street, and I would prefer, at this stage, not to involve them.' The butler's grey eyebrows shot up and he looked over Rhia's shoulder towards the gates. He stepped aside immediately to let them in.

Although the butler was hurrying, it seemed to take an age to reach the dining room, buried deep in the house. Blood-coloured walls and dark wainscoting rose on either side making Rhia claustrophobic. Her heart pounded. What if the others couldn't find their way in, or got lost in the house?

'There's no need to announce us,' said Isaac quietly, when they finally reached the right door. 'And, if you don't mind my offering you some advice, I suggest you hastily find yourself another employer.' The poor man merely shook his head in confusion and hurried away.

The dining room was dim, the curtains almost fully drawn. Mr and Mrs Montgomery, Mr Beckwith and Isabella all sat at one end of the long table. Two candelabras were lit as if it were a formal dinner.

When the door opened, they all looked up expectantly – as though their silence, rather than their conversation, had been interrupted. Prunella Montgomery looked dreadful. A strand of hair hung over her painted face, and even the most expensive powders and paints could not disguise the bloodless skin. The hand that clutched the stem of her claret glass had a visible tremor.

'Miss Mahoney!' Isabella stood up so quickly that she knocked her chair over. She ran across the room in a blur of buttermilk chiffon, and flung her arms around Rhia's neck as though she were the dearest of long-lost friends. 'I'm *so* pleased to see you! I didn't know you were in London!' She turned to her father. 'Papa! Have you kept it a secret from me? Is Rhia to come back to work at the emporium?'

'No,' said Rhia, 'I am not.' Isabella was playing the ingénue. Perhaps she always had. Her eyes had a desperate look that told worlds more than her incessant, meaningless chatter. Isabella knew, as everyone in the room knew, that something was wrong.

Mr Montgomery and Beckwith were on their feet, ostensibly polite, but Beckwith's usually impassive expression had a new alertness. The only person who barely stirred was Prunella, who took a large swallow of claret, then picked up a piece of bread and nibbled on it as though things were perfectly normal.

Mr Montgomery bowed, and smiled his captivating smile, but it was a mask and he was clearly on guard.

'Good afternoon, Isaac! What a surprise. And Miss Mahoney, how … delightful to see you returned to us safely.' He could not have looked less delighted.

'Greetings, Jonathan,' said Isaac. He frowned, choosing his

words slowly and carefully. 'We thought we'd call since your name came up today. Twice. Once in association with a counterfeiting racket in Sydney and once in connection with a murder.' Rhia had not expected Isaac to be so daring. She thought he would be careful until the rest of their party arrived.

Mr Montgomery kept smiling as though Isaac was playing some kind of prank. But his eyes darted to Beckwith, who put his hand on his waistcoat pocket. Beckwith was on edge, and for the first time Rhia saw that he was not, after all, a passive man. He suddenly looked as mean as a cornered stoat. No one moved or said anything.

Rhia noticed a movement out of the corner of her eye. The door opened and Michael, Dillon and Sid entered. They could have been waiting at the door for any length of time. Beckwith slid his hand into his pocket and pulled out a black pistol, which he pointed at Rhia. He wasn't looking at her, though, he was looking at Michael. Michael was holding his knife.

'You'd all best be leaving now,' Beckwith said slowly. His voice chilled Rhia more than the sight of his gun pointed at her breast. She had hardly heard Beckwith speak before, and now she knew why. Unlike Mr Montgomery, he had a distinctly northern accent. Did a bullet kill one instantly, or would she bleed to death? Ryan's prone body was like a photogenic drawing in her mind. Michael's knife was a primitive-looking weapon; it was the colour of ivory, and it had saw-like serrations an inch down either side of its deadly sharp point. It was aimed at Beckwith. 'I learnt to throw a knife from a real Australian,' Michael said steadily. 'They take aim at their prey while it's moving and they never, ever, miss their mark.'

Dillon was watching Beckwith, his eyes darted to Rhia; a wordless supplication to stay perfectly still. As if she wouldn't. She was made of stone.

The only sound was Isabella's soft whimpering. Prunella had put down her glass. Beckwith's hand stayed steady, pointing the pistol at her. Mr Montgomery's eyes were darting about as though searching for an escape route. There wasn't one. Sid, who'd rolled up his sleeves, blocked the door. He had his hands on his hips and he was leaning forwards slightly, like a rugby player hoping for a scuffle.

If she didn't say anything now, she may not have another opportunity.

'Did you kill Ryan Mahoney, Mr Montgomery?'

Rhia heard Isabella catch her breath.

Montgomery looked at her, hard and cold. She'd seen this side of him before, she remembered, at Isabella's party. Just a flash. But she had ignored it because she had been so taken in by the mask of success and respectability. 'I did not,' he said.

She nodded. 'Not personally. But it was your idea.' She looked at Beckwith. 'You shot him. You pointed that pistol at him, didn't you?' She marvelled at the steadiness of her own voice, as though it were coming from someone else entirely. Beckwith said nothing. He was not fool enough to admit to murder in the company of so many. His eyes strayed for only a second to Montgomery's though, and that was all it took. In a moment, Michael's knife was hurtling across the room. It hit Beckwith's forearm. The pistol dropped to the floor with a clatter and the arm that had been holding it was now hanging limply. The knife twisted and fell, but it had done its work. Beckwith groaned with pain and clutched his forearm with his other hand. His shirtsleeve was already soaked in blood. Michael moved quickly and took hold of him by his good arm. Montgomery made a move towards the door but Isaac stepped in front of him.

'Since we're all here,' said Dillon, 'I'd like to take a stab – no pun intended, Mr Beckwith – at what inspired the coining racket. I'd say you've had your work cut out, John Hannam, keeping up appearances and running a mercer's on Regent Street, not to mention a house in Belgravia, though I imagine your good wife's money has helped. Still, with the silver crisis and the downturn in trade, not to mention the shortage of China silk, you must have needed an injection of funds to keep up appearances. Lucky you had the benefit of a criminal past, isn't it? Oh, and did I say we know who John Hannam is?'

'I've no idea what you're talking about and I certainly don't have to tell you anything about my business affairs,' Montgomery spat, his face so twisted with resentment that it was hard to believe he was the genteel mercer whose lunch had been interrupted.

'Quite right, you don't. We have enough evidence. We even have Josiah Blake's letter, but you may have thought Rhia or Laurence had that anyway?'

Mr Montgomery looked as though he would happily kill Dillon as well, but he was outnumbered. He was white with fury, or fear, and he was visibly perspiring.

Prunella Montgomery picked up her wine glass. 'It seems that you've been found out, my dear. I knew some of it, of course, though I didn't imagine … this.' She flung her hand out in a wide gesture that almost knocked over one of the candelabras. 'A man cannot hide his true self from his wife, Jonathan. You've become careless. I might be a tippler, but I'm not entirely without sensibility. Not yet.' She looked away from him in disgust. 'When he is alone with Francis, he is not so careful of his manners,' she said, to no one in particular. 'I suppose I have wondered how long it would be before he went too far. And that nice young man …' She shook her head.

'Which nice young man, Mrs Montgomery?' Michael coaxed.

'The naturalist. It was botany, wasn't it?' She looked at Isaac.

'Yes, it was,' he agreed.

'Do you mean Mr Reeve?' Rhia would not have described him in the same way.

'Yes. He had been petitioning for our patronage for some time, and Jonathan, quite suddenly, decided to help him reach Australia. Now I understand why.' Prunella drained her glass and set it on the table. She cast one last look at her husband. 'What a pity you are not, at least, ashamed of yourself.' She rose slowly and with a slight totter. 'Come, Isabella, these gentlemen have business with your father.'

Prunella and Isabella left the room and Rhia caught Dillon's eye. She raised an eyebrow and he nodded. It was time to call the constables. If she was going to say something it would have to be now. 'It may have been your intent to ruin me, or maybe you had no intent but to get me out of your way, but what you have done is quite the opposite. I suppose, indirectly, you have done me a favour. I'll soon be selling my own cloth in London.'

'Don't be a fool,' he said. 'You would never survive. The trade is a man's domain.'

'Of course. So that is why the Thames is full of filth and the skies are dark with sulphur and lime. I met several women on the *Rajah* with a head for commerce.' (She thought better of mentioning Agnes's proposed business.) 'You'll soon find out what it's like to get to know people in prison. Most of them won't be real criminals, like you. By the way, Mr Beckwith, you dropped a calling card at China Wharf. You should be more careful.'

Rhia turned her back without giving Beckwith another glance. She couldn't stand to look at him.

On the drive, she signalled to the constables and went to wait in the carriage. She pulled her cloak together, and breathed in the cold. The sky was patterned with cloud as delicate as mother of pearl. The air was still. If today were a cloth, it would be chambertine; a blend of linen and wool; the sturdy fibres that had woven themselves through her life.

Soon, one of the constables galloped past, up the road, tipping his black cap at her as he passed. No doubt he had gone to get the police wagon. When the door of the carriage opened, Rhia expected that it would be one of the men, but it was Isabella.

'Do you mind if I sit with you?' Isabella looked as though she'd matured in the space of an hour, in spite of the frill of chiffon beneath her fur.

'Of course not.' They sat in silence for a moment. Rhia wondered if she should say something placatory about what was going on in the house. She couldn't think of anything. 'That's a pretty gown.'

Isabelle smiled weakly. 'To be truthful, I'm fed up with pretty things. Papa likes me in them, but I would prefer something more sophisticated.' She chewed on her lip. 'It seems that he is in trouble.'

'It does seem so.'

'Will I be permitted to visit him in prison?'

'I expect so. You did not marry, then?'

'No. Papa said he was not good enough for me, but I know that it's really because of money. It seems that Papa doesn't have much after all. I shall take ballet classes, that will cheer me. Mama says I may.' Isabelle looked at her hands. 'I'm so sorry, Miss Mahoney, about what happened to you. You did not deserve it.'

The black police wagon passed as they conversed about the most frivolous things Rhia could think of, and then Isabella said she had better go and say goodbye to her father.

'I hope you'll visit us, Miss Mahoney?'

'I'll be going home soon, but I'll be in London again, on business.' On business. She liked the way that sounded.

Isabella left and the men arrived. Isaac stepped up onto his chaise and offered to drive Sid home. Michael said he thought he'd sit up on the hammercloth with the driver. Dillon climbed into the carriage with Rhia.

They sat side by side, almost touching. Dillon's hand rested lightly on Rhia's. His fingers traced slowly along her wrist. He turned to her and ran his thumb down her cheek and across her lips, leaning towards her until she felt his warm breath on her face and his lips pressing on hers. They were softer than she had imagined. His hands slid to her shoulders and down her arms as though he were undressing her. They rested on her waist, pressing against her hips. Everywhere he touched, her skin came to life. The depth of the sea, the radiance of the moon and the strength of heaven had got her here, and she would never forget how this inner lightness felt. Perhaps Antonia had been right after all about the inner light.

They had rearranged themselves by the time they arrived at Cloak Lane. Michael stepped down and coughed loudly before he opened the carriage door. He shook Dillon's hand and said he hoped to see him in Ireland one day, then he left them alone beneath the carriage lamp.

Inside the circle of light, Dillon looked at Rhia quizzically.

'Might I visit you in Ireland?'

'You might,' she said.

'Then perhaps I shall,' he replied.

'You had damn well better,' she said.

# Merchant's Quay, October 1842

Michael Kelly sat on a pile of stones quarried from Belgard near Dublin; stones that were about to form part of the new Mahoney storehouse. He pulled out his tobacco tin and watched the scurrying activity of the quay. The never-ending rotation of commerce. Behind the row of red-brick stores was a tangle of masts and rigging; the sight that had once called him to adventure and the open sea. He breathed a sigh of completion. It was time to stay home now.

Not far off stood Dillon and Rhia. They'd been married in the summer, in Greystones chapel. It was a typical village wedding, everyone was welcome and there'd been a ceilidh on the green afterwards. Annie pulled him up to dance, and when he protested, Thomas and Fiona made him. So he danced with his wife and she looked as lovely in her yellow dress as she'd looked the day he first laid eyes on her.

She'd never looked better, though, than she had the day he got home. What a sweet day it had been. He'd left Rhia to take the carriage up the headland, and walked along the shale. Thomas was at the loom, and Annie was spinning, just as he'd imagined it for years. He walked right in, and they both looked at him, stunned, as though a stranger had walked into their parlour. Annie dropped her distaff to the floor. He'd never seen her do that, she was always so careful with her yarn. Then she was in his arms. They didn't sleep the first night. How could they? There was too much remembering to do. Remembering of each other. She didn't ask him if he'd stayed true, but if she'd been in any doubt of his love then he'd proved it that night and on many nights since.

Standing beside Rhia and Dillon were Bridget and Connor Mahoney. Connor still had his stick but he stood straighter these days. He didn't take much interest in the trade any more, but he didn't need to; not with Brigit and Rhia in the house. They were watching as the foundation stones were laid in the place where the ruined linen storehouse had been. Rhia had taken her old red cloak to the dyers quarter and now it was purple, and her hair was grown long again. They'd done well. They had a clipper at sea and another that should be leaving Sydney by now, and one about to depart Dublin for London. Antonia had found them plenty of English and continental buyers. She and Isaac were business partners now, and Michael wouldn't be surprised if they soon became more than that.

He had received a letter from Dan in Sydney, saying why didn't he send his cloth back to them, since good quality woven was still rare in the colony. Rhia was now insisting that she accompany the first shipment; though Michael could see her husband didn't think much of the idea. That wouldn't make any difference to her, though. She did as she pleased and Dillon seemed to like that about her. That was uncommon in a man, Michael was prepared to admit it.

Michael wouldn't be going back to Australia. Even coming to Dublin for a spell was too long to be away from home these days. Annie was waiting for him now, just as she'd done for all those years.

Rhia was looking towards St Patrick's, and Michael thought he saw her incline her head respectfully, but he couldn't be sure.

# Acknowledgements

I was very fortunate to view the Rajah Quilt at the National Gallery of Australia in Canberra, where it has been housed since it was discovered in an attic in Scotland in 1987. This was made possible by the good will of the Head of Conservation at the National Gallery, Deborah Ward, who also took the time to answer my questions about this historical textile, made on the transport *Rajah* in 1841. The Rajah Quilt is the only known surviving convict quilt. Stitched into its intricate design are the dreams and sorrows of but a few of the thousands of women who were transported to Australia during the eighteenth and nineteenth centuries. *The Silver Thread* is based very loosely on what is known about the voyage of the *Rajah* and the making of the quilt, and I have taken liberties. Not least amongst these, the fact that the *Rajah* sailed into Hobart rather than Sydney, and that, to the best of my knowledge, no murder took place on that voyage! There is also the matter of the London and North Western Railway, and of certain publications that were not quite in circulation at the time.

I consulted many sources in researching the factual aspect of this novel, but chief amongst these was Robert Hughes' *The Fatal Shore* and *Leviathan* by John Birmingham. My work was made easier by the effort of these authors. Any errors or inaccuracies are firmly my own.

As always, there are people without whose understanding

487

and support I simply couldn't have done. Thank you, firstly, Nick and Saoirse for allowing me to disappear occasionally, and Ali and Mike for Rose Cottage and a well-timed whisky or two. Thank you Bryon and Philippa for helping, and to Ngaire Macleod.

I'm grateful to colleagues, friends and fellow writers at Bath Spa University, including Richard Kerridge, Tricia Wastvedt and Tracy Brain, and for the solidarity of Brett Hardman, Suellen Dainty, Jenny McVeigh, Angela Lett, and Jack Woolf. Thank you, also, to the Babcary writers; Guy de Beaujeu, Shannon Slater and Wendy Teasdill.

I owe much to the patience and continuing support of Monika Boese and Siv Bublitz at Ullstein, and to Kirtsy Dunseath for her interest. The perception of Richenda Todd and Susan Opie was extremely helpful and much appreciated.

Huge thanks to Anthony Cheetham, Nic Cheetham and Mathilda Imlah at Head of Zeus, and particularly to Laura Palmer for her insight and hard work.

I am most of all grateful to my agent, Kate Hordern, whom I can't thank enough for her tireless industry, good sense and big heart. Her input, and her belief in this novel, was a great strength throughout.